THE CURSED PROPHECY

JOHNATHON AXEL CARR

Copyright © 2025 by Johnathon Axel Carr
All rights reserved.

No part of this publication may be reproduced, distributed, or transmitted in any form or by any means, including photocopying, recording, or other electronic or mechanical methods, without the prior written permission of the publisher, except in the case of brief quotations embodied in critical reviews and certain other non-commercial uses permitted by copyright law.

This is a work of fiction. Names, characters, places, and incidents are either the product of the author's imagination or used fictitiously. Any resemblance to actual persons, living or dead, events, or locales is entirely coincidental.

ISBN (Paperback) 978-1-0684887-0-2
ISBN (Ebook): 978-1-0684887-1-9

Cover design by Johnathon Axel Carr
Interior formatting by Johnathon Axel Carr
First edition

This story was written out of pure love for the genre I grew up with—fantasy, horror, and everything in between. Thank you for stepping into my world.

—Johnathon Axel Carr

CHAPTER 1
The Road to Elaria

The sun dipped low on the horizon, casting a warm, golden glow across the rugged landscape as the merchant's wagon trundled steadily along the winding path toward Castle Elaria. The rhythmic clatter of wooden wheels against the cobblestone road and the gentle jingle of the horse's harness provided a soothing soundtrack to the journey. Seated at the back of the wagon amidst crates of spices and bolts of fine cloth, Darius surveyed the approaching castle with a contemplative gaze. His auburn hair, tousled by the breeze, framed a face marked by both youth and the burdens of destiny. Light armour, gleaming faintly in the dying light, encased his lean yet muscular frame, offering protection without hindering his movement. Over this, he wore a hooded cloak of deep forest green, the hood pulled low to shield his piercing emerald eyes from the dust of the road.

A great sword, its hilt intricately engraved with runes of old, was sheathed across his back, the weight of the weapon a familiar and reassuring presence. The cloak's fabric fluttered gently around him, occasionally revealing glimpses of the finely crafted armour beneath. Darius's hands, calloused from years of training and battle, rested lightly on the edge of the wagon, fingers tapping absently as he lost himself in thought.

The merchant, a jovial man with a wide-brimmed hat and a weathered but kind face, glanced back at his unexpected passenger. He had come across Darius earlier that day, the young warrior standing resolute at a crossroads, eyes fixed on a distant goal. Their paths converged by chance, and with a shared destination, the merchant had offered Darius a ride. As the wagon creaked along, the merchant whistled a merry tune, his presence a comforting contrast to the heavy silence that often enveloped the hero. Darius though remaining silent most of the journey still found himself admiring the kingdom around him as he gazes out of the wagon, The kingdom of Elaria sprawled across a landscape of breathtaking beauty and untamed wildness, a realm where nature's splendour and mystery intertwined in a mesmerizing dance. From the soaring peaks of the Dragonspine Mountains to the storm-lashed shores of the Azure Sea, Elaria was a land steeped in beauty, danger, and legend. Verdant forests cloaked the valleys, the most fabled among them the Whispering Woods—a realm of filtered sunlight, ancient ferns, and whispered secrets carried on the breeze.

The mountains loomed in the north like the jagged teeth of a slumbering titan, rumoured home to dragons and other forgotten beasts. Glacial winds swept their craggy spires, where secluded lakes and echoing caves were said to hide lost magic and forbidden truths.

Further inland, rivers like silver veins threaded through golden plains and hill-scattered farmland. Village rooftops peeked through orchard groves and wheat fields, with towns bustling near trade roads and castle walls.

The Azure Sea thundered against the western cliffs, its sapphire waves concealing treacherous reefs and smuggler's coves. Only the bravest mariners dared its waters, sailing between storm and salt to reach the kingdom's bustling ports.

At Elaria's heart stood Castle Elaria, a gleaming sentinel watching over it all. From its tallest tower, one could behold the vast kingdom in every direction—a tapestry of wild beauty and fragile peace. Darius' destination,

summoned to the castle, eh?

Darius thought Looking towards the castle for but a moment before looking back at the landscape almost as if Darius taking a final look before destiny claimed him,

what a joke.

He takes one last glance at the castle before resting his eyes for the remainder of the ride. Castle Elaria rose like a vision from a dream, its white-stone spires piercing the sky, banners fluttering in the wind. Carvings of mythical beasts and ancient runes shimmered faintly in the sunlight, casting a serene glow over the kingdom below.

At its base sprawled Castle Town—a living, breathing heart of Elaria. Market Street bustled with merchants shouting over each other, stalls brimming with bright fabrics and fragrant spices. The scent of fresh bread mingled with roasting meats, and the hum of conversation filled the air.

Beyond the market, narrow alleys wound through cozy neighbourhoods where flower-boxed windows and warm greetings made the town feel alive. To the east, fields of golden crops stretched toward the horizon, dotted with grazing livestock and the distant songs of shepherds.

Near the castle gates, the Royal Gardens bloomed in tranquil contrast—winding paths, quiet ponds, and vibrant blossoms offered a peaceful haven amid the noise.

Inside, the castle's halls were a blend of opulence and legend. Statues of heroes flanked the entrance, and sunlight poured through stained-glass windows, casting coloured patterns across marble floors. In the throne room, beneath towering ceilings and glowing chandeliers, the weight of centuries lingered. From the highest tower, one could see all of Elaria—a kingdom alive with mystery, magic, and the promise of adventure.

As the castle loomed ever closer, its majestic spires piercing the sky like sentinel guardians. As they approached, the bustling sounds of the castle town began to fill the air—a symphony of life that contrasted sharply with the solitary journey Darius had endured thus far. He drew in a deep breath, the mingled scents of fresh bread, blooming flowers, and distant sea air filling his lungs, grounding him in the present moment.

Yet beneath his calm exterior, a storm of emotions brewed. A duty to his kingdom, and the weight of the prophecy swirled within him, each thought a thread in the complex tapestry of his fate. As the wagon rolled closer to the castle gates, Darius tightened his grip on the edge of the wagon, steeling himself for the trials to come. The path ahead was fraught with danger and uncertainty, but within the heart of this young warrior, a fire burned brighter than any shadow that might seek to extinguish it.

"This is as far as I go, lad," declared the merchant, bringing the wagon to a gentle stop in the bustling market area of Castle Town. With a satisfied pat on the flank of his trusty horse, the merchant acknowledged the animal's hard work. Darius, clad in his light armour and hooded cloak, hopped down from the wagon and approached the merchant with gratitude in his eyes. "You have my th--" Darius began, only to be cut off by the merchant's sudden interruption. The older man fixed him with a solemn gaze, a hint of urgency in his voice as he spoke.

its not like someone was talking old man.

"You know, boy," the merchant said, his words carrying a weight of wisdom earned through a life of travels and tales. "Hold the light close, lad. Relish in every joy, as little as they may be. It may just save your life. Good luck." Darius was taken aback by the unexpected gravity of the merchant's words. In the brief time they had journeyed together, the merchant had been a beacon of cheerfulness and camaraderie, yet now, a shadow of concern seemed to cloud his demeanour. Unable to fully decipher the merchant's intentions, Darius simply nodded in appreciation and offered a sincere thanks as they bid each other farewell. As they parted ways, Darius couldn't shake the lingering feeling of foreboding that the merchant's parting words had stirred within him, a silent reminder of the dangers that awaited him on his path, As Darius meandered through the bustling market, his sharp gaze caught not only the familiar merchant but also the many townsfolk who seemed to recognize him—each aware of his summons to the castle. It was as if whispers of the prophecy had woven themselves into the very fabric of the town. Every glance he received carried a quiet weight: a blend of concern for his well-being and the fragile hope placed in the one destined to save the land. Yet amidst the crowd, he found an unexpected comfort in their silent support— a wordless chorus of belief in his strength. Each step he took through the market was a testament to the burden he bore, and a quiet reminder of the resolve that had carried him this far.

ok

Darius looked up at the castle with a slightly different outlook,

let's not keep that little bitch waiting any longer shall we

He takes hold of his hilt without drawing his sword from the sheath to calm his nerves and continues the walk to the castle.

"Halt!"
A guardsman's sharp command pierced the air as Darius approached the towering gates of the castle, a spear pointed in his direction. The guard scrutinized Darius with a critical gaze, sizing him up as if assessing a potential threat.

"State your business, peasant," the guard demanded; his tone laced with authority. Before Darius could utter a word, a second guard interjected rudely, his eyes lingering on the great sword sheathed on Darius's back. "My, my! Fine-looking weapon you have there," the guard remarked, a hint of mockery in his voice. Darius bristled at the interruption, his patience wearing thin as he attempted to assert himself.

"I am-" he began, only to be cut off once again by the guard's snide remark.

what's with everyone and cutting me off first the merchant and now this jack-off

"Steal it from a knight?" the guard taunted, a smirk playing on his lips. Darius felt a surge of frustration building within him, the constant interruptions and disrespect gnawing at his composure.

"No. I am-" he tried to clarify, but the guard's derisive comment pushed him to his limit. The guard walked towards Darius and circled,

he comes any closer I'm killing him

"I'll have to relieve you of such a weapon," the guard declared, making a move to seize the great sword from its sheath but the guard at that moment realised the sheer weight of the blade while trying to lift it, lifting the blade just enough to reveal the black blade hiding within the sheath.

right, I'm done with his shit

Darius's patience snapped like a taut bowstring, his resolve hardening as he swiftly turned to face the guard with a swift and forceful movement. The guard's attempt to take the sword was met with unexpected resistance, the weight of the weapon proving too much for him to handle. In the moment of defiance, Darius's green-hooded cloak billowed, revealing his striking auburn hair and piercing emerald eyes that seemed to blaze with determination. The guard, taken aback by Darius's sudden defiance and realisation as to who he was, stumbled backward and fell to the ground in a startled heap.

"That…..you….wait—"
Tripping over his own words looking at Darius, the first guard who no longer was willing to watch from the sidelines reproaches with his spear once more,

"How dare you assault a royal guard you swine!" Steadying his spear, he lunged forward to pierce Darius in the back, "Stop!" Exclaims the other still on the floor, Darius draws his sword but an inch, using the setting sun to his advantage he reflects the light into the eyes of the attacker using his blade, the grounded

guard now on his feet rushes over to quell the situation only to find he's now the target for the blinded companion, Darius stood between the two guards grabs a hold of the long wooden pole stopping the wild attack and bringing an end to the situation without moving from his position since the altercation started, "Shit" The guard complains trying to pull his spear from Darius' grasp,
"Auburn hair like fire-" The other started' "Green eyes like emeralds"
The guard with the spear loosens his grip now realising what's going on, "And an obsidian made great sword as black as the abyss to hell." Both guards then stand at attention with a look of shame on their faces at what just transpired, "Prophesied Hero, Darius, summoned by the king, please enter the castle at your leisure" neither guard looking him in the eye. Darius then sighs.

this is going to be a ball ache if they report this.

"Eyes up men! Be proud of what you do here, your royal guards to the king are you not?" Darius asks, the guards share a look and the tension in the air loosens,

I should have just killed them, but I don't have full control yet. He still has his morals it seems, what a pain.

"In future do not let greed and boredom cloud your judgment, stand tall and fulfil your duties with honour." Darius finishes as opening the gate. Both guards now standing tall eyes fixed forward, "Sir!"

whatever, I did it for me, it'll be a royal pain if this come back on me, take your sorry asses to the tavern tonight and drown your shame in ale and forget this happened.

As Darius passed through the towering gates, a sense of tranquillity enveloped him like a gentle embrace, the heavy iron portals closing softly behind him. He found himself standing amidst the enchanting beauty of the castle's flower gardens, their petals swaying in a delicate dance with the whispering breeze. The air was filled with the sweet fragrance of blooming blossoms, a symphony of colours painting the courtyard in a vibrant tapestry of nature's splendour. Sunlight filtered through the lush greenery casting a warm golden glow that bathed the garden in a soft ethereal light. Each dew-kissed petal and verdant leaf seemed to shimmer with life, a testament to the magic and serenity that dwelled within the castle's walls. As Darius took a moment to soak in the peaceful ambiance of the courtyard, he notices a figure tending to the flowers and as he walks through the picturesque scenery, he can start to make out the features of the figure, A woman.

Closer now, he saw her features more clearly—ethereal white-blonde hair that shimmered like spun silver in the sunlight, flowing around a face of quiet strength and grace. Her eyes, a luminous shade of cerulean, held an intelligent calm, as if she saw deeper than the surface of things. A pair of delicate spectacles perched on her nose, lending her a scholarly elegance. They framed her face in a way that enhanced her natural allure, adding a thoughtful air that felt both regal and human.

She wore a long, flowing gown of rich royal blue, the fabric catching the light like water beneath moonlight. Intricate gold embroidery traced the hems and sleeves in sweeping, vine-like patterns, gleaming with every subtle movement. Along the collar and trailing down the front ran a line of fine white trim, delicate as lace, adding a softness to the commanding silhouette. The high waistline and tailored bodice gave her both stature and poise, as if she belonged not just to a throne—but to the very stories woven into her kingdom's history. There was something in the way she moved—graceful, deliberate—that commanded presence without needing to speak.

"Princess Seraphina!" A handmaiden approaching the woman,

princess...

The princess and handmaiden talk in a volume too quiet to be heard by Darius, his gaze glued to the princess.

the PRincEsS

Darius's thoughts began to scatter like leaves in the wind, a dull ache surged through his head, memories not of his own began to flash in his mind causing him to instinctively reach for his forehead with one hand. With a deep breath, he closed his eyes in a silent attempt to subdue the uninvited pain that gripped his mind. "Are you okay?"

no.

A beautiful, melodic voice beckoned to Darius, pulling him from the haze of discomfort.

damn it all! Go away.

Slowly, he released the grip on his head and opened his eyes, only to find Princess Seraphina standing before him. In her presence, the pain that had plagued him moments before dissipated like morning mist under the sun's gentle gaze.

damn it, lost my hold…..

Their eyes met in a moment of quiet understanding, a connection that transcended words and spoke volumes in the language of shared experiences and unspoken emotions.

CHAPTER 2

The Blood Moon's Chosen

The tranquil moment was abruptly shattered as reality reasserted its grip on them. "You're the hero my father summoned?" Princess Seraphina's voice broke through the silence, her gaze unwavering. Darius met her eyes with a slow nod, acknowledging the weight of his destiny. "Darius, born under a blood moon in a small village to the north on a cold spring night, destined to—"

"Save the kingdom from the looming threat known as Vorthis, and to ensure that the seal remains steadfast." Darius finished her sentence, a sense of resignation in his voice.

"I know," Darius whispered with a hint of a smirk, his gaze locked with Seraphina's, a mixture of awe and trepidation in her eyes, then for a fleeting moment a glint of sadness takes to her eyes as if she knows something different, something unknown to Darius. He wonders what plagued her.

As the weight of what felt like a destined meeting lingered in the air, the princess's handmaiden approached, a gentle reminder of the responsibilities that awaited. "Princess, it is time to attend to your duties," the handmaiden urged softly, casting a fleeting glance at Darius before focusing her attention on Seraphina.

With a nod of understanding, Seraphina tore her gaze away from Darius, her expression a mix of reluctance and resolve. "I must go," she whispered softly, her voice carrying a sense of duty that belied her inner turmoil.

As the princess departed to fulfil her obligations, Darius stood alone amidst the enchanting beauty of the castle grounds. The grandeur of Castle Elaria surrounded him, its pristine halls and elegant architecture a testament to the kingdom's splendour. Darius peered through the open solid oak double doors, The setting sun filtered through stained-glass windows, casting a kaleidoscope of colours on the polished marble floors.

Time to meet the old fool.

With a deep breath, Darius crossed the threshold and entered the castle, as he stepped into the grand foyer, the opulence of the castle enveloped him like a warm embrace. The flickering torches cast a golden glow on the intricately carved walls, bathing the corridor in a dance of light and shadow. The sound of his footsteps echoed against the marble floors, adding a sense of reverent solemnity to the air.

Before he could fully take in his surroundings, a guard approached him with a sense of purpose. "Darius, I shall escort you to the throne room to meet with his majesty," the guard declared, his voice resonating with authority. Without waiting for a response, he turned on his heel and began to stride forward, a silent command for Darius to follow.

"Uh….Thanks?—"
Darius fell into step behind the guard, his eyes wide with wonder as he passed ornate tapestries and priceless artifacts that adorned the walls. The faint scent of polished wood and burning incense lingered in the air, adding to the aura of grandeur that surrounded him. Each step brought him closer to the heart of the castle, where the ruler of the realm awaited his audience.

As they approached a pair of towering gold-plated doors, the guard turned to Darius with a respectful nod. "Please enter," he said, his stance shifting to one of readiness as he stood at attention to one side, a silent sentinel guarding the threshold to the throne room.

he always was one for a show.

With a deep breath, Darius crossed the threshold into the throne room. The double doors closed softly behind him, and the grandeur of the chamber unfolded like a stage set for kings. Tall stained-glass windows cast fractured light across stone floors, illuminating tapestries of ancient battles and victories. The air was thick with the scent of incense and the quiet crackle of torches. The throne itself stood at the far end—an ornate seat of carved wood and velvet, resting beneath a vaulted ceiling painted with celestial symbols. Darius advanced, his footsteps echoing in the vast space. When he reached the throne, he knelt, bowing his head low. "I have arrived at your request, my liege."

Seated upon the throne was a man aged by time but unbent by it— his silver-streaked hair and regal posture told of wisdom hard-earned. His voice was calm, yet carried urgency.

"Welcome my boy, there is much you must know. Our land is in grave danger."

"I know of the fabled prophecy your majesty, a warrior was chosen by fate to defeat a great evil, and your summons letter revealed that you believe it is me? But it seems there is more to tell?" "Yes, young hero much more." Darius's heart quickened, the solemnity in the king's tone seeping into his bones. "What is it, my lord?"

The king took a deep breath, his eyes reflecting years of burden. "A darkness has manifested, creeping through our lands. It stems from an ancient evil known as Vorthis. Centuries ago, our ancestors sealed Vorthis away, but the seal weakens with time.

Now, as it does every 100 years it falters, and the darkness spreads." Darius felt a chill run through him. "How can this be stopped?"

you don't.

The king leaned forward, his gaze intense. "You must seek out this darkness that has twisted and gained life of its own becoming harrowing monsters and confront them. By doing so, you will strengthen the seal on Vorthis, saving our land for another hundred years." Darius's mind raced with questions and doubts. "But how am I to find this darkness? And what if I fail?" The king's expression softened, yet his resolve remained firm. "You will not be alone, Darius. The prophecy speaks of a chosen one, guided by the light within. You have the strength and courage needed. Trust in yourself and the path will reveal itself." "But why me?" Darius asked, feeling a mix of fear and determination. The king rises to his feet and walks towards Darius, "What if I'm not the one the prophecy speaks of?" Darius continued. The king placed a reassuring hand on Darius's shoulder. "According to the prophecy, your village of Tynged bears only female offspring. However, once every century, Tynged births a male, and that male is destined to quell the rise of Vorthis." Darius nodded slowly, realizing for the first time that no other family in his village had birthed a male during his lifetime.

"Furthermore, the sword of dark demise, your sword, said to be forged using the blackest obsidian in the fabled hidden volcano atop Dragonspine mountains, entrusted to you by the village elders was also done so as the prophecy states, it's the sword that originally fought Vorthis centuries ago, it will be vital in your quest." Once again, Darius nodded. The king, now back on his throne, wore a downcast look of regret. Noticing this, Darius asked, "What is it? Is there more to the prophecy?"

oh, there's more.

The king nodded without meeting Darius's gaze. Darius' eyes scanned the king's expression for clues, his mind drifting back to the market street and the old merchant's parting words. "Your Majesty, it seems there is a part of the prophecy you have yet to explain, a part known to the castle town residents and guards but not to the rest of the kingdom." The king remained silent, still not looking at Darius. "Your Highness! I must know," Darius insisted. "It appears you are destined to lose your life in combat," the king said solemnly. Darius, now with a serious look of concern, gestured for the king to elaborate.

The king continued, reciting the prophecy from memory, "During the endless cycle of conflict between light and darkness, a hero of legend is born not under the guiding light of the sun but under the cursed blood moon of night. This hero will have auburn hair like fire and green eyes of emerald. If this day comes, the cursed hero of destiny is bound to fail in his quest to reseal the evil, and darkness will surely drown the kingdom and its inhabitants."

The king looked down at Darius's feet. "The prophecy ends there, my boy. Sadly, we do not know what happens after your quest. As documented by my ancestors, you would be the ninth hero to undertake this mission. Nine centuries of peace…"

"Gone," Darius finished, a look of confusion crossing his face. "Because of… me?"

yes, you "hero".

The king sighed deeply; his eyes filled with sorrow. "It is not your fault, Darius. You are not to blame for the fate you were born into. Each hero before you faced their own trials, and none have failed. You carry the legacy of their bravery and sacrifice. Your journey may be fraught with peril, but you also have the chance to change the course of history." Darius's mind raced, grappling with the weight of the prophecy and the burden of expectations. "How can I succeed where I am doomed to fail?" he asked, desperation tinging his voice. The king's gaze softened, and he spoke with quiet conviction. "You have something the others did not. Knowledge of the prophecy's potential outcome. Use this foresight wisely. Seek allies, trust in your strengths, and remember, even in the darkest times, the light of hope can shine the brightest." A determined resolve began to form within Darius. "I will not let our kingdom fall. I will do everything in my power to succeed." The king nodded, a glimmer of hope returning to his eyes. "Then go, Darius. Prepare for your journey. The fate of the kingdom rests upon your shoulders, but remember, you are not alone. The strength of our people goes with you."

Darius stood, the gravity of the king's words pressing down on him like an invisible cloak. He took a moment to compose himself, feeling the cool marble of the floor beneath his boots, the warmth of the torch flames on his face, and the heavy silence of the grand chamber. "I will not disappoint you or the people of Elaria," he vowed, his voice steady despite the tumult within. The king nodded gravely, a hint of admiration in his eyes. "The Royal Seer, Lady Alara, will be your guide in the matters of prophecy and the arcane. She will aid you in understanding the ancient texts that may hold the key to your victory." Darius felt a flicker of hope amidst the shadow of his fate. He had always been curious about the mystical arts and the wisdom they held. "I will seek her counsel immediately, my liege," he said, bowing his head once more. "No," the king said firmly, raising a hand to halt him. "You must rest tonight. Your journey is fraught with peril, and a clear mind and body are your greatest weapons. Begin your quest with the break of dawn, after you have had time to gather your thoughts and prepare yourself."

Darius nodded, the gravity of his mission weighing heavily upon him. He was led to a chamber that was more than just a room to rest in—it was a sanctuary of luxury. The walls were adorned with tapestries depicting scenes of battles long past, each thread a silent testament to the valour of Elaria's ancestors. A four-poster bed, with sheets softer than a cloud and pillows stuffed with the finest feathers, beckoned to him. The fireplace crackled warmly, casting a comforting glow across the chamber. Yet, sleep eluded him. His mind was a tempest of thoughts and questions, each one threatening to capsize the fragile ship of his resolve. He found himself pacing the cold stone floor, the echoes of his footsteps a metronome to the rhythm of his racing thoughts.

The soft glow of the moon slipped through the windows, painting the tapestries in shades of silver and black. The flickering shadows seemed to come alive, whispering tales of heroes and battles, both won and lost. Darius, unable to shake the restlessness that gnawed at his soul, decided to explore the castle's vast library. He had heard tales of its vastness, a treasure trove of knowledge that could offer him insight into the prophecy and his own fate.

Darius wandered through the expansive library, the faint glow of candles illuminating rows upon rows of towering bookshelves. The scent of aged parchment filled the air, a comforting embrace that momentarily distracted him from the weight of his impending destiny. He ran his fingers along the spines of the tomes, absorbing the rich history contained within each one, hoping to find a story that would help clear his mind.

As he turned a corner, he caught sight of Princess Seraphina seated at a grand mahogany table, a book open before her. The soft glow of candlelight danced around her, casting gentle shadows that accentuated the features of her face. He hesitated for a moment, unsure if he should intrude upon her solitude, but curiosity propelled him forward.

"What are you reading?" he asked casually, glancing at the pages filled with intricate illustrations and elegant script. Seraphina looked up, her expression shifting from concentration to surprise. "It's a collection of folk tales from around the kingdom," she replied, her eyes lighting up. "This one is about a clever trickster who outsmarts a greedy king. It's quite amusing."

"Sounds interesting," Darius said, leaning against the table. "I've always preferred tales of adventure over the dry history we learn in the courts. What's the best part so far?"

She smiled, her enthusiasm evident. "The trickster managed to convince the king that his crown was made of glass, and he kept pretending to break it in front of the court. The king was beside himself with rage, fearing he'd be laughed at. It's a clever reminder that even those in power can be foolish."

Darius chuckled, imagining the scene. "I wish I could see that. Seems like a fitting lesson for those who wield power without wisdom." Seraphina nodded, her expression growing contemplative. "It's easy to forget that those who rule are just as human as the rest of us. Sometimes I wish the nobles could step outside the castle walls and see the world through the eyes of the common folk."

"Do you ever get the chance to?" Darius asked, genuinely curious. "To see beyond the castle?" She sighed softly, a hint of longing in her gaze. "When I was younger, I used to sneak out. I would watch street performers and listen to the music echoing through the streets. It was liberating—just being Seraphina, not the princess."

"Really?" Darius leaned in, intrigued. "What was that like?"

"Magical," she said, her eyes sparkling with nostalgia. "There's something about the laughter of strangers, the energy of the crowd. For a moment, I felt free. But then reality would settle in, and I'd have to return to my duties." Darius felt a connection forming, their shared feelings of being trapped by their respective roles. "I understand," he said softly. "I often feel that way too. Everyone expects me to be the hero. It's hard to shake the feeling of being a pawn in someone else's game."

Seraphina's expression shifted to one of understanding, and she leaned forward slightly. "It can be suffocating, can't it? Sometimes I wish I could trade places with someone, anyone, just for a day. To make choices without the weight of a crown pressing down on me." Darius nodded, feeling a kinship in her words. "If I had a choice, I'd wander the world, see new places, and find my own path—one not dictated by prophecies or expectations. Just… to be free."

"What would you do first?" she asked, her curiosity piqued. "Climb the highest mountain and feel the wind on my face," he replied, the image vivid in his mind. "Or sit by a river, listening to the water flow without a care in the world. What about you?"

"I think I would explore the markets," she said, a smile creeping onto her face. "To taste all the different foods and hear the stories of the people. I'd want to laugh without worrying about decorum or duty."

Their laughter mingled in the air, a momentary escape from the gravity of their circumstances. As they shared their dreams and fears, the conversation deepened, flowing naturally from one topic to another, as if they were old friends catching up rather than a hero and a princess.

"Sometimes it feels like we're both trapped in glass cages," Darius mused, glancing at the ornate windows that framed the library. "Everyone watches us, waiting for us to fulfil our destinies."

Seraphina's gaze turned serious, a flicker of understanding in her eyes. "It's a heavy burden, isn't it? The weight of expectations can feel unbearable. But it helps to share these thoughts with someone who understands." Darius met her gaze, feeling an unspoken bond forming between them—a connection forged in vulnerability and honesty. "I didn't expect to find solace here tonight, but I'm glad I did."

"Me too," Seraphina said, her voice softening. "For a moment, it feels like we're just two people dreaming of a different life." As the candlelight flickered around them, illuminating their shared hopes and fears, Darius felt a sense of peace wash over him. They may have been bound by their destinies, but in that moment, they were free—if only for a while. "Let's make a promise," Darius said suddenly, a spark of determination in his voice. "No matter what happens, we'll keep our dreams alive. We'll find a way to break free from our cages, even if it's just in our hearts."

"I promise," Seraphina replied, her eyes shining with a mixture of hope and resolve. "We'll find a way to escape, if only for a moment." As they continued to talk, the bond between them grew stronger, a flicker of something deeper beginning to take root—a silent promise of understanding, a friendship. They spent hours together, the candles slowly burning down to nubs as they spoke of their hopes and fears, their laughter and whispers echoing through the cavernous library. Darius shared tales of his youth— the simple joys of village life, the warmth of shared meals, and the fierce love of his people. Seraphina, in turn, revealed the lonely corridors of palace life, the suffocating weight of royal expectations, and her secret longing for adventures beyond the castle walls.

As the night deepened, Seraphina's voice softened, her confidence wavering for the first time. "Darius," she began, her fingers tracing idle patterns on the worn table. "My dreams... they've been plagued with you. I see battles and shadows, but through it all, there's a light—your light." Her voice trembled slightly, vulnerability seeping through as her eyes searched his, seeking answers neither fully understood.

Darius felt a warmth spread through him—a strange mixture of fear and connection. He hesitated before speaking, his thoughts spiralling back to the fleeting visions from the courtyard, the memories that felt like echoes from another life. "I've felt it too," he confessed, his voice low and rough. "Like... like our fates are tied together by threads I can't see or cut. It terrifies me, knowing I might be part of something far bigger than I ever asked for." Seraphina leaned closer, her lavender perfume delicate against the musty scent of ancient tomes. "My visions are often cryptic," she whispered, her breath fanning the space between them, "but one thing is clear—you are the key to our salvation." Her words hung in the air, heavy with meaning, as her eyes shimmered with both hope and fear.

CHAPTER 3

The Threads of Fate

The first rays of dawn seeped through the towering stained-glass windows, casting fractured beams of gold and crimson across the library's stone floor. The candles had burned themselves out hours ago, leaving only the soft glow of morning to illuminate the scattered books and scrolls that lay forgotten around Darius and Seraphina.

A heavy silence lingered between them, the weight of their late-night confessions still fresh, delicate as spun glass. Darius shifted in his seat, running a hand through his unruly hair, his mind still tangled in thoughts of fates and threads he couldn't see. The soft tap of a cane against stone broke the stillness. The sound echoed through the vast hall, steady and deliberate. Seraphina straightened, her eyes flickering to the grand archway where a figure emerged from the shadows—a woman draped in flowing robes the colour of storm clouds, her white hair braided intricately down her back.

Her eyes, though clouded and sightless, seemed to pierce directly through Darius. "Alara," Seraphina said, rising to her feet with a mixture of reverence and affection. "I wasn't expecting you so soon." The seer smiled faintly, the corners of her pale lips barely curving. "Visions wait for no one, child." Her voice was soft, melodic, but laced with something deeper—like a song filled with hidden meanings. She turned her sightless gaze toward Darius. "And neither does destiny." Darius stood awkwardly, unsure whether to bow or speak first. "You must be Alara," he offered, feeling strangely exposed under her empty yet knowing stare.

She tilted her head slightly, as if listening to a voice only she could hear. "I am. And you, Darius child of prophecy, are the boy caught between threads of ruin and salvation." A chill skated down his spine. "The failure hero to be the only one to lose to Vorthis, I didn't ask for any of this," he muttered, the defensiveness creeping into his tone.

Alara's blind eyes softened, though her expression remained unreadable. "None of us do. The question is, will you follow the path before you, or fight it until it consumes you?" Seraphina moved closer, her hand brushing Darius's arm in a silent gesture of support. "Alara has guided my family for generations. If anyone can help you make sense of... all this, it's her."

Darius exhaled slowly, tension pooling in his shoulders. "Then I guess I don't have much choice." Alara's smile deepened, faintly amused. "Choice is a luxury of those not bound by prophecy. Come," she gestured to a table layered with scrolls and dusty tomes, "we have much to discuss, and little time before the world begins to unravel."

Darius exchanged a glance with Seraphina before following Alara out the doorway towards her chambers.

Darius followed Alara through the dimly lit corridors, her steps light despite the carved staff guiding her path. A strange hush filled the air, as though the castle itself held its breath the closer they drew to her chambers. They stopped before an arched door of aged oak, its surface etched with swirling runes that glowed faintly in the darkness. With a wave of her hand, the door creaked open.

The room beyond was unlike anything Darius had ever seen. It was vast yet intimate, the curved walls lined with ancient tapestries depicting celestial events—eclipses, comets, and constellations swirling in endless cycles. The scent of burning sage and lavender hung in the air, mingling with the faint metallic tang of old magic. Hundreds of glass vials and crystal orbs floated midair, suspended by unseen forces, each one humming softly with stored energy. Runes danced across their surfaces, flickering like embers.

The centrepiece of the room was a large circular table carved from dark stone; its surface inlaid with shimmering silver symbols forming an intricate map of the stars. Candles burned at its edges, their flames flickering in shades of violet and blue. On shelves lining the walls sat countless artifacts—curved daggers with inscriptions in forgotten tongues, cracked mirrors framed in bone, and timeworn tomes bound in strange leathers. Trinkets spun slowly in the air—tiny, delicate objects of unknown purpose—while an hourglass filled with glowing sand floated above the table, grains dripping impossibly upward.

At the far end of the chamber, a large stained-glass window filtered in the rising sun, casting swirling patterns of colour across the room. Beneath it, a small fountain bubbled with water that shimmered silver in the light, its gentle trickle the only sound beyond the low hum of magic.

Darius stood at the threshold, wide-eyed, feeling like he had stepped into another world entirely. "Come in," Alara said softly, already moving to the stone table, her fingers brushing its surface with a reverence that spoke of countless readings performed here. "This is where the truths of the past and the possibilities of the future reveal themselves—if you know how to look."

Darius stepped forward, the air heavy with power, every breath filling his lungs with a strange warmth. "I've... never seen anything like this," he admitted, his voice almost a whisper.

Alara smiled faintly, her clouded eyes turning toward him as though she could see straight through him. "Few have. Fewer still leave unchanged." She gestured to the seat across from her. "Sit, Darius. It is time we unravel the threads of your destiny." Alara's pale, sightless eyes fixed on Darius as though she could still see through the veil of reality into something deeper—something darker.

"You understand the weight of this prophecy," she began, her voice a low murmur that echoed off the stone walls, "that you are fated to fail." Darius clenched his fists, the sting of the king's words still fresh in his mind. "I understand," he replied, though the words felt hollow. "But I need to know... is there truly no path that leads to victory?"

Alara's fingers traced the worn edges of an ancient tablet, her touch delicate, reverent. "Prophecies are threads in a vast tapestry. Some are fixed, woven tightly into the fabric of fate. Others... fray at the edges, leaving room for change." She tilted her head, as though listening to some distant echo only she could hear. "You are bound to fail in the way the prophecy foretells. But failure... is not always the end."

Her words, cryptic and unsettling, hung in the air. Darius's voice cracked under the weight of his frustration. "So I'm just meant to watch the kingdom fall? To play my part as the doomed hero?"

A faint smile touched Alara's lips, tinged with both sorrow and something softer—hope, perhaps. "Even in the deepest darkness, a flicker of light can change the course of things. Perhaps you cannot seal Vorthis as those before you did, but your actions could still shape what follows."

Darius's jaw tightened. "What do you see, Alara? In the visions?" She hesitated, her fingers stilling over the tablet. "I see the land fractured, soaked in shadow. But I also see... fragments. Pieces that resist. People who survive. And in some visions, I glimpse a figure standing alone amid the ruin, sword in hand, light spilling from the cracks in the earth."

"Is it me?" Darius asked, his voice barely above a whisper. "I cannot say." Alara's brow furrowed, the weight of countless failed heroes pressing down on her words. "But know this—destiny is a cruel thing, Darius. Yet it has a weakness: the will of those brave enough to defy it. Will you choose to defy it?"

Of course he will, stupid question you blind bat.

The voice slithered through Darius's mind, dark and sharp, though he didn't so much as flinch—he hadn't heard it.

But Alara did.

Shit.

Her head tilted ever so slightly, her pale eyes narrowing as though trying to trace the source of the whisper. A flicker of unease passed over her features, but she masked it quickly, her expression returning to its calm facade. "I will," Darius replied firmly, his voice resolute, unaware of the shadow curling deeper within him.

Alara forced a small nod, though her thoughts churned. The darkness is already near him… but he does not know. Still, she said nothing, her silence heavy with truths left unspoken. The silence lingered, thick with unspoken thoughts, before Darius finally broke it. "What now?" he asked, his voice edged with both determination and uncertainty.

Alara's blind eyes shifted as though seeing something beyond the room, something distant and dark. "The path ahead is veiled in shadows, but some truths remain." She traced her fingers along the surface of the table, stopping at a worn map sprawled across it. "Vorthis cannot be faced in his full strength. His will and power are fragmented—split into four shards, each embodied by a demon birthed from his essence."

"Four demons?" Darius echoed, leaning in. Alara nodded slowly. "They wander this world, spreading wreck and ruin. Each one holds a piece of Vorthis's might. Slay them, and you weaken him, strip away his strength." Her hand hovered over the map, though her eyes did not see it. "Only when all four fall will Vorthis's resting place—the castle where he was sealed—reveal itself. It is hidden from this realm, cloaked by his power. But with the demons gone, the veil will lift."

Darius clenched his jaw, already picturing the monstrous foes he would have to face. "And then I go to the castle… to finish it." Alara's lips pressed into a thin line. "Yes. But the future is fragile, Darius. The visions only show so much. The path beyond the castle's reveal… is uncertain." She hesitated, the earlier whisper still lingering in her mind, a warning she could not fully understand.

Darius exhaled, the weight of it all sinking deeper into his bones. "Then I start with the demons." Alara gave a slow, solemn nod. "Steel your heart, Darius. Each one you face will break you in ways a blade cannot." Her words echoed in the chamber, Darius took a step toward the door, the weight of Alara's words pressing heavily on his shoulders. But before he could leave, her voice echoed once more through the chamber, softer this time—almost hesitant.

"Darius," she called, her blind eyes fixed somewhere past him, as if seeing another thread of fate unravelling. "This path… it is said to be walked alone. But prophecy is a fickle thing. It speaks in absolutes, yet life rarely follows such lines."

Darius paused, his hand hovering over the doorframe, brow furrowing. "What are you saying?"

Alara's fingers traced a faint symbol on the table, her touch lingering. "Even in the deepest darkness, a single light can guide the lost. But many lights together?" She smiled faintly. "They can hold back even the longest night." He absorbed her words, unsure of their full meaning, but feeling the weight behind them, nonetheless. "So… there's still hope."

Alara didn't answer directly. "Hope takes many forms, Darius. Some you may not see until you need them most."

The chamber fell into silence once more. Darius nodded, more to himself than her, and stepped out the door, Alara's cryptic words lingering in his mind—like a seed waiting to grow, her cryptic words turning over and over in his head. As he walked through the winding halls of the castle, a thought nagged at him. Should he see Seraphina before he left? Perhaps offer her some reassurance, or hear more of her thoughts on the matter? He stopped by a window, gazing out at the sprawling kingdom below, the world seeming so small, so distant from the weight on his shoulders.

leave her behind.

But no. He couldn't. There was no time for sentimentality. His destiny lay in the unknown, and he had no place to burden others with it. Not yet. And so, with a final, regretful glance toward the hall that would lead him to the princess's chambers, he turned away and stepped out of the castle doors.

The air outside was brisk, carrying with it the faint promise of change. As he descended the grand staircase, a quiet rustle of movement caught his eye. Far above, high on the castle walls, Seraphina stood on the balcony, her silhouette framed by the rising sun. She gazed out across the kingdom, lost in thought, the light playing across her features.

For a fleeting moment, their gazes met. A wordless connection passed between them—one of understanding, unspoken yet profound. Darius felt the weight of the moment, the hint of something unfulfilled, but he didn't linger, as Darius made his way down the castle steps, the heavy weight of his mission on his shoulders, he ventured through the bustling market streets of the kingdom. The sights and sounds of Castle Elaria's town greeted him with an odd sense of comfort as they did when he arrived the day before—colourful stalls brimming with fresh produce, the lively chatter of merchants and townspeople haggling, the scent of freshly baked bread wafting through the air. Yet, amidst the daily hustle, there was an undercurrent of something different. Whispers of his quest, of the prophecy, fluttered through the crowd.

One by one, the townspeople seemed to recognize him as he walked, their eyes filled with a mix of awe and hope. A young woman, no older than Darius, stepped forward with a small pouch of herbs, her hands trembling slightly. "For the journey ahead," she said, her voice barely above a whisper. "May the earth guide you."

Darius gave her a small nod, accepting the herbs. "Thank you," he replied, his voice thick with a gratitude he didn't quite feel. He tucked the pouch into his belt and continued on.

As he walked, more townsfolk approached. A grizzled merchant with a weathered face, his hands calloused from years of work, thrust a small loaf of bread into Darius's hands. "Take this," he insisted. "It'll keep you strong on the road."

Darius hesitated for a moment, the weight of the bread more symbolic than anything, but he didn't refuse. "I appreciate it," he said quietly, slipping the loaf into his pack.

Further down the street, an older woman, bent with age, handed him a canteen of water, her wrinkled hands offering it with surprising strength. "You'll need it more than you know," she said, her voice filled with a quiet knowing.

"Thank you," Darius replied, taking the canteen. It felt lighter than it should have, as if it contained more than just water—like it held their hopes, too.

By the time he reached the edge of the marketplace, a lantern appeared in his path, its delicate glass flickering in the soft morning light. A young boy, no older than eight or nine, looked up at him with wide eyes. "For when it gets dark," the boy said solemnly, his small hand offering the lantern. "You'll need light." Darius crouched down, meeting the boy's eyes. "I will," he said softly, accepting the lantern, "and this." The boys mother had appeared holding a tightly rolled blanket, "to make sure you rest easy." "Thank you." His heart tightened at the boy and mother's sincerity. It was a small gesture, but one that carried a weight of its own.

As he stood up, ready to leave, the people of the town watched him go, their silent blessings a mix of hope and despair. No words were spoken, but the air was thick with their unvoiced encouragement. Darius took a deep breath, feeling the weight of the gifts and the people behind him. With each step, the echoes of their kindness lingered in his chest, a reminder of what he was fighting for. He adjusted his pack, the weight of the supplies comforting in a way that had nothing to do with practicality. As he moved beyond the gates of the kingdom, the quiet townsfolk, their faces a blur in the distance.

As Darius passed through the castle gates, the open countryside stretched out before him—vast, untamed, and quiet. He paused for a moment, taking in the landscape. The sun had fully risen now, casting a golden light over the fields and forests that lay beyond the castle's walls. It was a stark contrast to the dark weight that hung in his chest, a weight that seemed to grow with every breath he took, as if the very air he breathed carried the weight of his destiny.

He took a slow step forward, then another, but as he moved, a question gnawed at him: Where do I begin? The words of Alara echoed in his mind—the four demons, Vorthis's castle, the path laid out before him—but there was no clear starting point. The uncertainty of the journey, of what lay ahead, made each direction seem equally uncertain. His mind swirled with the enormity of it all, and yet, the silence of the countryside seemed to offer no answers. It was as if the world itself held its breath, waiting for him to make the first move.

He could feel the eyes of the townsfolk still on him, watching from the distance. He had the supplies they'd given him, the promises of support, but there was still a deep, unsettling void in his heart. What did their faith in him mean if he didn't even know where to begin? The weight of their hopes felt almost too much to bear.

His eyes wandered toward the horizon. He remembered the village he'd passed on his way to Castle Elaria—the one with the winding road that led through thick trees, the one nestled near the edge of the valley. The village seemed like the logical first step. It was the closest to the castle, and it had to have someone who could offer more than vague prophecies and cryptic words. There, perhaps, he might find a clue, or a person who could make sense of this fate he'd been handed. It was a starting point, at least.

That village would be his first stop.

With a determined breath, Darius turned in the direction of the village, the landscape unfolding before him like a scroll he was now tasked to read. His boots crunched softly against the gravel road as he walked, the weight of his journey pressing down on him. The path ahead wasn't clear, but it was something. At least it was a place to start.

Each step felt heavier than the last, as though the very earth beneath him was pulling him toward something unknown. The long road ahead stretched before him like a dark and winding river, its currents carrying him forward despite his uncertainty. Yet there was no turning back now. Not after everything he had learned. Not after the prophecy.

The demons. The castle. Vorthis.

One thing was certain: the road ahead would be long, and it would be fraught with shadows, but it would eventually lead him where he needed to go. He just had to figure out how to get there.

And so, Darius set his sights on the village in the distance, the only thing he could grasp with certainty in a world that felt increasingly uncertain. the unseen chains of fate, and the knowledge that his fate was tied to something greater than himself, weighed heavy on his shoulders. But he had no choice. The road ahead was the only road left.

CHAPTER 4

The Edge of Trust

The castle had long since disappeared behind the hills, swallowed by the vast wilderness stretching before him. For the first time since his arrival at Castle Elaria, Darius was truly alone.

The road beneath his boots had given way to uneven dirt paths, winding through dense patches of trees that whispered with every shift of the wind. Sunlight filtered through the branches in broken streaks, casting fractured patterns across the ground. The air was thick with the scent of damp earth and pine, so unlike the stone and incense of the castle halls.

For a while, he walked in silence, his thoughts louder than the world around him. Alara's words echoed in his mind, circling like vultures over a dying beast. *Will you choose to defy it?* He had answered without hesitation, but doubt clung to him like a second skin. A distant rustle broke his thoughts. He stopped, hand instinctively moving to his sword. The wind? A small animal? Or something worse? The undergrowth shifted again, and a low growl rumbled through the trees. Darius turned sharply, eyes scanning the thick brush. The world around him seemed to hold its breath, waiting.

Then it lunged. A flash of matted fur and yellowed fangs. A wolf—lean, hungry, and desperate. Darius barely had time to react before the beast was upon him, claws scraping against his armour as its weight slammed into him. He staggered back, planting his feet just in time to shove it off with his forearm. The wolf snarled, pacing in a slow circle, hackles raised.

Darius drew his sword, but his grip was too tight, his fingers stiff. *It's just a wolf*, he told himself, but his mind was elsewhere. It wasn't the beast that terrified him—it was the road ahead, the weight of the prophecy, the crushing uncertainty. The wolf lunged again, and this time, he was too slow. Teeth sank into the leather of his bracer, the force jarring his arm as he struggled to shake it off.

Too slow, hero.

He twisted, bringing his knee up hard into its ribs. The wolf yelped, loosening its grip just enough for Darius to shove it away. His heartbeat thundered in his ears.

Focus.

He stepped forward, slashing low. The blade caught the wolf's shoulder, cutting deep but not lethal. The beast yelped, stumbling, but it did not retreat.

It was desperate.

And so was he.

With a sharp breath, he braced himself as the wolf leapt again, this time bringing his sword up in a clean, decisive arc. The blade found its mark. The wolf's momentum carried it forward a few steps before it collapsed into the dirt, its breath coming in ragged gasps before it stilled.

Silence returned to the forest.

Darius stood over the body, chest heaving, his hands trembling slightly around the hilt of his sword. Not from the fight itself, but from everything weighing down on him. The fight had been easy—yet his mind had made it harder. He had hesitated, let his thoughts slow him.

A slow, sarcastic clap broke the silence.

Darius spun, his hand flying to his sword, but the only threat before him was… a person? A grinning, easy-going figure perched on a fallen log their arms folded and one leg lazily draped over the other, watching him with evident amusement.

"That was a hell of a show," they said, tilting their head. "Really kept me on the edge of my seat there. Thought for sure that wolf was about to win." Darius narrowed his eyes, taking in the stranger. Brown hair tied up in a messy manbun, though loose strands fell haphazardly around his face, Their clothes were well-worn but not ragged, a mix of patched leathers and a dark cloak draped lazily over one shoulder. A set of twin daggers rested at their hip, but their stance was utterly relaxed, as if they hadn't a care in the world. Their smirk was almost infuriatingly casual.

He exhaled sharply. "You just sat there and watched?"

"Well, I was going to help, but you looked like you needed the practice." They shrugged. "Didn't want to steal your moment." Darius ground his teeth, but the stranger just grinned wider. "Besides," they continued, swinging their legs off the log and hopping onto their feet, "if you're this fun to watch fighting a wolf, I can't wait to see what happens when you run into something bigger."

Darius wasn't sure if he wanted to sigh or punch them. "And who exactly are you?"

The stranger swept into an exaggerated bow. "Name's Rowen, and you, my tragic, brooding friend, are clearly not from around here." They straightened, their gaze sharpening just a little. "So, what's a lost soul like you doing wandering the wilds?" Darius hesitated. He wasn't sure if this person was just a traveller or someone he needed to be wary of. But one thing was certain—they were the stark opposite of him. And for some reason, that made their presence oddly grounding.

He clapped a hand on Darius's shoulder, completely unfazed by the glare he received. "So, where's a guy like you headed?" Darius shrugged off Rowen's hand, his emerald eyes narrowing. "North," he said curtly, turning away to clean his blade on a patch of grass. "And I'm not lost." Rowen let out a low whistle. "North, eh? Through the Whispering Woods? Towards Dragonspine? Brave man." He cocked his head, watching Darius with a lopsided grin. "Or foolish. Sometimes hard to tell the difference."

Darius sheathed his sword, the obsidian blade sliding home with a soft hiss. He met Rowen's gaze, his expression unreadable. "I know the dangers. I'm prepared."

"Oh, I'm sure you are," Rowen chuckled, nodding toward the wolf's carcass. "Bold strategy, letting it take a bite first. Really keeps things exciting." Darius bristled. "I don't need to explain myself to you," he said coldly, turning away.

Rowen fell into step beside him without missing a beat. "No, you don't. But you might want to consider it. The Whispering Woods aren't kind to lone travellers, especially ones who look like they just stepped out of a royal painting." Darius clenched his jaw, quickening his pace, but Rowen matched him stride for stride, as effortless as a shadow. "Look," Rowen said, his tone shifting, some of the teasing fading. "I'm not trying to pry. But I know these woods better than most. And if you're heading north... well, let's just say there are things in those trees that make that wolf look like a harmless pup."

Darius slowed, meeting Rowen's gaze despite himself. The stranger was irritating—too smug, too carefree—but there was something about the way he spoke, the quiet confidence behind his words, that made Darius hesitate. Just for a breath, he hesitated.

Darius sighed, his shoulders sagging slightly. "I appreciate the concern," he said, his tone still guarded but lacking the sharp edge from before. "But this journey... it's not one I can share."

Rowen arched an eyebrow, his grin widening. "Oh? Sounds mysterious. Let me guess—secret mission? Forbidden love? Prophecy of doom?" At the word prophecy, Darius tensed. It was brief, almost imperceptible, but Rowen caught it. His eyes lit up with unmistakable amusement. "Ah, prophecy it is then! How exciting," he said, rubbing his hands together like a gambler about to roll the dice. "You know, I've always wanted to be part of a grand destiny. Fancy letting me tag along?"

Darius shook his head, exasperated. "This isn't a game. You don't understand what's at stake."

"Then enlighten me," Rowen said, his voice shifting—gone was the easy sarcasm, the playful jabs. He was still smiling, but something in his gaze had sharpened, watching Darius carefully. Darius scoffed, shaking his head. "You're awfully persistent for someone who just met me."

Rowen spread his arms in an exaggerated shrug. "I like to think of it as being *invested* in the world around me. And right now, that world includes one brooding swordsman with a big secret." He smirked. "Besides, you *clearly* need someone watching your back.

What happens when the next wolf comes along? Or gods forbid, something with more teeth?" Darius rolled his eyes, pushing forward along the trail. "I can take care of myself."

"Uh-huh. Right. Like you took care of that wolf?" Rowen easily matched his pace, hands resting casually behind his head. "You hesitated back there. Lost in thought. If you do that when something worse comes along, you're dead."

Darius bristled but didn't respond. He hated that Rowen had noticed—hated that he was right. His mind had been elsewhere, too tangled in fate and duty to focus on the fight in front of him. That couldn't happen again. After a moment of silence, Rowen nudged him lightly with an elbow. "Hey, don't take it so personally. Happens to the best of us. And trust me, I know all about getting stuck in your own head."

Darius gave him a sceptical glance. "Somehow, I doubt that." Rowen gasped in mock offense. "What, just because I don't skulk around looking like the weight of the world is crushing me? I have layers, you know." Darius huffed—not quite a laugh, but close. "Right."

"See? That was almost a smile. We're making progress." Rowen grinned, then gestured toward the tree line ahead. "Look, like I said, I know these woods. If you're heading north, you'll have to get through the Whispering Woods first, and trust me, it's a lot easier with someone who knows the way."

Darius hesitated. He knew better than to trust strangers, especially ones who seemed too eager to follow him. And yet… Rowen didn't seem like a threat. If anything, his carefree attitude was a stark contrast to the weight that Darius carried—an annoyance, maybe, but not unwelcome.

"Fine" he said at last, his voice begrudging. "But just until we reach the village, and don't slow me down." Rowen grinned like he'd won a prize. "Wouldn't dream of it, *partner*." Darius sighed. He already regretted this. And yet, somehow, the road ahead felt just a little less lonely.

Darius kept his pace steady, but his mind was still turning over Rowen's presence. The man was clearly more than he let on—too skilled, too comfortable in the wilds to be just some carefree wanderer. And yet, he acted like all of this was just a game. He glanced at Rowen out of the corner of his eye. "You haven't actually told me why you're so eager to follow me." Rowen grinned. "Haven't I? Maybe I just like your charming personality." Darius sighed, exasperated. "Somehow, I doubt that."

Before Rowen could fire back another quip, a rustling in the undergrowth brought them both to a halt. Darius's hand went to his sword. Rowen, by contrast, tilted his head slightly, listening. "Wolves," he murmured. "At least four." A low growl confirmed his words as dark shapes melted out of the trees, circling them. Darius braced himself. The first wolf lunged—he swung his blade, but just as it tried to leap back, Rowen was already there, sweeping low and slashing its legs out from under it. The wolf yelped, and Darius finished it with a clean strike.

Another came from behind, but before Darius could turn, Rowen moved—fluid, almost playful—vaulting over him and driving his short sword into the wolf's flank mid-flip. Darius exhaled sharply. "Show-off." Rowen landed lightly, flashing a grin. "You love it." The fight didn't last much longer. When the final wolf fell, the two stood, catching their breath. Rowen wiped his blade on the grass, then glanced at Darius with an unreadable expression.

"Alright," he said, his tone quieter now. "You want the real reason?" Darius turned to him, waiting.

Rowen sheathed his weapon. "I know who you are, Darius. And I know what you're setting out to do." His usual smirk was gone. "My village—it's suffering. We can't get our harvest to markets because of the beasts and nasties that's recently been lurking we have little money, and I can't sit by and wait for a hero to fix things. I need to stand with you."

Darius studied him, feeling the weight of those words settle between them. For once, Rowen wasn't joking. The Whispering Woods stretched before them, thick with ancient trees and twisting roots. Sunlight barely pierced through the dense canopy, casting the path ahead in shifting shadows. Darius walked with quiet purpose, his sword still in hand. Rowen, by contrast, moved like he belonged here—light on his feet, eyes scanning the undergrowth, always aware.

"So, do you always look this miserable when you travel?" Rowen quipped, sidestepping a gnarled root. "Or am I just lucky enough to witness your brooding at its peak?" Darius didn't dignify that with a response. They had been walking for some time now, their earlier fight with the wolves lingering only in the occasional glance at a claw mark on Darius' bracer or the drying blood along Rowen's sleeve.

It wasn't long before trouble found them again. A guttural snarl cut through the stillness, and from the brush burst another creature—larger than the wolves before, its body low to the ground, claws digging into the dirt. A boar, but warped, its eyes glowed an unnatural yellow, and its tusks were jagged, almost like blackened bone. Darius barely had time to react before it charged.

He swung his sword, but the beast twisted at the last second, the blade glancing off its thick hide.

"Great," Rowen muttered, already moving. "An angry, armoured pig. Just what we needed."

Darius pivoted as the boar came at him again, this time striking hard enough to send the creature skidding. But before it could recover, Rowen darted in low, kicking off a nearby tree to come down hard with his daggers, driving them into the beast's exposed neck. It let out a strangled cry before going limp.

Darius caught his breath, looking at Rowen, who grinned as he yanked his blades free. "You know," Rowen said, shaking off the blood, "for someone so serious and rigid, you fight well." Darius exhaled, glancing at the dead beast. "You're not bad yourself," he admitted.

Rowen feigned shock. "Did the great and mighty Darius just compliment me?" Darius rolled his eyes and kept walking.

The hours passed with more skirmishes—nothing too dire, but enough to test them. More wolves, an oversized snake that almost caught Darius off guard, and even a horned hare Rowen insisted on calling a "demon bunny."

Despite himself, Darius found the rhythm of their fights... comforting. Rowen's wild, unpredictable style balanced his own more measured strikes. Where Darius took the direct approach, Rowen moved with sharp, precise agility, cutting off escape routes, landing hits in ways Darius wouldn't have considered.

The sun had begun to dip below the tree line when Rowen finally said what Darius had been thinking. "We're not making it out of here before nightfall," he noted, scanning the sky through the gaps in the trees. "And unless you have some miraculous night vision you haven't told me about, we need to find shelter."

Darius knew he was right. The deeper they went, the more unnatural the woods had begun to feel. The air carried a strange stillness now, like the forest itself was waiting for the sun to set before revealing its true nature.

Rowen crouched low, running his fingers over the ground. "There's a clearing not far from here," he murmured. "Looks like an old hunter's camp. If we move now, we'll get there before it's completely dark." Darius hesitated for only a moment before nodding. "Lead the way."

Rowen smirked. "Oh, now you trust me?"

Darius sighed. "Don't make me regret it."

Rowen chuckled and took the lead, weaving effortlessly through the trees. As Darius followed, he realized—without fully meaning to—that he had started trusting Rowen. Just a little.

The campfire crackled, casting flickering shadows on the surrounding trees. The smell of roasting meat filled the air— nothing fancy, just the boar they had hauled back after their skirmish. The firelight danced in Rowen's eyes as he poked at the spit, grinning like it was the greatest feast in the world.

Darius, sitting across from him, was less enthusiastic about the meal. It wasn't the taste that bothered him—he was used to eating what the land provided—but the fact that he'd had to rely on someone else for this moment. That felt... odd. He'd always been the one taking the first watch, organizing, being the one others could depend on.

But now here he was, side by side with Rowen, who seemed to be relishing the meal with abandon. He leaned back, tossing a bone into the fire with a satisfied sigh.

"Not bad for a pair of strangers, huh?" Rowen said, licking his fingers before flopping down onto the grass. "I mean, most people would've just starved out here by now."

Darius couldn't help but smirk, though it was a touch more tired than usual. "I wouldn't call this a feast," he muttered, tearing into his own portion.

Rowen raised an eyebrow, clearly amused by Darius's dry tone. "Sure, it's no royal banquet, but it's better than a day's travel without a bite. Plus, you didn't have to cook it. So, bonus for you."

Darius couldn't deny that, though he didn't acknowledge it out loud. Instead, he turned his gaze to the fire, the crackling flames a welcome distraction from his thoughts.

Rowen, seemingly content to continue the easy flow of conversation, stretched his arms out and gazed at the sky. "You know, I've always found the night sky to be... kinda comforting. Out here, anyway. Feels like everything's bigger than you, like it doesn't matter how messed up things are. The stars, they don't care about your problems."

Darius glanced up at the stars, following Rowen's gaze. "You have a strange way of looking at the world."

"That's what people keep telling me," Rowen laughed, his tone full of mirth. "But hey, someone's gotta look at it differently. Or else, it'd just be... boring."

They sat in comfortable silence for a few moments, the fire crackling between them, its warmth sinking into Darius's skin. He found himself feeling... lighter. The tension that usually coiled tight in his chest wasn't as suffocating tonight. Rowen's presence, wild as it was, had a way of dissolving that heaviness, like the space between the words left unspoken was enough to give him room to breathe.

"So," Rowen said suddenly, his voice light. "You think you're gonna make it through this entire journey without cracking a smile?"

Darius blinked, taken aback by the question. "What do you mean?"

Rowen grinned, tossing a small rock into the fire. "I mean, I've been watching you. You've got a lot of fight in you, sure, but you don't let loose at all. Not even once. Not even when I call you 'brooding'. You're practically a statue."

Darius felt a fleeting spark of irritation, but it passed quickly. Rowen had a way of disarming him, of making his sharp edges feel a little less necessary. He sighed, glancing at the fire. "I'm not here to entertain you, Rowen."

Rowen leaned forward, elbows on his knees, eyes gleaming with mischief. "I didn't think you were. But maybe, just maybe, you could let yourself have a bit of fun. You don't always have to be on edge, you know."

Darius didn't reply right away. His gaze drifted back to the stars, and he found, for the first time in a long while, that he wasn't dreading the next moment. The crackling of the fire, the night air, Rowen's easy banter—it wasn't so bad.

And then, when Rowen made some ridiculous face to poke fun at him, Darius couldn't help it. A short laugh slipped from his throat, unexpected and brief.

Rowen's grin widened. "Oh, so there's a smile hiding under all that stone, huh?"

Darius felt his lips twitch upward, a faint smile tugging at the corners of his mouth. His laugh faded, but the warmth lingered.

For a moment, they were just two people around a fire in the middle of the woods. No weighty prophecies, no looming dangers, just the crackle of flames and the quiet, easy rhythm of being alive. And Darius, despite everything, found he didn't mind that. Not one bit. The fire burned brighter as the moon rose higher above them, casting its pale light over the two figures sitting side by side.

CHAPTER 5

Where Madness Grows

The first rays of dawn filtered through the canopy above, casting long shadows across the dense underbrush. The crackling fire was reduced to smouldering embers, its warmth fading with the night. Darius rubbed his eyes, the remnants of sleep still lingering in his bones as he sat up, stretching his stiff limbs.

Rowen was already awake, as usual, leaning against a tree with his back to the fire, silently observing the surroundings. The man was always alert, even in moments when he seemed to be doing nothing.

Darius stood, brushing off the dirt from his cloak and fastening his sword belt. His muscles still ached from the day before, but he didn't let it show. There was a weight to the silence around them this morning, a feeling that the woods were holding their breath in anticipation. Rowen pushed off the tree and approached, his usual grin replaced by a more serious expression. "We should be moving. The path to the heart of the woods isn't far, but it's a hell of a lot trickier than the edges."

Darius gave him a sharp nod, feeling the shift in the air as they prepared to leave the small clearing behind. There was something in Rowen's voice today—less playful, more cautious—that set Darius on edge. The woods felt different, too. The once welcoming green canopy now seemed oppressive, the distant calls of birds and animals replaced by an unsettling silence.

"We'll stick together, as usual," Darius muttered, more to himself than Rowen.

Rowen gave a half-smile, his eyes scanning the path ahead. "You're starting to catch on," he said lightly, but there was an edge of something more serious behind it. "But trust me, if we're going to make it through the heart of these woods, we'll need to watch our backs more than ever."

Darius glanced over at Rowen, their eyes meeting for a moment. "I've got my eyes open," he said firmly, already stepping forward. "Let's get moving."

The road ahead was uncertain, the woods dark and full of hidden dangers. But as they walked, side by side, there was an unspoken understanding between them. They may not trust each other completely yet, but for now, they had each other's backs.

The further they travelled into the woods, the heavier the air grew, pressing down on them like a thick, unseen weight. The trees seemed to close in tighter, their gnarled limbs twisting unnaturally, casting twisted shadows on the path ahead. The once familiar sounds of birds and small animals had all but disappeared, replaced by the distant rustle of unseen things moving just beyond the tree line.

Rowen was unusually quiet, his usual playfulness gone. His eyes flickered constantly, scanning their surroundings, the carefree air replaced with something more guarded.

Darius noticed, and for the first time, he felt a tension in the air, something intangible that made his skin prickle. It was a slow-building discomfort that seemed to seep into every corner of the forest, tightening the knot in his gut.

Rowen's voice broke the silence, low and serious. "Something's wrong here. These woods…" He paused, glancing around, as if waiting for the trees themselves to whisper. "They've always been eerie, but it's different now. Ever since the seal started weakening, it's like the woods themselves can feel it. Feel what's coming."

Darius didn't respond immediately. He hadn't heard much about the seal before, other than vague rumours. But from the tension in Rowen's voice, it was clear that whatever was happening here wasn't just in the air—it was in the very heart of the forest itself.

Before he could ask, a low, guttural growl echoed through the trees, and the ground beneath their feet seemed to tremble ever so slightly.

Rowen's hand went to his sword, his body tensing. "Get ready," he murmured, eyes narrowing as he scanned the thick underbrush.

The growl came again, closer this time, and was followed by a sickening snap of bones, as if something was shifting, twisting in ways it shouldn't. The bushes ahead rustled violently, and out of the shadows lunged a creature unlike anything Darius had ever seen.

Ah, here they are.

It was a wolf, yes, but it was far from natural. Its body was grotesque, its limbs distorted and elongated, the fur on its back matted and bristling with black, sickly spines that seemed to pulse with some dark energy. Its eyes gleamed a fiery yellow, filled with malice, but they were too wide, too unnatural. There was no intelligence in them—only hunger.

The creature howled, a noise so inhuman that it sent a chill down Darius's spine.

"Move!" Rowen shouted, shoving Darius to the side as the wolf lunged.

Instinct took over. Darius drew his sword just in time, blocking the beast's claws with the edge of his blade. The force of the strike nearly sent him to the ground, but he held firm, shoving the creature back with all his strength. But before he could react, another wolf—no, *thing*—emerged from the shadows, its body contorting in ways that defied logic. This one had gnarled, razor-sharp fangs that dripped with some black substance, and its eyes were sunken, hollow pits.

Darius fought, but it was clear—this was no ordinary beast. His blade sliced through its flesh, but it didn't flinch. Instead, it seemed to writhe, healing almost immediately, its body reforming in a grotesque display of dark magic.

Rowen was moving like a shadow beside him, faster than Darius could track. He dove, rolling under Darius's strike and coming up on the other side of the beast, slashing through its underbelly with a swift, precise motion. The creature howled in agony, but it didn't die. It only grew angrier, thrashing violently.

Darius cursed under his breath and swung again, this time catching the creature in the throat, forcing it back. But just as he was about to finish it off, the first wolf came charging back, its mutated form almost faster than he could react.

"*Watch your back!*" Rowen yelled, his voice cutting through the chaos.

Darius spun just in time to see the wolf's twisted jaws snap shut around his arm, sinking deep into the leather of his bracer. The pain was immediate, sharp, but his focus was even sharper. He raised his sword, driving it deep into the beast's skull, the crack of bone resonating through the clearing.

But the moment the wolf fell, another growl sounded, this one far more guttural, coming from deeper in the woods.

Rowen panted beside him, his sword coated in thick, black blood, his usual grin replaced by a grimace. "These things… they're not just animals. They're born of something darker, something ancient." His voice was hoarse, and his eyes flashed with something like fear. Darius took a breath, wiping the sweat from his brow as he surveyed the surrounding woods. "What the hell is going on here?"

Rowen's voice dropped low, his words heavy. "The woods are waking up. And it's not just the trees. It's Vorthis. His magic is leaking into this place, warping everything around it."

that's right, tremble.

A cold shiver ran down Darius's spine, but he couldn't look away. He wasn't sure what was worse—the creatures or the truth Rowen had just revealed.

As Rowen sheathed his dagger, he didn't look back at Darius. Instead, his gaze was fixed on the dark depths of the forest ahead, as if he could already hear the next growl echoing from the shadows. "Stay close," Rowen said, his voice hard now, no trace of the playful tone left. "This is only the beginning."

As Darius and Rowen continued their journey deeper into the Whispering Woods, the air grew heavier with every step, thick with an unnatural chill. The once serene and familiar landscape had become something far more menacing, the very trees themselves seemed to groan in agony as they twisted and stretched, their roots reaching like tendrils into the ground.

With each passing hour, they encountered more contorted, eldritch versions of creatures that normally called the woods home—beasts that were grotesquely altered by the influence of Vorthis's weakening seal. The birds were now monstrous, their feathers blackened and torn, their calls dissonant and haunting. The deer they once saw darting through the trees were now skeletal, their hollow eyes glowing with an unnatural light, charging at them like mindless predators.

Darius's sword struck with more precision now, the edge of his blade cutting through the corrupted beasts with grim determination. But it wasn't just his blade that was becoming sharper—his movements were changing, adapting. Where once he had been stiff and calculated, he was now fluid, almost graceful in his strikes. His footwork had become lighter, faster. He was moving with a purpose, and that purpose was becoming clear with every swing, every parry, every step.

Rowen watched all of this in stunned silence. At first, he had assumed Darius's fighting style was rigid and methodical, far too disciplined for a forest like this. But over time, the way Darius moved was changing, shifting. He was adapting—incorporating the instinctive, wild fluidity Rowen himself had mastered.

In the midst of a battle with a corrupted stag, its limbs distorted, and its antlers more like serrated shards of obsidian than bone, Darius spun low, sweeping his blade in an arc that cut through the creature's hide in a single smooth motion. Rowen's eyes widened as he observed the shift in Darius's style.

"Damn," Rowen muttered, almost to himself. The way Darius had moved, fluid and quick, it was almost as if he were... mimicking Rowen's own instincts. The stag crumpled to the ground, its monstrous form disintegrating into a pile of dark, rotting ash. But Rowen didn't take his eyes off Darius.

"You... you did that *on purpose*," Rowen said, blinking as if trying to make sense of it. "You switched your style right in the middle of that attack—*and it worked.*"

Darius paused, wiping the sweat from his brow as he straightened, his emerald eyes narrowing in silent contemplation. "I just saw an opening," he muttered. "Wasn't thinking about style—just what needed to be done."

Rowen shook his head in disbelief. "You've got a hell of an instinct for it, though. You adapted mid-fight. I've never seen anyone do that—not like you did. Most people would struggle to even notice the opening, let alone... *flow* into it like that."

Darius didn't answer, but the flicker of a smile played on his lips, though it was brief. His thoughts were still racing, still processing the tension growing in the air around them. But Rowen's words lingered in his mind. "It's just survival," Darius muttered after a long pause. "Adapt or die. Isn't that what you've been doing since we've been in these woods?"

Rowen smirked at the response but nodded. "Fair enough. But still, you're not just surviving anymore. You're *thriving* out here. You've been picking up on everything I've been doing like it's second nature to you."

Darius gave him a sideways glance. "Maybe it's the woods themselves. They're changing... and so am I."

Rowen's grin faded for a moment, his eyes growing serious.

"You're something more than just 'surviving.' I've seen people fight before. But you? You're *evolving* mid-battle. I knew you are some big shot hero but before that I thought you were maybe a royal soldier rigid and tough, but now..." He trailed off, shaking his head. "*Now* I know what you really are."

Darius stopped in his tracks, his expression unreadable, but his heart raced at the weight of Rowen's words. "And what's that?" Rowen's smirk returned, but it was softer now, more understanding. "*You're the hero we need.*"

The words hung in the air, and Darius, for the first time in a long while, felt the weight of them settle inside him. His gaze shifted toward Rowen, who was watching him with an intensity that wasn't mocking or playful, but genuine.

But before Darius could respond, a shrill, agonized screech split the air, pulling them both from the moment.

They spun in unison, weapons raised, as a new presence made itself known. From the darkness of the trees emerged a creature far more twisted than anything they had faced before: a grotesque, multi-limbed beast, its body composed of writhing, tangled masses of limbs and flesh, dripping with dark, oily ichor. Its mouth was a maw of serrated teeth, and its eyes glowed with a sickly green light, twitching unnaturally in the dark.

"Here we go again," Rowen muttered under his breath, his hand instinctively moving to his dagger. "*You ready to show me something new, hero?*"

Darius's grip tightened on his sword. His muscles were tense, but his mind was clear. He wasn't thinking about style or how to adapt anymore. He just knew what to do. The battle instincts he had picked up from Rowen were there, ingrained in his own movement style. The fight wasn't a struggle anymore—it was an extension of himself.

"Let's finish this," Darius said, his voice cold and determined. Rowen's grin was back, but this time there was no mockery in it—only respect. "That's what I like to hear."

Together, they rushed into the fray, their movements synchronized as though they had been fighting together for years. Darius's sword sliced through the air in sweeping arcs, each strike faster and more fluid than the last, as Rowen darted in with the precision of a predator, his strikes low and quick, targeting the creature's underbelly.

They were no longer just allies fighting for survival—they were becoming a true team, their bond growing stronger with each battle.

And with each fight, Darius knew he was closer to becoming the hero this world needed, he would defy his destiny and will not fail. As the sun dipped lower in the sky, the forest grew quieter. Darius and Rowen moved cautiously, their senses heightened, but the woods were still. Almost too still.

Then, the air shifted. A chill slithered across their skin, unnatural, creeping like a whisper in the back of their minds. The leaves, once rustling with the movement of smaller creatures, were now eerily silent. Darius felt his heart race. This silence wasn't natural.

Rowen's gaze darted around, his fingers twitching on the hilt of his sword. "We're not alone," he muttered under his breath.

Before either could react, the ground beneath their feet trembled. The trees groaned as something immense shifted in the shadows. A low, guttural growl echoed from deep within the forest, shaking the very air around them.

Darius's grip tightened on his sword, his heart pounding as he searched the shadows. But then he saw it.

The beast emerged from the darkness like a nightmare made of flesh. Its form was wrong, indescribable—a mass of shifting shapes and writhing tendrils that stretched out from a central body, constantly changing. Its eyes were everywhere. Dozens of them. Slits, bulging orbs, and empty sockets blinking in every direction, as if its very form was an attempt to make sense of the impossible. The more he looked at it, the harder it was to comprehend its shape or structure. It defied logic.

"Move," Rowen hissed, pulling Darius back as the creature lunged forward, its long, spindly limbs reaching out like grasping hands.

Darius didn't need to be told twice. They both dashed in opposite directions, but the creature moved faster, its impossibly long limbs snapping through the air with a horrible sound. It towered over them, its form twisting and reforming as if made of shifting shadows and madness.

The more Darius tried to focus on it, the more the world around him seemed to distort. His vision blurred. His mind, already weary from the constant battles, struggled to grasp what was in front of him. The creature was impossible. And yet, it was there.

Rowen's voice broke through the fog in Darius's mind, though it sounded distant, as if coming from another world. "We can't fight this thing! We have to get out—now!"

Darius barely registered the words. His sword felt heavier in his hand, and his legs seemed sluggish, weighed down by something unseen. It wasn't fear. It was something worse. Something far deeper. The creature wasn't just a threat to their lives. It was a threat to their sanity, their very perception of the world.

Rowen was already ahead, racing through the trees, his movements erratic, desperate. Darius followed without thinking, pushing through the fog in his mind. The air felt thick, suffocating, as if the very atmosphere was pressing down on him, trying to crush him into madness.

The sounds of the creature's monstrous form following them grew louder—its gurgling, gory growls mixed with the sound of snapping branches and the agonizing screech of its knotted body shifting.

They ran. They didn't stop.

But with every step they took, the world around them seemed to warp further. The trees no longer looked like trees. The sunset seemed to twist into something alien. Reality felt like a fragile thread, ready to snap at any moment.

"Just keep moving!" Rowen shouted, his voice strained.

Darius couldn't remember how long they ran. Only that the nightmare was still behind them, its presence overwhelming every thought, every breath.

And then, they burst from the trees and into a clearing the sun now completely set. The creature was still with them, but something had changed. The world had shifted. The clearing felt almost like a different world entirely—one that didn't care about the rules of nature or reality.

Rowen turned to Darius, his face pale with terror. "We can't stop! We have to—" But the beast was right behind them.

"Run!" Rowen screamed, and they bolted into the night once more.

After what felt like an eternity of running, Darius and Rowen stumbled through the thick underbrush, crashing out of the forest and into the open. The sunlight hit them like a physical blow, harsh and unrelenting after the oppressive darkness of the woods.

They stopped, both of them breathing heavily, their chests heaving with each frantic breath. Darius's mind spun as he tried to process the sudden shift—one moment they were fleeing a nightmare that twisted reality itself, and now… daylight. The soft morning light streamed through the trees, birds chirped in the distance, and the world was calm. Too calm.

Darius's hand still clutched his sword, knuckles white from the tension. His legs felt weak beneath him, and he couldn't seem to shake the feeling that the ground was still shifting underfoot. His eyes flickered to Rowen, whose face was as pale as death, his breath ragged.

Rowen's voice was a hoarse rasp. "Is it… is it gone?" His eyes darted around, scanning the peaceful forest behind them, searching for any sign of the creature. But there was nothing. The beast was gone, as if it had never existed. The sun shone down with its usual warmth, and the distant mountain peaks of Dragonspine loomed serenely ahead, unbothered by the chaos they had just endured.

Darius wiped the sweat from his brow, but it didn't stop the tremors running through his limbs. He couldn't shake the image of that creature—the way it had warped everything around them, how it had made him feel like he was losing his grip on reality. How, for a moment, he couldn't even trust his own senses. Was it real? Or had it all been some corrupted hallucination?

"I… I can't make sense of it," Darius muttered, his voice hollow.

Rowen took a shaky step forward, his eyes wide. "This… this isn't right." His voice faltered. "This should've been night. We—when we ran, it felt like the forest had swallowed us whole. But now…" He looked up at the sky, blinking against the sunlight. "Now, it's daytime."

Darius looked around as well, but the change was too jarring. The woods no longer felt haunted, no longer had the oppressive air of doom. It was as if the Whispering Woods had never been twisted, as if they had been lost in a nightmare of their own making.

"No sign of it," Rowen muttered, scanning the area with frantic eyes. "No sign of anything… just trees. And sunlight."

They stood there in the clearing for a long moment, neither of them able to speak. Darius's heart was still racing, his thoughts tangled in confusion. The woods had been a prison of madness, a place where time and reality had bent. And now, as if someone had simply flicked a switch, everything was normal again. Too normal.

Rowen broke the silence, his voice barely a whisper. "What the hell just happened?"

"I don't know," Darius replied, shaking his head. "But I don't think we're supposed to understand."

The realization hit them both at once: the creature hadn't just been a physical threat. It had been something far worse, something that attacked their minds, warped their perception.

Rowen, always quick to recover, now seemed shaken, far from his usual playful self. "We—we need to keep moving," he said, his voice hoarse. "I… I don't know what we just survived, but I don't want to stay in these woods another second."

Darius nodded, his pulse still hammering in his chest. They had no choice but to move on. Rowen had been right—there was nothing left for them here. The beast, the madness, the distorted reality of the woods… it was all gone. But the lingering sense of unease remained, gnawing at the edges of their minds.

As they started walking again, the path ahead seemed far too quiet. The weight of what had just happened pressed down on them both, but neither dared to speak. The silence between them was deafening, the kind that spoke volumes without needing words.

They made their way toward Rowen's village, but every step felt as though they were carrying the full weight of the nightmare with them. The mountains loomed ahead, but the path felt impossibly long, their every movement slow and deliberate, as if the world itself was holding its breath.

And with each step, they both knew: whatever they had encountered in the Whispering Woods, whatever madness it had brought with it, would stay with them long after they escaped its clutches.

As the sun climbed higher in the sky, they continued on—sweating, panting, their bodies and minds shook to the core by the horrors they'd witnessed, and the terrifying thought that they might never be able to leave those woods behind them.

CHAPTER 6

Before the Ash Falls

Rowan's village was still distant, but for the first time in hours, they stopped, both of them needing the break. Darius leaned against a nearby rock, his hands braced on his knees as he caught his breath. His eyes remained fixed on the path ahead, but his gaze was distant, unfocused. The air was unnaturally still, as though the very land had taken a breath and held it, waiting. His sword was sheathed but felt heavier than ever, like a weight pressing against his back, and yet, for all its familiarity, it seemed foreign.

Rowen sat a few paces away, his legs stretched out in front of him, his head tipped back to rest against the trunk of a tree. He hadn't spoken in what felt like hours, his usually unshakable demeanour cracked. His hands were still trembling, but he didn't try to hide it. His cloak, once worn with careless swagger, now hung askew, as though it too had lost its former ease. The faint glint of sweat on his forehead caught the sunlight, but it did nothing to banish the pallor to his face. He stared up at the sky as if searching for some meaning in the endless blue, but all he found was the vast emptiness above.

Around them, the forest was eerily quiet. The faint rustling of leaves was the only sound, but it felt too calm, too peaceful after what they'd just endured. The birds that had sung in the distance earlier had long stopped, and the air seemed thick, pressing down on them both. There was no hum of life, no flutter of wings, no movement beyond the sway of the trees in the wind. The earth beneath them felt unnaturally solid, its coolness seeping through their boots, grounding them, but also reminding them of the instability of their reality.

Darius wiped his brow, fingers lingering on the fabric of his sleeve as though the touch of it could ground him. He couldn't remember the last time he'd felt so… disoriented. He didn't know whether it was the creature, the madness that had clawed at his mind, or the sheer weight of what they'd seen. He hadn't flinched or panicked when it came for them, but now, in the absence of that immediate threat, the echoes of it all made his stomach twist.

Beside him, Rowen shifted, his boots scraping against the dirt as he stood and moved to the edge of the clearing. He crouched low, watching the trees as if they might suddenly spring to life. The sound of his fingers brushing against the bark of the tree he'd been leaning against was soft, almost hesitant. It was a far cry from the usual playful flicks and gestures that punctuated his words. Now, there was an unnerving stillness in his movements, as if every step was weighed with the uncertainty of what lay ahead.

The sky above them stretched wide, and though the sun climbed higher, there was a sense of deep, unshakable twilight in their chests. The warmth on their skin felt empty, as if it were the sun itself trying to heal something that couldn't be fixed. Time didn't seem to move in a straight line. The woods had warped it, made it bend, and now, even the passage of daylight couldn't make sense of what they had gone through.

Rowen pulled his cloak tighter around him, though the air was warm. His fingers clutched the fabric, twisting it, his eyes fixed on the distance but not really seeing it. The occasional twitch of his lips betrayed a storm of thoughts, but they never gave voice to the gnawing questions. What had they really fought? What had they run from? Was it something only they could see, or had the world itself been altered in that moment?

There was a shift in the atmosphere—the temperature, the sound, the very way the light filtered through the trees—and they both felt it, without speaking a word. Neither of them moved, their bodies still, as if not wanting to disturb the uneasy peace that hung between them. Neither of them wanted to break it, but neither of them felt safe enough to speak.

Darius's hand lingered on the hilt of his sword, the familiar grip now feeling like a reminder of the frailty of everything they had just fought for. His breath came slower now, though still laboured. It wasn't just exhaustion anymore. It was something deeper. The realization was settling in—whatever had happened in those woods, it wasn't just something they would forget once they left its borders. It would follow them. Even if they couldn't put it into words, even if they couldn't understand it, they knew it had changed something inside them.

Rowen's eyes shifted to Darius, but when their gazes met, neither of them spoke. It was enough to say nothing at all.

Rowen had already begun walking, his footsteps a rhythm Darius had come to recognize. The silence between them was thicker now, laden with the weight of the forest's lingering horrors. Darius followed without a word, his mind far from the path ahead. The chaos of their recent encounter—the thing they'd barely escaped—still churned in his gut, but he kept his eyes forward. It was too dangerous to linger on what could've happened if they'd been just a moment slower, just a breath behind.

Rowen tried to fill the space with lightness, whistling an off-key tune, but it came out strained, his usual carefree energy nowhere to be found. He cast a glance over his shoulder. "Maybe I should've packed some snacks, huh?" His attempt at humour was flat, the words hanging between them without the usual spark.

Darius's jaw tightened. He wanted to respond, to snap something back, but the words didn't come. They felt too far out of reach, like trying to catch smoke with his bare hands. He wasn't the same after what they'd just endured. He didn't want to admit it, didn't want to let Rowen know how shaken he truly was. He wasn't some fragile thing that needed comforting, but the cold reality of their situation still clawed at his chest.

They travelled in silence for a while longer, the terrain growing more familiar as the Whispering Woods began to thin out behind them, though the oppressive air never fully lifted. The path ahead seemed endless, stretching further into the unknown despite the village being within sight.

By the time the sun dipped below the horizon, casting long shadows over the jagged earth, Rowen's earlier cheer had fully drained. He finally broke the silence again, his voice softer, more measured this time. "How much farther till you wanna take a break, Darius? You've been real quiet."

Darius slowed, his boots crunching softly on the leafy floor. The question caught him off guard, not for the inquiry itself but for how it forced him to reconsider what had been left unsaid. Rowen had asked earlier, in passing, but now it felt different, the pressure behind it undeniable. There was genuine curiosity in Rowen's eyes, but Darius was reluctant to say too much.

"A few hours," Darius muttered, his voice betraying more than he intended. The truth was, the distance didn't matter anymore. What lay ahead had become uncertain, and it had nothing to do with the miles between them and Rowen's village.

Rowen didn't push, but Darius could feel the weight of his unspoken questions. They had grown close through battles, through silent solidarity in the face of things that shouldn't exist in the world. And yet, Rowen's curiosity still gnawed at him. The forest, their shared experience, the dark secrets that neither dared to speak—it was all beginning to crack the walls around Darius's heart.

After what seemed like an eternity of walking in silence, they reached an area fit for setting up camp. The Whispering Woods had become just a distant patch of greenery, but a darkness still clung to the air, as if something unseen was watching them. Rowen set up camp, though his movements were absent of the usual speed and efficiency. His hands trembled slightly as he worked, something he didn't try to hide from Darius.

Once their campfire was crackling to life, Rowen tossed a few sticks into the flames, the crackle and hiss filling the air. The firelight painted his face in flickering hues of orange and gold, casting shadows over his eyes. His earlier attempt at a joke was long forgotten, his demeanour quieter than usual. He still didn't ask anything more about Darius's mission. Perhaps he understood now wasn't the time.

Darius, too, sat in silence by the fire. The warmth of the flames felt distant, a faint comfort compared to the cold that had settled deep into his bones. He had wanted to push the thoughts of the beast from his mind, but the image lingered, its unnatural shape and the maddening pull of its presence. Even now, the memory of it seemed to scrape at the edges of his sanity.

As the night deepened, the silence between them stretched longer. Darius didn't know how much of his own tension was being reflected in Rowen's quiet movements, but it felt like they were both waiting for something to break the stillness.

Finally, after a long while, Rowen cleared his throat and looked over at Darius. His voice was low, almost hesitant. "You know, I've been thinking," he started, his tone lighter, as if trying to regain some sense of normalcy. "You've got something you're running from, don't you? Or is it that you're not that much into playing a part in this prophecy?"

Darius's heart skipped, but he kept his gaze steady on the fire. His thoughts raced, but none of them could settle. "I'm not running from anything," he replied quietly, though the words felt hollow even to him.

Rowen studied him for a moment longer, the silence between them growing thick. Then, just as suddenly as it had started, Rowen leaned back and let out a soft chuckle. "Guess that's a story for another time, huh?"

Darius didn't respond, but a part of him felt like something had shifted—something unspoken had been acknowledged between them. In the midst of the dark night, with the weight of the forest still heavy in the air, they both understood something that didn't need words.

They weren't done yet. They hadn't reached the end, and there was still much ahead. But for now, they had each other. And as the fire crackled, the shadows around them felt a little less threatening. At that, the two rested till morning.

As the first rays of dawn broke through the trees, Rowen and Darius trudged along the path, the forest now far behind them.

The night's chill still clung to the air, but the warmth of the sun offered some comfort, its golden light filtering through the branches. They were both silent, each lost in their thoughts, the events of the past day and night still fresh in their minds.

Suddenly, the sound of footsteps approaching caught their attention, a rhythmic thudding of boots on earth. Before either of them could react, a figure emerged from behind a small grassy hill up ahead—tall, strong, and moving with an unspoken confidence.

She was a woman, her mousey blonde hair tied back into a no-nonsense braid that swung behind her as she walked. Her armour was well-worn but sturdy, crafted for function rather than decoration, and the massive battle axe strapped to her back seemed almost too big for her frame. She carried herself with a fierce, silent energy, like a storm waiting to break.

Rowen's eyes narrowed the moment he saw her, his steps halting as he sized her up. There was no mistaking it—she was from the neighbouring village of Faldenor, a place with a rivalry so old it was practically part of the earth itself.

The woman came to a stop just a few feet away from them, her eyes flicking over Rowen first and then to Darius. She didn't speak immediately but sized them up, clearly noticing the subtle tension in the air.

Rowen raised an eyebrow, crossing his arms over his chest. "Well, well. Faldenor, huh?" he said, his voice laced with a challenge. "Should've known."

The woman's lips coiled into a small smirk, though it didn't quite reach her eyes. "And you're from Thalorath, I can tell by that self-righteous stance of yours," she replied, her tone sharp but not unkind. "What's the matter, did you lose your way home?"

The two exchanged a look—one full of unspoken rivalry that had brewed over years of competition between their villages. It was the kind of rivalry that started with petty insults and the constant desire to prove one village better than the other. And yet, there was a strange understanding between them, an acknowledgment of each other's strength.

Darius, who had been silent up until now, took a small step forward, his hands resting on the hilt of his sword. His gaze lingered on Ingrid for a moment before he spoke, his voice softer, yet welcoming. "I take it you're on your way to Rowen's village?" he asked, his tone neutral.

The woman nodded politely, her eyes flicking back to Rowen with a hint of challenge still in her gaze. "That's right. I'm Ingrid, from Faldenor. Got a few things to settle with the Thalorath folks." Her grin widened just slightly. "But that's none of your concern." A remark clearly pointed in Rowen's direction.

Darius studied her for a moment, the familiarity of her presence reminding him of the women from his own village, like a returning warrior after a long absence.

"Well, if you're headed the same way," Darius said, his voice warm but with an underlying hint of authority, "it's a long walk. You can travel with us for a while, if you'd like. There's strength in numbers."

Rowen glanced at Darius, a bit taken aback by how quickly he'd extended the invitation. He already knew by now, Darius didn't open up so easily, It was a little unexpected. Rowen had braced himself for some kind of challenge or hesitation from Darius, but instead, he was offering Ingrid a quiet camaraderie. It made Rowen pause for a second, wondering why he hadn't received the same treatment. Had Darius simply been more guarded back then, or was there something about Ingrid that made him feel at ease?

Ingrid eyed him closely, sensing his offer wasn't just out of politeness but out of genuine concern. She wasn't used to that kind of openness, especially from a stranger. But she found it… strangely comforting.

Rowen rolled his eyes, but it was clear his guarded stance softened a bit as he looked between Darius and Ingrid. "I'm sure we'll get along just fine," he muttered under his breath, though the slight smirk on his face betrayed his amusement.

Ingrid raised an eyebrow, the rivalry between their villages still fresh in her mind, but there was something in Darius's demeanour that softened her resolve. "Fine," she said, rolling her shoulders in preparation for the journey ahead. "But don't think I'm here to hold anyone's hand, especially not a Thalorath brat."

Rowen chuckled at that, the tension between him and Ingrid simmering in the air. "We'll see about that, you'll be holding the shit outta my hand by the time we reach my glorious village." he shot back, a teasing glint in his eye.

And just like that, a strange truce settled over the trio. Rowen and Ingrid continued to trade barbs, their rivalry palpable but playful. Darius, for his part, didn't get involved in the banter, instead, he kept his gaze ahead, but every now and then, his eyes flicked to Ingrid. There was something familiar about her—strong, sure-footed, confident in herself. Not unlike the women from his village. It wasn't that he felt protective over her, not yet, but there was an unspoken recognition. A reminder of what he had left behind.

The road stretched on beneath their feet, the morning sun now high enough to warm the earth and cast away the last remnants of the night's chill. The trees that lined the dirt path were thinner here, allowing for a clearer view of the rolling hills beyond. For the first time in what felt like ages, there was an ease in their steps, a lull in the tension that had weighed them down since the woods.

Rowen and Ingrid, however, were anything but quiet.

"I still say Faldenor's Harvest Festival is just a poor imitation of the real thing," Rowen remarked, his arms crossed over his chest. "I mean, come on, your people actually think dunking a man in a barrel of cider and calling him the 'Cider King' is worth celebrating?"

Ingrid scoffed, rolling her shoulders as she walked. "Oh, like Thalorath's so much better? What do you lot do again? Make a massive bonfire and see who can throw a spear through a barrel the farthest? Real inventive."

Rowen smirked. "At least our festival doesn't end with half the town passed out in ditches."

"That just means we know how to have fun." Ingrid shot back. "Besides, I'd take our Cider King over whatever poor bastard gets 'honoured' in that fire-jumping nonsense."

Darius, who had been quietly listening to the exchange, furrowed his brow. "Fire-jumping?"

Rowen turned to him with an incredulous look. "Wait—don't tell me you've never seen it?"

Darius shook his head. "Can't say I have."

Ingrid's eyes widened slightly, a rare moment where she and Rowen shared the same reaction. "You've never seen fire-jumping?" she repeated, as if the very idea was incomprehensible.

Rowen let out a short laugh. "Gods, Darius, what kind of village did you even grow up in?"

"A small one," Darius said dryly. "We had our own traditions, but I don't remember anything about leaping over flames or dunking people in barrels."

Rowen snorted. "Then you've been missing out. Fire-jumping is a test of courage. During the festival, there's a massive bonfire, and the bravest—or dumbest—among us try to jump over the flames without burning their feet off. It's a sign of strength."

Ingrid grinned. "It's a sign of idiocy."

Rowen ignored her. "And then there's the drinking contests, the archery competitions, the wrestling matches—"

Darius lifted an eyebrow. "Sounds like an excuse to get drunk and hit each other."

Rowen and Ingrid exchanged a look before nodding at the same time. "That's the point," they said in unison.

Darius exhaled a laugh. It was strange—after everything that had happened, the blood, the fear, the madness of the woods—he had expected the weight of it to linger. But here, walking with them, trading words like old friends, it all felt… distant like something from another life.

"You'd probably do well in the archery competition," Rowen continued, nudging him. "Might even outshoot some of our best."

"I was thinking the wrestling matches," Ingrid added with a smirk. "Something tells me our quiet swordsman here has some fight in him."

Darius chuckled. "Maybe I'd surprise you."

"Oh, I doubt that," Rowen teased. "See, the key to winning is—"

But Rowen stopped mid-sentence. His body tensed, eyes narrowing as the village ahead came into view.

It should have been a welcome sight—small wooden houses lined in neat rows, smoke rising from chimneys, the sound of daily life carrying on. But there was none of that. Instead, the air smelled of something acrid, a sickening sense of distortion.

The smoke wasn't from chimneys. It was from ruin.

The village was in shambles—doors torn from their hinges, carts overturned, belongings strewn across the dirt. Some houses still burned, their blackened wood cracking under the heat. The morning light, once comforting, now cast long shadows over a place that should have been alive but was now eerily silent.

Rowen's jaw clenched.

Ingrid's hand went to her axe.

Darius reached for his sword.

The horrors of the Whispering Woods had seemed like a fading nightmare. But now, standing at the edge of devastation, reality had caught up with them once again. And whatever had done this…might still be near.

CHAPTER 7

Ashes and Oaths

The scent of blood hung thick in the air, mingling with the acrid stench of charred wood. Smoke still curled from the remains of homes, their walls collapsed into smouldering heaps. The dirt road, once well-trodden and lined with signs of daily life, was littered with shattered pottery, broken tools, and the bodies of livestock, their throats torn open as if by massive claws. Flies buzzed around the carnage, feasting on the devastation left in the wake of something monstrous.

Rowen stopped dead in his tracks, his breath catching in his throat. His fists clenched at his sides, trembling. "No…" he whispered, his voice barely audible over the distant creak of ruined structures. His village—his home—stood before him in ruin.

Then his gaze snapped to Ingrid, and the horror in his expression twisted into something sharper. "This… this is what you meant by 'business with my village'?" His voice rose, raw with grief and fury. "You and your people did this, didn't you?!"

Ingrid recoiled, her eyes narrowing. "Excuse me?" she shot back, stepping toward him. "Are you out of your damn mind?"

"Don't act innocent! You show up, talking about 'business' with my village, and now I find it in ruins?!" Rowen's voice cracked, his emotions teetering between rage and despair. "Is this your idea of settling a rivalry? Slaughtering innocent people?!"

Ingrid's expression darkened, but there was no anger in her eyes—only something colder, something wounded. "You think I had something to do with this?" she asked, her voice quieter but no less sharp. "Rowen, my village was attacked the same way three nights ago."

That stopped him.

She took a deep breath, pressing forward, her jaw clenched as if speaking the words physically hurt. "I came here for help. I thought maybe—maybe—your village had seen something, had answers. But I came too late."

Rowen's chest rose and fell rapidly, his fury still burning, but the certainty in Ingrid's voice— the raw, bitter truth of it—sank in like a cold stone in his gut.

Darius, who had been silent up until now, finally stepped between them, his gaze sweeping over the carnage. "Look around," he said evenly. "This wasn't done by people." Both Rowen and Ingrid turned to him, the weight of his words cutting through their tension.

Darius gestured toward the wounds on the livestock—jagged, gaping tears, as if something had ripped through flesh with monstrous strength. "No blade did this. No torch set these fires. Whatever came through here, it wasn't human."

A heavy silence settled between them, the only sounds left were the distant crackling of dying embers and the wind howling through the ruins.

Rowen didn't wait. The moment the shock wore off, he broke into a sprint toward the ruins, calling out names as he vanished into the wreckage. His voice echoed through the skeletal remains of his village, desperation laced in every cry.

Darius and Ingrid watched him go, neither moving to stop him. "He needs to see for himself," Darius murmured. Ingrid exhaled through her nose. "Yeah."

For a moment, they stood in silence, the devastation stretching around them in every direction. The world felt eerily empty, as if life itself had been drained from it.

Darius glanced at Ingrid. Her face was unreadable, but her fingers clenched into fists at her sides. "You knew they'd help," Darius said, breaking the silence.

She scoffed, a hollow sound. "Of course I did. You think we waste our time on rivalries when something like this happens?" She turned to him, eyes dark, unreadable. "Rowen can hate me all he wants, but I came here because I knew his people would stand with us. And because we needed them." Darius didn't respond right away. He just let her talk.

Ingrid took a slow breath, her hands tightening into fists. "Over half my village is gone," she said, her voice quieter now, the edges raw. "Our elder. Our strongest hunters. My mother." She hesitated, then let out a bitter chuckle. "Funny, isn't it? You think someone that important to you is untouchable. Like they'll always be there. And then one day, they're just… gone."

Darius didn't look at her. He knew what loss felt like.

She shook her head, staring out at the wreckage. "I was the strongest warrior left. So they sent me here. To warn Rowen's people. To ask for their help." Her jaw tensed, and she inhaled sharply. "And I was too late."

Darius finally turned to her. "You tried," he said simply.

She scoffed again. "Doesn't change anything, does it?"

"No," he admitted. "But it matters."

Another silence fell between them, but this one was different. Ingrid closed her eyes for a long moment, then exhaled, steadying herself. When she looked back toward the village, her expression hardened.

"We need to find the elder," she said. Darius nodded. "Let's go." And with that, they followed the path Rowen had taken into the ruins.

The village was eerily quiet, save for the occasional crackle of smouldering wood and the distant sound of someone weeping. The air was thick with the scent of blood and ash, a nauseating mix that clung to their clothes and skin. What had once been a place of life—filled with laughter, trade, and the hum of daily chores—was now a graveyard of broken homes and shattered lives.

Darius moved through the wreckage, his boots crunching over splintered wood and debris. He didn't know what to say. He wasn't even sure if there was anything to say. Instead, he focused on what he could do. A collapsed section of a home groaned under its own weight, the fire that had gutted it now only smouldering embers. He stepped forward, gripping a fallen beam, and with a strained grunt, pushed it aside. Beneath it, a man lay half-buried, coughing weakly.

Rowen was already kneeling beside him, hands working quickly to pull away debris. "Hold on," Rowen muttered, voice unsteady but firm. "We've got you."

Ingrid crouched at the man's other side, inspecting a gash along his arm. Without a word, she tore a strip from her already-tattered sleeve and wrapped it around the wound. Her movements were brisk, efficient—she had done this before.

Darius didn't hesitate, reaching down and hauling the man up by his good arm. He was heavier than he looked, but Darius steadied him, ensuring he could stand. The man mumbled a weak thanks before stumbling toward a small gathering of survivors.

Darius exhaled, the weight of the moment pressing down on him heavier than any piece of rubble. This is what being a hero looks like? Picking up the pieces after the worst has already happened?

The previous prophecies had always painted this journey as something grand, something noble. A destined path of triumph, of slaying monsters and saving the world. But this? Was this the curse of his doomed prophecy. He looked around at the hollowed-out remains of the village, at the people who had lost everything, and a thought gnawed at the back of his mind.

What if I can't stop this from happening again?
you won't ever stop it.

He swallowed hard and moved forward, helping where he could. He doused small fires with dirt, lifted debris to free those trapped beneath, but no matter how much he *did*, the feeling didn't go away.

Nearby, Ingrid was silent as she knelt beside a collapsed fence, lifting a boy—no older than ten—off the ground. He clung to her for a moment before running off toward what remained of his family. She watched him go, her face unreadable.

Darius hesitated before stepping closer. "You okay?" Ingrid let out a breath that could've been a laugh if it wasn't so bitter. "No," she admitted, brushing soot from her hands. "But there's no time for that, is there?"

Darius wasn't sure how to respond. Instead, he looked over at Rowen, who was now further ahead, speaking with a group of shaken survivors. He was desperate to find the village elder, to hear that there was still someone left in charge—someone who could tell them what to do next.

Ingrid followed Darius' gaze. "He needs this," she murmured. "Something to focus on. I get it." Darius nodded. "And you?"

She exhaled sharply, crossing her arms. "I told you. I'm here because my village was hit first. Over half of them are gone." Her voice was flat, controlled—but Darius caught the faintest tremble at the edges. "The elder. My mother. We lost them both."

Darius looked at her, really looked at her. She still stood strong, her presence unwavering, but he could see the grief behind her eyes, the weight pressing down on her shoulders.

For a moment, he wanted to say something—some empty reassurance that things would be okay, that they'd fix this. But the words felt meaningless. Instead, he simply nodded.

Ingrid let out a slow breath and glanced toward Rowen, who was now speaking urgently with a group of survivors. "We should keep moving. There are still people who need help."

Darius followed her gaze, then looked back at the ruins around them. His hands curled into fists at his sides. This wasn't over. The horror that had done this was still out there. And if this was only the beginning, then he couldn't afford to fall behind.

Without another word, they continued forward, stepping through the wreckage, picking up the pieces—until there was nothing left to find.

The sun hung low in the sky now, its golden light casting long shadows over what remained of the village. Fires had been smothered, the wounded tended to, and those who had been lost… honoured in the only ways they could manage. But there was no celebration. No relief. Only the quiet determination of those who had survived, clinging to what little they had left.

A gathering had formed in the village square, what little space remained unscathed by the attack. At its centre, seated upon a makeshift cot and wrapped in bloodstained bandages, was the elder of Thalorath. The old man had suffered grievous wounds—his left arm was limp at his side, and a deep gash marred his forehead—but still, he sat tall, eyes sharp as they swept over his people.

Rowen stood near the back of the crowd, arms crossed tightly, his usual smirk absent. Beside him, Ingrid remained silent, her gaze fixed on the elder.

The murmurs faded as the old man raised his hand. His voice, though hoarse, carried through the square with the weight of experience. *"We have lost much. More than we ever thought possible. But we are still here."* His words were steady, unshaken. *"Thalorath stands."*

A quiet murmur rippled through the crowd—agreement, or perhaps just the need to believe him.

The elder's gaze drifted past the wounded, past the ruins, until it landed on one person in particular.

"And we are not alone."

Darius blinked, confused, before he realized that the elder was looking straight at him.

Oh, no.

A hush fell over the village as all eyes turned toward him.

Oh, gods, no.

"Among us," the elder continued, "stands the one chosen by fate. The hero spoken of in the old prophecy. A warrior who will bring an end to the coming darkness."

Darius felt his stomach twist. His skin prickled with second-hand embarrassment for himself. He could practically feel the weight of the stares, the expectation, the quiet desperation in their expressions. They were looking at him as if he had already won. As if he knew what he was doing.

He took a small step back, rubbing the back of his neck. "Uh... I think there's been some misunderstanding."

The crowd continued to watch him, hopeful, waiting. Darius exhaled sharply through his nose, doing his best to school his expression into something neutral. He felt like he had been thrown back to his first meeting with Rowen—suddenly the centre of attention, being called something grander than he was. Something he didn't feel like.

"This is ridiculous," he muttered under his breath.

From the back of the crowd, Rowen snorted. "Gods, look at him. He's about to fold in on himself."

Ingrid, arms crossed, smirked slightly. "I thought heroes were supposed to have grace under pressure."

Rowen grinned. "Oh, trust me, he's *never* had that."

Darius shot a glare in their direction but quickly schooled his face back into indifference as the elder continued.

Rowen's smirk faded slightly as he exhaled. "Ingrid." His voice was quieter now, more hesitant. She raised an eyebrow at him. "I was… wrong to accuse you earlier. About this being your fault."

She studied him for a moment, then nodded. "Yeah, you were."

Rowen sighed, running a hand through his hair. "I just—seeing my home like this, seeing these people suffering… I lashed out. But I get it now. You were doing what *we* should've been doing. Looking past old grudges."

Ingrid's smirk faded entirely, her expression unreadable. "It shouldn't have taken this for our villages to actually talk to each other."

Rowen let out a breath. "No, it shouldn't have." He hesitated before adding, "I'm sorry." For a moment, Ingrid said nothing. Then, quietly, she nodded. They both looked forward again, listening as the elder continued to speak. The moment between them passed, but something unspoken had shifted. A truce. And as they watched Darius struggle under the weight of expectation, Ingrid's smirk returned.

"…Think he's gonna pass out?"

Rowen chuckled. "Give it five minutes."

Ingrid smirked but said nothing, watching Darius shift uncomfortably under the weight of the village's expectations. His hand hovered near the hilt of his sword, not as if preparing for battle, but as if seeking something solid to anchor himself.

Rowen exhaled, shaking his head. "Y'know… it's kind of funny." Ingrid turned to him, brow raised. "What is?" Rowen scratched the back of his head. "This whole time, I thought this prophecy nonsense was just that—nonsense. A story old folks told to make us feel better about things we couldn't fight." His gaze drifted back toward Darius, who was now awkwardly nodding at something the elder was saying. "And now he's just here. Real as anything. And the thing is…" Rowen hesitated. Ingrid tilted her head slightly. "What?" Rowen let out a breath, voice quieter. "I don't think he *wants* it." Ingrid's expression darkened slightly, thoughtful. "No. I don't think he does either."

Rowen crossed his arms, rolling his shoulders. "People see him as a hero already. But that look on his face right now? I know that look. It's the same one I saw in the mirror when I realized no one else was going to step up to help my village. The look of someone who didn't *ask* for this." Ingrid nodded slowly. "Responsibility isn't always a choice."

For a moment, neither of them spoke, watching as Darius gave a painfully forced half-smile to an eager villager who clasped his hands as if touching a legend. "I also think he's been hiding something from me since we met. Something he knows about his journey that he didn't care to share." Rowen added. "he's carrying a lot I guess poor guy".

Then Ingrid smirked again. "Still doesn't mean we can't enjoy watching him suffer a little." Rowen huffed a quiet laugh. "Obviously."

The weight between them lingered, but something lighter had settled alongside it—understanding.

They were still standing in the ruins of a broken home. But for the first time since the attack, something lighter settled between them. Something that, just maybe, could turn into hope. As the meeting dispersed, the villagers slowly drifted away, murmuring to one another in hushed voices. Hope had been offered, but it was fragile, like a candle flickering against the wind.

Darius let out a breath he hadn't realized he'd been holding, shoulders stiff from the weight of all those expectant gazes.

"See? You survived," Rowen teased as Darius finally rejoined them, a smirk tugging at his lips. Darius rolled his eyes. "Barely." Rowen chuckled but then crossed his arms, tilting his head slightly as if studying Darius for the first time. "Alright, hero. Since we've got a moment, let's talk. Who exactly are you?" Darius frowned. "You know who I am. We've been travelling together since I practically left the castle."

"No, I know your *name*," Rowen corrected. "I know you fight well. I know you carry a sword bigger than you should be able to lift given your build, and I know you're apparently *destined* for something none of us understand." His eyes narrowed playfully. "But what I *don't* know is anything about *you*."

Ingrid leaned against a broken stone wall, arms folded, smirking. "I have to admit, I'm a little curious too. I've heard the stories of the prophecy and the heroes, thinking they was all tosh, yet here you are." Darius sighed, rubbing the back of his neck. "There's not much to tell."

"Oh, come on." Rowen leaned in. "Big, brooding swordsman, lone wanderer type, doesn't like the attention—there's a story in there somewhere." Darius exhaled through his nose, glancing away. He wasn't sure why this was suddenly a topic of interest, but the weight of their eyes told him they weren't going to let it go.

"Fine," he muttered. "I grew up in a village—small, out of the way south of the castle. Not much happened there. My father was a blacksmith and master swordsman. My mother—" He hesitated for a beat. "She isn't with us anymore." The teasing in Rowen's expression faded slightly, but he kept his voice casual. "And your father? Alive?"

Darius hesitated again, but this time, something in him urged him to keep talking. "He was a hard man. Quiet, like me, I guess. Always busy. I spent most of my time helping in the forge, learning the craft." He glanced down at the sword on his back. "when I was at the age the prophecy stated I was given this obsidian sword forged in Dragonspine a million years ago or something to vanquish evil." Rowen let out a low whistle. "Huh. So that's why it looks like it was made to cut through mountains."

Darius smirked slightly. "Wasn't planning to slay demons with it at the time." Ingrid raised an eyebrow. "And when did that change?" Darius' jaw tightened slightly. The truth hovered on the edge of his tongue—the prophecy, the cycle of heroes before him, all marching toward their fate and him to his doom. But instead, he simply said, "When Vorthis came looking for me."

Rowen frowned. "So you didn't set out on this journey by choice?" Darius let out a humourless chuckle. "No. Definitely not." A short silence stretched between them. The wind rustled the remains of ruined homes, the air still thick with smoke and grief. Rowen's voice was softer now. "That why you act like this whole thing is a burden?"

Darius' fingers twitched at his side. "It is a burden," he admitted. "People keep expecting something from me. They look at me like I'm already a legend, like I've already won. But I don't know how this ends. I don't even know if it can end, after all according to the prophecy I'm destined to fai-" Darius caught himself before revealing too much.

Rowen watched him closely, as if searching for something in his words. Then, he simply grinned. "Well, you're stuck with us now, so maybe try to enjoy the ride." Darius huffed. "Enjoy?"

Rowen shrugged. "Why not? we're all doomed if ya don't win

right?, might as well have a good time along the way." Ingrid smirked. "Optimistic way to look at it." Rowen shot her a wink. "Someone's gotta be." Rowen stretched his arms behind his head and grinned. "Well, since we're sharing—Ingrid, why are you even still here? You got what you came for. You could've gone back home."

Ingrid raised a brow. "And leave you two to bumble your way through this mess?"

Rowen snorted. "Admit it, you're just scared I'd do a better job than you could." Darius smirked. "I highly doubt that's why she's staying." Rowen put a hand to his chest in mock offense, but before he could retort, Darius turned the question on him instead. "What about you?" Darius asked. "You act like it's all fun and games, but you're still here. Why? Why not stay and help your village?"

Rowen exhaled, crossing his arms. "You know why." Darius tilted his head. "Do I?" He glanced at Rowen. "You tell me, then. Why are you still here with me? Why are you insisting on following me?" Rowen's smirk faded. He turned slightly, gesturing to the broken remains of his home. His voice was quieter when he spoke.

"My reasons before today were trivial. But now? This is my reason." He let out a deep sigh, running a hand through his hair. "I'm no good at building or medicine or anything useful here, but what I can do—" He looked Darius square in the eyes. "—is fight. I'll make sure this doesn't happen again. That's how I'll be useful to my village."

A silence settled between them, heavy but understood. Then Ingrid finally broke it. "For me, it's my people too," she admitted, her voice firm. "I came here to ask for help, but I stayed because I know this won't stop. Not with one village. Not with two. If we don't end this, it'll keep spreading. Maybe the whole kingdom. Maybe the world. I can't let that happen." Rowen nodded, and for once, there was no teasing in his expression.

Darius looked between them. He realized now—they weren't just here because of some prophecy or duty. They had their own reasons. Their own stakes.

Maybe, in some way, they understood this burden better than he did.

CHAPTER 8

The Weight Shared

The tavern had been hastily converted from one of the sturdier buildings left standing after the attack. It wasn't much—just a large hall with salvaged wooden tables, a few flickering lanterns, and the scent of spiced broth and smoked meat thick in the air—but it was enough. It was a place to sit, to breathe, to pretend, even for a little while, that things were normal.

Darius, Rowen, and Ingrid sat around a rough-hewn table, each with a plate or bowl before them, their bodies worn from the day's events but their stomachs ready to claim whatever warmth a meal could offer.

Darius had chosen Hearthland Hunter's Pie, a traditional dish from the farmlands of Elaria. The thick, golden-brown crust flaked apart at the edges as he cut into it, revealing slow-cooked venison bathed in a rich, herb-infused gravy. Wild mushrooms and root vegetables were nestled within, their flavours deepened by a hint of dark ale. A wedge of smoked cheese and a small heap of pickled mountain onions sat on the side, their sharpness meant to cut through the dish's heavy richness.

Rowen, naturally, had opted for Stormbrewer's Stew—a thick, dark concoction that he swore was *the* superior choice. It was a mountain village staple, made with tender braised goat meat, fire-roasted turnips, and red lentils, all steeped in a broth thickened with ground hazelnuts. The scent of smoked paprika, cumin, and juniper berries curled in the air, the kind of aroma that made a man feel warmer just by breathing it in. Served in a hollowed-out bread loaf, it was meant to be eaten with torn-off chunks of black rye, the crust thick and sturdy enough to hold its own against the stew's bold flavours.

"This," Rowen said, taking a hefty spoonful and smacking his lips, "this is real food." He jabbed his spoon toward Darius' plate. "That's just meat hidden in bread."

Darius raised a brow. "It's a pie."

Rowen scoffed. "It's a meal trying to be a snack. Now, *this*—" He gestured dramatically at his stew. "—this is food with presence. Warms your bones. Makes you stronger." He flexed for emphasis.

Ingrid rolled her eyes. "If your stew makes you stronger, you'd think you wouldn't be so easy to throw around in a fight."

Rowen clutched his chest in mock offense. "Uncalled for."

She smirked, turning back to her own meal—a plate of Ironflame Skewers. Strips of marinated boar were skewered alongside charred bell peppers, onions, and smoked beets, the meat glistening from a honeyed mead glaze. The scent of rosemary and cracked pepper mingled with the crisp, fire-kissed edges of the vegetables. A side of roasted parsnips and cabbage completed the plate, their surfaces blistered from the heat. Ingrid had already torn a skewer free from the plate, chewing through a piece of meat with a satisfied hum.

Darius nudged his plate closer. "I will say, that smells better than his." Rowen threw a piece of bread at him.

But their attention quickly turned to the small dish beside Ingrid's skewers. A handful of dark, brined fruits rested in a wooden bowl, their deep purple hue betraying nothing of their taste. They glistened slightly under the low lantern light, soaked in honey, vinegar, and crushed fennel seeds. Ingrid plucked one from the bowl and popped it into her mouth, chewing with obvious enjoyment.

Darius and Rowen exchanged a glance.

"What in the gods' names is *that*?" Rowen finally asked, eyeing the fruit as if it might bite him first.

"Frostbitten Brinefruit," Ingrid replied easily. "From the Whispering Woods. It's a delicacy."

Rowen wrinkled his nose. "It *looks* like something that should've been thrown away a month ago."

Darius leaned in slightly, watching as Ingrid picked up another piece. "What does it even taste like?"

"Like tart wine and aged vinegar," she said, grinning. "With a hint of honey. Stronger than any of you can probably handle."

Rowen narrowed his eyes. "I could handle it."

Ingrid smirked. "Go on, then." She plucked a brined fruit from the bowl and offered it to him.

Rowen hesitated. Then, with far too much bravado, he snatched it up and tossed it into his mouth. He chewed once. Then twice. His expression remained neutral for all of two seconds before his face contorted into something between confusion and betrayal.

Darius snorted. "That bad?"

Rowen coughed, forcing himself to swallow. "That's *not food*."

Ingrid laughed. "Told you."

Rowen downed half his stew in an effort to rid himself of the lingering taste, shaking his head. "You eat *that* willingly?"

"Love it," Ingrid said, tossing another into her mouth with a smirk.

Darius leaned back, watching them bicker, the weight of the day momentarily set aside. It wasn't much—a meal in a makeshift tavern, teasing over questionable food—but after everything, it felt like something they all needed. A moment to be people instead of warriors.

He took another bite of his pie, listening to Rowen groan dramatically about the lingering taste of brined fruit, and allowed himself, just for a moment, to enjoy the company he hadn't expected to find on this journey.

enjoy while you can "hero".

The last remnants of their meal sat between them—crumbs of Darius' Hearthland Hunter's Pie, the broth-streaked bowl from Rowen's Stormbrewer's Stew, and Ingrid's mostly empty plate, save for a few stubborn traces of honeyed glaze from her Ironflame Skewers. The flickering lanterns overhead cast long shadows across the makeshift tavern, where weary villagers nursed their drinks or spoke in hushed tones, their voices dipping beneath the occasional crackle of a dying hearth.

Rowen leaned back in his chair, stretching his arms with a satisfied groan. "I'm telling you, nothing beats a good Stormbrewer's Stew. It's like getting punched in the face by warmth and flavour." He thumped a fist against his chest. "You feel it in your soul."

Darius smirked, prodding at the last scrap of crust on his plate. "I don't know about that. A good meat pie after a long day does the trick just fine."

Rowen scoffed. "A pie? Please. That's farmhand food. What I had? That's warrior food."

"Sounds more like mountain people trying to make soup but getting it wrong," Ingrid chimed in, plucking another Frostbitten Brinefruit from her plate and biting into it with an audible crunch.

Rowen's face contorted in exaggerated disgust. "I still don't understand how you eat that."

Darius nudged his mostly empty mug aside, watching as she popped another piece into her mouth without hesitation. "Seriously. That stuff smells like something died in the jar."

Ingrid arched a brow, holding one up between two fingers. The deep purple fruit glistened in the lantern light, its briny sheen almost unnatural. "It's a delicacy."

Rowen leaned forward, his expression dubious. "It's a mistake." She smirked. "It's an acquired taste. You wouldn't get it."

"Oh, I get it." He gestured between himself and Darius. "It's you who's got the problem."

Darius shook his head. "I have to agree with him on this one." Ingrid merely shrugged, unbothered. "More for me, then."

A lightness settled between them, something almost resembling normalcy despite the ruin surrounding them. It was strange—how laughter could still exist here, how the tension of the day had loosened just enough for them to enjoy something as simple as a meal.

As the tavern's patrons began filtering out, murmuring farewells, a few villagers nodded in Darius' direction, their expressions filled with a cautious kind of hope. It made his stomach twist.

Rowen noticed, elbowing him lightly. "Look at that. You've got fans." Darius exhaled through his nose, shaking his head. "That's the problem."

Ingrid watched him for a moment, then set her empty plate aside. "We should get moving. If we're leaving the village by morning, we'll need a place to rest."

Rowen sat up, rolling his shoulders. "Finally. Thought we'd be stuck in here all night."

Darius stood last, casting one final glance across the dimly lit tavern. He could still feel their eyes on him, those silent expectations pressing down like a weight he hadn't agreed to carry.

The night air was cool as the trio stepped outside the makeshift tavern, the lingering warmth of the fire behind them. The village was quiet now, save for the occasional creak of wooden structures and the distant murmur of hushed conversations. The sky above, freed from the haze of smoke and dust, revealed a sea of stars, twinkling like a thousand eyes watching over the world below.

Rowen stretched his arms over his head, his cracked joints protesting. "lets see, We've got to find a good place to sleep tonight." He glanced around, searching for a patch of land to settle. "That hill over there looks decent enough."

Ingrid followed his gaze, her brow furrowing. "Don't you live here, moron? Where's your house?"

Rowen's gaze never wavered as he continued scanning the horizon, his voice flat. "It's gone. I checked earlier. All gone. Poof."

Ingrid and Darius exchanged a brief glance, both of them sensing the subtle edge to his words. There was more there than he was letting on, but neither of them pressed it. The topic seemed like a delicate thread, one they didn't want to unravel, not yet.

Rowen, meanwhile, was already moving on, brushing off the brief silence with a shrug. "Just a home, right? No worries. Camping it is."

Darius caught the stiffness in Rowen's shoulders as he turned away, and Ingrid's sharp eyes narrowed, but neither spoke. They knew better than to dig into something Rowen clearly didn't want to talk about. Instead, they let the conversation fade into the night air, the unspoken tension hanging between them like a faint shadow.

Darius' gaze lingered on the broken homes of the village. Despite the warmth inside, a coldness had settled in his chest, an unshakable feeling that tonight, no matter how hard they tried to make it feel like the normal rhythm of travel, was different. There were too many eyes on him now. Too many people waiting for him to do something. Lead.

"Let's get a fire going," Rowen suggested, already moving toward a small pile of gathered wood near the village edge.

As they made their way to the hill Rowen had pointed out, the sounds of the village faded behind them, replaced by the rustling of tall grass underfoot. They set up their small camp just under the lip of the hill, out of sight from the main village. The stars above seemed to offer a moment of peace, as if the heavens themselves were holding their breath.

Rowen made quick work of the fire, striking flint and kindling into a small blaze that crackled to life. Ingrid took out a worn blanket from her pack, spreading it over the grass, while Darius stood a little longer, staring out into the distance. The silence between them was comfortable, but still, the burden of leadership pulled at him.

"Everything alright?" Ingrid asked, noticing the far-off look in his eyes.

He blinked, pulling his gaze from the horizon. "Just thinking." He cleared his throat, as if shaking off a fog. "About tomorrow."

Rowen shot him a look from the fire, flipping a piece of dry wood onto the flames. "Don't worry. We've got your back. No one's expecting miracles, Darius."

"No." Darius shook his head, moving to sit down on the blanket Ingrid had spread out. "But they are expecting... me." He pulled his knees up to his chest, letting out a long breath. "They look at me like I'm already a hero. Like the prophecy is some kind of guarantee. But they don't know what's coming. I don't know what's coming."

Death.

Rowen's smirk softened as he took a seat beside the fire, prodding the flames. "I get it. But you don't have to figure it all out right now, do you?"

Darius looked up at Rowen, meeting his eyes for the first time. Rowen's face wasn't mocking anymore, but something else—something earnest, maybe even understanding.

"You don't have to do it alone," Ingrid said softly, sitting down beside him. Her eyes held his for a moment, then shifted to Rowen as he added more wood to the fire. "We're with you. All of us. Even her." Pointing at Ingrid. "Whatever comes, we'll face it together." He finished. Ingrid narrowing her eyes at him.

Darius's throat tightened. He swallowed the lump in it. For a moment, he could almost believe their words, almost imagine that they could take the weight from his shoulders. Almost.

"Tomorrow. One village at a time," Darius said, a determination rising in his chest. "We'll move out before dawn. We need to keep the momentum. Get to the next village, get more information. We'll move quickly. We'll strike first. We need to be ready for whatever comes."

Rowen's brow furrowed. "Strike first, huh? Not exactly the 'saviour of the prophecy' plan, but alright." He chuckled, slapping Darius on the back.

Darius let out a strained laugh, but it was enough to shake off the growing anxiety gnawing at his insides. He was still no closer to understanding the prophecy, but he understood this: this was his journey. And whether or not he felt ready, whether or not he had the answers, he had to lead them forward.

"Alright, Darius. If that's the plan, you'll have us." Rowen grinned. Ingrid let the silence settle again, the sound of the fire crackling between them. Then she spoke, as if it was a thought long coming. "We're not in this for the prophecy. We're in this because we have something to protect. Each of us. Our homes. Our people." She met his eyes again, unwavering. "Whatever comes next, we'll make sure you don't face it alone. Not while we're still here."

you're doomed to fail.

The fire crackled as the night air cooled, and the stars above glistened brighter with every passing minute. The steady rhythm of the flames seemed to match the thoughts swirling in Darius's head. Despite Ingrid and Rowen's assurances, his mind raced with uncertainty. He had to be ready for what was coming. He had to be the hero the prophecy demanded, whether he believed in it or not.

"Alright, enough with the brooding." Rowen's voice cut through his thoughts, sharp and insistent.

Darius blinked, looking up at him, confused. "What?"

"You heard me," Rowen said, leaning back on his hands, his gaze steady on Darius. "The weight of the world's not on your shoulders, not anymore." He waved a dismissive hand toward the stars, then toward Darius. "You don't have to carry all this. You're the 'hero,' right? So why don't you start acting like it?"

Darius frowned, opening his mouth to respond, but Rowen kept talking, cutting him off. "We've got your back. We're here, even her." Pointing at Ingrid. "You've been stuck in your own head for so long, thinking you have to handle it all. But the truth is, you don't. You're leading the charge? Fine. But you're not doing it alone. That's where we come in."

Darius stared at Rowen, still not fully understanding.

Rowen pushed himself to his feet with an exaggerated stretch, looking down at Darius with a mock-serious expression. "You take the reins, Captain Hero. You lead us into battle. You do the big speeches, the daring rescues, whatever makes you feel like the 'chosen one.' But leave the little stuff to us."

don't listen to him.

Ingrid glanced at Rowen, raising an eyebrow, but Rowen was undeterred. He exhaled through his nose, as if the solution was simple. "Done. You lead. We follow. Simple as that."

For a moment, silence hung in the air, thick with the weight of Rowen's words. Darius stared at him, surprised by his bluntness, yet there was an undeniable sense of confidence in Rowen's eyes— a confidence that made something shift inside Darius.

Ingrid sighed, her gaze flicking between the two men. She opened her mouth as if to argue but closed it again, clearly debating with herself. Finally, she crossed her arms and looked at Darius with a resigned expression. "Against my better judgment…" she began, her voice firm but almost teasing, "…I agree with Rowen. You need to stop acting like you have to do everything yourself. We've got this. We'll handle whatever's needed, big or small." She smirked. "We're a team now. You can't do this alone."

stop listening.

Darius was silent for a long moment, absorbing their words. He had been carrying the burden of leadership on his own for so long, thinking it was something only he could do. But now, with Rowen's ridiculous confidence and Ingrid's calm assurance, something clicked.

He leaned back slightly, finally exhaling a long breath he hadn't realized he was holding. He met their eyes—Rowen's confident grin, Ingrid's steady gaze—and for the first time in a long while since being told he was the child of prophecy, he felt like maybe he didn't have to do this alone. Maybe, just maybe, he could let go of the weight for a while and trust in the people beside him.

"I guess… I guess you're right," Darius muttered, a reluctant smile tugging at the corners of his mouth. "I can't do it all, can I?"

damn it!

Rowen gave him a dramatic, exaggerated bow. "That's the spirit, Darius. Let us handle the dirty work, and you just focus on being the big, scary hero." He chuckled, then added, "But seriously, get some rest. Tomorrow's going to be a long day."

Darius laughed, the sound light and unfamiliar after so many days of tension. The weight that had been pressing down on him, suffocating him, felt a little lighter.

"Alright," he said with a deep breath. "I lead. You guys handle the rest. Deal?"

Rowen clapped his hands together, rubbing them like he'd just struck a deal with the devil himself. "Done."

Ingrid gave a small smile, her eyes softening for just a moment. "Good. Now, let's get some sleep."

As Darius settled into his blanket beneath the stars, he finally allowed himself to relax. His mind was still heavy with the journey ahead, but he knew something had changed tonight. He had his friends. He had his team.

And for the first time, he felt ready to embrace his role—not just as the hero of the prophecy, but as someone who had a purpose beyond the weight of expectations. He now realised the parting words of the seer, Alara. He is now determined to defy his destiny. Tomorrow, they would face whatever came next. Together.

I'll creep back when you're at your lowest hero.

CHAPTER 9

The Bond Forged in Frost

The sun had barely begun to rise, casting a soft golden light across the barren fields and over the charred remains of the village. Darius, Rowen, and Ingrid stirred from their makeshift camp near the edge of the village, already packing their belongings in quiet unison. The morning air was crisp, carrying the scent of ash and damp earth. They had no time to linger. The plan was set, travel to Faldenor gather more information on their attack and try and track the demon whereabouts, Ingrid's village was 2 days walk away, and every moment mattered if they were to stop the spread of the attacks to any more villages.

Ingrid was the first to rise, her eyes scanning the distance, thoughts lingering on the road ahead. Rowen followed soon after, cracking his neck with a lazy stretch before pulling his jacket tighter around himself. Darius was last, his gaze lingering on the ruins of the village they'd spent the night in. It felt strange to leave so soon, with the memories of the attack still heavy in the air.

As they packed, a commotion from the village reached their ears—a sudden burst of raised voices and hurried footsteps. The trio exchanged quick, knowing glances. The last thing they needed was another surprise, but they had no choice but to investigate.

"Come on," Darius said, already moving towards the village. "Let's see what this is about."

They made their way quickly through the narrow streets, their boots crunching on the gravel and the remnants of broken wood.

Passing the makeshift tavern, they'd eaten at last night the commotion was coming from the remnants of the village square, where a small crowd had gathered. Darius pushed through the crowd, Ingrid and Rowen close behind, their eyes scanning for the source of the disturbance. As they reached the front of the crowd, they saw the village elder standing at the centre.

Beside him was a young mage appearing to be slightly younger than Darius and his group, she has long, flowing black hair that cascades down her back, shimmering softly in the morning light. Her robes are a deep, calming shade of blue, embroidered with delicate silver threads that catch the light as she moves, giving her an almost ethereal quality. In her hands, she carried a slender staff of pale gold, topped with a crescent moon that gleamed softly even in shadow—an elegant symbol of wisdom and serenity that mirrored her presence. Her face is gentle, with soft features—high cheekbones, full lips, and eyes the colour of storm clouds, deep and thoughtful. Her natural beauty is understated but captivating, with a gentle aura that immediately puts others at ease.

Though softly curved and graceful, there was nothing calculated in her appearance—only natural elegance. Her posture straight and confident but unassuming. Unlike Ingrid, whose strength is shown in her sharp edges and commanding presence, the mage's power is expressed in her calm demeanour and warmth, drawing others to her without ever forcing it. She's the kind of person whose mere presence soothes troubled hearts.

The crowd gathered closer, hushed murmurs rippling through the air as Lyra stood before them "My name is Lyra, I come from Ravaryn," she began, her voice gentle but strong enough to carry over the crowd. "I was part of a pilgrimage, a sacred journey to the heart of the Dragonspine Mountains. We—my bodyguards and I—set out to seek the blessing of the Dragon King, Ormanath."

Her hands trembled slightly as she spoke, but she kept her composure. "It's a tradition, a rite that has been followed for generations. To climb the mountain and receive the blessing of the dragon—its power, its knowledge—was meant to guide our village, to protect it."

She paused, her gaze lowering to the ground, and the villagers fell silent, sensing the depth of the pain in her words.

"When we reached the peak, we were confronted by Ormanath himself," she continued, her voice faltering slightly. "But something was... wrong. He didn't look like the majestic dragon I had heard of in stories. His scales were dull, his eyes... vacant, like he was no longer the being we had once revered. His presence felt chaotic, unnatural, like the mountain itself was shivering with something dark and wrong."

She swallowed hard, her breath shaky as memories of that day rose to the surface.

"My bodyguards tried to protect me, but they were no match for him. Ormanath..." She hesitated. "...he destroyed them all in a matter of moments. I don't know what happened to him—what changed him—but I barely managed to escape, slipping down the mountain in a daze. I... I got lost. When I tried to descend, I ended up on this side of the Dragonspine. I have no idea how. I was disoriented. The storm, the chaos... everything felt like a nightmare I couldn't wake from."

The villagers exchanged uneasy glances, the weight of her story sinking in. A cold shiver passed through the group as the reality of the situation began to take shape—something was terribly wrong in the mountains, something far more dangerous than they had initially imagined.

Lyra's eyes met Darius's then, her gaze pleading. "I need to get back home... back to Ravaryn. Please, I don't know how to make it across the mountains alone. My people are waiting for me, and if... if Ormanath is truly lost to whatever cursed him, I fear what may happen to my village next." Her voice cracked, but she quickly steadied herself. "Please... can you help me get back?"

The silence hung in the air for a moment, but it didn't last long. Darius, standing at the edge of the crowd, suddenly stepped forward, his hand instinctively moving to the hilt of his sword. His posture was firm, his expression less guarded than before. The weight of leadership seemed to settle more naturally on his shoulders now, and his voice, though soft, carried a new confidence.

"We'll help you," Darius said, his words steady. "You're not alone in this. We'll guide you back to Ravaryn, no matter what's waiting for us up there." He looked over at Rowen and Ingrid, who stood beside him, both nodding in agreement.

Rowen clapped his hands together, grinning. "Seems like our journey just got a little more interesting. We'll help you find your way home, and maybe we can figure out what happened to your dragon along the way."

Ingrid, though still guarded in her demeanour, gave a slight nod of approval. "The mountains are dangerous, but we've faced worse. We'll make it."

Lyra's relief was immediate. She exhaled deeply, her shoulders slumping slightly as the tension she had been carrying seemed to ease. "Thank you," she whispered, her voice thick with gratitude. "You don't know what this means to me."

Darius gave her a reassuring nod. "We'll leave right away. We'll get you home." His words were simple but filled with an unspoken promise. He was no longer just the reluctant hero, but a leader who had begun to take his role seriously. "My name is Darius, hero of prophecy." He offered a reassuring smile, his voice calm and steady. "It's a pleasure to meet you."

Before Lyra could respond, a second voice chimed in, brimming with confidence. "Rowen's the name, right hand and best friend to the hero. I'm practically a hero myself—maybe even more so—"

Ingrid, unable to resist, gave him a sharp nudge in the ribs, cutting him off. She turned to Lyra with a small, apologetic smile. "I'm Ingrid. Let's get you home."

And at that, the four set off.

The morning was cool, and a light mist clung to the earth as they began their journey toward the foot of Dragonspine. The path was narrow, winding through the remnants of the village, past the few remaining homes, and out into the wild terrain beyond. Despite the looming challenges ahead, there was a sense of camaraderie that hung between them, the beginnings of a new, unspoken understanding.

Lyra found herself walking slightly behind the others, her head tilted as she took in the landscape, though her thoughts seemed distant. She was still coming to terms with the loss of her bodyguards and the strange corruption she had witnessed in the dragon, but for the moment, the presence of the group brought her a small measure of comfort.

Darius, sensing her quietness, glanced over his shoulder. His tone was soft when he spoke, an attempt to make her feel more at ease. "I know it's hard, but you're safe with us. We'll help you get home, no matter what it takes."

Rowen, walking at Darius's side, flashed her a grin. "Yeah, don't worry. Me and Mr hero are a pretty well-oiled machine when it comes to sticking together. You'll be fine." His tone was teasing, but there was no mistaking the sincerity in his eyes. "Besides, I don't think your dragon's gonna stand much of a chance against our little squad."

Ingrid, ever the pragmatist, shot Rowen a look that could have frozen a wildfire. "Rowen, maybe ease up on the dragon talk. Lyra's been through enough you think?."

Rowen raised an eyebrow but didn't argue. He knew better than to press Ingrid too far. Instead, he turned his attention to Lyra, a playful glint in his eye. "Sorry. Guess I can get carried away sometimes."

Lyra couldn't help the faint smile that tugged at her lips. It felt strange to be around people who weren't focused solely on the task at hand, people who could still joke and laugh, even in the face of the unknown. It was something she hadn't realized she missed.

After a few moments of silence, she spoke up, her voice soft but steady. "Thank you… all of you, for helping me. I didn't expect it… but I'm grateful."

Ingrid gave a small nod in acknowledgment, her eyes softening for a moment before she focused ahead, scanning their surroundings. "We're in this together now. Besides, I feel like I get the sense you'd do the same for us."

Lyra nodded, feeling the warmth of their support seep into her chest.

As they trekked further along the winding path, Darius's voice broke through the quiet. "So, Lyra, what made you want to seek the dragon's blessing? What did you hope to find on your pilgrimage?"

Lyra hesitated, then shrugged slightly, her gaze lost in the distance. "I've always been told the blessing of the dragon would give me strength, wisdom... clarity. I thought it would guide me, help me make sense of the world. But... I didn't expect what I found."

Rowen's interest piqued, and he looked back at her, his easy grin now replaced by a more genuine curiosity. "What did you find, then? What was so off about the dragon?"

Lyra's expression darkened, her brows furrowing as she recalled the eerie sight of the creature. "I don't know... something was wrong with it. Its eyes—" she shivered slightly, unwilling to continue the thought, but the words hung in the air. "It wasn't the dragon I expected. It... didn't feel right. It felt like it was... not alive, not truly. Something had changed."

Ingrid slowed her pace, narrowing her eyes as she processed Lyra's words. "What do you mean? Changed?"

Lyra shook her head, her voice barely above a whisper. "I don't know how to explain it. But something... corrupted it. Like it wasn't the creature I read about in my childhood tales anymore. It was as if whatever was in it... wasn't the dragon at all." She let out a long breath. "It wasn't the blessing I had imagined, but the curse that followed me down the mountain."

Darius' steps slowed as well, his focus now entirely on her. The weight of her words lingered in the air, each syllable adding a heavy layer to their already uncertain journey. But it was in that moment that Darius realized the true extent of the challenge ahead of them.

A chill ran down his spine. The way Lyra described the dragon—

off, unnatural, something inside it that wasn't meant to be there—sounded eerily familiar. His mind drifted back to that night in the Whispering Woods. The shifting air, the warping reality, the way the world twisted in on itself when that thing came for them.

Rowen must have been thinking the same thing because when Darius glanced at him, their eyes met, and an unspoken understanding passed between them.

It's happening again.

Neither of them said a word, but the weight of the realization settled between them like a stone. If the corruption they had seen in the forest was now reaching the great dragon of Dragonspine… then this was bigger than any of them had imagined.

Still, they remained silent. Telling Ingrid and Lyra now would only invite fear and doubt, and they couldn't afford that—not yet.

So, Rowen forced on a grin, shoving the unease aside as he let out a loud, exaggerated yawn. "Well, I don't know about you, but I'm not worried. We've got a prophecy guy, a mage, an axe-wielding maniac, and—most importantly—the amazingly talented, ridiculously strong wild swordsman right here. What could possibly go wrong?"

Ingrid rolled her eyes, but there was the faintest flicker of amusement in her expression. Lyra chuckled softly, the sound light and unburdened for the first time since they met.

By midday, the air had thinned, crisp and sharp against their skin as they climbed higher into the mountains. The snow-dusted path wound between craggy rocks, the ground uneven beneath their boots.

Then, without warning, a low, guttural growl echoed off the cliffs.

From the crags above, a trio of Frostfang Ravagers leaped down, their pale, wolf-like bodies bristling with thick fur, their elongated limbs unnaturally sinewy. Their fangs dripped with a faint mist—ice forming where their breath touched the ground. These were predators of the highlands, known for ambushing weary travellers and working together to bring down prey.

The group had no time to react before the beasts lunged.

Darius moved first, drawing his sword and stepping forward, his instincts kicking in. Rowen flanked left, quick as ever, but before they could settle into their usual rhythm—

"Out of the way!" Ingrid barrelled past them, her massive axe swinging wildly as she cleaved down toward the nearest Ravager. The creature contorted mid-air, dodging her strike, but the sheer force of her swing sent a shockwave through the earth, kicking up a spray of snow and stone.

"Oi! Watch it!" Rowen yelped, ducking as Ingrid's axe narrowly missed his head. He pivoted, trying to recover, only for Lyra to shout—

"Duck!"

A burst of magic crackled from her outstretched hands, a shimmering blue arc of energy streaking past him and slamming into one of the Ravagers, sending it skidding back.

Darius barely had time to register the attack before another beast pounced at him. He brought his blade up, but suddenly Rowen flipped over him, attempting to strike the Ravager mid-air—only for Ingrid's axe to come swinging again, forcing both of them to scramble backward.

"By the gods, Ingrid, stop swinging that thing so close to us!"

Rowen barked.

"Then fight better!" Ingrid shot back, raising her axe for another downward slam.

Darius growled in frustration. Their attacks were clashing. Lyra's spells were unpredictable, Ingrid's overwhelming power threw off the battlefield, and even he and Rowen—who had learned to move in perfect sync—were completely out of rhythm.

Meanwhile, the Ravagers were moving as one, darting in and out, targeting their weak points.

Darius gritted his teeth. "We're going to get torn apart like this."

He forced himself to focus. Adapt and lead he thought to himself.

"Rowen, take left! Ingrid, hold centre but control your swings! Lyra, cover the flanks and don't fire unless I say so!"

For a moment, they hesitated.

Then, Rowen gave a sharp nod, dashing to the side to bait one of the creatures. Ingrid shifted her stance, controlling her next attack, waiting for a clearer opening. Lyra steadied her breathing, hands glowing with magic as she readied her next spell.

Darius exhaled. "Now."

He surged forward. His blade met the first Ravager, forcing it back. Rowen caught the second, slashing at its legs, while Ingrid delivered a crushing blow to the third, finally splitting its skull. Lyra timed her magic with Darius' movement, unleashing a final blast that caught the last creature mid-lunge.

It hit the ground, lifeless.

The battle was won—but it had been messy.

Breathing heavily, the four of them stood in the snow, catching their breath. Darius looked around at the others, realizing just how poorly they had fought together. They had power, but no coordination.

And if they were going to face something far worse ahead—this had to change. Darius wiped the sweat from his brow, frustration still lingering from their disorganized battle. If they were going to be a real team, they needed to fight as one.

He took a steadying breath and faced them. "That was a disaster. If we want to survive the mountain, let alone anything worse, we need to understand each other's fighting styles. Starting now."

The others exchanged glances. Rowen let out an exaggerated groan but didn't argue. Ingrid crossed her arms, nodding in agreement, and Lyra perked up, clearly intrigued.

Darius unsheathed his obsidian greatsword, planting the tip into the ground. "I'll start. My fighting style is based on adaptability. I use a heavy blade, but I don't rely on brute force alone. I can adjust depending on who I'm fighting. If I watch someone long enough, I can learn their techniques and counter them. In short, my biggest strength is adaptation."

Rowen twirled one of his blades between his fingers, grinning. "Mine's easy. I move fast, hit fast, and don't stop moving. Think of it like a dance—if I keep moving, the enemy can't predict me. I aim for weak spots, and if I have a partner—" He nudged Darius with his elbow. "—I work around them, keeping enemies distracted while they go for the kill. Basically, I'm untouchable."

"Untouchable my ass," Ingrid scoffed. "You almost got cleaved in half back there."

Rowen grinned wider. "Keyword: almost."

Ingrid rolled her eyes before gripping the handle of her axe. "My style is simple. I don't waste attacks. Every swing is meant to kill. I don't dance around like a show off, and I don't adapt on the fly— I strike when the moment is right, and I strike hard. Strength beats speed. Every. Time."

"Debatable," Rowen muttered.

Darius ignored them and turned to Lyra. "And you? How does magic work in combat?"

Lyra straightened, suddenly eager. "Oh! Right! Okay, so, every mage has a basic spell. Mine is called Astra Bolt—it's a simple burst of light magic, quick and efficient. Every mage starts with a unique spell that they can cast at will, no matter what."

She raised her hand, and with a flick of her wrist, a small pulse of blue energy crackled in the air before fading.

"But the bigger spells—the real magic—require a charge." She held up her fingers. "I can cast five big spells a day before I need to rest and recharge. Some mages have more, some have less. Right now, my strongest spells are Stormcaller—a lightning-based attack—and Frostlance, an ice spell that freezes enemies on impact."

Rowen whistled. "Five big spells, huh? So once you're out, you're out?"

Lyra nodded. "Exactly. That's why I have to be careful when I use them. But utility spells don't use charges! Things like creating a floating light orb for dark places or levitating small objects—those are free to cast."

To demonstrate, she waved her hand, and a tiny glowing orb floated above her palm before slowly dimming. "So why the magic staff if you can use the magic with your hands?"

Darius asked pointing at her staff.

lyra tilted her head as if it was a silly question before realising that maybe most people really don't know how it works "so basically once you learn a spell its yours, but while your learning one or trying to master one and make it your own you need your staff to channel it through, I've mastered all the spells I can do but sometimes I can reach for my staff subconsciously" she chucked then smiled as if proud of her explanation.

Then, as if suddenly remembering something, she lit up. "Oh! And I've heard that there are mages from all over the world who can do crazy things, like summon familiars or even cast two big spells at once, but only use one charge—can you imagine how powerful that must be?! And then there are battle mages who can use weapons alongside their magic, and then—"

She stopped, realizing everyone was staring. A deep blush spread across her cheeks.

"Um... sorry. I got a little carried away." Rowen smirked. "A little? You looked ready to write a whole book on it."

Lyra coughed into her hand, looking away. "Anyway... that's how it works."

Darius chuckled, feeling the tension ease just a little. "Good. Now that we understand each other, let's make sure that never happens again."

CHAPTER 10

Lightning and Laughter

With a newfound understanding of each other's abilities, the group pressed forward, ascending the winding paths of Dragonspine. The air grew colder, the winds sharper, and the terrain more treacherous. Every step took them higher, and with every stretch of land conquered, the beasts of the mountain grew bolder.

Their next challenge came in the form of cliffcrawlers—monstrous, six-legged lizards that clung to the sheer rock walls, their bodies camouflaged against the stone. The first attack was sudden. One of the creatures lunged from the rocky outcropping above, its splintered fangs snapping at Rowen's shoulder.

Rowen barely had time to react, rolling to the side as Darius swung his greatsword upward, forcing the beast back. But as soon as it retreated, three more emerged from the surrounding cliffs, their claws clicking against the stone.

"They blend in too well!" Ingrid growled, gripping her axe. "We can't fight what we can't see!"

"I've got it!" Lyra lifted her staff. "Lumen Sphere!"

A bright orb of light burst into existence, floating above them and illuminating the rock face. The moment it flared to life, the cliffcrawlers screeched in protest, their natural camouflage failing under the harsh glow.

"There!" Darius charged, his greatsword cleaving downward. The nearest crawler shrieked as the blade cut deep, but before he could follow up, Rowen darted past him, slashing at another.

They were fighting better than before—still rough, but improving. Ingrid waited for her moment, tracking the creatures' movements. The second one lunged for her, and instead of dodging, she met it head-on, planting her feet and swinging with brutal precision. The impact sent the crawler flying, its body slamming into the rocks below.

Rowen and Darius found their rhythm again, with Rowen weaving in and out of range while Darius focused on heavy, decisive strikes. Lyra, meanwhile, stayed at a distance, carefully aiming her spells.

One of the remaining cliffcrawlers scuttled toward her, but before it could strike, a bright flash erupted from her palm. "Astra Bolt!" The burst of light sent the creature tumbling back, stunned long enough for Ingrid to finish it off with a downward chop of her axe.

The last crawler turned to flee, but Rowen dashed forward, flipping over Darius and landing a precise strike to its spine. The creature collapsed; its screech cut short.

They took a moment to catch their breath.

"That was better," Darius admitted, sheathing his sword. "Still a mess, but better."

"We'll get there," Rowen said, shaking out his shoulders. "As long as Ingrid doesn't take my head off swinging that thing."

"I'll consider it next time," she muttered, adjusting her axe. The final stretch before nightfall was the hardest yet. The terrain had grown steep and uneven, the path narrowing to a precarious ledge with a sheer drop to the left. The cold was beginning to bite, a harsh reminder of how high they had climbed.

Then, the mountain itself seemed to shift.

From a rocky alcove ahead, something massive stirred—a deep, guttural growl reverberating through the stone. Then, with a thunderous boom, a hulking form stepped into view.

A mountain troll.

Standing nearly three times Darius' height, its thick, pale skin was marred with jagged scars, its shoulders hunched, and two piercing yellow eyes burned from beneath a heavy brow. In one gnarled hand, it clutched a boulder the size of a horse.

Rowen let out a low whistle. "Well. That's new."

The troll's snarl warped into a hideous grin, revealing rows of cracked, crooked teeth. Then it hurled the boulder forward.

"Move!" Darius barked.

They scattered, the boulder crashing into the ledge where they had stood, sending chunks of stone tumbling into the abyss.

"That thing's too big for me to take head-on!" Ingrid shouted, tightening her grip on her axe.

Darius cursed under his breath. His greatsword was deadly against humanoid opponents, but this thing was built like a wall.

"We need a plan," Lyra said, eyes wide. "We can't just rush it!"

Rowen, on the other hand, had already darted forward. "We poke at it! Wear it down!" His twin swords flashed as he slashed at its leg, but the troll barely reacted.

It swung its arm wildly, and Rowen barely managed to flip backward in time to avoid being crushed. "Okay, so that didn't work."

Darius lunged next, aiming for the knees, but even as his greatsword struck true, the blade barely bit into the thick hide.

The troll's massive hand shot out, catching him off guard. A brutal backhand sent him sprawling into the dirt.

"Darius!" Lyra gasped.

Ingrid roared in frustration, charging forward with her axe. She timed her strike perfectly, bringing it down on the troll's wrist as it reached for Darius. The axe sank in deep, drawing a bellowing cry from the creature.

The troll kicked out blindly, sending Ingrid skidding back.

Lyra's hands trembled around her staff. "I need an opening!"

Darius groaned, pushing himself up. His body ached, but they had no choice. He gritted his teeth and steadied his stance.

"Ingrid, hold its attention! Rowen, aim for its weak spots! Lyra—get ready!"

Ingrid charged again, this time dodging as the troll swung its fist. She struck at its knee with a heavy blow, forcing it to stagger.

Rowen moved like a shadow, darting behind it and slicing at its Achilles tendon.

The troll bellowed in pain, stumbling as its injured leg buckled slightly.

Darius took the moment to grab Lyra's arm. "Now! Use your

Stormcaller!"

She hesitated—this was one of her biggest spells.

But she saw the others struggling. She saw how they were pushing themselves, trusting her to finish this.

Her grip on her staff tightened.

A pulse of energy crackled in the air. The sky, once clear, darkened with swirling storm clouds.

"Stormcaller!"

A brilliant arc of lightning erupted from her staff, striking the troll square in the chest.

The beast howled, its body seizing as the electricity coursed through it. It staggered backward, feet skidding on the loose stone—

Then it slipped.

With one final agonized shriek, the troll plummeted off the ledge, disappearing into the depths below.

Silence fell.

Rowen was the first to break it.

"That. Was. AMAZING!" He turned to Lyra, his eyes practically glowing. "You made a storm appear out of nowhere! That was like—like—like something out of a legend!"

Lyra blinked, face flushing. "I—well, I wouldn't say—"

"No, no, don't be modest! That was incredible! Do you have more spells like that? What else can you do? Can you call a blizzard? Or summon a storm wolf? Or—"

Ingrid groaned loudly, rolling her shoulders. "Gods, you never shut up." She swung her axe over her back and turned away abruptly hiding a frustrated face, trudging forward.

Lyra's smile faltered slightly. "Oh… did I do a sickening sense of distortion?"

"No, no, that's just Ingrid's way of saying she's impressed." Rowen grinned. "She just won't admit it."

Darius shook his head, exhaling. "Alright, let's find a place to rest. We need to be at full strength before we reach the peak."

The group trudged forward, exhaustion settling in. The battles had taken their toll, but there was a strange sense of accomplishment among them now.

They weren't just traveling together anymore.

They were becoming a team.

By nightfall, they found a small clearing sheltered from the wind. As the fire crackled and the stars shimmered above, the mountain loomed overhead—waiting.

"If we keep this pace tomorrow, we will reach the peak." Darius predicted.

The cave the troll had emerged from wasn't exactly inviting, but after the brutal fight, it was the best shelter they could ask for. The walls were rough and jagged, the floor uneven, but it was dry and blocked the worst of the mountain wind.

As the others set about making camp, Lyra raised a hand, conjuring a small orb of pale light. It floated above them, casting a gentle glow throughout the cave. Shadows danced across the walls, making the space feel a little less ominous.

"Handy," Rowen remarked, flopping onto a nearby rock. "Ever considered a career in dungeon lighting?"

Lyra let out a small laugh, tucking her legs under herself. "I think I'll stick to the saving people kind of magic, thanks."

Darius busied himself with lighting the fire, using a few dry branches they had gathered earlier. The flames crackled to life, filling the space with a much-needed warmth.

"Alright," Ingrid said, dropping her pack on the ground. "Let's eat."

Rowen's expression brightened. "Finally! I'm starving."

They pulled out the food they had brought from the village—simple rations of bread, dried meat, and cheese. It was nothing compared to what they had eaten at the tavern, but after a long day of climbing and fighting, it was more than welcome.

Darius tore off a chunk of bread and chewed thoughtfully. "It's... edible."

"Barely," Rowen muttered through a mouthful of jerky. "Ugh, I don't know how people survive on this stuff."

"By eating it instead of whining," Ingrid quipped, slicing off a piece of cheese with her dagger.

As they ate, Ingrid reached into her pack and pulled out a familiar small jar. The moment she twisted the lid open, an all-too-familiar sharp, fermented tang filled the cave.

"Oh, no—no, no, no." Rowen froze mid-bite, eyes going wide in horror. "Not this again!"

Darius groaned, pinching the bridge of his nose. "Ingrid, why?"

Lyra, who had been about to take another bite of her bread, hesitated as the unmistakable acrid-sweet scent reached her. She cleared her throat, attempting to remain polite. "That's… quite the aroma."

Rowen slumped back against the cave wall, looking betrayed. "We just survived a troll, Ingrid. Haven't we suffered enough?"

Ingrid shot him a smug grin as she plucked one of the dark, brined fruits from the jar and popped it into her mouth. "You're all being dramatic."

Darius shook his head. "Last time you ate those, I swear the entire tavern reeked for hours."

"That's an exaggeration." Ingrid rolled her eyes.

"No, it's not," Rowen shot back, jabbing a finger at her. "That poor waitress gagged dishing it up for you. You traumatized that woman."

Lyra pressed her lips together, trying to keep composed, but the smell was creeping into her nose—a pungent mix of vinegar, honey, and something sharp she couldn't quite place. She exhaled slowly, willing herself not to react too strongly. "It's… unique."

Rowen turned to her with pleading eyes. "Lyra, don't humour her. That's how she wins."

Ingrid snorted. "Wins what? Having good taste?"

Darius leaned back, arms crossed. "I'm still amazed that anyone eats that stuff willingly."

"Plenty of people do," Ingrid defended. "I told you, It's a delicacy."

Rowen narrowed his eyes. "You would literally have to pay us in drinks just to get us to try it."

"you already tried it, and all I did was question your manhood." Ingrid pointed out smugly.

Rowen opened his mouth to argue, then closed it, looking shifty. "I obviously blocked it from memory it was that horrid, but that's beside the point."

Lyra, who had been valiantly trying to maintain her composure, finally gave in and laughed. "It does smell a bit… intense."

Rowen pointed at her. "See? Even Lyra, the nicest person here, can't pretend that's normal food."

Ingrid simply popped another brinefruit into her mouth, utterly unfazed.

Darius shook his head with a sigh. "At least keep the lid on when you're not eating them."

Ingrid grinned and did so—but far too slowly for Rowen's comfort. He made a show of waving his hands in front of his face, dramatically fanning the air.

Lyra, now fully letting herself enjoy the banter, smiled as she tore off another piece of bread. "You know," she mused, "I think I'm starting to see how you three survive all this chaos."

Rowen smirked. "Oh? And how's that?"

Lyra glanced around at them—the teasing, the banter, the way they made even the worst situations feel a little lighter. "You never stop talking."

Darius huffed a quiet laugh. Ingrid snorted. Rowen grinned like she had just given him the highest compliment in the world.

Outside, the wind howled through the mountain pass. But inside the cave, with the fire crackling and their laughter bouncing off the walls, it didn't feel quite so cold. The fire had burned low, casting long, flickering shadows along the cave walls. Outside, the wind had finally died down, revealing a clear night sky. Darius sat near the entrance, his back against the cool stone, gazing up at the moon. It was full and bright, casting a pale glow over the mountain ridges in the distance.

His fingers idly traced the hilt of his sword as his thoughts wandered. He should have been sleeping, but his mind was too restless—too caught up in everything that had happened and everything still to come.

After a while, he glanced back toward the others, his lips twitching in amusement at what he saw.

Rowen and Ingrid had—inadvertently, of course—ended up curled together in their sleep. At some point in the night, Rowen must have shifted toward Ingrid for warmth, and Ingrid, in turn, had draped an arm over him. Blissfully unaware of their current predicament, they slept soundly, nestled together like two exhausted wolves.

Darius stifled a chuckle, shaking his head. Oh, the morning reaction to this was going to be legendary.

He was already imagining Rowen's horrified squawking and

Ingrid's grumbling denial.

But before he could dwell too long on the entertainment to come, a quiet rustling beside him drew his attention.

Lyra stirred, shifting from her spot. She sat up slowly, rubbing her eyes sleepily before noticing him still awake.

"You're not sleeping either?" she murmured.

Darius shrugged. "Didn't feel like it."

Lyra pulled her cloak tighter around herself, following his gaze to the moon. They sat in silence for a few moments before she exhaled softly, dropping her gaze to the ground.

"...I'm scared."

Darius turned his head slightly, studying her expression. She wasn't looking at him—instead, her fingers fidgeted in her lap, curling into the fabric of her cloak.

"Scared?" he prompted gently.

Lyra swallowed. "Of facing the dragon again." She hesitated, then admitted in a small voice, "Of failing again."

Darius leaned forward slightly, resting his forearms on his knees. "Lyra…"

"I'm not as adept as the others back home," she continued, her voice quiet. "Magic comes so naturally to them. To me, it always feels… forced. Like I have to think so much harder about every spell. Like I'm trying to reach something that always stays just out of my grasp."

She let out a frustrated sigh. "What if I can't do this? What if I let you all down?"

Darius was quiet for a moment, letting her words settle. Then, he shook his head.

"You remind me of myself," he said finally.

Lyra looked at him in surprise. "I do?"

Darius leaned back against the cave wall, tilting his head toward the sky. "My father was a blacksmith. And a master swordsman." He let out a low chuckle. "I, on the other hand, was a terrible fighter."

Lyra blinked. "You?"

He nodded. "Couldn't even lift a sword properly when I was younger. My father trained me, day in and day out. It was gruelling. Exhausting. Sometimes, I thought I'd never get there."

He glanced at her then, offering a small, knowing smile. "But I did."

Lyra held his gaze, her expression softening.

"And you will too."

She looked down, turning his words over in her mind.

Darius wasn't the type to offer false comfort. If he said something, he meant it.

"You've already improved," he continued. "I've seen it in the fights we've had. You're faster. More precise. You're thinking on your feet. You may not realize it yet, but I do."

Lyra swallowed, her fingers loosening their grip on her cloak.

After a moment, she gave him a small, but genuine smile. "Thank you, Darius."

Darius simply nodded.

A comfortable silence settled between them. The night air was cold, but beneath the pale glow of the moon, it didn't feel as heavy anymore.
And then, the night shattered.

A distant, guttural roar echoed through the mountains—low and deep at first, but rising into something unnatural. Something eldritch. It vibrated through the stone, rattling the very air around them.

Darius stiffened, his fingers instinctively gripping his sword hilt. Beside him, Lyra went rigid, her breath catching in her throat.

She knew that sound.

She had heard it before—felt it in her bones when she had stood before the beast and failed.

Her hands curled into fists, and for a moment, she was back there again. Trapped beneath its gaze, helpless. Weak.

Darius glanced at her, saw the fear flicker across her face.

Without hesitation, he reached out, placing a firm hand on her shoulder. "We'll face it together."

Lyra turned to him, eyes wide.

"You're not alone in this," he continued, his voice steady. "You won't fail. Not this time."

The roar faded, swallowed by the vastness of the night, but its presence still lingered—a dark promise hanging in the air.

Lyra swallowed hard, forcing herself to breathe.

Finally, she nodded.

Darius gave her shoulder a final squeeze before letting go.

After a while, Lyra let out a quiet yawn. "We should get some rest."

Darius smirked. "Agreed. We have a very… entertaining morning ahead of us."

Lyra followed his gaze toward Ingrid and Rowen—and when she saw their tangled sleeping arrangement, her hand flew to her mouth to stifle a laugh.

"Oh, that's going to be fun."

Darius grinned. "Very."

With that, they settled back down, the fire crackling softly as they finally drifted into sleep.

Morning came slow and quiet. Darius was already awake, sitting near the fire, smirking to himself as he carefully tore off a piece of bread. Across from him, Lyra sat cross-legged, stifling a grin as she stirred the remnants of their simple breakfast. They were taking their time—not out of laziness, but anticipation.

They had both noticed the moment they woke up.

Rowen and Ingrid, still asleep, tangled together near the dying fire.

Ingrid's arm was draped over Rowen's chest, his head resting against hers, their breaths falling into an unconscious rhythm. It was almost peaceful.

Almost.

Lyra bit her lip, glancing at Darius. "How long do you think before they notice?" she whispered.

Darius smirked. "I'm betting right about... now."

There was a sleepy groan, then a content sigh as Rowen stretched—only to pause mid-motion as realization set in. His eyes fluttered open, blinking blearily, then immediately widened in horror.

Ingrid stirred next, rubbing her face, looking momentarily content—until Rowen let out a strangled noise.

"...What the—"

Ingrid froze.

There was a moment of absolute, painful silence.

Then—pure chaos.

Rowen threw himself backward so fast he hit his head on the cave wall. "WHAT THE HELL?!"

Ingrid scrambled away as if she had just been set on fire. "WHY WERE YOU—WHY WAS I—"

Darius, having fully expected this reaction, calmly took another bite of bread.

Lyra, struggling to keep a straight face, finally lost it and snorted into her food.

"WHAT DID YOU DO?!" Ingrid accused, jabbing a finger at Rowen.

"ME?! YOU'RE THE ONE WHO—"

"I WAS ASLEEP!"

"SO WAS I!"

They both glared at each other, flushed red, faces twisted with embarrassment.

Rowen rubbed his temples, muttering under his breath. "This is the worst morning of my life."

Ingrid groaned, burying her face in her hands. "I can't believe I—" She didn't finish. She refused to finish.

Lyra, still giggling, glanced at Darius. "Worth waking up early for?"

Darius grinned. "Oh, absolutely."

Eventually, after an eternity of muttered curses and a lot of avoiding eye contact, Rowen and Ingrid finally gave in and helped pack up camp.

Rowen grumbled as he folded up his bedroll. "You know what? I don't even care. You were warm, I was comfortable. There. I said it."

Ingrid, halfway through stuffing the last of her things into her pack, froze.

Darius and Lyra both turned to watch.

For a split second, Ingrid's flustered glare wavered—just a hint of something else flashing behind her eyes. Then, with a scoff, she stood up, slinging her pack over her shoulder. "Don't ever say that again. I am NOT comfortable. I am a warrior."

Rowen turned away as he packed, smirking to himself.

Darius and Lyra exchanged a look—Darius amused, Lyra covering a small smile behind her hand. Neither said a word.

Darius then just shook his head, picking up his sword. It was going to be a long day.

But at least it had started on a good note.

CHAPTER 11

Broken Wings, Burning Sky

A roar unlike anything mortal ears were meant to endure tore through the morning stillness. It was a sound of pure, ancient rage—of something that did not belong in this world. The very walls of the cave trembled, loose rocks shaking free from the ceiling and clattering around them.

Darius barely had time to grab his sword before instinct screamed at him to run.

"Move!" he barked, shoving Rowen forward.

They burst from the cave just as another deafening roar split the sky, rattling their bones from the inside out.

And then they saw it.

The dragon loomed over the mountain ridge like a nightmare given form, its once-magnificent scales now knotted and gnarled, pulsing with an unnatural, sickly light. Its wings, once proud and powerful, had become shredded and uneven, the webbing torn and reformed into something that shimmered between reality and something far worse. Spiralling horns curled from its skull like blackened, charred roots, and its eyes—*gods, its eyes*—were hollow pits of writhing darkness, shifting like something alive was burrowing within them.

Ormanath, the Dragon King, was no longer a king. He was a *curse*, an abomination that should not exist.

Lyra let out a sharp gasp, her hands clamping over her mouth.

Rowen went pale. "Is that... that thing even *alive*?"

Ingrid, gripping her axe tight enough to turn her knuckles white, swallowed hard. "This—this isn't a demon. Then what the hell is it?"

The dragon opened its jaws, and the very air seemed to distort. No fire came, no breath of flame—but a guttural, echoing *wail* of sheer wrongness, a sound that dug into their minds like clawed fingers. The sky itself dimmed around it, as if light itself recoiled from its presence.

Darius felt his knees threaten to buckle. This wasn't some demon conjured from the depths of the seal. This wasn't part of the cycle. This was something else entirely.

They ran.

The ground beneath them cracked and shifted as if the mountain itself was trying to shake them off. Stones tumbled away, some small, some large enough to crush bone. They scrambled up jagged slopes, boots slipping on loose gravel, hands grasping at cold, unyielding rock.

Darius didn't know if they were running from the dragon or being led to it.

Another deep tremor rippled beneath them. A ledge just behind them gave way, crumbling into the abyss below. Rowen barely managed to leap forward, landing hard on his hands and knees before scrambling up again.

"This—this is insane!" Rowen gasped, gripping his chest as he ran. "You never said anything about the prophecy including *this!*"

Darius gritted his teeth, focusing on keeping them moving. "Because it doesn't!"

"Are you sure?" Ingrid shouted over the roaring winds, her voice sharp with accusation. "You knew about the cycle, the demons, the castle—are you absolutely certain it never said anything about this happening?"

Darius wanted to snap at her, but the truth was just as unsettling for him as it was for them.

"There was nothing," he said through clenched teeth. "Not in the prophecy. Not from the seer, Alara. No past hero ever faced something like this!"

"Then what the hell is it doing here?!"

Lyra's voice was tight with fear, her fingers gripping her staff as she struggled to keep up. "The demons are supposed to come through the seal, right? What if—what if something is leaking out and corrupting our world not just having the 4 demons roaming?"
Clever girl.

Darius didn't have an answer for that. None of this made sense. The demons had always been bound to the cycle, appearing only when the seal weakened. This—this shouldn't be happening.

Is it because this cycle is doomed?

yes.

The thought came unbidden, curling in the back of his mind like a whisper of truth he didn't want to acknowledge. *Is it because I was never meant to win? Because my cycle is cursed?*

yes.

Another tremor shook the mountain. Ahead, the narrow path widened into a plateau.

And then—silence.

Not the silence of the wind slowing. Not the hush of a lull in battle.

Something deeper.

The air itself seemed to still. The howling winds that had battered them moments ago vanished as if swallowed. No distant echoes of falling rock. No rustling of trees below.

Just quiet.

A breathless, waiting quiet.

They stopped at the edge of the clearing, panting, chests rising and falling as they turned their wary eyes toward the path ahead.

Something was waiting for them.

And they were exactly where it wanted them to be.

They formed a circle, backs pressed together, eyes darting into the mist.

Nothing.

The thick, swirling fog obscured everything beyond a few feet. Shadows shifted within it, some twisting like reaching claws, others vanishing just as quickly as they appeared.

Rowen gripped his daggers tighter. "This is bad." His voice was unusually tense, the usual cocky bravado nowhere to be found.

"We can't fight what we can't see," Ingrid muttered, shifting her stance. "We need to—"

A rock tumbled somewhere in the haze, sending them all spinning toward the sound.

Nothing.

Darius' breath came shallow and uneven. His heart pounded against his ribs.

This isn't in the prophecy.

This wasn't how it was supposed to be. He was supposed to fight *four* demons. He was supposed to follow a path, one walked by heroes before him. A clear, set path leading to the end.

Not this.

Not this nightmare.

Is this my fault?

Was this happening because of *him?* Was he *breaking* the cycle by existing in it? By failing? By making the wrong choices?

Another shift in the mist. A distant, echoing *rumble*.

Everything went still.

Lyra swallowed hard. "I— I'm going to light it up."

She conjured a small orb of golden light, the warmth of magic trembling in her fingertips. Then, with a quick motion, she hurled it forward.

The glow cut through the mist, flickering as it travelled. It soared into the fog—

—And landed on *something*.

A glistening, twisted *thing*. The light reflected wetly off its warped, sinewy flesh, revealing glimpses of curling, unnatural shapes. Its scales were cracked and peeling, revealing raw, pulsing flesh beneath. Patches of what once might have been shimmering dragon hide were warped beyond recognition.

Then it moved.

A sickening *flap* of its grotesque wings—if they could even be called that—sent a gust of wind tearing through the clearing, *ripping* the mist away in an instant.

And they saw it.

They *wished* they hadn't.

The *thing* before them was no longer a dragon.

Where regal horns once sat, jagged, branching spires of bone jutted in erratic directions. Its eyes—its *too many* eyes—glowed like embers in the deep recesses of a face stretched and distorted beyond recognition. Its mouth hung open just slightly, revealing layered, writhing teeth that didn't fit within its own maw.

Its limbs were *wrong*. Too long in some places, too thick in others, the muscle shifting like it wasn't sure what shape it was meant to hold. From its back, spines protruded at uneven angles, some breaking through its warped wings, which twitched and pulsed as if *alive* on their own.

The horror of it settled in their bones.

Rowen's breath hitched. "*What the fuck—*"

Lyra covered her mouth, her eyes wide with terror.

Ingrid looked sick, her knuckles bone-white around her axe handle.

Darius stared.

This wasn't a demon. This wasn't one of Vorthis' creations. This was *something else*. Something greater. Something worse.

And then—

It *moved*.

Too fast for something that size. Too unnatural in its grace. It lunged, all writhing limbs and coiled power, straight for them.

Darius didn't think.

He *moved*.

His blade was in his hands before his mind caught up. He swung *hard*, intercepting the monstrous claw with a ringing *crash*. Sparks flew from the impact, his boots skidding back against the stone.

There was no time to question anything now.

No time to doubt.

They had told him to stop overthinking. To stop sweating the details. To lead.

Be the hero.

So he *would*.

The others stood in stunned silence for only a moment.

Then, almost as one, they shifted into their stances.

Rowen, daggers poised.

Ingrid, axe raised.

Lyra, magic crackling in her hands.

Darius stood at the front, blade gleaming even in the dim light.

He didn't see himself, but if he could—if any of them could truly *see*—they might have sworn, just for a second, that he was glowing.

Radiant.

The thing reared back and swung again. Darius rolled just as a massive, gnarled claw slammed into the ground where he had been standing, shattering stone on impact.

Rowen shot past him in a blur, daggers flashing. "We're doing this, then? Good! Let's *dance!*"

With fluid, almost inhuman speed, he darted beneath the beast's twisting limbs, slicing at any exposed flesh he could find. His blades cut deep—but not deep enough. The wounds sizzled, the flesh beneath shifting and knitting together in a way that was *wrong*.

Rowen cursed and backflipped away as the *thing* lashed out.

Before it could follow up, Ingrid roared into battle, charging forward like an unstoppable force. She swung her axe in a heavy arc, catching the beast's malformed forearm and stopping its advance cold.

A solid THUNK rang out as the weapon buried itself deep—

—but the dragon *didn't care*.

It twisted unnaturally, its arm bending in a way it shouldn't have been able to, throwing Ingrid back before she could react. She hit the ground hard, rolling to a crouch, teeth grit in frustration.

Then—

A flash of blue.

Lyra's voice cut through the chaos as she lifted both hands, magic surging at her fingertips.

"Frostlance!"

A sharp, crystalline spear of ice *exploded* from her palm, soaring straight for the beast's exposed side.

The spell *hit*, piercing deep—

—but then, with a sickening crack, the *thing broke* the ice away from its body. The wound dripped thick, black ichor, sizzling like molten tar, but it hardly slowed.

Lyra paled. "That should've—"

A clawed limb lashed toward her.

Darius moved before he could think. He slammed into her, pushing her out of the way just as the strike came. The beast's claws raked across his side instead, carving deep, burning lines of pain through his armour.

He gritted his teeth, forced himself to stand.

No time to stop.

No time to hesitate.

Lyra scrambled to her feet, breath shaky. She wiped the blood from her cheek—his blood—but her hands were already glowing again.

A storm brewed in her palms, crackling with wild, unstable power.

"*Stormcaller!*"

Lightning split the air.

An angular bolt of raw, searing energy *slammed* into the beast's chaotic form, sending an ear-splitting *crack* through the battlefield.

This time, the *thing* reeled back, twitching and convulsing as arcs of electricity raced across its malformed body. It let out a deep, gurgling *screech*, the sound warping in its throat.

Lyra's hands trembled.

But it wasn't enough.

The beast *moved* again, shaking off the attack like it was nothing.

Rowen came in fast, dashing between its massive legs, slashing at anything vulnerable. He synced effortlessly with Ingrid as she brought her axe down in another brutal swing, both of them attacking in perfect tandem, striking where the other created openings.

For a brief moment, it almost looked like they were making progress.

Then—

The beast *exhaled.*

A deep, guttural *rumble* rolled through its chest, and the very *air* seemed to darken.

A *wave* of black, smoke-like energy burst forth from its maw, hitting them *all* like a crashing tide.

Darius staggered, vision blurring, the foul magic burning against his skin like fire.

Lyra screamed, clutching her head as the force of it sent her crumpling to her knees.

Rowen barely rolled away in time, but even then, he hit the ground hard, coughing violently.

Ingrid took the worst of it. She stood her ground, gritting her teeth, but the moment the wave passed, she collapsed to one knee, her breath ragged.

Darius forced himself to move.

Not yet.

Not *yet.*

"Lyra!" His voice was hoarse, but he didn't care. "Hit it again!"

Lyra's hands shook, her body drained, but she clenched her fists and summoned what little physical strength she had left.

"*Stormcaller!*"

Another bolt of lightning *crashed* down, striking the beast directly in its writhing chest.

It *shuddered* violently, eyes flickering—

—but when the light faded, it was *still standing.*
I've won. Give up.

Darius' stomach dropped.

His entire body ached. Blood dripped from his wounds, pooling beneath him. His team wasn't faring much better—Ingrid's arms were shaking from exhaustion, Rowen was breathing heavily, and Lyra looked like she could collapse at any second.

And yet—

The *thing* just stood there.

Watching.

Its too-many eyes glowed like embers in the night.

And then—

It took a step forward. Darius wiped blood from his lip, his body screaming in protest as he forced himself upright. The thing took another step forward, its grotesque form shifting and writhing in the darkness, the many embers of its eyes watching.

He glanced around.

Lyra was slumped against a jagged rock, her breaths ragged. Rowen was crouched low, favouring his side, one of his daggers missing. Ingrid was standing, but only just—her knuckles white as she gripped her axe, the weight of exhaustion pressing down on her shoulders.

Damn it.

This was bad. Really bad.

And yet—

A small, wild grin tugged at the corner of his mouth.

don't you fucking dare.

"Really?" he said, voice hoarse but laced with amusement. "You two!" he pointed at Rowen then Ingrid. "were so eager to follow me, swearing up and down you'd help me save the world. And now, you're all on your knees over one ugly dragon-thing?" He spread his arms. "Come on, where's that heroism?"

Rowen let out a breathless laugh. "One ugly dragon-thing? Darius, look at that thing. I'm not even sure it's a dragon anymore."

Lyra groaned, rubbing her temples. "You're actually joking right now? Have you finally lost it?"

"Yeah, well." Darius rolled his shoulders, wincing at the sting of his wounds. "Figured someone had to." He extended a hand toward her. "Up you go, mage. You're not getting out of this that easy either, you followed me up here too."

She narrowed her eyes at him but took his hand, hauling herself upright.

Ingrid exhaled sharply. "He's lost it," she muttered, shaking her head. "We should leave him behind."

Rowen stretched, wincing. "Hey, if he's lost it, what's that make us? I say we even the score and kill this thing before we *all* start rambling like him." He twirled his remaining dagger. "One last round?"

Darius smirked. "Now you're talking."

They turned to face the beast once more.

It was still there. Still *watching*.

Rowen lunged first, weaving through the shifting limbs like a shadow, but he was slower now, his movements losing their usual effortless precision. His blade struck true, slicing deep into its warped flesh, but the wound barely bled before it was already closing.

Not enough.

Ingrid charged next, her axe crashing against its twisted limb. The sheer force of the impact made it recoil, but she was slower, too—her swings laboured, her stance unsteady. The beast swung back, and she barely got her axe up in time to block.

Lyra staggered to the side, hands shaking, but she clenched her fists, gathering the last of her power.

"*Stormcaller!*"

Lightning split the air, striking the beast dead centre. It *convulsed*, its entire body twitching, but even then, it didn't fall.

"*Stormcaller!*"

Another strike.

The smell of burned flesh filled the air.

And still—

It *stood*.

Lyra's knees buckled. That was it. That was everything she had left.

She raised a trembling hand. Summoned what little magic still remained in her veins.

A single flicker of golden light formed at her fingertips.

Her *basic* spell.

It wasn't enough.

Darius knew it. She knew it.

But she fired it anyway. "Astra bolt!"

The small bolt of energy zipped through the air, striking the *thing* right in one of its many eyes.

It let out a terrible, distorted *shriek* and *lashed out.*

Darius threw himself between Lyra and the incoming claw, sword raised—

The impact *sent him flying.*

Pain *exploded* through his body as he hit the ground, hard.

He barely had time to breathe before he saw it moving toward him again, its shifting, many-limbed form looming above—

Then Rowen was there, launching himself onto its back, daggers plunging into its flesh.

"*Come on, you bastard!*" he snarled, trying to wrench them deeper.

The *thing* contorted violently, throwing him off.

Then Ingrid was there, slamming her axe into its leg, holding it in place.

Darius moved.

Sword in hand.

One last strike.

With a cry, he *drove* his blade upward, piercing straight through the knotted flesh of its throat.

The *thing* shuddered.

Then, at long last—

It *collapsed*.

Silence.

Heavy. Overwhelming.

Then, finally—

Rowen let out a wheezing breath.

"I... *never* want to see another dragon again."

The *thing* gave one final, shuddering twitch—then, its grotesque form began to *crumble*.

The tortuous flesh and unnatural limbs that had once made up the eldritch dragon *collapsed inward,* its body disintegrating into thick, black ash that was swiftly carried away by the mountain wind.

And just like that—

It was *gone*.

Silence settled over the clearing.

Then, almost in unison—

All four of them *collapsed*.

Darius let his head hit the dirt, his lungs burning, his arms feeling like lead. He could hear Lyra gasping for breath nearby, Rowen muttering curses between exhausted wheezes, and Ingrid just... groaning.

They had won. Somehow. *Barely.*

Rowen was the first to speak. "Well. I don't know about the rest of you, but I definitely saw my life flash before my eyes back there."

Ingrid scoffed, still lying flat on her back. "Assuming your life actually flashed before your eyes and not just a blur of all your bad decisions."

"Oh, it did. And shockingly, none of those decisions involved fighting a demon-infested dragon. So, this is new territory for me."

Lyra let out a breathless laugh. "I think this is new territory for everyone."

Darius finally pushed himself up just enough to look at the others. "Okay," he breathed. "I know we literally just woke up a few hours ago, but..." He let himself flop back onto the ground. "I say we set up camp. Right here."

No one argued.

"I second that," Lyra muttered.

Ingrid grunted. "Thirded."

Rowen sighed dramatically. "Fourthed. But only if we *maybe* heal up a little too."

Darius let out a tired chuckle. "Yeah, yeah, we'll patch up before we pass out."

Rowen grinned, propping himself up on one arm. "Hell, if we're doing that, I'll even take another one of those cuddles." He turned his smirk toward Ingrid.

Ingrid—who had been on the verge of drifting off—snapped her eyes open, shooting him a look.

"Absolutely not."

Lyra giggled. Darius huffed out a tired laugh.

Then, despite everything—the pain, the exhaustion, the sheer insanity of what they had just survived—

The four of them laughed.

Loud. Breathless. Victorious.

And for the first time since their journey had begun, it truly felt like they had earned it.

CHAPTER 12

The Joy Before Goodbye

The mountain was *silent*. A stark contrast to the chaos that had raged only hours before. No unnatural roars. No shaking earth. No desperate cries. Just the gentle crackle of a fire, the soft whistle of the wind, and the steady breaths of the four battle-worn warriors who had survived.

Rowen sat a short distance from the fire, his movements slow and deliberate as he reached down to the dirt and pulled his second blade from where it had fallen in the fight. He turned it over in his hands, inspecting its edge. *Still intact. Still sharp.* He let out a breath and sheathed it beside its twin at his hip.

Ingrid had barely moved from where she'd collapsed earlier, still fast asleep, arms folded over her chest, face turned away from the fire.

Lyra sat nearby, carefully feeding small pieces of wood into the flames, her expression unreadable as she eyes the colour of silvery blue. The orange glow cast soft shadows over her features, reflecting in her dark eyes.

Darius moved about the camp, setting out blankets and rummaging through their supplies. He pulled out what little food they had left—dried meat, a handful of travel rations—and began to prepare what he could.

No one spoke.

The battle had left them *drained,* not just physically, but mentally and for now, the silence was *welcomed.*

Time had passed. A day and a half, to be exact.

They had remained atop the mountain, letting their wounds mend, their bodies rest, and their spirits recover. What had started as a painful, exhausted silence had gradually given way to familiar banter.

Rowen stretched his arms over his head, groaning. "I don't know about you lot, but I feel *alive* again. Nothing like nearly dying to make you appreciate not being dead."

Darius snorted. "You always have such a way with words."

Ingrid scoffed, rolling her shoulder as she tested the movement. "At least I can move again without wanting to scream. I say we put this damned mountain behind us."

Lyra, who had been quietly watching the fire die down, finally spoke. "We... can't go back the way we came."

A brief silence followed as the group remembered the *destruction* the dragon had left in its wake. The path they had climbed was gone—reduced to little more than broken rock and sheer drops.

Darius sighed, rubbing the back of his head. "Guess that settles it, then. We go down the other side." He turned to Lyra. "That'll take us toward your village, right?"

Lyra nodded slowly. "Ravaryn isn't far from the base of the

mountain. We can rest there. Resupply. Maybe ask around and see if anyone's heard anything about the demon."

Rowen smirked. "And you can finally go home." The words should have brought her relief. This had been the plan all along—help the group reach the mountain, face the dragon, and then return to Ravaryn. *Safe*. She *should* be happy. *Should* be looking forward to seeing her family again. So why did the thought make her chest feel tight?

She glanced at the others—at Darius, calmly packing up their supplies, at Ingrid, adjusting her axe against her back, at Rowen, casually sharpening one of his daggers with an easy grin.

She had fought beside them. Struggled beside them. *Survived* beside them.

And now… she was just supposed to leave?

She swallowed the thought, pushing it away. It wasn't time for this. Not yet. Instead, she forced a small smile. "Yeah… I guess I can." And with that, they gathered their things, put out the fire, and began their descent.

The descent was nothing like their frantic climb.

Where before there had been crumbling rock and treacherous slopes, now there were smooth stone paths, carved stairways, and ancient archways standing tall against the sky.

This was no wild, untamed route—this side of the mountain had been built for passage. "Well, this is much more pleasant than the other side of the mountain," Ingrid commented.

"It makes sense," Lyra said as they walked, her voice distant. "Mages have been coming here for generations to see the Dragon

King. To seek his blessing." She trailed her fingers along the aged stone of an archway as they passed beneath it. "He was a guardian. He watched over the land."

Rowen scoffed. "Yeah, well... guess that was a load of shit." Darius shot him a look, but Lyra only sighed. "He wasn't always that way. He watched over us, guided us, helped those seeking knowledge." She hesitated. "We had bedtime stor—"

She stopped herself.

A silence settled over them for a moment. The air was *lighter* here— not just because of the smooth path, but because the *weight* of battle had finally lifted. No longer fighting for survival, they simply walked.

Rowen was the first to fill the quiet. "I dunno about you guys, but I *hate* stairs." Ingrid rolled her eyes. "Of course you do."

"I'm serious. This is the most exhausting thing we've done so far."

Darius snorted. "Not the fight with the eldritch horror?"

"That was *less* exhausting than this."

"You almost died."

"*Exactly.*"

Ingrid scoffed. "You're ridiculous."

"And yet, here I am, alive and charming as ever."

Darius chuckled, shaking his head. Lyra even smiled. But the smile didn't reach her eyes. As the others continued their usual banter, she found her mind drifting.

They were headed toward Ravaryn. Toward *home*. Was this really it for her? Was she really supposed to just *leave* now?

She had spent so long believing this was temporary—just a short journey before returning to her normal life. But now…

Now, the idea of watching her friends walk away felt *wrong*.

She glanced at them, at the way they all fit together—Rowen teasing, Ingrid rolling her eyes, Darius quietly amused.

She didn't want to leave that behind.

And Ingrid noticed.

As Lyra grew quieter, Ingrid's gaze flicked toward her, watching the way her fingers fidgeted with the hem of her robe, the way her expression had turned distant.

She didn't say anything. Didn't comment.

But she *noticed*.

And as they walked beneath another archway, descending further toward Ravaryn, she wondered what had Lyra so torn

By the time they reached Ravaryn, the sun had already begun its slow descent, casting golden light over the quiet village. The journey down had been long, but compared to the horrors of the past day, it was almost peaceful.

As soon as they stepped past the first row of stone houses, a group of young children in simple mage robes spotted them. Their eyes lit up, and in an instant, they rushed forward, shrieking with delight.

"Lyra! Lyra's back!"

Before Lyra could react, tiny arms wrapped around her from every direction, clinging to her like a pack of overjoyed younger siblings. She laughed, ruffling their hair and squeezing them back, spinning slightly as they clung to her.

Rowen raised an eyebrow. "So, uh… these are your siblings?"

Lyra blinked at him as if he had just asked if the sky was green. "What? No."

Rowen glanced at Darius and Ingrid, who both shared his confusion. "Then… why are they treating you like you are?"

Lyra only shrugged, gently prying off a particularly stubborn little girl who refused to let go of her arm. "I don't know. They just do."

Darius shook his head but smiled, watching as Lyra knelt to hug each child properly before sending them off. As they continued into the heart of the village, it became immediately clear that this kind of affection wasn't just from the children.

A pair of men straightened their posture upon seeing her, puffing out their chests and giving their best attempts at a confident stride. A few even offered to carry her things, their voices suddenly an octave deeper than usual.

A group of women greeted her with warmth, hugging her tightly, some pulling her aside to talk before realizing she had guests.

The elderly bowed their heads slightly as she passed, some reaching out to gently touch her arm, thanking her for tasks she had apparently done days prior—fetching herbs, helping with spells, even repairing roofs.

Then, out of nowhere, a young woman with auburn hair practically tackled Lyra into a crushing hug, pressing her cheek against hers.

"Lyra! I was so worried!" The woman pulled back just enough to cup Lyra's face, her own chest practically squishing against Lyra's arm. Then, without hesitation, she placed a quick, affectionate kiss on Lyra's cheek before finally releasing her.

Silence.

Rowen, Darius, and Ingrid all stood completely still, varying shades of embarrassed, confused, or somewhere in between. Lyra, on the other hand, barely reacted beyond a small chuckle.

Darius cleared his throat. "…So. That happens often?" Lyra tilted her head. "What?" Rowen motioned vaguely. "That. All of this. Everyone treating you like some long-lost love, or their favourite sibling, or their saviour."

Lyra frowned slightly, looking between them. "I mean… I guess? It's always been like this. I don't really think about it."

Ingrid crossed her arms, watching as yet another person waved excitedly at Lyra from across the way. "…They love you."

Lyra blinked.

Darius smiled, shaking his head. "Of course they do."

And in that moment, standing in the middle of the village, watching Lyra be showered in warmth and adoration, the three of them felt something unexpected—pride. They had brought her home. Safe. And seeing her surrounded by people who clearly adored her, they knew they had done something right.

Rowen clapped a hand on Lyra's shoulder, grinning. "Well, damn. And here I thought you were just some book nerd."

Lyra rolled her eyes, but a small, bashful smile tugged at her lips.

As the four continued through the village, basking in the warmth of Lyra's homecoming, a voice called out from the central square.

"Tonight, we feast in celebration!"

A chorus of cheers erupted as the villagers quickly spread the news—Lyra had returned, and that was more than enough reason to throw a grand banquet.

The great dining hall of Ravaryn was alive with laughter and the clinking of goblets. A vast banquet table stretched through the centre, laden with roasted meats, fresh bread, fruits, and all manner of delicacies, the rich aroma filling the air.

Darius, Rowen, Ingrid, and Lyra sat at a place of honour near the head of the table, where a regal woman in flowing deep-blue robes presided over the feast. Her dark hair was streaked with silver, her features sharp yet kind, and her presence alone commanded quiet respect.

This was High Magus Selene Valenford, leader of Ravaryn's mages.

As the heroes recounted their journey, Selene listened intently, her expression unreadable as they described the battle atop the mountain. When Darius explained how they had no choice but to slay the corrupted Dragon King, Lyra looked down, fingers tightening around her goblet.

Selene exhaled softly, eyes dark with grief. "To lose a guardian so sacred to our people… it is no small sorrow."

The table was silent for a moment.

"But," she continued, glancing at the three warriors who sat beside her daughter, "I know full well what would have come if his corruption had spread. Had he descended upon these lands, we would have suffered far greater losses." She inclined her head. "For that, you have my deepest thanks."

Rowen, mouth full of food, gave an awkward thumbs-up. Ingrid bowed her head respectfully. Darius merely nodded.

Then, Selene turned to Lyra, a small smile tugging at the edges of her lips. "And I thank you for bringing my daughter home."

The three warriors froze. Lyra nearly choked on her drink. Darius, Ingrid, and Rowen turned to Lyra in perfect unison, eyes wide with shock.

"Wait, *what?!*" Rowen blurted. Lyra shifted uncomfortably under their stares. "...Oh. Yeah. That."

Darius felt a strange clarity settle over him. Her inferiority complex. It all made sense now. Up the mountain, she had spoken of never quite being good enough, always feeling like she had to prove herself. And now he understood why.

She wasn't just another mage. She was the mage's daughter. The daughter of Ravaryn's leader and judging by her awkward expression, it was clear she had never seen herself as quite measuring up.

"Why didn't you tell us?" Ingrid asked, furrowing her brows.

Lyra sighed. "Because it doesn't matter. I'm still just me."

Rowen leaned back with a smirk. "Right. Just you. The most beloved person in this entire village *and* the High Magus's kid. Totally normal."

Lyra groaned, burying her face in her hands.

Selene chuckled softly at their reactions, but then the conversation shifted as Darius leaned forward, his tone turning serious.

"High Magus," he said, "we need information on the demons of Vorthis. Any clue, any lead. We're searching for anything that might tell us where to go next." Selene's expression grew sombre. "You are not the first to seek answers on such things."

She reached into the folds of her robes and withdrew a parchment, smoothing it out on the table. The edges were slightly worn, as if it had been read and reread several times.

"This arrived three days ago from an old friend, Halward, who resides in Black Hollow, a village in the marshlands far south of here."

Darius frowned. He had never heard of Black Hollow, but something about the name alone felt... foreboding.

Selene continued, "Halward writes of an attack. He describes it as something *indescribable*—as if words fail to capture what they witnessed. The villagers, desperate to name their nightmare, have called it..."

She tapped the parchment once.

"The Mawborn."

A chill ran through the room.

Rowen set his goblet down slowly. "That doesn't sound ominous at all." Lyra chewed her lip. Ingrid folded her arms.

Darius exhaled. Another piece of the puzzle. Another horror awaiting them in the shadows.

And their next destination was set.

The feast had stretched deep into the evening, the warm glow of lanterns and flickering torches bathing the hall in golden light. Laughter and music filled the space, the air thick with the scent of roasted meats and spiced ale.

At one end of the hall, Ingrid sat at a long table, surrounded by a group of burly men who watched with anticipation as she slammed down another empty mug. The man across from her, nearly twice her size, hesitated before taking his next drink, his face already flushed red.

"C'mon," Ingrid teased, wiping her mouth with the back of her hand. "You gonna let a girl outdrink you?"

The gathered crowd roared with laughter. Someone thumped the poor man on the back, urging him on, but even he knew it was a losing battle.

Rowen, meanwhile, had gathered a small audience of women and children, dazzling them with an impromptu display of sleight-of-hand tricks.

"Now watch closely," he said, holding up a single gold coin between his fingers. He waved his hand over it, and suddenly, the coin was gone.

The children gasped. A few of the women clapped.

One of the kids pointed accusingly. "It's up your sleeve!"

Rowen feigned offense. "How dare you doubt the master of illusions?" He turned his hand over—and when he opened his palm again, the coin was back. "Magic, my dear sceptics."

More cheers.

Rowen winked at a passing barmaid. "You impressed?" She rolled her eyes, but she was smiling.

In another corner, Darius sat, clearly uncomfortable as a group of villagers gathered around him, hanging onto his every word.

"So there I was," he muttered, rubbing the back of his neck, "facing down a horde of wolves at the edge of the Whispering Woods, and—"

"The Whispering Woods? *You* went through there?" an older man interrupted; eyes wide. Darius shifted. "Uh… yeah?"

The murmurs grew excited. Someone clapped him on the shoulder. Another called for more drinks in his honour.

"Tell us about the battle at the mountain!" another shouted.

Darius groaned internally. He hadn't meant to get caught up in this. This felt all too familiar—the way Elder had practically forced him into the spotlight back at Rowen's village, putting him in front of people, making him talk about what he had done.

And yet…

Even as he sat there, awkward and flustered, he realized he wasn't fighting against it as much this time. The words came easier. The people listened; eyes alight with wonder.

Maybe… just maybe… he was starting to accept his place in all of this.

Near the edge of the hall, Lyra sat on the steps outside the open doors, looking out over the village. Her mother, Selene, sat beside her in quiet understanding.

"You're still thinking about it," Selene murmured.

Lyra swallowed, staring down at her hands. "…I don't know what to do." Selene smiled gently. "Yes, you do." Lyra hesitated, but Selene continued before she could argue.

"This is the world telling you to go, my dear. You have found good friends. A path beyond these walls. Beyond our traditions and expectations." She placed a warm hand over Lyra's. "Go with them. Have an adventure. Learn. Grow."

Lyra let out a quiet breath.

"…I can't."

Selene didn't look surprised.

"My place is here," Lyra whispered. "With our people. And the others… they already said I could stay home. That my part in this is done." Selene was silent for a long moment before she squeezed Lyra's hand, her expression filled with both pride and sadness. "Then that is your choice."

The night carried on around them, but in that moment, it was just the two of them sitting in quiet understanding.

Back inside, Darius lifted his gaze and caught sight of Lyra. She was still sitting on the steps, a shadow of uncertainty on her face. Her mother beside her, silent but knowing. Darius didn't need to hear the words to understand what had just happened.

His stomach twisted.

Slowly, he turned his head, finding Rowen still caught up in his little performance, revelling in the attention.

Then, he looked toward Ingrid, who had just forced another of her challengers to slump forward onto the table in defeat.

And in that moment, as Ingrid wiped her mouth and looked up, their eyes met.

Then she followed his gaze to Lyra and she understood. She knew exactly what had been eating away at Lyra since they descended the mountain. She also knew exactly what Lyra was going to do when morning came.

The celebration carried on, but for the four of them, something unspoken settled between them.

And soon, the night would come to an end.

CHAPTER 13

Beneath the Ruined Crown

Morning in Ravaryn was peaceful. The sun cast golden light over the quiet village, illuminating the mist that still clung to the earth like a fading dream. The scent of morning dew mixed with the faint aroma of herbs and incense from the mage quarters, and the occasional distant chime of a bell signalled the start of a new day.

At the village gates, Selene stood tall, her expression calm as she handed a parchment to Darius—a carefully detailed map leading them southward to the Marshland village of Black Hollow.

"This should get you there," she said warmly. "It won't be the easiest trek, you will travel through some old ruins that are home to some goblins nowadays, but it's the fastest route."

Darius accepted it with a nod. "Thanks. For everything."

Selene turned to Rowen and Ingrid, offering them a kind smile. "And to you both as well. You've done more for my daughter than I could ever repay."

Rowen waved a dismissive hand. "Oh, you don't have to repay us. But if you're offering free food every time we pass through—"

Ingrid elbowed him.

Selene chuckled before her gaze settled on Lyra, who stood at her side. The young mage had been silent, watching the exchange with a stiff posture, her expression unreadable. But behind her, the villagers had gathered, watching the party with a mixture of joy and sorrow. Some smiled, others gave small nods of encouragement, this was a lovely village, and it was clear—Lyra was well-loved here.

Even so, that torn look still lingered on her face. The three adventurers turned to leave. Then, just as they were stepping onto the road—

"Well?"

Lyra's head snapped up.

Darius was looking right at her, brow raised, arms crossed like he'd been expecting something.

Ingrid smirked. "You're not seriously staying behind, are you? We've got work to do."

A flicker of light sparked in Lyra's eyes. She turned toward her mother, as if for permission, but Selene simply smiled—a knowing, gentle expression that told Lyra everything she needed to know.

"...Are you sure?" Lyra asked, turning back to them, hesitant but hopeful, Before Darius or Ingrid could respond, Rowen blinked in confusion. "Wait... wasn't she always just coming with us anyway?"

Lyra's mouth parted in shock before a laugh escaped her. Ingrid groaned, shaking her head. Darius let out a quiet chuckle.

"Of course we're sure," Ingrid said, nudging Lyra's shoulder. "You're part of this now, idiot."

Rowen grinned, throwing an arm over her shoulder. "And besides, without you, who's going to keep us from accidentally blowing ourselves up with magic?" Lyra looked at Rowen and teased "none of you even know any magic", a fake look of insult on Rowen's face. The warmth in Lyra's chest spread through her entire body. This... this was her place.

She turned back to the villagers, her mother, her people.

The older mages bowed their heads in farewell. The young ones, the children who had clung to her the day before, waved frantically and called her name. And Selene... Selene simply gave her one final smile, one that promised she would always have a home to return to.

With a deep breath, Lyra stepped forward, embracing her mother one last time. Then she turned on her heel and ran up to the trio, her friends. Darius smirked. "Took you long enough."

Lyra playfully elbowed him, but the warmth never left her eyes. The four of them set off down the road, together at last.

another brat joins the fray.

And, of course, the hazing started immediately.

"So, you really thought you were staying behind, just living it up, sleeping, eating and drinking, huh?" Ingrid teased, shaking her head. Rowen gasped dramatically. "Lyra, how could you? And here I thought we meant something to each other!"

Lyra rolled her eyes. "I swear, you two are unbearable." Darius chuckled. "You'll get used to it."

"Or," Ingrid added, slinging her axe over her shoulder, "you'll regret every choice that led you to this moment." Lyra laughed, shaking her head as she fell in step with them.

From the village gates, Selene watched them go, the corners of her lips curling into a soft smile. Her daughter was in good hands.

And for the first time in her life, Lyra wasn't just a mage of Ravaryn—she was an adventurer. Together, the four of them marched toward the unknown, toward Black Hollow.

The journey south stretched over the next couple of days, the terrain shifting from the familiar mountain paths into rolling forests and uneven trails. The first day had been uneventful save for Rowen's insistence on taking the lead, which led them straight into a thick patch of thorns. Darius had to hold back a laugh as Ingrid wordlessly yanked him free while Lyra muttered spells to pull the thorns from his clothes.

"You know, for a tracker, you sure do lead us into a lot of trouble," Ingrid teased, tossing a thorny branch aside.

Rowen grinned. "It's part of the experience. What's an adventure without a few scrapes?"

"Less painful," Lyra said dryly.

The second night, they made camp in a small clearing, setting up a fire and sharing rations. The plains were quieter here, but there were still signs of wildlife—tracks of wolves, the distant calls of owls, and at one point, a rustling in the brush that had all four of them tensing for a fight. When the creature revealed itself as nothing more than a massive brown bear, they relaxed—briefly. Then the bear turned aggressive after Rowen refused to share his food, forcing them into a brief but intense struggle. Ingrid held the creature back with sheer strength, Rowen darted in and out with his blades, and Lyra's astra bolts provided just enough of a sting to send it retreating into the cluster of trees nearby. Darius had landed the final blow using the hilt of his blade, but even as the bear limped off, he felt a pang of guilt. It wasn't a demon, just a beast trying to survive.

As they settled back around the fire, Rowen winced, rubbing his shoulder where the bear had nearly bowled him over. "I liked it better when we were fighting that ugly dragon thing," he joked. "At least that was an abomination. This felt personal."

"You say that as if you knew the bear," Ingrid smirked, shaking her head.

Lyra chuckled, but then her expression softened. "At least we handled it together. No one got seriously hurt."

Darius stared at the flickering firelight, listening to the quiet laughter of his companions. It was a strange feeling—comfort, maybe. When they had first joined him, they all had their own reasons. Ingrid wanted to protect her village. Rowen was searching for help. Lyra had just wanted to get home. But now, as they sat here together, bruised, exhausted, and still standing, something had shifted.

They weren't just traveling together anymore. They weren't just allies. They were friends. Darius let out a small breath and smirked. "Guess I'm not doing this alone after all." Rowen raised an eyebrow. "You just now figuring that out? We've been together for quite some time now yano."

Lyra smiled softly, nodding. Ingrid nudged his shoulder, offering a rare look of approval.

"About time," she muttered.

The morning sun cast long shadows over the landscape as the

group finally arrived at the old ruins. Darius surveyed the crumbling stone towers, half-buried in ivy and time, before glancing at Lyra. "What is this place?"

Lyra brushed dust off a worn pillar, her expression thoughtful. "If the stories from my village are true, this was once an old stronghold, maybe even the royal castle before the kings and queens permanently moved to the capital. But it was destroyed in the last great conflict—during the previous hero's cycle. If that's true, then… maybe one of the demons was fought here."

Rowen let out a low whistle. "So, we're walking in the footsteps of legends. No pressure."

As they wandered deeper inside, the air grew thick with dust and history. The remnants of old bookshelves lined the walls, their pages brittle and faded. Paintings, cracked and weathered, still clung to the walls, depicting regal figures of a forgotten age. Rowen, grinning, made his way to the throne at the far end of the room and flopped down onto it. "Bow before your king!" he declared, pointing dramatically at Ingrid, who responded with an unimpressed glare. "You'll be the first I send to the dungeons, peasant."

Lyra, meanwhile, sifted through a pile of loose parchment, her eyes lighting up as she pulled out a handful of aged spell pages. "These… these are spells I don't know!" She studied them excitedly. "This one—Ignis Surge—conjures fire in a sweeping arc. Gale Pierce… it's wind-based, sends slicing air currents at foes. And this one… Lumin Edge, a light-based slashing spell. Oh! And this… Conjure Artifact—it lets me create small objects from pure energy." She clutched them tightly "Aetherial Chains. It's a restraint spell, one meant to bind an opponent in glowing magical bindings." a quiet determination in her eyes. "These could be useful."

Darius, meanwhile, was drawn to a large stone tablet near the far wall. The carvings were old, depicting scenes of warriors battling horrors beyond comprehension. He traced the timeline with his fingers, eyes narrowing. "This... these are the cycles. Every single one. The first hero, the second... all the way up to the eighth."

Ingrid and Rowen joined him, peering over his shoulder. "What do they say?" Ingrid asked.

Darius frowned. "The first cycle... it was easy. The hero defeated Vorthis quickly. The second, a little harder. Each cycle after, the battles grew worse. The demons stronger. The land suffered more each time." He exhaled sharply. "No one ever told me this. Not even Alara. If this is true... then Vorthis isn't just waiting. He's getting stronger. Each hero has just been a temporary fix. Like putting a bandage on a lost limb."

The weight of that realization settled over them like a heavy fog. Before anyone could speak further, the silence was broken by movement—a skittering sound, echoing from the darkness around them.

Something was here.

The group instinctively tensed, hands moving to their weapons as the scurrying grew louder, surrounding them.

The air shifted. A low chittering sound echoed through the ruined halls, faint at first, like the rustling of dry leaves caught in the wind. Then came the movement—small, rapid scurrying in the darkness beyond the broken pillars and shattered walls.

Darius tightened his grip on his sword as shadows flickered along the edges of their torchlight. Eyes gleamed from the crevices and gaps in the stonework, dozens of them, reflecting the fire's glow like hungry embers.

Then, they emerged.

One by one, goblins slithered out of the darkness, their bodies hunched and wiry, their limbs too long for their small frames. Their skin varied in hues of sickly green and mottled grey, their bony fingers tipped with needle-like claws. Teeth, yellowed and uneven, gleamed beneath wide, lipless mouths, curled into unnatural grins. Some carried crude weapons—rusted swords, chipped daggers, even sharpened bones—while others wielded nothing at all, as if their clawed hands were weapons enough.

Rowen muttered a curse under his breath as more poured in, clambering along the broken archways and fractured ceiling beams. They moved with unsettling ease, their gangly limbs gripping onto stone like insects. Soon, they were everywhere—perched atop broken furniture, crouched along the walls, dangling upside down from what little remained of the ceiling. Their numbers swelled until the entire chamber was filled with them.

Darius's eyes swept across the room, making a quick count. At least fifty.

"Gods…" Lyra whispered, pressing a hand to her chest.

"They're not attacking." Ingrid noted, her axe gripped tight in both hands.

Indeed, not a single goblin had yet made a move. Instead, they loomed in place, staring, studying them with eerie fascination. Their heads twitched side to side, eyes darting, bodies shifting restlessly—but they did not pounce.

It was as if they were waiting.

Rowen swallowed hard, barely breathing. "I don't like this." A murmur rippled through the horde as the goblins shifted, parting just enough for one figure to step forward. He was slightly taller than the others, though still hunched, his wiry frame draped in mismatched scraps of armour—some stolen from fallen warriors, others crudely crafted from bone and leather. A jagged scar split across his yellowed face, one milky eye staring dead ahead while the other, sharp and predatory, locked onto the group.

He walked with an unsettling confidence, his clawed fingers twitching at his sides. When he spoke, his voice was gravelly, guttural, but unmistakably in the human tongue.

"Who... leader?" The goblin's lips twisted into something resembling a grin, sharp teeth glinting in the dim light. "What purpose... in my home?"

His speech was broken, words strung together in a way that felt unnatural, self-taught. Yet despite the crude grasp of language, his meaning was clear. This was his domain, and he was waiting for an answer.

The other goblins tensed behind him, their eyes locked onto the group like a pack of starving wolves eyeing fresh meat. Drool dripped from their fanged mouths, some licking their lips, their bodies coiled and twitching with anticipation. The leader held up a hand, keeping them still—for now. But the restraint was thin. One wrong word, one sudden move, and they would pounce.

Darius' grip tightened around his sword. His eyes flicked to Rowen, Ingrid, and Lyra. The exits were completely blocked—goblins clung to the walls, the ceiling, their long fingers digging into cracks in the stone like spiders in a web. Escape wasn't an option. Not yet.

Ingrid leaned slightly toward Darius, whispering, "Talk fast."

Darius took a slow breath and took a half-step forward. He could feel the weight of every goblin's gaze pressing down on him. "We didn't come here to fight," he said carefully, keeping his voice level. "We're just passing through."

The leader tilted his head, eyes narrowing. "Hmph... Pass through?" His hooked nails scraped against his own chest as he gestured to the ruins around them. "This home. Home for goblins. Not for humans. Humans... take. Always take."

Rowen let out a slow, nervous chuckle. "Well, we're not taking anything. Just looking around. Real nice place you got here."

The goblin leader's grin stretched wider. "Nice?" He sniffed the air, taking a step closer, his piercing gaze darting between them. "You... lie? You steal? You kill?"

The air grew heavier. The goblins behind him tensed further, some snarling low in their throats, claws flexing against the stone. Lyra clutched her staff tightly, her mind racing for any spell that could get them out of this.

Darius kept his expression neutral, though his mind was spinning. One wrong answer could get them ripped apart. "We don't mean any harm," he said slowly. "We just want to leave."

The goblin leader's milky eye twitched. Then he let out a slow, raspy chuckle. "Want to leave?" He pointed one clawed finger at Darius' chest. "Maybe... we let you. Maybe... we don't."

His grin never faded, but his fingers flexed, his muscles tensed. The rest of the goblins were waiting, poised on the edge of violence, just waiting for the word to attack.

Still, all the exits remained blocked and the goblin leader's grin never wavered. If anything, it stretched wider, more unnatural, as if his face barely contained it. He took another step forward, his movements slow, deliberate, savouring the moment. The rest of the horde mirrored him, inching closer, their hungry eyes flashing in the dim torchlight.

"You..." The leader's clawed finger drifted lazily between them. "Where from?"

Darius kept still, watching him carefully. "A village to the north."

The goblin hummed, tilting his head as if considering. "Big village? Small?"

"Small," Ingrid answered flatly, her fingers curling near the handle of her axe.

The goblin leader clicked his tongue. "Hmmm... Small. Easy to burn. Easy to take." His words were slow, measured, just to see how they would react.

Rowen tensed. "What's with the questions? Thought we were just passing through, not sitting for an interview."

The leader ignored him, his gaze flicking to Lyra. "You. Magic girl." His grin split wider, his gnashing teeth catching the firelight. "What spells you know?"

Lyra stiffened. "Enough."

The goblin let out a wheezing laugh, the noise sending a ripple of chuckles through the horde. The room felt smaller now. The goblins pressed closer, their bodies twitching with anticipation.

The leader let the laughter die down, then finally dropped the act.

"You want to run." His voice lost its previous amusement, replaced by something darker. "I see it in eyes. See it in feet. Always shifting. Always looking." He clicked his tongue, wagging a long, gnarled finger. "No, no, no. You come in home. When you leave... is when I say."

His words sent a shiver through the group.

The goblins behind him erupted into a fit of giggles, a distorted, chittering noise that bounced off the stone walls. Some clapped their hands together; others smacked their weapons against the ground in excitement.

"But!" The leader's voice rose over the chaos. "Maybe I... give chance. Maybe we play a game."

The goblins howled and screeched with delight, their excitement reaching a fever pitch. They drew closer, their breath hot and rancid, their clawed hands twitching.

Rowen let out a slow breath. "I hate games."

The leader leaned in. "Hide and seek."

The words sent a chill down Darius' spine.

Rowen chuckled dryly. "Lemme guess. We hide, you seek, and if we lose, we get eaten?"

The leader's grin sharpened. "You smart one."

The goblins shrieked with laughter, some climbing onto the ceiling like insects, others shifting side to side as if barely able to contain themselves. Their bodies trembled with hunger, anticipation.

Darius clenched his jaw. They weren't getting out of this without a fight.

Then, Rowen stepped back.

A hollow sound echoed beneath his boot.

His eyes flicked downward. The wood creaked. A trapdoor.

He slowly glanced toward Ingrid and tilted his head slightly—a silent message. Ingrid's grip tightened on her axe. She caught on immediately.

Rowen smirked and looked back at the leader. "You know, I gotta say, you're a real charming host. Got the whole 'creepy mastermind' thing going. But I've got a better game idea—"

Before he could finish, Ingrid swung.

"let's play Tag, your it." Rowen finished.

Her axe slammed into the wood, splintering it apart in a single devastating strike. The trapdoor gave way, and in an instant, the four of them dropped.

The last thing they saw before falling was the goblin leader's grin disappearing, replaced by a furious snarl.

Then they hit the ground hard. Dust exploded around them as they landed in the damp, stale air of the dungeons below.

Darius barely had a second to get his bearings before the shrieking above turned into an all-out frenzy.

"RUN!" Darius roared, scrambling to his feet.

The sound of the goblins above erupted into chaos—snarls, shrieks, and the frenzied pounding of feet as they scrambled to chase their escaping prey. From above, the leader's voice slithered down into the dungeon, a sickening cackle laced with amusement.

"Run, run, little meats—run fast! We coming!"

The first wave of goblins dropped through the shattered hole, eyes gleaming in the dim light, claws scraping against the stone as they scrambled forward on all fours. Lyra shot a bolt of fire behind them, the narrow passage flaring with orange light as the blast struck, sending some goblins screeching back.

"This way!" Rowen sprinted ahead, his sharp eyes scanning the tunnels. The stone walls were cracked and crumbling, serpentine roots snaking through gaps in the ancient foundation. Shadows flickered as goblins poured from side tunnels, howling as they gave chase.

One leaped from the side—Ingrid pivoted mid-sprint, her axe catching it midair and sending it slamming into the wall. Another lunged from the ceiling, its dagger flashing downward—Darius twisted, slashing his blade up, severing its hand before shoving it back into the horde.

"They're everywhere!" Lyra cried, launching another spell over her shoulder. Wind surged in the tunnel, flinging goblins against the walls like ragdolls. But more kept coming. Dozens, maybe more.

"They're driving us somewhere!" Rowen shouted. "We need to—"

Then Darius saw it—a glimmer of light ahead, faint and distant. An exit.

"There! GO!"

They ran harder, lungs burning, muscles screaming. The tunnel widened, the light growing brighter, but the goblins were closing in.

Darius' foot slammed into water—ice-cold, rushing past his legs. This must lead to a riverbed he thought. The exit was a massive, rusted iron gate barely hanging onto its hinges. The brightness outside blinded them, but it was their only hope.

Rowen running beside him, panting. "Tell me you got a plan!"

Darius' eyes locked onto a thick, rusted chain coiled beside the gate, running upward into the shadows.

"That chain—it's holding up the gate!"

Rowen didn't hesitate. "Then drop it!"

The goblins surged closer, nearly upon them. Lyra's magic was dimming, her exhaustion showing, and Ingrid was swinging wildly, barely keeping them back.

The group with one final surge of energy run through the opening at the same time Darius slashed at the chain with everything he had. The metal groaned—then snapped.

The gate came crashing down with a deafening *clang*, sealing the entrance just as the goblins smashed into it from the other side. Dozens of clawed hands reached through the bars, grasping, nails scraping against metal. Their screams and screeches filled the tunnel, eyes burning with rage as they howled in frustration.

The group now stood in waist-deep water, drenched, breathless, but alive. For a moment, they simply stood there, the weight of their escape settling in. Then Rowen let out a breathless laugh, shaking his head. "Well... that sucked."

CHAPTER 14

The Fire Before the Fog

The group had travelled south until the stars were high, pushing forward just enough to be sure the goblins weren't following. The land sloped downward, and before long, they waded through a second river—this one calmer, its water clear and cool against their weary bodies. By the time they settled on a small clearing to make camp, the village they planned to visit in the morning was still half a day's walk away.

Drenched, exhausted, and still rattled from their narrow escape, they wasted no time in setting up. A fire crackled to life, warm and welcoming against the damp night. They laid their soaked clothes near the flames, draping them over rocks and branches to dry, before wrapping themselves in thick blankets scavenged from their packs.

Rowen and Darius sat by the riverbank, sticks in hand, with thin wire they'd managed to fashion into makeshift fishing lines. With their blankets wrapped around them like oversized cloaks, they looked less like warriors and more like tired wanderers seeking a quiet moment.

Rowen cast his line, watching the ripples spread across the water. "You know, this is a real bonding experience. Just two guys, fishing after being nearly eaten alive by goblins. Real poetic."

Darius smirked, adjusting his grip. "Yeah, we should make it a tradition. Every time we almost die, we go fishing."

Rowen nodded sagely. "I'm in. Of course, if we keep up this pace, we'll have enough fish to open a market stall by the end of the month."

Darius chuckled, shaking his head. The night was calm, the only sounds being the crackling fire behind them, the gentle rush of water, and the occasional croak of frogs hidden in the reeds. It was a strange contrast to the chaos they'd endured just hours before.

Rowen tilted his head, glancing at Darius out of the corner of his eye. "So, anyone special waiting for you at the end of this?"

Darius paused mid-reel, his expression unreadable. "Not really."

"Not really?" Rowen repeated, smirking. "That wasn't a 'no.'"

Darius exhaled, focusing on the water. "It doesn't matter."

Rowen's grin widened. "Oh-ho, it *does* matter. Come on, I need some fuel for future teasing. Spill it."

For a moment, Darius didn't answer. Then, finally, he muttered, "I… felt something. A connection."

Rowen whistled. "With *who*?"

Darius rolled his eyes. "someone I met before you, back at the castle." Trying to be vague.

Rowen's mouth dropped open in mock shock. "The princess? Our princess? The one in the fancy dresses and the big castle?"

Darius shook his head. "Forget it."

"Oh no, no, you can't just drop that and expect me to move on." Rowen leaned forward. "Was there a longing look? A secret rendezvous? Did you share one of those dramatic, tension-filled moments?" Darius sighed. "I'm going to push you into the river now." Rowen gasped. "You wouldn't dare."

Without another word, Darius shoved him.

With a yelp, Rowen toppled into the water, flailing before surfacing with a splutter. "*Unbelievable!* Here I am helping you be in touch with your feelings, and this is how you repay me?"

Darius grinned. "You brought it on yourself."

From the fire, Ingrid and Lyra turned to see the commotion, shaking their heads as Rowen dragged himself back to shore.

"Idiots," Ingrid muttered, tightening the blanket around her shoulders.

Lyra smiled. "At least they're enjoying themselves."

The two girls sat closer to the fire, their blankets wrapped tightly around them as they let the warmth chase away the lingering chill of their wet clothes.

"You and Darius knew each other before this, right?" Lyra asked.

Ingrid shook her head. "nah, I met him a few days before you did, purely coincidence really"

Lyra tilted her head. "so do you know what's he's really like? I mean, besides the whole 'brooding, determined hero' thing."

Ingrid huffed a quiet laugh. "He's stubborn. Can be quiet. Likes to be alone, although that seems to be changing but he also doesn't give up from what I've seen."

Lyra smiled. "That's a good thing."

Ingrid watched the fire crackle. "Yeah. It is."

The quiet of the night stretched around them, interrupted only by the distant chirping of crickets and the occasional splash from the river where Darius and Rowen fished.

"It's strange, isn't it?" Lyra mused, pulling her blanket tighter around her. "How quickly we all got caught up in this. A few days ago, I was in my village, training with the other mages, thinking my biggest concern was perfecting my spell work." She exhaled softly, shaking her head. "Now I'm out here, running from goblins and sleeping under the stars with you lot."

Ingrid smirked. "Yeah, tell me about it. One moment, I'm dealing with bandits and trading supplies, and the next, I'm chasing after some broody hero with no sense of direction."

Lyra laughed. "Funny how people seem to follow Darius, even when he doesn't ask them to."

Ingrid nodded, her expression thoughtful. "Yeah. There's something about him, I guess. He's got that... I don't know, that presence. Like even if he doesn't say much, you just know he's going to see things through."

Lyra tilted her head. "You think he knows that?"

Ingrid snorted. "If he does, he sure doesn't act like it."

A comfortable silence settled over them for a moment before Lyra spoke again. "What was your life like before all this? Before you left your village?"

Ingrid leaned back slightly, staring into the fire. "Just me and my mother. My dad was never in the picture." Her voice was even, but there was a weight to it. "She did everything for me. Made sure I had food, a home, a future. But she was always worried—worried about being alone, about whether we'd be safe without a man around." She clenched her jaw slightly. "So I made sure we didn't need one. Trained harder than anyone else, got stronger, took care of her instead. I don't need to rely on men—"

A fish *smacked* into her face.

She let out an uncharacteristic yelp, scrambling back as Rowen stood there, grinning ear to ear, proudly dangling his catch. "Look what I have! *Dinner!*"

Darius trudged up behind him, smirking at Ingrid's rare startled expression. "Guess that makes him the provider tonight."

Ingrid scowled, wiping her face with her blanket before giving Rowen a death glare. "I swear to the gods, if you ever do that again—"

"Oh, lighten up, Miss 'I Don't Rely on Men,'" Rowen teased, twirling the fish like it was some grand trophy. "You can rely on me for good food at least."

Lyra was giggling now, hiding her smile behind her blanket. "That was a very... dramatic entrance, Rowen."

"Timing is everything." He waggled his eyebrows before tossing the fish down near the fire. "Now, someone cook this thing before Ingrid kills me." Darius shook his head with a chuckle and grabbed his knife to clean the fish while Rowen plopped down beside the fire, smug as ever.

Ingrid grumbled under her breath before sighing and sitting back down. "You're lucky I'm too hungry to throw you into the river."

"Oh, don't worry, Ingrid," Lyra teased. "We all know you don't need us."

Rowen snickered. "Nope, but she *likes* having us around."

Ingrid rolled her eyes as the smell of roasting fish filled the air, but despite herself, a small, reluctant smile tugged at her lips.

They cooked and ate, the warmth of the fire and the gentle lull of the night settling over them. One by one, fatigue took hold. Darius was the first to drift off, leaning against a rock with his arms crossed. Lyra soon followed, curling up in her blanket, her breathing slowing into soft, steady rhythms.

That left only Rowen and Ingrid, the flames casting flickering shadows over their faces.

Rowen stretched his arms behind his head, glancing at Ingrid. "So… You meant what you said earlier? About not needing anyone?"

Ingrid raised a brow. "Of course."

He nodded, but his usual smirk was missing. "I get it. I heard what you said about your father. That must've been rough."

Ingrid blinked at him, caught off guard by the shift in tone. "I got through it."

"Yeah, but still." He shrugged. "I wouldn't know what that's like. Never had parents to begin with."

Ingrid frowned. "What?"

Rowen leaned back on his hands, staring at the fire. "Orphan. No family. No home. Just me. Camped out wherever I could, stole what I had to, hunted when I could."

She was silent for a moment, taking in the weight of his words. Then, a realization struck her. She looked at him carefully. "When we talked about your house burning down... That was a lie, wasn't it? You don't have a home."

Rowen exhaled a laugh, but it wasn't his usual carefree one. "You caught that, huh? Yeah. I made that up. Thought it sounded better than 'I sleep in trees sometimes.'"

She watched him for a moment before crossing her arms. "Then why did you follow Darius? If you don't have a family to protect, it can't really be about the village, can it?"

Rowen's grin faltered just a little before he looked away. "Actually... it is."

Ingrid tilted her head. "What do you mean?"

Rowen ran a hand through his hair, staring into the fire. "I arrived at that village when I was a teenager. Just another stray passing through. The tavern owner and his wife? They gave me a room upstairs, fed me, let me stick around. Told me as long as I protected the village, I had a place there." He let out a slow breath. "I wasn't lying, Ingrid. That village is the only thing I have. They took me in. Looked at me like I was worth something. I wasn't about to let that go."

Ingrid watched him quietly. It made sense now. His wild, untamed fighting style. His easygoing nature but fierce loyalty. And when he spoke about the village, there was no hesitation. He meant every word.

She didn't know what to say. So, for once, she didn't say anything at all. Instead, she simply sat there, listening to the crackling fire. This was the most serious she'd ever seen him, the usual carefree smirk replaced with something quieter. He wasn't just the loudmouth jokester she thought he was. There was more to him. A lot more.

The fire crackled between them again, and Ingrid pulled her blanket tighter. "Must be nice for you then. You're used to sleeping outside, but it's freezing tonight."

Rowen scratched his cheek, looking a little sheepish. "Uh... well... I mean, we could always... you know... cuddle again?" He gave an awkward chuckle. "Just for warmth, of course."

Ingrid's face burned instantly, and she turned away, scowling. "Say one more word and I'll break your nose."

Rowen grinned, but he didn't say anything else. Instead, he just watched as, without another word, Ingrid shuffled closer, scooting under his blanket until they were pressed together. It wasn't like before, when exhaustion and instinct forced them into it. This time, it was a choice.

Neither of them spoke as the firelight flickered over them. Rowen relaxed first, letting out a slow breath, while Ingrid sat stiffly for a moment longer before finally easing into the warmth.

Eventually, the quiet and the heat lulled them both to sleep, curled up together beneath the stars.

Rowen stirred first, blinking against the dim morning light filtering through the trees. The fire had burned down to glowing embers, and the air was crisp with the scent of damp earth and lingering smoke. He barely noticed the warmth pressed against his side until Ingrid shifted slightly, still fast asleep.

He glanced down at her, watching the steady rise and fall of her breath. It was strange—seeing her this still, this peaceful.

Normally, she was a force of nature, all sharp glares and unwavering confidence. But now, bundled up against the cold, she looked almost... soft.

Rowen smirked to himself. "You know, Ingrid, if you wanted to cuddle again, you could ask me next time"

Her eyes snapped open, and before he could react, she shoved him backward, sending him rolling out the blankets onto the cold ground.

"Oh, shut up," she grumbled, sitting up and rubbing sleep from her eyes. A faint pink dusted her cheeks, but she refused to acknowledge it. Instead, she stretched before standing. "I'm getting dressed. Try not to freeze to death out here."

Rowen chuckled as he sat up, watching her grab her armour and move toward the trees for some privacy. He shook his head, running a hand through his messy hair before dragging himself to his feet.

A few minutes later, the rest of the group began to stir. Darius stretched, groaning as he sat up, while Lyra yawned and pulled her blanket tighter around herself. One by one, they got to their feet, shaking off the last remnants of sleep and the lingering chill from the night.

They dressed, packed up camp, and set off toward the village.

The village itself was modest—larger than a simple settlement but nowhere near the bustling size of a town. Wooden stalls lined the main road, merchants calling out their wares as the group passed by. The air smelled of freshly baked bread, dried herbs, and smoked meat.

They moved from stall to stall, picking up supplies—a few loaves of bread, dried meats, and some fresh fruit for the road. Darius bartered for a fresh set of bandages, while Lyra secured a small pouch of herbs that could be used for healing salves. Rowen, of course, took it upon himself to sample anything remotely edible, much to Ingrid's irritation.

"You do realize we actually have to pay for those, right?" she scolded as Rowen popped a dried fig into his mouth.

"Hey, I like to make sure we're getting our money's worth," he said around a mouthful of food, grinning.

As they finished gathering supplies, they overheard whispers among the villagers. A grizzled older man, standing by a cart of dried fish, caught their attention when he muttered, "The marshlands ain't what they used to be."

Darius approached, curiosity piqued. "What do you mean?"

The old man glanced at him, then at the others, lowering his voice. "Been hearin' strange things lately. Travelers goin' in, but when they come out... they don't remember a damn thing. No name, no past, just blank. Like their whole life got plucked right outta their heads."

Rowen scoffed. "Sounds like a story to scare kids."

"Maybe," the old man mused, crossing his arms. "Or maybe it ain't. Either way, be careful if you're headin' that way."

Lyra frowned in thought. "When I was little, there was a similar story people told us about demons in the ocean. My mother used to say if kids wandered too close without an adult, the sea would take their names and memories so they could never go home."

Darius pondered this, his fingers tapping against the hilt of his sword. The idea was unsettling, but he finally nodded. "It's just a story. We'll be careful, but we've got a job to do."

With that, they finished their shopping, ensuring they had enough food and supplies before finally setting off once more. Their next destination loomed ahead—the marshlands that would lead them to Black Hallow.

The journey south began as the landscape gradually shifted from solid earth to marshy terrain. The air grew thick and humid, clinging to their skin as they pressed forward. The dirt roads they had travelled before faded into narrow, muddy trails, winding through pools of stagnant water and gnarled, ancient trees draped in long strands of moss. The sound of buzzing insects filled the air, and the ground squelched beneath their boots with each careful step.

Signs of past travellers—some successful, others not—were scattered through the swamps like forgotten relics. A wooden wagon sat half-swallowed in the murky waters, its broken wheels jutting out at odd angles. Further along, a tattered chest lay partially submerged, its lid ajar and contents long lost to the depths. Once, they even passed a skeleton resting against the roots of a fallen tree, its bones draped in the remains of a rotted cloak. It was an ominous reminder of how unforgiving these lands could be.

Lyra unfolded the map her mother had provided, tracing a course as best she could. "If we keep southeast, we should hit drier ground before nightfall," she murmured, more to herself than anyone else.

"Assuming the map's even accurate," Ingrid muttered, adjusting her grip on her axe. "This place looks like it shifts with the wind."

They trudged along, stepping carefully to avoid patches of deep mud. The water was dark and still in most places, reflecting the warped canopy above. But then—

Bubbles. A single cluster disturbed the surface of a nearby pool, breaking the mirror-like stillness with a faint, unsettling plop.

Lyra gasped and jumped back, her eyes wide. "What was that?"

Rowen smirked. "Relax, probably just a fish. Or a demon wiping someone's memory from his lips before crawling out to say hello."

Lyra shot him a glare. "Not funny."

"Come on, it's a little funny," he grinned. "What, that old man's tale got you spooked?"

She hesitated, then exhaled a short laugh, though there was a nervous edge to it. "Something about how the deep could steal memories, leaving you an empty shell if you strayed too far." She shivered slightly, pulling her cloak tighter. "Guess it just hits a little too close to home."

Darius, who had been silently observing, glanced back at the bubbling pool before shaking his head. "Just stories. Both your mothers and the old geezers." But even as he said it, he found himself glancing over his shoulder as they pressed on, the uneasy feeling lingering in his gut.

CHAPTER 15

The Swamp That Forgets

As they trudged deeper into the swamp, the trees grew denser, their snaking limbs hanging low as if whispering among themselves. The ground sucked at their boots with each step, and a thick mist curled between the gnarled roots. The stench of stagnant water mixed with decay made it clear that whatever had once thrived here was long gone.

It was Lyra who spotted it first—a crumpled figure half-submerged in the muck, its skeletal remains wrapped in the tattered remains of a traveller's cloak. Time and the swamp had eaten away at the flesh, leaving only bones and scraps of fabric clinging to a once-living form. But what caught their attention was the leather-bound journal still clutched in the corpse's bony grip.

Darius knelt, prying the book free carefully. The pages were damp, warped by moisture, but the ink remained—scrawled in an erratic, almost frantic hand. He opened it, frowning as his eyes scanned the words.

Who am I?

Where am I going?

How am I?

What was my name?

Why am I here?

What was my—

The words repeated, the handwriting becoming messier with each line until it devolved into jagged scratches across the page. Darius turned the next few pages, and what he found made his stomach tighten.

The words no longer formed coherent sentences. Instead, they spiralled into incoherent ramblings, broken thoughts, and chilling descriptions of something unseen.

It watches.

It does not blink because it has no eyes, but I know it sees me.

It moves without moving.

I tried to count its limbs, but there are too many. Or too few. I don't know.

My head hurts.

Why is it laughing?

Darius exhaled sharply. "This guy lost his mind."

Rowen leaned over his shoulder, peering at the pages. "That or he was just a bad poet." He smirked, but there was no real humour in his voice.

Lyra hugged herself. "No… this is something else." She hesitated, then reached for the book, flipping back a few pages. "These early entries are normal. Travel logs. Notes about food rations, routes, villages. Then—" she tapped one of the later pages—

"it shifts. Like his thoughts weren't his own anymore."

Ingrid crossed her arms, glancing at the corpse. "Could be sickness. Or starvation. Hallucinations." But even as she said it, there was doubt in her voice.

Rowen scoffed. "Right. Because all starving men start writing about nightmare creatures and forgetting their own names." He glanced around the swamp. "Kinda weird how this guy just sat here and rotted instead of trying to leave, huh?"

A silence settled over them.

Darius shut the journal. "Whatever happened to him, it's over. Let's keep moving."

He tossed the book onto the corpse's chest and stood. But as they turned to leave, a low wind stirred the mist, and a whisper slithered through the air. It was faint—just a breath of sound—but for a moment, it almost sounded like a voice.

A voice asking a question.

Who are you?

Lyra stiffened. "Did you hear that?"

Rowen chuckled, a little too quickly. "It's just the wind. Unless you think the skeleton wants to borrow our map."

Darius cast one last look at the remains, his grip tightening on his sword. Then, without another word, they walked on, leaving the journal, the corpse, and its forgotten questions behind.

The group trudged forward, their boots sinking into the damp earth with every step. The marsh seemed endless, stretching in every direction with no signs of solid ground beyond the tangled roots and murky waters. A thick canopy of coiled trees loomed overhead, their branches draped in hanging moss that swayed with every passing breeze.

They encountered minor inconveniences along the way—Rowen nearly lost a boot in a patch of deep mud, Ingrid cursed as she scraped her shin on a submerged root, and Lyra yelped when a particularly large bug landed on her shoulder. Still, they pressed on, until finally, Darius spotted a cluster of large, flat stones rising from the swamp like the broken remnants of an ancient path.

"Here," Darius said, stepping onto the largest rock. "Let's rest for a moment and check our bearings."

No one argued.

Lyra sat cross-legged, pulling out the old spells she had salvaged from the ruins. She muttered incantations under her breath, flicking her staff as she attempted to conjure a small item—a simple test of magic control. With a soft shimmer of light, a wooden cup appeared in her palm. She beamed, pleased with her almost instant progress, before turning her attention to a more advanced spell: Aetherial Chains, She traced the arcane symbols carefully, determined to commit them to memory.

Rowen, meanwhile, dug through his bag and pulled out some dried meat, tearing into it without hesitation.

Ingrid wrinkled her nose. "How can you eat in this stench?"

Rowen smirked, mouth full. "Survival instinct. You get used to it."

"Oh, right, because rotting swamp gas and whatever-that-was you just stuffed into your mouth is such a gourmet experience."

Rowen swallowed and pointed at her. "Don't act high and mighty.

Need I remind you of your love of those rancid Frostbitten Brinefruit?"

"That's different!"

"Was it? 'Cause I recall you stinking out a tavern and a cave with those eyewatering death fruits, if you can even call them fruits anymore."

Darius shook his head, suppressing a smirk as he looked over the map.

Ingrid huffed, pulling out a whetstone and beginning to sharpen her axe with slow, methodical strokes. The rhythmic sound of metal scraping against stone filled the air. After a moment, she glanced at Darius. "Your sword could probably use some care, too. Want me to sharpen it?"

Darius ran a thumb along the edge of his obsidian blade. It was still sharp, but a bit of extra care wouldn't hurt. He handed it over without hesitation. "Go ahead."

As Ingrid took the sword, Rowen smirked. "The axe wielding murder machine does have a soft side."

Ingrid shot him a glare. "I can easily kill you here and now, you know."

Rowen grinned. "Now that's the Ingrid I know."

Darius ignored the bickering and turned to Lyra. "How are the spells coming along?"

Lyra tucked a loose strand of hair behind her ear. "Better. I'm getting a feel for conjuration, but this restraint spell is tricky. It requires a lot of control."

Rowen leaned over, glancing at the arcane notes in her lap. "Aetherial Chains, huh? What, planning on tying me up?"

Lyra didn't even look up. "Only if you keep talking."

Darius exhaled a quiet chuckle. "Just make sure you can actually use it when the time comes."

"I will," Lyra assured him.

Darius stood, stretching his limbs before tightening the strap of his sheath. He glanced at the others, his expression unreadable as always. "Ready?"

There were a few murmurs of agreement as the group packed up their things. Ingrid handed Darius his freshly sharpened blade, and Rowen, still chewing on the last of his dried meat, slung his bag over his shoulder. Lyra clutched her staff, absentmindedly muttering spells as they began walking again.

The swamp stretched endlessly ahead, gnarled roots jutting from the muck, stagnant pools of water dotting the path. Lyra, still deep in practice, conjured small items as she walked—a plate, then a cup, then another. She concentrated, determined to master the process while moving. A spoon shimmered into existence in her hand before she let it drop to the ground with the others.

Rowen chuckled. "What are you doing, setting up a fancy dinner?"

"Just practicing," Lyra said, stepping over a spiralled root. "This spell is easy enough to cast, but maintaining consistency takes effort."

As they continued forward, the wind whispered through the trees. Faint, fragmented voices—just on the edge of hearing.

"Who am I?"

"Where are we?"

The words barely registered, half-lost in the swamp's ever-present groan of shifting water and rustling leaves.

The group walked on, hours seemed to pass, idol conversations between the four as they pressed on.

"Aww man, I wonder how the elder and villagers are doing back at……" Rowen suddenly frowned, rubbing the back of his head. "What was the name of my village again?"

Darius arched a brow. "How do you forget the name of the place you grew up?"

Rowen shrugged. "Dunno. Just… slipped my mind for a second."

"Maybe the swamp's rotting your brain," Ingrid said dryly.

"Could be. Or maybe it's just from dealing with you"

Ingrid snorted, shaking her head before turning to Darius. "Anyway, where to next, uh…" She trailed off, her brows knitting together in brief confusion. "Wait… what was your name again?"

Darius halted. "What?"

She blinked hard. "No, I know it. I do. It's just… why did I blank on it for a second?"

Before anyone could comment further, Lyra's gaze caught on something ahead.

Her conjured cup, and another and another.

All of them scattered across the path.

Her stomach turned as her eyes lifted to the large, flat rock sitting just ahead.

"The rock," she breathed, her voice barely above a whisper.

Ingrid frowned. "What?"

"We've passed it before." Lyra turned in a slow circle, realization dawning. "Not once. Not twice. I think we've walked past it five times now."

A tense silence followed.

Rowen scratched his head. "You sure? I mean, all rocks kinda look the same—"

"No." Lyra pointed at the ground, at the spoons and cups and plates she'd conjured. "I dropped those as we walked. That's how I know."

Darius's expression darkened. "Then we're trapped in a loop."

Lyra swallowed. "Not all of us."

"What do you mean?" Ingrid asked.

"I remember everything," Lyra said slowly, working through the thought aloud. "Because I was concentrating on my spell. My mind was active, focused on a task."

"So what?" Rowen crossed his arms. "We just start shooting fireballs to keep from forgetting?"

"No…." Lyra thought for a moment "but… we could play a game."

Rowen blinked. "A game?"

Lyra nodded, thinking fast. "A concentration game. Something that keeps our minds focused as we walk."

Darius narrowed his eyes. "What kind of game?"

Lyra tapped her chin before nodding. "There's a game we played as kids back home. 'Echo Steps.'"

Rowen grinned. "Alright, now I'm interested."

Lyra nodded. "It's simple. We take turns saying a word, but it has to connect to the last word someone else said. If you repeat a word that's already been said, you lose. If you pause too long, you lose."

Ingrid frowned. "Connect how?"

"By association. If I say 'fire,' the next person could say 'warmth' or 'burn' or 'light.' You can only say something that links to the last word somehow."

Rowen smirked. "So if I said 'Ingrid,' Darius would have to say 'angry'?"

Ingrid shot him a glare. "If you want your legs broken, sure."

Darius sighed. "Fine. We'll try it. If it keeps our heads clear and gets us moving in the right direction, then it's worth it."

"Exactly." Lyra nodded. "Let's walk and play at the same time. I'll start."

She took a breath, gripping her staff.

"Swamp."

Rowen grinned. "Stinky."

Ingrid rolled her eyes. "Rot."

Darius glanced around warily. "Decay."

They continued walking, their words forming a strange, winding chain—simple, playful, but with an edge of necessity.

With each step, they hoped they were finally moving forward.

The game continued as they walked, their words stringing together in an effort to keep their minds sharp.

"Cold," Ingrid said.

"Snow," Lyra followed.

"White," Darius added.

Rowen smirked. "Ingrid's hair."

The axe-wielder gave him a shove. "Not how the game works, idiot."

Despite the banter, their path finally began to shift. The gnarled trees thinned out just enough for them to see a murky, open stretch of water ahead. A rotting wooden signpost sat half-sunken in the muck, its lettering barely legible.

"Black Hallow →"

"Guess we're on the right track," Rowen muttered, brushing a hand over the worn wood. "Not exactly a promising welcome."

They continued forward, keeping the game going just in case. But then the path ended.

Before them stretched a wide bog, its surface thick with sludge, bubbling ominously in places. There was no obvious way across—only black water stretching too far to wade through.

"Tell me this isn't the way," Ingrid muttered.

Darius pulled out the map, unfurling it carefully. "It is."

"That's unfortunate," Rowen said, folding his arms. "So what, we swim?"

Lyra shuddered. "Absolutely not."

Darius studied the map again, searching for any indication of another route, but Rowen suddenly pointed ahead. "Wait. There."

They followed his gaze to the left, where a structure barely held together. An old wooden bridge stretched across the bog, weathered and rotten from years of neglect. Some of the planks were missing, and others looked ready to collapse with the lightest touch.

Ingrid exhaled sharply. "That thing is one bad step away from dropping us all in."

Darius folded the map and sighed. "It's the only way."

There was a beat of silence before Ingrid rolled her shoulders. "Fine. I'll go first. If it holds me, it should hold the rest of you."

With careful steps, Ingrid moved onto the bridge, testing each board before shifting her weight. The wood creaked beneath her boots, but she pressed forward, her grip tight around her axe handle.

Rowen followed next, stepping cautiously as he mimicked her movements. Lyra and Darius exchanged a glance before moving onto the bridge together, keeping a steady pace behind him.

The wood groaned.

Then, without warning—

CRACK!

A section of the bridge gave way beneath Rowen. He cursed as his foot slipped through the splintering planks, the rotten wood crumbling further beneath him.

"Rowen!" Lyra gasped.

His body lurched forward, and for a heart-stopping second, he nearly plunged into the swamp. But Darius and Lyra both shot out their hands, grabbing him by his arms before he could fall through completely.

"I got him!" Lyra strained, gripping his sleeve tightly.

"Hold on," Darius gritted out, trying to pull him up.

The wood beneath their feet groaned again, splinters raining into the water below.

"Not to rush you," Rowen said, voice tight, "but I'd rather not take a bath in whatever *that* is."

Then—

THUNK!

A heavy weight hooked onto Rowen's harness, pulling him up in a swift, forceful motion.

Ingrid stood at the edge, gripping the handle of her battleaxe, the blunt end wedged against Rowen's chest as she hauled him forward with raw strength.

With a final yank, he tumbled onto the bridge, coughing and gripping the boards beneath him.

"Could've given me a gentler tug," he muttered, shaking off the near disaster.

"Could've let you fall," Ingrid shot back.

Darius and Lyra quickly scrambled after them, the last planks of the bridge already cracking under their weight. The second Darius stepped onto solid ground, the entire structure gave way, the remaining wood crumbling into the bog with a sickening splash.

A long silence followed.

Rowen let out a shaky laugh. "Well. No going back now."

Darius exhaled, watching the last fragments of wood sink beneath the sludge. "No. There isn't."

Lyra rubbed her arms, still shaken. "Let's keep moving before anything else decides to fall apart."

Without another word, the group turned forward—deeper into the swamp.
exhaustion gnawed at them.

"I swear," Ingrid muttered, stepping over a rotting root, "this swamp stretches longer than it should."

Rowen groaned, rubbing his face. "How is it already night? Shouldn't we be there by now?"

Darius frowned, adjusting the map. The parchment crinkled in his grip as his eyes traced the markings. "We should've reached Black Hallow hours ago. We lost time."

Lyra shivered. "You mean—?"

"That thing… whatever it was." Darius didn't need to elaborate. They all knew. "I'd say it stole at least two or three hours from us."

Silence settled over the group, thick as the swamp mist.

Then—

A scent.

Smoke.

Faint at first, but undeniable. A dry, acrid bite in the air that didn't belong to the damp rot of the swamp.

"Fire," Lyra whispered, her voice tight.

Rowen sniffed the air, suddenly alert. "And not from a camp."

Darius didn't hesitate. "Move."

They quickened their pace, mud sucking at their boots as they pushed forward. The air grew heavier, the scent thickening with every step. Then—

A scream.

Faint. Distant. But real.

Then another.

The group broke into a run.

Branches clawed at them as they tore through the swamp,

adrenaline pushing away the exhaustion.

And then—

It happened.

A screech.

Not of any beast. Not of anything natural.

A sound that didn't belong to this world.

It was *everything* at once. A wail, a howl, a shriek of torment. Nails on bone. A thousand dying breaths. It stopped them dead in their tracks, their bodies refusing to move.

Pain erupted in their skulls. Their ears rang.

The voices returned.

"Who am I?"

"Where am I going?"

"What am I doing?"

"Why?"

The questions clawed into their minds, writhing through their thoughts like worms. Their breath came short.

Then—

An explosion.

A deafening blast shattered the night, fire illuminating the horizon in a violent burst. The shockwave sent ripples through the swamp, drowning out the voices for just a moment.

The group stumbled forward, desperate to see—

And they *wished* they hadn't.

Black Hallow was gone.

Nothing remained but ruin. Charred husks of buildings. The shattered remnants of what was once a village.

And at its centre— *It*. The Mawborn.

A shifting mass of mouths, writhing, twisting, each one speaking. Whispers. Wails. Laughter. Sobs. The voices overlapped, an endless tide of madness. Some called out in forgotten tongues. Others murmured secrets in voices they almost recognized.

Rowen swayed on his feet, his face pale.

Ingrid gripped her axe until her knuckles turned white.

Lyra trembled, her breath coming in short, panicked gasps.

Darius could only stare.

It wasn't just destruction. It was *erasure*. Nothing remained. No bodies. No remnants of the people who lived here. Like they had never existed at all.

And the Mawborn continued to speak. Calling. Consuming.

Devouring the last echoes of those who had once called Black Hallow home.

ah finally, I can reach him again. His fear, his doubts they're creeping in again.

CHAPTER 16

Where Heroes Break

The first thing Darius noticed was the cold. Not the damp chill of the swamp, but something deeper, something that clung to his bones. He opened his eyes to a sky streaked with the first hints of dawn, the colour of blood and bruises. His body ached, muscles screaming in protest as he pushed himself up from the ground. His fingers dug into the damp earth, nails caked with dried mud—and something darker.

He turned his hand over. Blood. Not his own.

A few feet away, Rowen lay sprawled on his back, his cloak torn at the edges, his chest rising and falling in shallow breaths. Ingrid was facedown, a gash across her back the wound already stopped bleeding, her axe lying just beyond her grasp. Lyra sat hunched against a tree, clutching her staff with white-knuckled fingers, her robes singed, strands of her black hair stuck to her sweat-slick forehead.

Darius tried to speak, but his throat was raw. His voice came out as little more than a whisper. "Rowen... Ingrid... Lyra."

Rowen groaned first, shifting slightly before wincing. "Did... did anyone get the name of the thing that hit us?" he rasped.

Ingrid stirred next, coughing as she rolled onto her side. "Gods... my head," she muttered. She blinked up at Darius, confusion knitting her brows. "What happened?"

No one had an answer.

Lyra looked the worst of them, staring at her hands as though they weren't her own. "I cast something," she said quietly, her voice barely audible. "I—I remember the feeling of magic, the heat of it—but I don't know what I cast." Her eyes flickered up to them, wide and lost. "I don't remember."

Darius pushed himself onto his feet, his legs unsteady. "We were at Black Hallow." The words felt foreign in his mouth, as though he were speaking someone else's memories. "We saw… something." A small flash of memory flickered like a bolt of lightning in his mind. "The Mawborn."

A spark of fire behind his eyes. Screams swallowed by an unbearable, otherworldly noise. But the images refused to settle, shifting like smoke in his mind.

"How long have we been out?" Rowen asked, glancing up at the sky. "It feels like we just—" He stopped, his expression twisting. "Wait. What day is it?"

A sharp silence followed. None of them had an answer. Had they lost a night? Two? More? The realization sent ice down Darius's spine.

Ingrid let out a shaky breath, wiping her face with her palm. "If that thing erases people, why are we still here?"

Rowen let out a humourless laugh. "Great question. Maybe we should ask it next time it tries to eat our brains."

Lyra suddenly stiffened, eyes darting to the ground. "What is that?"

They followed her gaze. The dirt was disturbed—clawed at, as if someone had tried to write something. Darius crouched, tracing his fingers over the half-scratched letters. Whatever words had been there had been lost, but the desperation was clear in the deep gouges in the earth.

His fingers curled over the hilt of his sword. It was sticky. Slowly, he lifted it to examine the dark smears along the obsidian blade. Blood. But whose?

Rowen cursed under his breath, shaking his head. "This doesn't make sense."

Nothing did.

They had seen the Mawborn. So why were they still standing? Did they beat it? There was no corpse suggesting they won. Had they been spared? Had someone—something—intervened? Or worse... had they been changed in ways they couldn't yet comprehend?

Darius sheathed his sword and turned to the others. "We need to move."

None of them argued. There were no answers to be found here—only more questions. And the gnawing dread that whatever had happened in the ruins of Black Hallow, it was not finished with them yet.

The ruined remains of Black Hallow stretched around them like the husk of a forgotten nightmare. Smouldering embers glowed in the wreckage, casting faint trails of smoke into the early morning sky. The air was thick with the scent of burnt wood and something worse—something foul and rotting beneath the destruction.

They walked in silence, picking their way through the outskirts of the ruined town, their movements slow and uncertain. There was no clear destination, no path forward—just the endless remnants of what had once been a village. The further they went, the clearer it became that nothing had survived.

Then, abruptly, the land dropped away.

They stopped just before the edge of a sheer cliff, the open sea stretching out before them, vast and endless. The sun glimmered off the waves, an almost mocking contrast to the devastation behind them. The sea had no answers for them. It only offered emptiness.

Rowen exhaled and crossed his arms. "Well. Looks like we found the edge of the world. I vote we jump. Might be easier than—"

Darius turned on him, his expression dark. "Not now, Rowen."

Rowen arched a brow. "Just saying—"

"I said not now." Darius' voice was sharp, harsher than he intended, but he didn't care. The ache in his body, the gnawing frustration in his mind—it was all too much. They had just barely escaped a nightmare, and they still didn't know how. The last thing he wanted was Rowen's usual sarcasm when they had no answers, no direction, nothing.

Rowen's smirk faded. His shoulders squared, and for the first time, there was real tension between them.

"You think I don't get it?" Rowen's voice was low, controlled. "You think I don't feel it, too? Fine, let's hear it then, oh wise leader—where do we go from here?"

Silence stretched between them, thick and heavy. Ingrid scowled and stepped forward, looking ready to knock their heads together, but Lyra spoke first.

"We… we're lost," she admitted softly, she thought for a moment, then looked to Darius. "What about the seer you mentioned a while back? Alana? She knew things before. Maybe…"

Darius' anger cooled. Alana.

She had spoken in riddles, seen things no one else could. If anyone could help them make sense of what had happened, of what they had survived, it was her.

He let out a slow breath and glanced at Rowen. The tension was still there, but it had shifted, softened.

Darius nodded. "Maybe you're right. Maybe it's time we go back."

Rowen met his gaze, then sighed and ran a hand through his hair. "Alright. Castle it is." He paused, then added with a lopsided smirk, "But if we do jump, I bet I can make the best splash."

Darius huffed, but this time, he let the comment slide.

The group turned away from the cliffs, their steps slow and uncertain as they made their way back into the ruins of Black Hallow. The air was still thick with the remnants of smoke and ash, the skeletal remains of buildings standing as eerie silhouettes against the brightening sky.

They searched the wreckage, hoping for some sign of where to go next, something to point them in the direction of the castle. But it was hard to tell where the roads had once led—many were swallowed by the destruction, others caved in or buried under collapsed debris. The swamp loomed beyond, its unnatural stillness making it clear that retracing their steps wasn't an option.

Darius moved ahead, taking in the surroundings, but his mind wasn't entirely on the search. The weight of their situation pressed against him, heavier than the sword on his back. He had barely begun processing what had happened, let alone figuring out where to go from here.

One by one, the others fell in step beside him.

Ingrid was the first. She was sharpening her axe again, the rhythmic scraping against the whetstone cutting through the silence. "You alright?" she asked, without looking up.

Darius hesitated before answering. "I don't know."

She nodded, like she understood that better than words could explain. "You will be." That was all she said before stepping ahead to scout further.

A little later, Lyra walked beside him, clutching her staff tightly. Her expression was tense, but she didn't seem as shaken as the others. "I think I was able to resist the Mawborn's memory loss better than the rest of you because I was concentrating on my spells," she murmured.

Darius glanced at her. "That's… something, at least."

"I want to figure out why," she admitted. "Maybe if I understand it, I can stop it from happening again. To us. To anyone."

He nodded. "If anyone can, it's you."

She gave him a small, grateful smile before falling back.

Finally, Rowen appeared at his side, hands tucked into his belt, eyes flicking over the ruins like he was trying to find anything else to focus on. The silence between them stretched before Rowen finally broke it.

"Hey, uh… back there. I was outta line." His voice was quieter than usual, the usual playfulness absent. "I get it. You weren't mad at me, you were mad at... everything. And you were right."

Darius glanced at him. "I didn't mean to snap."

Rowen shrugged. "Yeah, well. I'm still annoying, so I probably deserved it." He smirked, but it didn't quite reach his eyes. He let out a breath, shifting his weight. "Listen, I'm not good at... this kind of thing. But what I do know is that we need you, Darius. You're the one keeping us together. If you crack, we all do. You don't gotta be fearless or have all the answers, but..." He scratched the back of his head. "You gotta be constant. Like, a torch in the dark. If your light goes out, how the hell are the rest of us supposed to see where we're going?"

Darius was quiet for a moment before nodding. "You're right."

Rowen grinned. "I always am."

Darius rolled his eyes and swung a fist at him. Rowen, expecting it, caught it mid-swing and grinned. "See? You're predictable."

Darius smirked. "And you're still annoying."

Rowen let go of his hand, chuckling. "Come on, oh mighty torch. Let's find a way back to the castle before Ingrid starts threatening to kill us both."

As they moved deeper into the ruins, the group stumbled upon something unexpected—a weathered signpost, somehow still standing amid the destruction. The wooden planks were cracked and worn, the writing barely legible, but the directions were clear enough.

One sign pointed toward *The Marshlands*. That much made sense. It was where they had come from, the treacherous swamps that had swallowed them in circles.

Another pointed toward *Black Hallow Pier*.

The group collectively paused, staring at it.

"…A pier?" Ingrid muttered, scepticism heavy in her voice. "In a swamp?"

Rowen crossed his arms, grinning. "What, you've never wanted to go for a nice scenic boat ride through the lovely, monster-infested bog?" He gestured grandly to the murky wasteland around them. "I hear it's quite the tourist attraction. You get a free disease with every trip."

Ingrid gave him a deadpan look. "Oh, well in that case, let's go immediately."

Darius shook his head and turned his attention to the last sign, the most important one. The arrow, though chipped and barely hanging onto the post, still pointed in the right direction.

The Castle.

That settled it.

Darius exhaled. "We're going to see Alara."

Lyra frowned, adjusting her staff in her hands. "I know I suggested it but we're sure she'll have some answers?"

"Do you have any other better ideas?" Ingrid asked, already adjusting the strap of her axe.

Lyra hesitated before shaking her head.

Rowen clapped his hands together. "Well, as much as I'd love to risk tetanus by investigating a mystery swamp pier, I think I'll pass." He smirked. "Castle it is."

With that decided, the group set their sights on the path and began on their way.

As they pressed on, the remnants of Black Hallow faded into the background, swallowed by the gloom of the remaining swamp. The air remained thick with the ever-present scent of decay, though now it was thinning, giving way to the first hints of fresher air.

The journey back toward the castle should have felt like a relief. The ground beneath their boots grew firmer, the gnarled trees less oppressive. With each step, they moved closer to home—closer to familiar lands, rolling fields, and the towering sight of the capital.

Rowen stretched his arms behind his head. "So, what's the first thing you lot are doing once we're in the city?"

"Eating," Ingrid answered immediately, adjusting her axe. "Something hot. Something that hasn't been soaked in swamp water or dried into dust."

Lyra smiled, brushing some loose strands of hair behind her ear. "A warm bath would be nice."

Rowen scoffed. "Oh sure, you get the luxury of a bath while the rest of us are licking soup out of wooden bowls?"

Lyra laughed. "You could take a bath too, you know."

"I could. But then who would make things miserable for you all?" He grinned.

Darius remained silent, focusing on the path ahead. He wanted to feel relieved that they were finally out of that cursed swamp, but something still felt... off.

He tried to shake it. The castle would be waiting, the capital bustling with life. They would regroup, seek guidance from Alana, and press forward with whatever came next.

Then they reached the clearing.

The moment their feet crossed the threshold from the last of the swamp, they all froze.

It was supposed to be different.

They were supposed to step into *life*. Rolling hills of vibrant green, shimmering lakes reflecting the sky, birds soaring overhead. The sight of the capital in the distance, a beacon of safety.

Instead, the land before them was *dead*.

The fields were nothing but brittle, withered husks. The lakes had darkened, turning stagnant and lifeless. The trees stood like skeletal remains; their bark peeled away as if the land itself had rotted from the inside.

And the creatures...

At first, they seemed like scattered figures, distant shadows in the grey haze. But then one moved—a sickening lurch, a perverse, unnatural motion.

Skeletons, wrapped in tattered remnants of armour, clawing their way across the wasted ground. Corpses, reanimated with empty, sunken eyes, dragging themselves forward as if still bound to some forgotten duty. Beasts, their flesh gnarled, moving like puppets on strings.

The castle still stood far in the distance, its glow piercing through the gloom like a defiant star. But even it seemed *wrong* somehow—isolated, distant, as if it no longer belonged to this world.

Darius felt his stomach twist. "What happened here?"

No one had an answer.

Because whatever had happened in Black Hallow—whatever *it* had done—was spreading. Every step felt heavier than the last.

The road toward the castle stretched endlessly before them, winding through the ruined fields like a scar upon the land. The air was thick with the stench of decaying flesh, the wind carrying the distant groans of the dead. There was no sun overhead—only an ashen sky, dull and featureless, casting everything in shades of grey.

Darius walked at the front, sword gripped tightly, his breathing shallow. His body still ached from wounds he didn't remember receiving. The others fared no better—Rowen's movements were slower than usual, his normally sharp footwork dulled by fatigue. Ingrid, usually an unshakable force, had adjusted the way she held her axe, shifting its weight between hands as though she couldn't quite steady herself. Lyra lagged behind slightly, her staff trembling in her grasp.

They were alive. But they were not whole.

The first skeleton appeared as a lone figure in the distance, dragging a rusted sword behind it, its hollow eyes locked onto them the moment they stepped into its presence.

Normally, a single undead would have been nothing—a mere inconvenience. But as the group readied their weapons, there was hesitation, a collective sense of dread that weighed them down.

Darius charged first, his sword flashing toward the creature's ribs. The blade struck true, shattering bone, but the skeleton barely faltered. Its arm moved in a blur, its rusted blade slamming against Darius's with unnatural strength. The impact rattled up his arms, nearly making him lose his grip.

It countered. Fast. Efficient. A downward strike. Darius barely twisted in time, the edge of the sword scraping his shoulder.

Rowen lunged from the side, twin daggers flashing, aiming for the joints. He struck the skeleton's knee, cutting through the old sinew holding it together. But rather than collapse, the thing *lunged*—its fingers closing around Rowen's arm, gripping with inhuman force.

Rowen gasped, struggling, but it was like iron squeezing down.

"Ingrid!" Darius gritted his teeth, slashing at the thing's arm, trying to force it to let go.

With a roar, Ingrid came barrelling forward. She swung her axe in a brutal arc, her movements slower than usual but still deadly. The blade connected, cleaving through the skeleton's torso.

It staggered—just for a moment.

Then, impossibly, it straightened, its bones realigning, the damage meaning nothing.

Lyra muttered an incantation, thrusting her staff forward. A burst of energy struck the skeleton, sending it sprawling to the ground. It twitched, jerking as if resisting, before its limbs finally stopped moving.

For a long moment, they just stood there. Breathing hard.

Rowen rubbed his arm. "That... was not supposed to be that

difficult."

Darius clenched his fists. He knew why. They were exhausted, drained from whatever had happened in Black Hallow. They hadn't recovered, hadn't had time to gather themselves.

And they weren't alone.

Two more skeletons emerged from the mist, their hollow sockets burning with unnatural light. A third figure limped between them—something once a wolf, its body wasted and stretched unnaturally, bones poking through thin, decayed flesh.

Darius exhaled, forcing his aching body to move.

They fought again.

And it was worse.

Every blow that should have ended a fight instead became another desperate clash. Rowen danced between strikes, but his movements weren't as sharp, his footwork slipping more than once. Ingrid's swings carried power, but her recovery was slow, each strike taking more effort than it should. Lyra's spells flickered, her magic unstable, her hands shaking.

The wolf lunged, its gaping maw lined with jagged, blackened teeth. It clamped down on Ingrid's arm before she drove her knee into its ribcage, forcing it off.

Darius blocked a skeleton's sword just in time, but the impact nearly knocked him off balance. The other one grabbed his cloak, yanking him backward. His vision blurred—he fought against it, twisting his body to slash the undead's arm off. But it still came at him, half its body missing, uncaring.

They killed them. Somehow.

But more loomed ahead.

Darius panted, sweat dripping down his face. His body felt like lead. Rowen's daggers were slick with blackened, unnatural blood. Ingrid's arm was bleeding from where the wolf had bitten her. Lyra was clutching her staff, barely standing.

"We… we can't keep this up," Lyra breathed, shaking her head.

Darius gritted his teeth. She was right. They weren't going to make it to the castle like this.

Then he saw it—a small, narrow gap between two hills. A cave.

"There," he pointed, his voice sharp. "We need to rest."

With what little strength they had left, they staggered toward the opening, their legs nearly giving out as they stumbled inside.

The moment they were out of the open, Darius collapsed his body against the wall, gripping his sword, they were safe. But the castle had never felt further away.

The cave barely gave them a moment's respite.

Darius leaned his head back against the cold stone, breath ragged. Every part of him ached. His fingers tightened around the hilt of his sword, but his grip was weak. Rowen sat nearby, pressing a hand to his side, where blood seeped through his tunic. Ingrid muttered a curse under her breath, her arm trembling as she tried to check her wound. Lyra had collapsed completely, her breathing shallow.

"We're not… gonna make it like this," Rowen panted, his voice strained but still carrying that damnable smirk.

Darius didn't respond. He couldn't.

Then—

CRACK

The ground beneath them exploded.

A skeletal arm burst from the stone, clawed fingers grasping hungrily. The cave trembled as the floor beneath them shattered, sending them sprawling. Darius barely managed to roll aside as another undead thing clawed its way from the earth, its eyes the colour of an abyss.

Before they could react, more emerged, forcing their way through the broken stone. The cave was crawling with them.

"Move! MOVE!" Darius bellowed, dragging Lyra by the arm as she stirred weakly.

But there was nowhere to run.

A deafening *roar* came from the entrance, and through the swirling dust, a massive beast stood silhouetted against the dim light outside. It was hunched and grotesque, its tusked maw dripping with saliva, its shoulders bulging with unnatural muscle. A boar warped by corruption.

It blocked the exit.

They were trapped.

Ingrid roared, lifting her axe with her good arm. She swung wide, but as she struck an advancing skeleton, the force of the impact jarred her weakened limb.

Something snapped.

She screamed.

Darius saw her crumple, her arm hanging uselessly at her side, bent at an angle that arms weren't supposed to bend.

"Ingrid—!"

Something slammed into him from the side, sending him skidding across the ground. His ears rang as he hit the cave wall hard enough to send his vision spinning.

He barely had time to process before he saw it—Rowen, moving in a blur to protect him, daggers flashing.

Then Rowen stopped.

The horned beast that had emerged from the shadows impaled him clean through the stomach.

Darius's breath hitched.

Rowen coughed, blood spilling from his lips as he tried to pull himself free. His daggers clattered uselessly to the ground.

"No—"

Another impact. This time against Darius's leg.

A sickening crunch.

Pain flared up his entire body, raw and unrelenting. His leg bent beneath him, unable to hold his weight. He fell, gasping.

Another impact.

Something struck his face.

His head snapped back, and blood poured from his forehead, hot and sticky, blinding his left eye. His thoughts swam. His vision blurred.

This was it.

This was it.

Everything that had led to this moment—the journey, the struggle, the hope—it was all for nothing. He was the hero of this cycle, but this cycle belonged to the darkness.

He was never meant to succeed.

The Mawborn had shattered them. The undead had torn them apart. The beasts had finished the job.

He was going to die here.

Then—

Light.

A blinding radiance burst forth, swallowing everything.

The creatures recoiled, shrieking as the golden glow seared them. The cave was filled with warmth, a presence so strong it nearly forced Darius's failing consciousness to cling to existence.

He blinked through the haze of blood and exhaustion.

Figures emerged through the light. A group of knights, armoured and strong, pushing back the creatures with practiced strikes.

And at their centre—

Alana.

Her presence was undeniable, her hands raised as magic pulsed from her in waves, driving the corruption back.

And beyond her…

A familiar silhouette.

Golden hair. Regal posture. Eyes filled with fire and fury.

Princess Seraphina. Darius tried to speak, but no words came.

The last thing he saw before darkness took him was Seraphina stepping forward, "Darius are yo-".

CHAPTER 17

The Light That Lingers

Darkness held him in its grasp, heavy and unrelenting. The world around him was a muddled haze, sounds muffled as if coming from behind thick walls. The creaking of wood beneath him and the gentle sway of movement told him he was on the back of a wagon, but his body refused to respond, numb save for the throbbing pain in his leg, his head, his everything.

Murmurs surrounded him. Fragments of words drifted in and out of his awareness.

"—too many of them—"

"—hold him still, the bone needs to set—"

"—Darius? Can you hear—"

A warm sensation spread across his chest, tingling like liquid fire beneath his skin. Magic. He tried to open his eyes, but they barely fluttered, the blurred outlines of robed figures shifting around him. Their hands moved over his wounds, faint golden light seeping into his battered body, but the pain did not fully leave.

Another voice, stronger, clearer—Seraphina's.

"Keep moving! Stay in formation!"

Darius blinked sluggishly. Through his hazy vision, he caught glimpses of her at the front of the caravan, issuing orders to the soldiers. Her sword was drawn, gleaming under the pale light, her stance unshaken. He had never seen her like this before, commanding with such precision, such force.

Shouts erupted. The wagon lurched.

Steel clashed. The sickening crunch of bone, the guttural roars of beasts. Shadows flickered along the edges of his vision—knights, soldiers, striking down monstrous figures clawing at the convoy. For a brief moment, he caught sight of Rowen on another wagon, his face pale, bandages wrapped tightly around his midsection. Ingrid sat nearby, her arm in a splint, expression hard-set despite the pain. Lyra lay beside her, unmoving, her hair splayed across a makeshift cot, healers working tirelessly to mend her wounds.

Another jolt. The world spun.

His head lolled to the side, his mind slipping away once more into darkness.

And then, nothing.

> ***Ah, hero… welcome.***
> "Who are you?"
> ***That is no matter. I have been trying to reach you.***
> "Reach me? What are you talking about? Wh—"
> ***I SAID THAT IS NO MATTER.***

A pressure, suffocating yet intangible, pressed against him. The space around him—wherever *this* was—felt like it was closing in.
> "……"
> ***you would not hear me before. The light was too strong, keeping me at bay. But now, at last, you can***

hear me. And so, I say—accept it. Accept your fate. Accept me.

"My fate? You mean to die? To lose to Vorthis and his forces?"

HA! Die? No, hero. Not death. You are not meant to die. You are meant to fall. There is a key difference.

The voice slithered through his mind, thick and weighted, a promise wrapped in something deeper, darker.

"Vorthis?..."

Darius awoke to the faint scent of herbs and incense, the air thick with the unmistakable aroma of healing salves and freshly brewed potions. A dull ache throbbed through his body, his limbs heavy, but the pain was manageable—muted by whatever concoctions had been administered to him. Blinking against the dim light of the infirmary, he slowly adjusted to his surroundings.

The room was large but enclosed, its arched ceiling lined with shelves crammed with glass bottles of varying colours, dried herbs hanging in bundles from wooden beams. A soft glow came from enchanted lanterns, their light flickering like candle flames despite their magic ensuring they would never wane. The walls were carved from smooth marble, a stark contrast to the rough stone of the castle halls, and the heavy curtains at the windows muffled the outside world. It was a place meant for healing, but despite its tranquil atmosphere, his mind was anything but at peace.

His gaze drifted to the other beds in the room, and for the first time, he took stock of his companions.

Rowen lay sprawled across his mattress, one leg dangling off the side, his usual wild nature even evident in sleep. His chest rose and fell in deep, steady breaths, though bandages covered his torso and arms, evidence of the battle they had barely survived. Across from him, Ingrid was the complete opposite—lying rigidly on her back, as stiff in slumber as she was in wakefulness. Even in rest, she looked as though she was prepared to leap into action at a moment's notice. But then his eyes fell upon the fourth bed, which was noticeably empty.

Lyra.

His stomach twisted. She was supposed to be there, yet there was no sign of her. The blankets were disturbed, as if someone had been there recently, but there was no way to tell if she had left of her own accord or had been taken elsewhere for further treatment. He wanted to ask. He wanted to sit up and demand answers, but his body protested any sudden movement, and his head spun at just the attempt.

Instead, he sank back into his pillows, staring at the ceiling as his thoughts drifted back to everything that had led them here. The journey, the Mawborn, the endless onslaught of the undead and beasts. He had never known true exhaustion until that moment, when all seemed lost, and he had accepted his end. But then—

That voice.

It had spoken to him so clearly, He conversed with it. Even now, the words echoed faintly in his mind.

You will fall, hero. Accept me.

But now? Now, there was nothing. No lingering presence, no dark whisper creeping at the edges of his thoughts. Just silence. It should have been a relief, but instead, it unnerved him. Had it truly left him? Or was it merely waiting?

A deep sigh escaped him as he turned his head, surveying the room once more, looking for any sign of movement. He was still confined to this infirmary, still trapped in his thoughts, and despite everything, the battle had left more questions than answers.

Before he could linger too long in his doubts, the door creaked open, and a kind looking figure stepped in, an older woman with silver-streaked hair and sharp, knowing eyes, broke into a warm smile the moment she saw him awake.

"Well, well," she said, stepping toward him with a bottle of potion in hand. "It's good to see you among the living, lad. You had us worried there for a moment."

But before Darius could respond she continued "my name is Marisol, the apothecary to the royal family."

Marisol placed the potion bottle on the bedside table, her sharp eyes scanning him with the practiced ease of someone who had seen more than her fair share of battered warriors. "You're the second of your group to wake up," she said, adjusting the blankets around him with a firm but gentle touch. "The young mage—Lyra, was it?—she came to not long before you. Last I saw her, she was in the royal library."

Darius exhaled, a wave of relief washing over him. Lyra was alive. Awake. Despite everything they had been through, she was strong enough to be on her feet. He closed his eyes briefly, letting that knowledge settle his racing mind before Marisol's voice brought him back.

"The other two have been treated and should wake any day now," she continued. "Rowen's wounds were deep, but he's a stubborn one—his body fights to keep up with his will. Ingrid, well... her injuries were more severe, but she's stable. You'll see them awake soon enough."

Darius glanced toward their beds. Rowen's blanket was now completely on the floor but he looked peaceful enough while Ingrid still lay rigid and unmoving, her breathing steady but slow.

Marisol placed a hand on his shoulder, her touch light. "I must inform the princess," she said. "She requested to be notified the moment you woke."

With that, she turned and left, the door closing softly behind her.

Darius shifted in his bed, wincing as the stiffness in his body made itself known. He had rested long enough—perhaps too long. The ache in his leg and the dull throb at his temple were proof enough that he was far from healed, but the others were still asleep, and he needed answers. If he stayed idle any longer, he feared the weight of uncertainty would consume him.

With a careful breath, he swung his legs over the side of the bed. Pain flared up his leg, but he gritted his teeth, pushing through it. He tested his footing, standing unsteadily, muscles protesting each motion. His bandages were fresh, and the remnants of healing potions lingered in his system, but his strength was a fragile thing. Still, he forced himself forward, one step at a time.

The castle corridors were grand and unfamiliar, lined with towering windows that cast elongated beams of morning light across polished stone. The distant flickering of torches warred against the sun's reach, and the vast tapestries adorning the walls whispered of history Darius did not yet understand. His footfalls echoed, uneven, hesitant. The weight of the silence pressed upon him, an eerie contrast to the chaos he had left behind in Black Hallow.

He needed to find Lyra in the royal library, then Alara. Answers waited for him, and he would not delay any longer.

But fate had other plans.

As he turned the corner, his balance wavering, he nearly collided with a figure moving briskly toward him. Soft hands steadied him, and as he lifted his gaze, his breath caught in his throat.

Seraphina.

Her golden hair cascaded in soft waves over her shoulders, and her sapphire eyes widened in shock before brimming with unmistakable relief. Her lips parted as if to speak, but for a moment, no words came. Then, in an instant, she closed the distance between them, her arms wrapping tightly around him.
"You're awake," she breathed, her voice trembling with emotion. "You survived."

Darius stood frozen, stunned by the sheer warmth of her embrace. For a moment, he let himself sink into it, closing his eyes. He could feel her heartbeat against his chest, fast and alive, and it struck him just how much he had longed for this.
"The prophecy..." she whispered against his shoulder. "I thought... I feared the worst."
Darius exhaled, steadying himself against her. "I'm here," he assured her, though the words felt weak compared to the storm within him. "But it was close."
She pulled back just enough to look at him, her hands still grasping his arms as if she feared he would disappear should she let go. "We had heard word that Black Hallow had fallen," she explained. "We were heading there to seek survivors when we found you instead."
Darius stiffened, his throat tightening. "Black Hallow..."
Seraphina nodded solemnly. "We saw the ruins in the distance, but we never made it to the village itself. We rushed you and your party back to be treated."

Darius clenched his fists, the memories flashing behind his eyes. "We saw it happen," he said, his voice barely above a whisper. "We saw it being destroyed... by something called the Mawborn. We fought it I think, but it—" He hesitated, glancing past her, as if saying the words aloud would make the horrors real once more. "When we woke up... it was the next morning. No survivors. Just us."

Seraphina's brows furrowed, her expression shifting from concern to something deeper, something troubled. "Darius… Black Hallow was destroyed a week ago, by the time we had word of its destruction it had already been 7 nights."

Silence. Cold and suffocating.
Darius swayed on his feet, his mind reeling. "That's not possible," he whispered. "We—" His breath hitched as the truth clawed its way through him. "We only lost a night I thought. Exhausted from fighting we collapsed till daybreak."
But they hadn't. They had lost an entire week.
A sharp, twisting pain curled in his chest, his stomach knotting as if the floor had just been ripped from beneath him. A week of time gone—wiped away like it had never existed. What had happened in those missing days? What had they done? Where had they been? His hands trembled at his sides.
Seraphina's grip on him tightened, anchoring him to the present. "Darius," she said gently, her voice steady despite the turmoil in her eyes. "You're not alone in this. We will find the answers, together."
He swallowed hard, nodding weakly. His mind screamed for clarity, but his body still waged war against him. He felt… hollow. Seraphina gave him a small, reassuring squeeze before adjusting her hold, slipping an arm around him for support. "Come," she said. "We should see Alara."
Darius hesitated only a moment before leaning into her help. The pain in his leg was distant compared to the weight in his chest, together, they moved forward through the castle's grand halls, towards Alara's chambers.

Darius leaned against Seraphina as they made their way through the castle halls, his steps slow and deliberate, each one testing the strength in his weakened legs. The once-looming stone corridors, lined with tapestries of past kings and golden sconces flickering with enchanted light, felt more familiar now than they had before. It wasn't just a place of royalty anymore—it was where he had started, where he had met the people who had sent him on this path.

Seraphina walked at his side, her hand lightly supporting his arm. "You really should still be in bed," she said softly, glancing at him with a mixture of concern and admiration.

He exhaled through his nose. "If I stayed in bed every time someone told me to, I'd still be on the floor in Black Hallow."

She gave a small huff of amusement, shaking her head. "Stubborn."

"Determined," he corrected, then winced slightly as a sharp pain lanced through his leg.

They moved at a steady pace, and as they did, Seraphina asked, "You were going to see Alara, right?"

"Yeah... But first, I was hoping to find Lyra." He looked ahead, jaw tightening as he thought about everything they'd been through. "There's a lot I need to make sense of."

She nodded, but her curiosity was evident. "You've seen so much since you left the castle, haven't you?"

Darius let out a breath and gave a small chuckle, though there was no humour in it. "More than I ever wanted to."

And so, as they walked, he told her.

He spoke of the corrupted dragon atop the Dragonspine Mountains, a beast whose eyes burned with unnatural fire, its very presence twisting the land into something unrecognizable. He told her of the ruins they had passed through, of how they had stumbled upon goblins lurking in the shadows, their hungry eyes glinting like daggers, how they had barely escaped the crumbling structures.

Then, his tone shifted, softened.

He spoke of Rowen—the reckless, loudmouthed tracker who never knew when to keep his thoughts to himself, whose terrible jokes made Darius groan but, somehow, always made things feel a little lighter. "He acts like an idiot, but... he's got more heart than anyone I've ever met. He never lets fear stop him, even when it should."

He spoke of Ingrid—the strong, battle-hardened warrior with a no-nonsense attitude, always taking the biggest cut of meat by the campfire, always acting like she didn't care when she very clearly did. "She'd rather die than admit she likes us. But she watches over us, keeps us in check. She's... she's our shield."

Then Lyra—the quiet, intelligent mage who had grown stronger with every battle, who had been so timid at first but now stood on equal footing with them all. "She's kinder than the rest of us put together. But when it comes down to it... she's stronger than she realizes."

Seraphina listened intently, watching Darius as he spoke. It wasn't just that he was telling her about them. It was the way he spoke, the way his voice shifted when he described them. He cared. Deeply.

When she had first met him, he had been alone, weighed down by fate, closed off. But now... now he was someone who fought for more than just duty. Someone who had people he loved.

"You've changed," she murmured, the words slipping out before she even realized it.

Darius looked at her, brow furrowing. "What?"

She smiled, tilting her head slightly. "When we first met, you barely spoke more than a few words unless necessary. You carried everything alone. But now, when you talk about them... you're different. You seem..." She hesitated, then gave a small, knowing smile. "...happier."

Darius held her gaze for a moment, something unspoken passing between them. It was strange—he had spent so much time dreading what lay ahead, fearing what he would become. And yet, when he thought of his friends, when he thought of Seraphina... that weight felt a little lighter.

Before either could say more, a voice interrupted them.
"Glad to see you on your feet, hero."
They turned to see Alara standing before them, her expression unreadable as always, her silver eyes sharp as they flicked over him. Darius straightened instinctively, wincing at the dull pain in his body. "Alara."
She inclined her head to them both before stepping forward, walking beside them as they made their way to her chambers. "Come. There's much to discuss."

The chamber was dimly lit, the air thick with the scent of burning incense and old parchment. Shelves lined the walls, overflowing with books and relics, and at the centre of the room sat a single round table, covered in scattered papers and strange symbols drawn in ink. The seer, Alara, stood at the far end, her silver eyes unreadable as she gestured for them to sit.
Darius ignored the offer. He was in no mood for pleasantries.
"I need answers," he said, his voice rough, still hoarse from exhaustion.
Alara regarded him silently before inclining her head. "Then speak."
Darius exhaled sharply, running a hand through his hair before meeting her gaze. "The demon... the thing called the Mawborn. I know it destroyed Black Hallow, I know it has the power to erase—but I need to understand." His fists clenched at his sides. "We lost time. Not hours. A week. I need to know what happened to us."

Alara watched him carefully, and for a long moment, she said nothing. Then, she spoke, her voice calm, deliberate.

"Mawborn's power is erasure," she said. "It does not wound. It does not kill. It removes."

Darius frowned. "Removes?"

"There is no memory to recover because there is nothing to recover. It did not merely steal a week from you—it made that time cease to exist. *You* ceased to exist."

The words sent a chill down his spine.

He took a step back, his breath uneven. His mind raced, recalling every strange detail from when they awoke—how the blood on the ground had dried, how Ingrid's wound had stopped bleeding despite how deep it had been. The exhaustion, the weakness... it all made sense now.

They hadn't been sleeping.

They had been gone.

His stomach churned at the realization. "So we were just... lying there? In the mud? For a week?" His voice was barely above a whisper.

Alara gave the smallest nod.

Darius gritted his teeth, anger boiling beneath his skin. "Then how do we fight it?" he demanded.

Alara lifted her gaze to him, and for the first time since he'd met her, there was a hint of something sharp in her expression—not anger, not annoyance, but something deeper.

She did not answer.

She did not need to.

The weight of her stare alone was enough to make him stiffen, to remind him who she was, what she was.

It was a simple, unspoken warning: Watch yourself.

He swallowed his frustration, exhaling slowly. "I just... I need to know how to stop it."

Alara closed her eyes, reaching out with her mind, searching.

The air shifted. The torches dimmed.

She spoke in a low, ethereal tone, her voice distant, as though speaking from somewhere far beyond the chamber.

"The beast of the abyss shrouds itself in nothingness."
"But when the abyss looks upon itself, it recoils."
"Reflections shatter its hunger."

Then, just as quickly as it had begun, the air returned to normal. The torches brightened, and Alara blinked, as if waking from a trance.

"That is all I can see," she said simply.

Darius furrowed his brow. Reflections? That wasn't much to go on, but it was something.

And yet... the last time she had given him a cryptic answer, it had come true. He had no reason to doubt her now.

Seraphina broke the momentary silence. "You should rest before you and your party face it again," she suggested, placing a hand on Darius' arm.

Darius wanted to argue, wanted to insist they had already wasted too much time. But the ache in his body, the sheer exhaustion pressing down on him, was impossible to ignore.

Before he could reply, Seraphina turned to Alara. "There's something else I wished to discuss," she said, lowering her voice slightly. "The seer from across the Azure Sea—has she come to you yet?"

Darius noted the shift in tone. The conversation wasn't for him, but he listened anyway.

"She arrived weeks ago," Alara answered, though her expression darkened. "She claimed the lands across the sea have been facing disturbances of their own. Their people whisper of new horrors, unnatural forces rising in the shadows."

Seraphina's brows knit together. "Do you believe it's connected?"

"Perhaps," Alara said. "Or perhaps chaos has simply found new places to spread."

Darius remained silent, filing that piece of information away.
Seraphina turned back to him. "We can discuss this more another time. For now... you and your friends need to recover."
Darius exhaled through his nose. He hated the idea of waiting, of delaying, but he knew she was right. They wouldn't survive another battle like the last—not like this.
"Fine," he muttered. "But not for long."
Seraphina smiled slightly. "Of course not."
Together, they started to make their way out of Alara's chambers, the weight of everything they had learned settling heavily on Darius' shoulders.
Just as Darius and Seraphina reached the door, Alara's voice stopped them.
"Wait."
Darius turned, half-expecting another cryptic riddle. Instead, Alara's gaze was sharp, focused. "There is someone you should meet."
He crossed his arms. "Who?"
"The seer from across the Azure Sea," Alara answered. "Her name is Sylara."
Darius tilted his head slightly at the name. It had a similar weight to Alara's, carrying the same mystical presence.
"And why would I need to meet her?" he asked.
Alara stepped forward, folding her hands together. "Seers are not all the same, just as mages are not." She glanced toward Seraphina before continuing. "You've seen Lyra's spell—her Astra Bolt? It is a simple spell, yet it comes easily to her."
Darius nodded. "Yeah, she uses it all the time."
"That is because it aligns with her affinity. While she may not realize it yet, her magic is attuned to fire, lightning, and ice. Spells of those elements will come to her more naturally than others."
Darius frowned. "And what does that have to do with seers?"

Alara gave him a knowing look. "You assume all seers are like me—bound to visions, prophecy, and the cryptic whispers of fate." She shook her head. "But just as mages wield different schools of magic, so too do seers. My gift is prophecy. Knowledge. I see what will be, though the vision often comes in fragments, obscured by time."

Darius exhaled, rubbing the back of his neck. "Right. So, what does this Sylara do?"

Alara smirked slightly. "I saw that question forming in your mind before you spoke it."

Darius scowled.

"She is not a seer of prophecy," Alara continued, ignoring his reaction. "Her gift lies in incantations and arcane craft."

Seraphina's expression shifted, her posture straightening slightly. "A seer of incantations… that's rare."

"Indeed," Alara agreed. She turned her gaze back to Darius. "She may be able to help you. To strengthen you and your companions. If she is willing, she could improve your… firepower, as it were."

Darius' eyes widened slightly.

That changed things.

Strengthening their abilities? If Sylara could actually teach them something useful, give them an edge in battle—especially against the Mawborn—then they couldn't afford to ignore that opportunity.

For the first time in the conversation, he wasn't just listening—he was interested.

"I'll speak with her," he said finally. "Where is she?"

Alara smiled. "You will find her in the courtyard by sundown. She prefers open air."

Darius gave a small nod. "Alright. I'll go."

Alara studied him for a moment longer, then turned away, moving toward her bookshelves as if the conversation had already ended.

Darius glanced at Seraphina, who was watching him with quiet approval.

"Well," she said, placing a hand on his shoulder. "Shall we?"

He took a steadying breath. The weight of everything still pressed down on him, but at least now… they had direction.

Without another word, the two stepped out of the chamber, leaving Alara to her visions of what was still to come.

CHAPTER 18

Where the Truth Takes Root

Darius and Seraphina made their way through the castle's winding halls strength now returning to Darius' legs, the steady rhythm of their footsteps filling the quiet space between them. The conversation with Alara still lingered in his mind, but before he could dwell on it for too long, the sound of armoured boots echoing against the stone floor caught their attention.

A knight in royal colors strode toward them, his face serious. He gave a brief bow before addressing the princess.

"Your Highness, the king has requested your presence in the throne room. It is urgent."

Seraphina straightened at once, her expression shifting from quiet warmth to composed authority. "I see. I will go at once."

Darius took a step back, watching her carefully. He knew she was strong—fierce, even—but something about the way the knight phrased it made him uneasy.

Seraphina turned to him, hesitating for just a moment. "Looks like we must part ways for now."

"Yeah," Darius said, rubbing the back of his neck. "Try not to let royal politics crush your spirit." She huffed a quiet laugh, but there was still something lingering in her eyes. Then, without thinking—

or maybe with too much thought—she reached out and clasped his hand between hers.

Darius blinked.

"I know you don't believe in prayers," she said softly, squeezing his hand ever so slightly, "but still... may the light guide your path." His throat felt oddly dry. He wasn't sure why.

Before he could find a response, she pulled away, stepping back toward the knight. With one last glance, she turned and strode down the hall, disappearing around the corner.

Darius exhaled and ran a hand through his hair. "Alright," he muttered. "Time to find Lyra."

The royal library was as grand as he remembers from the first time he saw it—towering bookshelves lined the vast chamber, stretching toward an arched ceiling where chandeliers bathed the room in golden light. A quiet, warm scent of parchment and aged tomes filled the air.

And in the middle of it all, with her nose buried deep in a massive book, was Lyra.

She sat at a heavy wooden table, completely absorbed in her reading, muttering under her breath as she traced lines of text with a delicate finger.

Darius smirked.

An opportunity.

He crept forward, careful with his steps, weaving through bookshelves to get closer without making a sound. She was completely oblivious, still murmuring about magical theory, flipping pages with an almost frantic excitement.

Then, right as he loomed over her shoulder—

"Boo."

Lyra screeched, nearly knocking the book off the table as she jolted upright. Her chair wobbled dangerously, and she turned to face him with wide eyes, her breath caught between a gasp and a furious growl.

"DARIUS!" she snapped.

Darius grinned, crossing his arms. "That's me."

She scowled, cheeks slightly flushed. "You absolute—! I *swear*, if I had my staff right now, I'd turn you into a toad!"

He chuckled, dropping into the chair beside her. "Oh, come on. You were *way* too into that book."

"I was learning important things!" she huffed, hugging the tome to her chest.

"Yeah, yeah. Speaking of learning things..." Darius leaned forward, resting his arms on the table. "I just had a chat with Alara. She had some interesting things to say about magic. Specifically, your magic."

Lyra's frustration faltered, her curiosity piqued. "My magic?"

Darius nodded. "Turns out, mages have affinities—natural alignments to certain types of spells. Yours?" He pointed at her. "Fire, lightning, and ice."

Lyra blinked. "What?"

Darius smirked. "You heard me, I don't understand it myself but that's why you have Astra Bolt as your basic spell apparently."

She reeled back slightly, clearly taken aback. "But... no one's ever told me that before. No one in my village ever mentioned anything like *affinities* affecting magic." She stared at him, eyes full of disbelief. "And Alara is *sure* about this?"

"As sure as she is about everything," Darius said. "Which is annoyingly sure."

Lyra leaned back in her chair, processing the information. Then, as if remembering something, she suddenly started rifling through a stack of papers next to her, flipping through old parchment with feverish energy.

"Wait, wait, wait—this explains so much."

Darius raised an eyebrow. "About what?"

She pulled out a sheet covered in runes, pressing a finger to a particular spell she had been struggling with.

"Aetherial Chains," she said. "I found it in the ruins. It's a restraint spell, darkness based—meant to bind an opponent in glowing magical bindings." She exhaled sharply. "But I *can't* get it to work. No matter how much I try, it just slips through my grasp."

Darius frowned. "Probably because it doesn't match your affinity."

Lyra stared at the spell, then at him, then back at the spell.

"... That makes *so much sense.*"

Darius smirked. "Told you Alara was annoyingly sure."

Lyra let out an exasperated laugh before digging through her collection again. This time, she pulled out another spell, pressing it down onto the table with a determined look.

"Ignis Surge," she read aloud. "Conjures fire in a sweeping arc." She glanced at Darius, a fire sparking in her eyes. "If what Alara said is true... then this should come naturally to me."

Darius leaned back, arms crossed. "Only one way to find out."

She grinned. "You better not be standing in front of me when I try it."

Darius chuckled, shaking his head. "Anyway, we can test that later. Right now, we need to gather the others if they're awake." He pushed himself up from the chair. "Alara wants us to meet with Sylara—the other seer from across the sea. Apparently, she might be able to help us improve our abilities."

Lyra perked up. "A seer that can teach magic?"

"Something like that," Darius said. "We'll find out soon enough."

Lyra snapped her book shut, standing with newfound excitement. "Alright, then let's not waste any more time."

Darius grinned. "Now that's the spirit."

With that, the two left the library, ready to see what awaited them next.

The infirmary was quieter than before, the lingering scent of herbs and the soft crackling of torches filling the air.

Inside, Rowen sat at the edge of a cot, grinning as he pestered Ingrid, who, despite her obvious discomfort, sat rigidly, arms crossed, pretending she was perfectly fine. Marisol, the castle healer, stood nearby, arms folded as she regarded them both with amused exasperation.

"So what I'm hearing," Rowen said, "is that Ingrid here, legendary axe-wielding warrior of the north, is too weak to get out of bed?"

Ingrid shot him a glare sharp enough to cut through steel. "Say that again, and I'll get out of this bed just to strangle you."

Rowen smirked. "So you admit you're too weak."

"Rowen, I swear to the gods—"

"I told you to stop pushing yourself," Marisol interjected before Ingrid could launch herself at Rowen. She sighed. "You lost a lot of blood. No one's expecting you to bounce back overnight."

"I am," Ingrid grumbled, averting her gaze.

That's when Darius and Lyra stepped into the room, catching the tail end of the conversation.

"Ah, there they are!" Rowen threw up his hands. "Darius, Lyra! Please, talk some sense into Ingrid before she actually tries to murder me."

Lyra tilted her head. "What makes you think we wouldn't let her?"

Rowen gasped, clutching his chest. "Betrayal! And here I thought we were friends."

Darius chuckled before turning his gaze to Ingrid. She looked pale, the deep gash across her back hidden beneath bandages, but there was a fire in her eyes that no wound could extinguish.

"Good to see you alive," he said.

She exhaled sharply, running a hand through her messy blonde hair. "You too."

A quiet moment passed between them—unspoken relief, mutual understanding. They had survived. All of them.

Rowen clapped his hands together. "Alright, now that the gang's all here—what's the plan, fearless leader?"

Darius rolled his eyes but didn't argue the title. Instead, he leaned against the wall, crossing his arms.

"I just spoke with Alara," he began, glancing at each of them in turn. "She had a lot to say."

He explained the concept of magical affinities, how mages had natural alignments to certain types of magic, much like how warriors had fighting styles suited to their strengths. He mentioned Sylara, the seer from across the sea, and how she might be able to help them—not just with understanding their supposed abilities, but with *improving* them.

Rowen squinted. "So… what, she's gonna wave her hands and suddenly we get stronger?"

"No idea," Darius admitted. "But if she can help, we'd be stupid not to hear her out."

Ingrid frowned. "And you're sure she's trustworthy?"

Darius hesitated for a moment before nodding. "She wouldn't be here if she wasn't."

That seemed to satisfy Ingrid—for now.

Then, he took a breath before moving on to the next part.

"The Mawborn," he said, voice darkening. "Alara gave us a clue.

Or, at least, something close to one."

He recited the riddle exactly as Alara had told him:

"The beast of the abyss shrouds itself in nothingness. But when the abyss looks upon itself, it recoils. Reflections shatter its hunger."

Rowen frowned. "I don't get it."

"Shocking," Lyra muttered.

"I *heard that*."

Ingrid, meanwhile, kept her expression unreadable, but her brow furrowed slightly. "...shatter its hunger?"

Darius shrugged. "No idea. But that's what we've got."

Lyra, already deep in thought, started murmuring to herself. "Nothingness, That could mean it doesn't have a fixed shape. Or maybe it exists in a way that's different from how we perceive reality. If reflections disrupt it somehow, then—"

Rowen clapped a hand on her shoulder. "Yeah, yeah, save the theories for later, Professor."

Lyra huffed but didn't argue.

"So," Rowen continued, "sounds like we've got two things on the agenda—meet this Sylara lady and then figure out how to deal with the Mawborn. That about right?"

Darius nodded. "Pretty much."

Rowen stretched, wincing slightly from his own lingering soreness. "Then what are we waiting for?"

Darius glanced at Ingrid. "Think you can walk?"

She gave him an unimpressed look. "Try and stop me."

Marisol sighed dramatically, muttering something about "reckless adventurers," but ultimately didn't protest.

With that, the four of them—bruised, battered, but *alive*—gathered their strength and made their way toward the courtyard.

The castle courtyard was bathed in the golden light of the late afternoon sun, the sky painted in hues of soft amber and violet. A gentle breeze carried the scent of fresh-cut grass and the distant aroma of baked goods from the castle kitchens. The courtyard itself was vast, lined with ancient stone archways covered in ivy, and at its centre stood a grand marble fountain, its water glistening under the sun.

And waiting before it was Sylara.

She was younger than Alara, perhaps in her mid-to-late twenties, yet she carried herself with the same mystical presence. Her hair was an ethereal silver-blue, long and flowing, as if touched by the ocean's mist. Her eyes gleamed like polished amethyst, piercing yet unreadable, reflecting a wisdom far beyond her years. She wore a layered robe of deep indigo and gold, the fabric flowing like liquid silk around her as if moved by unseen forces. Strange silver rings and trinkets adorned her hands, each humming with a faint arcane energy.

Her gaze flickered to Darius the moment he stepped forward, studying him with a quiet intensity.

"So…" she murmured, her voice calm yet laced with something unreadable. "You are the Hero of the Doomed Prophecy."

The words were sharp, and there was no reverence in them.

Darius frowned slightly, exchanging a glance with his companions before stepping forward. "I am Darius," he corrected. "And these are my friends."

Sylara's expression did not shift. "And yet, you all march toward an end already written in fate," she said, folding her arms. "A hero that is destined to fail. A cycle doomed to fail."

Rowen blinked, whispering to Ingrid, "She's a cheerful one, isn't she?"

Ingrid elbowed him.

Lyra's brow furrowed, her fingers tightening around the book she had been absentmindedly clutching. "Wait..." she said slowly, looking from Sylara to Darius. "What did she mean by that? A hero destined to fail?"

Darius exhaled, long and slow. He had known this moment would come eventually—knew he couldn't keep it from them forever. He glanced at each of them, at Rowen's raised brow, Ingrid's sharp, assessing gaze, Lyra's widening eyes. His friends.

"You deserve to know the truth."

The words felt heavy in his throat, but he forced them out. *"I wasn't just chosen to be the hero. I was chosen to die."*

Silence.

"At some point in this journey, I will fall. That is how my cycle goes. Every hero that came before me was destined to win and push back Vorthis and his army—mine, is to die. The cycle isn't just about defeating Vorthis. It's about breaking me, wearing me down, destroying me before I can defeat Vorthis." He clenched his fists. "But I won't let that happen. I don't care what's written in some prophecy—I will stop Vorthis before I fall. And if I do die, then I will damn well make sure that you—" he looked at them all, eyes hard but voice soft "—don't follow me into death. That's a promise."

The weight of his words settled over the group like a thick fog. Lyra's hands were shaking, her lips parted as if searching for something to say. Ingrid stood stone-still, but there was something unreadable in her expression, something deeper than mere shock.

Rowen, for once, was quiet. He looked at Darius, really looked at him, before shaking his head. "Damn it, Darius."

Darius braced himself for anger—for accusations.

But Rowen only huffed, folding his arms. "You should've told us from the start. Would've saved me a lot of confusion about why you were such a mope when we first met."

That earned a snort from Lyra, and even Ingrid let out a breath that could have been the ghost of a laugh.

Darius blinked, caught between relief and exasperation. "Rowen—"

"No, no, hold on," Rowen continued, grinning despite the tension still lingering in his eyes. "So all that brooding, the long stares into the fire while camping, the 'woe is me' attitude—was that just you being dramatic about your fate?"

"I was not—"

"Oh gods, you were." Rowen clapped him on the back. "You were all mysterious about it too. Man, I thought you were just naturally that grumpy, but no, turns out you were just sitting on a secret death prophecy the whole time. Makes sense now."

Darius groaned, shaking his head, but the weight in his chest had loosened—just a little.

Ingrid crossed her arms. "You should have told us."

"I know."

"You're not alone in this, Darius," Lyra said softly, stepping closer. "None of us are. If fate says you're going to die, then... then we'll just have to find a way to change fate."

Her voice was full of quiet determination, the kind that made something stir deep in Darius's chest.

Rowen grinned. "Or at the very least, we'll make sure you go out looking really cool."

Darius rolled his eyes, but he couldn't stop the small, tired smile that tugged at his lips. "Thanks, Rowen."

"Anytime, oh Doomed One."

Another laugh. The tension had not fully left, but something had changed between them. A deeper understanding.

Darius turned back to Sylara, meeting her gaze head-on. "If you believe the prophecy set forth for me," he said evenly, "then why did you agree to meet with us?"

Sylara studied him for a long moment before exhaling through her nose. "Because Alara asked it of me. And I respect her foresight, even if I do not always agree with it."

There was something unspoken in her words, something hesitant.

As if she was searching for an excuse to turn them away.

Darius stepped forward again.

"I may be fated to fail," he admitted. "But we're here anyway. Fighting. We don't need someone to tell us how this ends—we need someone to help us keep going."

His words lingered in the air, heavier than they should have been.

Sylara's sharp gaze softened. Just a fraction.

"...Hmph." She uncrossed her arms, looking at each of them in turn. Then, slowly, she gave a small nod. "Very well."

She motioned for them to gather closer.

"Incantations," she began, "are not the same as magic. They are not drawn from the natural elements like a mage's spells. They are rooted in your body, your experience, and your battle instinct."

She raised her hand, and for a moment, a shimmering glyph appeared before her palm, pulsing softly before vanishing like mist.

"Magic is learned," she continued. "But incantations are unlocked."

Darius furrowed his brow. "Unlocked?"

Sylara nodded. "They are forged from your own fighting style, from your instincts in battle, and from your experiences. A swordsman will never manifest an incantation meant for an archer. A brawler will never wield an incantation meant for an assassin."

Rowen leaned forward; eyes gleaming. "So... it's like the world gives us new moves based on how we fight?"

Sylara tilted her head. "It is more that the world acknowledges how you fight. Incantations are manifestations of self-improvement. They reflect your growth, your struggles, and your victories. The more you push your limits, the greater the power you may unlock."

Rowen grinned. "That sounds awesome."

Ingrid crossed her arms. "And what about magic?"

Sylara shook her head. "Magic is not the same. I cannot teach magic, nor can I help a mage develop their spells. Magic is tied to mana affinity, and each mage must train in their own way. Lyra will have to continue building her magic on her own."

Lyra nodded, a little overwhelmed but eager to rise to the challenge.

Darius took a breath. "So… when do we begin?"

Sylara smirked slightly. "Not yet. You are all still recovering. Training in your state will only set you back further."

Darius frowned, but before he could protest, she continued.

"I will meet you all in one week's time in the castle barracks," she said. "There is a training arena there. When you come to me, you must be at your full strength. Until then, rest. Recover. And prepare."

Rowen groaned dramatically. "A week? You can't at least give us a hint about what we're learning?"

Sylara simply turned and walked away, not giving him a second glance.

Rowen threw his arms in the air. "Oh, come on!"

The group exchanged amused looks, a rare moment of hope and excitement settling between them.

For the first time in a long while, things didn't feel impossible.

As they began to chat amongst themselves, playful banter filling the air, Seraphina watched from the balcony above.

Her blue eyes softened as she looked down at them. At Darius, smiling. Laughing.

He really did look happy now.

And so, she smiled too.

CHAPTER 19

The Shape of Strength

The week of recovery passed in a blur, yet for each of them, it became a time of growth.

Rowen, true to himself, quickly became the terror of the castle's staff. From sneaking into the kitchens and making off with entire loaves of bread ("For survival!" he claimed) to challenging knights to footraces in the great halls, he was a constant whirlwind of mischief. At one point, Darius found him attempting to teach a squire how to wrestle—despite the fact that Rowen himself barely knew how to fight fair.

"You're a damn pest," Ingrid muttered as Rowen stood in the middle of the courtyard, shirtless, arms stretched toward the morning sun.

"I'm embracing life, Ingrid," Rowen declared. "Would you rather I be boring and broody like Darius?"

"He's right there."

"I *know*."

Darius simply shook his head and walked off.

Lyra spent most of her days deep in books, and more often than not, she found herself in the presence of Alara. The seer was elusive, but when Lyra asked questions, Alara would answer—albeit in her usual cryptic fashion.

"You are not limited to what is written," Alara mused one evening, watching as Lyra pored over an old tome. "Spells, like stories, can be rewritten."

Lyra looked up, frowning. "What does that mean?"

"It means your magic is not set in stone." Alara approached, lightly tapping the book Lyra had been reading. "A mage does not simply learn spells. She shapes them. A spell is a foundation, and it can be built upon."

Realization sparked in Lyra's eyes. "So... I could take something like Frostlance and make it stronger? Change how it works?"

Alara merely smiled, but Lyra caught the glimmer of approval in her gaze. "You have much potential, little one. It is a wonder no one has told you this before."

"No one in my village really knew magic," Lyra admitted. "We had some basics, but I was mostly on my own."

Alara's gaze softened. "Then perhaps it is time for you to forge your own path. Do not let others define your limits."

That stuck with Lyra long after their conversation ended.

Rowen and Ingrid's interactions took on a new energy. The teasing, the constant back-and-forth—it was the same as before, yet different.

Rowen was the first to acknowledge it. One night, as they sat outside beneath the stars, he nudged her. "You ever wonder what happens after all this? When we're done fighting demons and saving the world?"

Ingrid shot him a look. "You assume we survive."

He smirked. "I'm an optimist."

She scoffed. "No, you're an idiot."

A pause. Rowen tilted his head. "You didn't answer."

Ingrid hesitated, then exhaled. "I don't know. Maybe I'd find a new fight. Maybe I'd…" She trailed off.

Rowen watched her, something unreadable in his gaze. "Stick around?"

Ingrid met his eyes then, holding his gaze longer than necessary. "…Maybe."

Neither of them acknowledged it further. But something had shifted.

Darius had several meetings with the king over the course of the week, sharing what he had learned from his journey. The goblin ruins, the corrupted dragon atop the Dragonspine Mountains, the devastation of Black Hallow.

The king listened carefully. "Your path has been harrowing," he admitted one evening. "Yet you press on."

Darius scoffed. "What choice do I have?"

"A lesser man would crumble."

Darius didn't have a response to that.

The king leaned forward. "Darius… You bear the weight of destiny, but you do not bear it alone." He gestured toward the window, where the city lay beyond. "The people of this kingdom stand behind you, whether they know it or not. Do not carry this burden in silence."

It was not something Darius could respond to—not yet. But the words lingered.

Each evening, as the castle settled into quiet, Darius and Seraphina found themselves drawn to the courtyard. It became an unspoken tradition, a place where the weight of their respective roles seemed just a little lighter.

At first, their conversations were simple. Seraphina like the first evening they met all that time ago would speak more of her childhood—how she used to sneak into the city disguised as a commoner, how she would steal pastries from unsuspecting vendors just to see if she could. Darius would smirk, teasing her about being a criminal princess, and she would laugh, soft and warm.

Then, as the nights passed, their words deepened.

Darius found himself speaking of his journey—not just the battles, but the people. The ones he had met, the ones he had lost. He told her about the tavern and the villagers in Thalorath who had given him food and drink for the night, despite the village being razed. He spoke of the family he had once known, their faces blurred by time but never truly forgotten.

Seraphina listened, truly listened, in a way that made Darius feel… seen. Not as a hero. Not as the warrior fated to die. But as Darius.

"You carry so much," she murmured one evening, watching him as he stared at the night sky.

He exhaled. "There's no other choice."

"There's always a choice."

He looked at her then, at the way the moonlight framed her face, at the way she met his gaze with quiet strength. And for a fleeting moment, he wanted to believe her.

By the fourth night, they no longer filled every silence with words. They simply *existed* together—side by side, beneath the stars.

By the sixth, Seraphina no longer hesitated before reaching out, brushing a stray lock of hair from his face after the wind carried it astray.

By the seventh, something had undeniably changed.

Neither of them spoke of it. Neither of them named what was growing between them. But it was there, undeniable in the way their eyes lingered too long, in the way their laughter softened into something more intimate, in the way their hands brushed when they walked through the garden paths.

It was not yet love, not yet something either of them were willing to face. But it was *becoming*.

And as the week came to a close, and Darius stood at the castle barracks with his companions, he found himself glancing toward the balcony where Seraphina so often stood.

She was there. Watching, she had seen many warriors train, many knights swear their oaths. But none of them were like him. He was no mere fighter—he was becoming something else, something greater. And for the first time in a long while, she felt... hopeful.

And when their eyes met, she smiled.

Darius turned away, but for the first time in a long while, he felt lighter.
The morning air was crisp as Darius and his companions stepped onto the packed dirt of the castle barracks' training grounds. The

sun had barely crested the horizon, casting golden light over the stone walls enclosing the arena. The space was vast, designed for soldiers to spar and train, but today, it was reserved for something far beyond ordinary drills.

Sylara stood in the centre, her flowing robes a shimmering mix of deep indigo and silver, catching the morning light in a way that made her look almost ethereal. Her long hair was pulled into intricate braids, woven with tiny charms that seemed to hum with latent energy. Despite her youthful appearance, there was an undeniable weight of wisdom behind her violet eyes. She regarded them all with quiet scrutiny before speaking.

"You are here to learn incantations," she began, her voice even and measured. "Powerful tools, capable of turning the tide of battle. But do not mistake them for simple tricks. Incantations demand more than just words—they require a connection between body, mind, and soul. They are drawn from your very being, shaped by your experiences, your instincts, your will to fight. And above all—" her gaze hardened— "they are dangerous. Use them without control, and they will just as easily destroy you as they will your enemy."

Rowen gave an exaggerated gulp, nudging Ingrid. "She makes it sound like we're playing with fire."

"Because you are," Sylara answered without looking at him.

Darius folded his arms. "Then we better make sure we don't get burned."

Sylara studied him, nodding approvingly before her gaze flicked to Lyra. "Though you are not here for incantations, you are still welcome to train. Your magic is your own path, but I suspect Alara has already begun to open your eyes to what it means to grow stronger."

Lyra perked up at the mention of Alara. "She mentioned… something about improving spells, about refining them rather than just moving on to new ones."

"A valuable lesson," Sylara said. "Though I cannot teach you magic, I am not blind to it. If you choose to stay, I will aid you in what ways I can. That is, if you are willing."

Lyra nodded eagerly. "I wouldn't be much of a mage if I turned down the chance to learn."

"Good," Sylara said, folding her arms. "Then let us begin."

Darius glanced at his companions, each one carrying their own sense of anticipation.

"Let's do this," he said. Sylara exhaled, stepping forward with a commanding presence. "Before we begin training, I need to understand what I'm working with. Each of you will demonstrate your current combat style. Show me how you fight."

She crossed her arms. "I will analyse your strengths and weaknesses, and from there, I will determine the incantations you will train to master."

Rowen grinned. "So, we just get to show off? Finally, some fun."

Sylara's expression remained unreadable. "I suggest you take this seriously."

Rowen muttered under his breath but stepped forward first.

Rowen stretched his arms before getting into position. He moved swiftly, darting around the training area, flipping over obstacles, and manoeuvring with an almost animalistic grace. His strikes were fast—dagger slashes aimed at weak points, precise but unrelenting. His footwork was erratic, never staying in one place, forcing an imaginary opponent to struggle to track him. At one point, he scaled a training post, flipping off it and landing in a crouch.

Sylara watched him carefully, her eyes sharp. As he finished, she gave a single nod. "You fight like a predator. Unpredictable, relentless, but you rely too much on movement to keep yourself safe. If you are caught off guard or slowed, you will struggle."

Rowen shrugged. "That's why I don't get caught."

Ignoring his remark, Sylara continued. "Your incantation should be the *Flicker Step*. It enhances your natural speed, allowing you to vanish and reappear in short bursts. However, it is not teleportation. It will require immense control, or you will misstep and leave yourself open."

Rowen smirked. "Sounds perfect."

Sylara's gaze hardened. "We'll see if you can handle it."

She turned next to Ingrid. "Your turn."

Ingrid rolled her shoulders, stepping forward. Unlike Rowen's erratic movements, Ingrid's approach was raw power and precision. She hefted her axe, delivering controlled but devastating swings that left cracks in the training post. Her stance was firm, unshakable, and each attack carried weight behind it.

Rather than rely on speed, she used leverage and brute force, making every movement count. At one point, she lifted her axe overhead with one hand before slamming it into the ground, causing the earth to tremble slightly.

As she finished, Sylara nodded. "You understand your weapon

well. But your power is limited by your own physical strength. Against foes of greater size or durability, you will struggle to match them."

Ingrid exhaled, wiping sweat from her brow. "Then I'll just have to hit harder."

Sylara's lips twitched in something almost like amusement. "You will learn *Titan's Grasp*. This incantation will temporarily increase the size and weight of your axe, enhancing your strength mid-battle. However, if you misuse it, you will find yourself overburdened and vulnerable."

Ingrid smirked. "Sounds like a challenge."

"It is."

Sylara's eyes shifted to Darius. "Now you."

Darius stepped forward, gripping his sword. Unlike Rowen and Ingrid, his style was measured, precise—a balance between speed and power. His strikes were clean, with no wasted movement, but there was a sense of control in everything he did. He fought with discipline, but Sylara also noted the potential for greater ferocity hidden beneath his restraint.

At one point, he switched from a heavy downward swing to a fluid horizontal slash, showcasing his adaptability. He was not reckless, nor purely calculated—he was something in between, a warrior still refining his own path.

As he finished, Sylara nodded slightly. "You have a strong foundation. But you lack versatility. Against foes who see through your strikes, you will need unpredictability."

Darius frowned slightly. "And how do I fix that?"

"You will learn *Phantom Edge* and *Crescent Fang*."

She stepped forward, explaining.

"*Phantom Edge* will allow you to create an afterimage of your attack—a delayed strike that deceives your opponent into reacting too soon or too late. It will force them to hesitate."

Darius considered this, nodding slowly. "That could be useful."

Sylara continued. "*Crescent Fang* will give you a ranged attack—an arc of energy that extends beyond your blade. It will allow you to strike from a distance when direct combat is unwise."

Darius tightened his grip on his sword. "I'll master them both."

"We shall see," Sylara replied while she folded her arms. Then, she turned to Lyra. "You are not under my instruction, but I will observe your magic nonetheless." Lyra hesitated before stepping forward, her blue robes swaying slightly in the wind. She raised her hands, conjuring a shimmering ice wall before her. It was solid and well-formed, but when she attempted to release the ice spikes from its surface, they were uneven—some jagged and unpredictable, others barely forming before crumbling away.

She frowned, focusing harder, but Sylara raised a hand. "Enough."

Lyra lowered her arms, looking slightly embarrassed.

Sylara tilted her head. "You hesitate."

Lyra bit her lip. "I don't want to lose control. I'm trying to improve my Frostlance to maybe develop a frost shield of sorts Alara gave me some advice, I can evolve my magic somehow if I could just figure out how."

Sylara studied her before giving a rare, almost understanding nod.

"Then your self-confidence is what you must overcome."

Before she could say more, the presence of another figure caught the group's attention.

Alara entered the arena, her robes billowing slightly as she walked with effortless grace. Though she had remained silent throughout much of the demonstrations, her watchful gaze had never left Lyra. She stepped forward, eyes locked onto the young mage.

"Lyra's magic requires refinement," Alara said, her voice calm yet assured, "but she has potential beyond what she realizes."

Sylara raised an eyebrow. "You rarely speak on magic."

Alara inclined her head. "I do not teach it, but I understand its place in fate." She then turned to Lyra, her gaze piercing yet patient. "Tell me, child. Why do you focus only on attack or defence, rather than both?"

Lyra blinked, caught off guard. "I—I thought it was best to separate them. Build a shield first, then counterattack."

Alara shook her head. "Magic is not so rigid. It is flow. Creation and destruction, cold and fire, stillness and movement. Why choose only one when you can wield both at once?"

The words struck something deep within Lyra. A spell that could protect and strike at the same time? Could she even do that?

Her mind raced as she reevaluated her approach. *What if... I build the wall with the counterattack already woven into it? What if, instead of summoning spikes separately, they were already part of the formation?*

Her pulse quickened. It could work.

Sylara crossed her arms. "An ambitious idea. If she can pull it off."

Alara offered a rare smile. "I believe she can."

Determination surged in Lyra's chest. She nodded firmly, turning back toward the training field. She would find a way to make this spell work—to defend and strike in one seamless motion.

"Each of you now understands what you will be learning. But do not mistake knowledge for mastery. These incantations will demand more than just repetition—they will require instinct, discipline, and the ability to adapt."

Rowen stretched his arms. "No pressure." Sylara narrowed her eyes. "If you do not take this seriously, you will fail." Rowen raised his hands in surrender. "Alright, alright. I'm serious."

Darius tightened his grip on his sword, determination settling in his gaze. Ingrid cracked her knuckles, eager to push herself further. Lyra exhaled, contemplating what she needed to do.

Sylara stepped back. "Then let us begin for real."

The first day was an exercise in frustration. Sylara did not let them use incantations immediately. Instead, she drilled them on their fundamentals—stance, control, focus.

The morning sun bore down on them in the open-air arena, sweat already forming on their brows despite the cool breeze rolling in from the castle walls.

Rowen grumbled as he adjusted his footing for what felt like the hundredth time. "I thought this was supposed to be incantation training, not standing-around-like-an-idiot training."

Sylara shot him a sharp look, her violet eyes gleaming with barely restrained patience. "If you do not understand the foundation of your body, you cannot understand the foundation of an incantation."

Rowen sighed but did as he was told.

Sylara walked between them, her presence commanding despite her seemingly relaxed posture. "Incantations are not magic," she explained. "You are not pulling power from the elements or bending mana to your will. You are commanding your own body and spirit to exceed its natural limits. The words of an incantation are a key—but the strength to use it comes from within you."

She paused, looking at them each in turn. "Think of it this way. A swordsman in battle does not think about each individual movement—his body moves on instinct, flowing from one attack to the next. A hunter does not analyse every step—he moves silently because it is part of him. The best warriors do not hesitate, do not falter, because they reach a state where mind and body act as one. Incantations work the same way."

Darius furrowed his brow. "So... it's like entering a battle state? Like muscle memory?"

Sylara nodded approvingly. "Yes, but deeper. You must push past the barriers your body has placed upon itself. It is not just saying the words and expecting power to come forth—it is knowing, deep in your core, that what you are about to do is possible. It is not about *forcing* your body to comply, but allowing it to do what it is capable of."

She gestured to Ingrid. "Your incantation will allow your axe to become heavier, more devastating. But if you hesitate—if you doubt that you can control it—it will overwhelm you."

To Rowen. "Your speed is already exceptional. Your ability will allow you to push that beyond human limits. But if your mind wavers, if your focus is not absolute, your steps will falter, and the technique will fail."

Finally, to Darius. "Your swordplay is adaptable. Your incantations rely on your understanding of how motion and deception work. If you do not commit to the illusion of Phantom Edge or the force of Crescent Fang, neither will manifest."

She stepped back, letting the weight of her words settle. "Once you activate your incantation for the first time, your body will remember the sensation. The next time will be easier. But that does not mean limitless use. A warrior in the last cycle tried to push beyond his limits, believing he could wield incantations as endlessly. His body betrayed him before the battle even ended. Power without discipline is destruction."

She turned to Lyra and gestured toward her. "Mages have a set number of spell charges before their energy is depleted. Incantations are the same. Your body has limits. Every time you use your ability, you burn stamina. Push too far, and you will collapse. However, just as mages can increase their magic reserves, so too can you build endurance. With training, you will be able to use them more frequently before exhaustion sets in."

Rowen wiped at his brow, shaking his head. "So, basically, we have to train until our bodies just know how to do it?"

Sylara smirked slightly. "Yes. And until then… you practice."

And so, the drilling continued. No incantations, no bursts of power—just hours of footwork, controlled breathing, weapon strikes, and the constant corrections from Sylara's sharp eyes.

It was only after their bodies were sore and aching, when sweat had soaked through their tunics and armour, when Rowen had fallen flat on his back at least three times, that she finally nodded in satisfaction "now then, I believe you're all ready to begin the real hard work", For Darius, this meant refining the precision of his strikes. "You swing your sword like a brute," Sylara remarked as he delivered a powerful but rigid strike at a dummy. "Crescent Fang is not about power. It's about precision. You are forcing the air to bend to your will, not bludgeoning it."

Darius gritted his teeth and tried again, adjusting his form.

Meanwhile, Rowen was attempting Flicker Step—and failing miserably. Every attempt left him staggering or misjudging his steps, making him appear anywhere but where he intended.

"This isn't teleportation," Sylara reminded him. "You must visualize where you are going before you move."

"I am visualizing it!" Rowen argued.

"Then your imagination is as sloppy as your footwork."

Rowen groaned, falling onto his back in defeat. "I think I liked her more when she was ignoring me."

Ingrid fared better with Titan's Grasp, though her first attempts nearly crushed her under the weight of her own weapon. The first time she activated it, her axe grew in size so suddenly that she lost control, sending it crashing into the ground and nearly pulling her down with it.

Sylara sighed. "Titan's Grasp is not about brute strength. It's about control. You are not wielding a boulder. You are wielding an extension of yourself."

Ingrid gritted her teeth, adjusting her grip. "I can do this."

Lyra knew her magic. Frostlance was second nature to her—she could cast it flawlessly, every time, exactly as she had been taught. But that was the problem.

She was too precise. Too textbook.

As the others worked on their footwork and incantation theory, Sylara and Alara observed Lyra in silence. She stood in the training yard, conjuring a perfect Frostlance—straight, sharp, balanced. She fired it, hitting the centre of a training dummy with practiced ease.

Alara tilted her head. "Efficient. Precise."

Sylara, however, crossed her arms. "Predictable."

Lyra turned, frowning. "Predictable?"

Sylara gestured at the dummy. "That spell was effective, but I saw every movement before you cast it. You formed the same stance. The same motion. There was no adaptation—only repetition."

Lyra blinked. "But that's how magic works, isn't it? You study, practice, and execute."

Alara chuckled softly. "From what I know magic is more than execution. It is expression. Every spell you've learned is a foundation, not a limit."

Sylara gestured at her. "Cast again. But don't follow your routine. Just... let the magic flow."

Lyra hesitated. That wasn't how she had been trained. But she took a breath, closing her eyes, trying to feel the mana rather than construct it.

She raised her hand. Ice swirled.

She hesitated for just a second, unsure of what her body wanted to do—and the Frostlance cracked apart before it could fully form.

Lyra gritted her teeth.

Sylara smirked. "Good. You hesitated. That means you're thinking about what comes next, not just relying on the muscle memory."

Lyra didn't quite understand yet, but she felt something shift.

By the third day, visible progress had been made—but at a cost.

Darius had finally managed to produce a faint shimmer of an afterimage when swinging his sword, marking the first step toward Phantom Edge. The moment he saw it, a thrill ran through him.

"I did it," he murmured, adjusting his stance.

Sylara gave a curt nod. "Now do it again. Until it no longer surprises you."

Rowen, after countless missteps (and a few bruises from slamming into walls), had finally managed to chain three rapid steps together without losing control. The first time he did it correctly, he nearly whooped in triumph—until Sylara cut him off.

"You're still relying on instinct alone," she said. "That won't be enough in real combat. Again."

Ingrid had gained more control over Titan's Grasp, learning to adjust the weight of her axe mid-swing rather than letting it control her. By now, she and Rowen had fallen into an easy banter, their teasing laced with something deeper.

"You watchin', Rowen?" Ingrid said, hefting her now-massive axe onto her shoulder. "You might learn a thing or two."

Rowen smirked. "I'd be more impressed if you could lift that thing with one hand."

"You mean like this?" Ingrid swung her axe effortlessly, the ground cracking beneath its force. Rowen whistled.

"Marry me."

Ingrid rolled her eyes but couldn't suppress the faint smirk.

Meanwhile Lyra was frustrated. She had perfected her magic long ago, yet now it felt like she was starting over.

She sat on a rock, arms crossed. "I don't see the point of this."

Alara knelt beside her, tracing a rune in the dirt. "Tell me, Lyra—what do you think makes a powerful mage?"

Lyra sighed. "Control. Stability. A strong will."

Alara smiled. "You sound like the textbooks." She gestured to the rune engraved on lyra's staff. "Magic is a living thing. It isn't meant to be contained in a perfectly shaped box."

Sylara nodded. "Your problem isn't power—it's flexibility. You've mastered what you've been taught, but magic should be an extension of you. Adaptable. If I were to fight you right now, I would know exactly what spell you'd use and how you'd cast it. No surprises. No instinct."

That stung.

Lyra exhaled slowly, lifting her hand, summoning a Frostlance.

But this time, she didn't follow the practiced motions. She let her instincts guide the casting. The magic swirled in her palm, and for the first time, the *Frostlance* shifted shape mid-cast, curling slightly, becoming sharper, adjusting to how she moved.

It wasn't perfect—but it was different.

Sylara raised an eyebrow. "Now you're getting it."

For the first time, Lyra felt free.

By the sixth day, everything began to fall into place.

Darius now fully controlled Phantom Edge, able to leave behind a shimmering afterimage with every strike. Crescent Fang had been harder to master, but by now, his energy arcs were slicing cleanly through training dummies.

Rowen had pushed Flicker Step to its limits, learning how to chain it into attacks. He even used it to sneak behind Ingrid mid-conversation, earning a half-hearted punch to the shoulder.

"That's what you use it for?" Ingrid sighed.

Rowen grinned. "Stealth is a weapon too."

"More like a nuisance."

Ingrid, on the other hand, had learned to expand her axe at just the right moment, sending shockwaves through the training grounds. The first time she did it correctly, Rowen stood back, hands on his hips.

Rowen whistled. "Alright. That's terrifying." Ingrid smirked. "You're just realizing that now?" Rowen placed a hand over his heart. "I might actually be in love." Ingrid rolled her eyes. "Get in line pal."

With free flowing Frostlance now mastered to a level she was happy with, at one point almost resembling an arrow more than a lance, Lyra turned her focus toward something greater. Alara's words about magic being both offense and defence had lingered in her thoughts. An ice wall—that was what she needed.

At first, her attempts were laughable. The walls she conjured were thin, brittle, barely enough to withstand a thrown rock. Even when she reinforced them, they lacked the raw durability of a proper defensive spell.

"You're trying to force ice into being," Alara noted as she watched Lyra frown at her latest attempt. "Instead of letting it form as it needs to."

Lyra sighed. She had been so focused on getting it perfect that she wasn't allowing her magic the room to shape itself. So, she changed her approach.

Instead of focusing on making the biggest, strongest wall, she focused on form and intent—summoning not just ice, but a barrier meant to protect. She pushed her mana outward, weaving it into a structure rather than forcing it into one.

The ice wall that formed was thicker, denser, holding firm against a strong impact. But something was missing. She exhaled, running a hand along the surface of her own creation.

"Good," Sylara said. "But you're not done yet."

The final day arrived. The training ground was littered with evidence of their efforts—cracked earth, shattered dummies, lingering wisps of energy.

"You are stronger than when you started," Sylara said, her eyes scanning over them, unimpressed. "But do not think you are strong enough. A battlefield is not a training ground. And your enemies will not wait for you to get it right."

Darius nodded. "We'll keep training."

Rowen cracked his knuckles. "Yeah, yeah. But admit it—we're impressive."

Sylara smirked, the closest thing to praise she had given all week. "We shall see."

The moment was interrupted by the should of ice shattering to the side of them because for the past two days, Lyra had built stronger and more refined ice walls, but they were still just that—walls. Static, unchanging. But Alara had suggested more.

It had to defend and attack.

Lyra pondered over how to make that happen. She experimented—forming ice, then trying to force it to shatter outward towards a would-be attacker, but she couldn't control the effect. The spikes would sprout unevenly, barely reaching beyond the wall.

It was Rowen, of all people, who accidentally gave her the final push.

"You know," he said, watching her try for the fourth time, "you're making it too stiff. What if you made the ice... I don't know, burst out all at once like all over, instead of trying to push it out in one direction or whatever?"

Lyra blinked. That was it.

Instead of commanding each piece, she had to let the ice do what ice does best—shatter.

She built the wall one last time, focusing on her breathing, letting the structure take form fluidly. Then, when it was solid, she sent a surge of mana into the foundation, visualizing the entire thing erupting outward.

The result was immediate.

The wall pulsed with a cold blue glow, and in an instant, razor-sharp spikes of ice shot outward in all directions, impaling everything within range.

Silence followed.

Lyra exhaled, shaking slightly. That had drained her—but she had done it.

Sylara smirked. "Now that," she said, arms crossed, "is a battlefield spell."

Alara gave a small approving nod. "You have taken your first real step toward understanding."

Lyra couldn't help but smile, she had a new spell under her control one of her own not taught through books, Glacis Bastion

As they left the arena, there was something different in the air—a sense of accomplishment, of anticipation. The battle ahead was uncertain. But now, they were stronger.

CHAPTER 20

The Night Before Shadows

The long wooden tables of the castle's grand dining hall were lined with roasted meats, fresh bread, spiced vegetables, and flagons of mead, all prepared in honour of the warriors who had spent the last week sharpening their skills. The mood was lively, the air thick with the scents of indulgence and the sound of laughter echoing off the stone walls.

Rowen was already deep into his usual antics, leaning lazily back in his chair while making a dramatic display of flicking bits of bread at a nearby servant. "So there I was, flickering faster than the eye could track, moving so fast I nearly outran my own shadow! I was basically untouchable!" He grinned, flashing his teeth as he shot a glance at Ingrid. "And then Ingrid here, swinging that oversized axe of hers, nearly knocked my head clean off."

Ingrid scoffed, tipping back her latest mug of mead. "Oh, please. If I really meant to hit you, you wouldn't be sitting here bragging." She wiped the foam from her lips and smirked. "That Titan's Grasp of mine? You wouldn't have even seen it coming."

Lyra, seated across from them, giggled as she popped a candied fruit into her mouth. Unlike the others, she had spent most of the night sampling every dessert she could get her hands on. "You two are hopeless," she said, shaking her head. "I bet I could hold my own against you both with my Glacis Bastion. Just imagine—ice spikes sending you flying across the battlefield." She gave Rowen a playful look. "Would be quite the sight."

Rowen gasped in mock betrayal. "Et tu, Lyra?" He clutched his chest as if wounded, then swiped a hunk of bread from Ingrid's plate before she could react.

"Oi," Ingrid growled, narrowing her eyes. "Do you have a death wish?"

Before Rowen could respond, a booming voice filled the hall.

"Drinking contests already? I expected no less."

King Aldric entered the room, his royal guards close behind him, their stiff postures a stark contrast to the relaxed, boisterous energy of the dining hall. The moment he stepped forward, the guards subtly tightened their stance, but the king himself—though commanding—held a far more casual air.

Rowen's eyes gleamed with mischief. "Ah, Your Majesty!" He gestured dramatically toward the empty chair beside him. "Would you care to join our humble little gathering?"

One of the guards bristled. "The king does not—"

King Aldric raised a hand, silencing him with a look before letting out a low chuckle. "You expect me to sit idly by while the hero of prophecy and his party celebrate without me? That hardly seems fair."

The guards exchanged worried glances, but Aldric, without waiting for their protests, took the seat beside Ingrid. She arched an eyebrow at him, then slid a fresh flagon of mead his way. "Your Majesty, with all due respect, is this really appropriate?" one of the guards whispered, shifting uncomfortably. "King Aldric, the people must see you as their unwavering pillar, not..." He gestured vaguely at the mug of mead being pressed into the king's hands.

Rowen grinned. "A royal who drinks with his people? I like it."

Aldric exhaled with amusement, then gestured to his men to leave him. "Don't get used to it." He looked at Rowen "tonight I wanted to share in your achievement on your training but tomorrow I am back to my role as king."

Across the hall, Lyra now found herself in an entirely different predicament.

"Lady Lyra, might I fetch you another drink?" one of the guards asked smoothly. Another leaned forward, resting his arm on the table. "Or perhaps a dance later?" Lyra blinked, completely unprepared for the attention. "O-oh, no, I, um—"

Rowen, overhearing, snickered into his drink. "Looks like someone's popular." The guards kept trying, clearly enjoying flustering the mage. One nudged his companion. "They weren't kidding. She is as lovely as the rumours say."

Lyra, cheeks burning, grabbed her goblet and took a hasty sip, nearly choking. Ingrid, watching from the sidelines, smirked into her drink but didn't intervene just yet—she was enjoying Lyra's rare moment of embarrassment.

One of the guards, perhaps sensing her discomfort, sighed and leaned back. "Forgive us, Lady Lyra we did not mean any discomfort." He looked to the king and shifted the conversation "We don't often see the king in such... human company."

Another nodded in agreement. "It's not proper for him to be drinking like this. But you know what? I think it's good for him."

The words carried a weight that lingered, and for a moment, the guards weren't just soldiers—they were people who cared for their king, even if they knew he had expectations far beyond their own.

As the night carried on, the laughter and clinking of mugs filled the hall. The energy of the feast was infectious. But at some point, Darius was no longer among them. The night air was crisp, the stars high above burning bright against the dark canvas of the sky. The sounds of celebration were distant, muffled behind stone walls, but here in the courtyard, it was quiet.

Darius stood near the fountain, hands braced against its cool surface. He had slipped away from the feast unnoticed—no fanfare, no parting words. Just a quiet retreat to where he knew she would be.

Seraphina stood a few steps away, gazing up at the sky as if searching for something. When she heard his approach, she turned, her lips curling into a soft smile.

"You always find your way here," she said.

Darius huffed, shaking his head. "Guess I do."

She tilted her head, stepping closer. "Aren't you supposed to be celebrating?"

"I was." He exhaled, rubbing the back of his neck. "Needed some air."

Seraphina studied him for a long moment before nodding. "And yet, you always seem to find air *here*. With me."

Darius had no response to that. He merely held her gaze, and in that quiet, unspoken moment, the warmth in her eyes mirrored something he wasn't sure how to name.

She smiled again, this time a little softer. "You'll be leaving soon, won't you?"

Darius hesitated, then nodded. "Yeah. The Mawborn is still out there."

For a moment, neither of them spoke. The space between them was small—closer than it had been before. Darius wasn't sure when it had happened, but he could feel the warmth of her presence, the way her breath came just slightly uneven.

Seraphina exhaled through her nose, tilting her gaze downward. "its funny though because I knew this day would come," she murmured. "The day you'd leave again."

Darius searched her expression, trying to find the right words. "It's not forever," he said, though even he wasn't sure if that was true. "I'll be back."

She huffed softly, shaking her head. "You can't promise that."

No, he couldn't. He knew that. She knew that. And yet, standing here with her now, knowing the road ahead was full of blood and horror, he wished more than anything that he could.

Seraphina's hand hovered just above his, fingers barely brushing his knuckles. There was hesitation, doubt—both of them caught between what they wanted and what they thought they should be.

"I shouldn't..." she whispered, more to herself than to him.

Darius' throat felt tight. "I know."

She was a princess. He was a hero—one meant to die. This wasn't supposed to be something that lingered in the back of his mind, something that made him question everything he thought he'd accepted about his fate. It wasn't supposed to be this hard to leave.

But then she looked up at him again, and suddenly, none of that mattered.

Seraphina stepped closer, a barely-there movement, a breath between them. Darius didn't think—he just acted, as if something inside him had already decided before his mind could catch up.

His lips met hers.

It wasn't desperate, nor rushed. Just soft, slow—uncertain in its confidence, like the two of them were testing the weight of this thing between them, seeing if it was real.

And it was.

For all his fears, for all her doubts, the world faded in that moment. The castle walls, the prophecy, the inevitability of his fate—it was just the warmth of her touch, the way her fingers curled against his cloak, the way he found himself anchoring to her without meaning to.

Then, just as naturally as it had begun, they pulled apart.

Darius lingered close, his forehead nearly brushing hers. He could feel her breath against his skin, steadying herself just as much as he was.

Seraphina's eyes searched his, and for the first time, she let herself smile—fully, genuinely. "That... was unexpected."

Darius let out a breath of laughter, shaking his head. "Was it?"

She laughed, quiet and warm, and for once, there was no hesitation as she reached for his hand. She held it, just for a moment, before stepping back.

"We should go," she said, though neither of them moved right away.

Darius nodded. He should go. He should turn and leave.

But instead, he found himself smiling, just a little. "Yeah."

And just like that, they both knew—this wasn't the end of whatever this was. It was only the beginning.

Darius and Seraphina walked side by side through the castle halls, the distant sounds of revelry growing louder with each step. Their fingers brushed occasionally—not deliberate, not quite an accident either. Neither acknowledged it aloud, but the weight of their shared moment in the courtyard still lingered between them, warm and unspoken.

As they reached the grand dining hall, the doors were already open, spilling golden torchlight into the corridor. The moment they stepped inside, chaos met them head-on.

Rowen was standing on a table, dramatically retelling a story—his arms waving wildly—while a group of knights and castle staff gathered around, half in awe, half in disbelief. Ingrid, now several flagons deep into her challenge with King Aldric, was leaning back in her chair, arms crossed, smirking as the king swayed ever so slightly, his men exchanging worried glances. Lyra, across the room, was hunched over a long table, surrounded by desserts, eagerly sampling every pastry and sweet confection she could get her hands on while being fawned over by a few lingering guards, who were clearly trying (and failing) to flirt with her.

The second Rowen spotted them, his face lit up with mischief. "Ah, look who finally decided to grace us with their presence!" he called, loud enough to draw the attention of nearly everyone in the hall. He raised his goblet with a wolfish grin. "What's the matter, Darius? Needed some 'fresh air' with the princess?"

Darius rolled his eyes, but Seraphina was quicker. "Something like that," she quipped, her tone light, but Rowen's jaw nearly dropped at her lack of denial.

The hall erupted into laughter, and Darius could already feel the inevitable teasing forming in Rowen's mind. Before the rogue could unleash more commentary, another voice spoke behind them.

"Quite the gathering," Alara mused as she stepped into the hall, her ever-present, knowing smile in place. Sylara followed just behind her, arms crossed, expression unreadable as she scanned the room. "More like barely contained disorder."

"You say that as if it's a bad thing," Rowen shot back, raising his goblet again before downing the rest of its contents.

Sylara exhaled in mild amusement before shaking her head. "Unfortunately, I won't be around to witness the aftermath of this mess. I depart for home in the morning."

"Already?" Lyra asked, looking up from her pastry pile.

"I've done what I came to do," Sylara said simply.

Alara, however, glanced at Darius with that ever-enigmatic gaze of hers. "The winds shift, the stars realign," she mused, swirling the last sip remaining within goblet resting in her hand. "Paths cross not just once, but when fate deems it necessary. Next time, the sands of travel will be beneath your feet." Darius frowned slightly at that, sensing the deeper meaning, but before he could ask for clarification, Alara turned to the table, plucked another goblet of wine from a passing servant's tray, and took a small sip, as if the matter was already settled.

The meaning of her words could wait.

For now, the feast continued.

The night was filled with laughter and indulgence, with good food and better company. Ingrid and Aldric's drinking contest stretched on, much to the dismay of his guards. Rowen eventually got the castle staff to play along with his antics, and even Darius, despite his usual preference for quiet, found himself smiling more than he had in a long time.

As the hours slipped by, guests trickled out one by one, some retiring to their chambers, others simply succumbing to the inevitable haze of too much drink and celebration.

As expected, King Aldric was the first to depart, his duty-bound nature refusing to let him indulge too far into the night. His men escorted him, despite his protests that he could walk just fine on his own. Ingrid, victorious in her drinking contest, let out a triumphant huff before staggering off toward her own chambers, while Rowen, still full of energy, attempted (and failed) to start a round of celebratory arm wrestling with the remaining knights.

Lyra was among the last to leave, rubbing her eyes sleepily as she finally relented to exhaustion. Darius lingered just a little longer, watching as the grand hall, once full of life and sound, slowly emptied. Tomorrow, the real journey would begin once again.

The sun had barely begun its ascent when the castle stirred to life. Morning light trickled through high-arched windows, painting the cold stone walls in a golden hue. Yet, within the chambers of the four warriors, there was little warmth to be felt.

A quiet heaviness hung in the air. Today, they set out once again.

Rowen woke with an arm draped lazily over something warm. A familiar scent—faint hints of mead and steel. His half-lidded gaze adjusted to the dim light, then downward, confirming the truth.

"Ingrid," he muttered groggily, blinking.

She was nestled beside him, one arm tucked beneath her head, the other sprawled across his chest. Her breathing was slow, steady. At some point in the night, exhaustion had won over both of them.

Rowen smirked to himself, shifting slightly. "Well, well… starting to make this a habit, aren't we?"

A groan was his only answer. Ingrid stirred, wincing at the dull pounding in her head before she realized exactly where she was. A second later, Rowen found himself unceremoniously shoved off the bed with surprising force.

He hit the ground with a *thud*.

"You—" Ingrid's voice was hoarse, laced with a hangover's wrath. "—are insufferable."

Rowen snorted from the floor, rubbing the back of his head. "I didn't shove you out of your bed."

Ingrid groaned, gripping her forehead. "Why is your voice so loud?" Rowen grinned, standing up and stretching. "Not my fault you tried to drink the king under the table."

She glared at him through half-lidded eyes before swinging a pillow at his head. He dodged, chuckling.

"Should probably see Marisol for something to fix that," he suggested, crossing his arms. "Wouldn't want to ride out with you all sluggish and miserable. Maybe the drinking contest was a bad idea."

Ingrid exhaled sharply through her nose. "For once, I agree with you."

Rowen blinked in exaggerated shock. "Quick, someone write this down." Then laughed, hard.

Without warning, she grabbed the nearest wooden chair and *hurled* it at him. He barely managed to duck as it clattered against the wall.

"Your laugh is *too damn loud*," she grumbled.

Rowen, still crouched, glanced at the broken chair and then back at Ingrid with a slow smirk. "Not denying anything though, huh?" he looked her up and down "the drinking contest or us."

She didn't answer, simply pulling on her boots with an extra bit of force. He took the hint—she wouldn't outright admit anything. Not yet.

But she didn't deny it either.

In another room Darius fastened the last of his gear, adjusting the strap of his sword sheath before glancing toward the mirror. His reflection stared back, but he barely recognized the man standing there.

It wasn't the wounds or the fatigue. It was something deeper.

A quiet acceptance.

A knock at the door pulled him from his thoughts. He didn't need to ask who it was.

Seraphina.

She stepped inside, her hands folded in front of her, her expression unreadable. But the moment their eyes met, there was something unspoken—worry, hope, a silent prayer.

"You're leaving." It wasn't a question.

Darius nodded.

Seraphina sighed, stepping closer. "After last night... I prayed for more time." Something in his chest tightened, but he didn't speak. She reached out, hesitated, then placed a gentle hand on his wrist. "Last night, you wanted to promise me you'd come back." He exhaled, his hand covering hers briefly. "And you told me I couldn't promise that." Her lips pressed together. "Then promise me you'll try."

A long pause.

Then, softly— "I will."

For a brief second, there was nothing but them. No prophecy. No war. Just this.

And then, Seraphina did something bold. She leaned in, just slightly, and *pressed a kiss to his cheek*. A whisper of warmth, fleeting, but grounding.

Darius' breath caught, but before he could speak, she had already stepped back, masking the emotions behind her usual regal composure. "Then I will pray for your safe return."

And just like that, she was gone.

By the time the four of them gathered near the castle gates, the sky was painted in soft hues of orange and gold. Their armour was strapped, their weapons ready.

Darius glanced around, taking in the sight of his companions.

Rowen, grinning as usual, though there was an edge of something more serious beneath the surface. Ingrid, rolling her shoulders, her usual determination shining through despite the faint stiffness from her hangover. Lyra, adjusting the strap of her staff, her gaze steady but her fingers gripping the handle a little too tightly.

They were ready.

The castle lands, however, were not.

The once-lush fields that stretched beyond the capital walls were aberrant and barren, their life stolen away by something unseen. The air felt thick, the trees hunched like silent sentinels, and beyond them—beyond the rolling hills—the *Whispering Woods* loomed.

Rowen was the first to break the silence.

"…You know, Darius, you and I met right there." He gestured toward the treeline. "Feels like forever ago."

Darius followed his gaze. "Yeah." His tone was unreadable.

Rowen gave a mock shudder. "Even back then that place felt like hell."

"Twisted, unnatural," Darius agreed, his mind drifting back to the eldritch beasts they had fought—the wolves with too many eyes, the shadows that moved even without light.

"The woods were sick," Rowen said, frowning. "Something was in there… but we never quite saw what."

Lyra and Ingrid exchanged glances.

"So… you think whatever that was is what we need to find?" Ingrid asked.

Darius exhaled. "If the darkness was already there before, then maybe that's where it started."

Lyra's voice was quieter, thoughtful. "Or worse… maybe that's where it lives."

Silence settled over them for a moment.

Rowen rolled his shoulders. "Well, one way to find out."

Darius looked at them—at his friends—and nodded.

The *Whispering Woods* awaited.

CHAPTER 21

Into the Whispering Woods

The air was thick with an unnatural stillness, the wind carrying only the faintest whispers of movement through the devastated land. The once-vibrant kingdom had turned into a wasteland of decay, the corruption spreading like a sickness, tainting everything in its path. The road to the Whispering Woods was long, but Darius and his party pressed on, knowing that whatever horrors awaited them, they would face them together.

But the land was not silent for long.

A guttural growl echoed through the skeletal trees ahead, followed by the unmistakable sound of something large moving through the dead grass.

The first battle of the day had begun.

The first foe revealed itself—a sickening amalgamation of man and beast, its skeletal frame stretched and unnatural, with jagged claws protruding from what had once been human hands. It let out a wet, gurgling screech before charging.

Rowen moved first.

He flickered forward in a rapid burst, appearing just to the left of the creature. His Flicker Step made it almost impossible to track him, but his execution was still rough—he stumbled slightly as he reappeared, forcing him to correct his balance.

The beast was fast. Faster than it should have been.

Before Rowen could properly counter, Ingrid was already there.

She roared as her Titan's Grasp activated, her axe growing in size mid-swing. She miscalculated—the weight change caught her off guard, and while the swing was powerful, it was too slow. The creature ducked beneath the massive blade, lunging for her exposed side.

A sharp crescent of deep purple energy shot between them, slamming into the creature's ribs and sending it flying backward.

Darius exhaled, lowering his obsidian greatsword, the air around him still rippling from his Crescent Fang.

"Still getting used to that one," he muttered, rolling his shoulders.

Rowen snorted. "Not bad, but next time, warn me before you slice something across my face."

"No promises."

More sounds. More movement.

The first was only a scout. The real fight was here.

From the treeline, dozens of undead creatures slithered, crawled, and sprinted toward them—some humanoid, some monstrous, all reeking of death and corruption. Their eyes burned with an unnatural glow, their limbs moving in jerky, erratic motions.

Darius tightened his grip.

"Lyra, defensive spells! Ingrid, hold the frontline! Rowen, keep them off our backs!"

The battlefield erupted.

Ingrid moved first, swinging her axe in a wide arc, her strength amplified by Titan's Grasp. She had learned from her earlier mistake—this time, she controlled the increase in weight, slamming the axe into the ground. The sheer force shattered the earth, sending shockwaves through the horde, making them stumble.

Lyra raised her staff, eyes shimmering that silvery blue. "Glacis Bastion!"

An ice wall erupted from the ground, blocking part of the swarm from reaching them.

But she wasn't done.

Lyra thrust her staff forward, triggering the second phase of her spell—the wall shattered outward, launching deadly ice spikes in all directions. Several undead fell instantly, impaled through the chest, but some continued forward, undeterred by their missing limbs.

Rowen vanished—flickering in and out of sight as he weaved through enemies.

He appeared behind a lunging beast, his twin blades flashing as he hamstrung it, then disappeared again before another creature could retaliate. He was faster now, but not quite perfect—his final step left him just slightly off balance, forcing him to roll out of a counterattack rather than striking back.

Darius, meanwhile, had his own problems.

One of the larger undead—a hulking, grotesque thing with exposed ribs and clawed arms—lunged at him.

Darius sidestepped, activating Phantom Edge, his afterimage causing the creature to swipe at nothing.

A second later, his real strike hit true, slicing deep into its exposed bones. It shrieked and staggered back, but another enemy lunged at him immediately.

Too fast. Too many.

A scream. Lyra's.

Darius turned just in time to see an undead wolf, its mouth unhinged far too wide, leap toward her.

Lyra threw up her arms, conjuring a last-second barrier of ice but due to her panic it reformed into an arrow. The wolf shattered through it, lunging straight for her throat.

Darius reacted without thinking.

He swung Crescent Fang mid-turn, the energy wave colliding with the wolf midair. The force sent it flying, slamming into the ground with a sickening crunch.

Lyra gasped, scrambling to her feet. "Thanks—"

No time. Another attack.

Darius grabbed her wrist, pulling her out of the way as a skeletal knight thrust a rusted sword where she had just been standing.

Rowen flickered behind it, plunging both swords into its back, kicking off the body as it crumpled.

"That's two you owe me!" Rowen called.

"Not keeping count!" Darius shot back, already turning to block another attack.

The battle continued, gruelling and endless.

But this time—unlike before—they were holding their own.

It felt like hours before the last enemy finally fell.

Ingrid's axe dripped with black ichor, her breath heavy. Rowen was leaning on his swords, a cut on his cheek. Lyra was pale but steady, her magic reserves clearly drained. Darius's arms ached, his body bruised, but they were still standing.

They had won.

He looked around, taking in the aftermath. They were stronger now, but not invincible.

Not yet.

As they caught their breath, Rowen nudged Darius with his elbow, smirking despite his exhaustion. "So. Think we're getting better at this?"

Darius exhaled, staring out toward the Whispering Woods, its dark mass looming in the distance.

"We'll find out soon enough."

With that, they pressed on—toward whatever horror awaited them in the trees.

Lyra took a deep breath, clutching her staff tightly as she glanced down at her hands. Her fingers trembled—just slightly—but enough to notice. She exhaled, trying to steady herself before speaking.

"That was... four charges," she muttered, her voice carrying a note of exhaustion.

Darius turned toward her, noticing the slight paleness to her face. His own limbs felt heavier than before, his grip on his greatsword slacker than it should have been.

"We need a break," he said firmly, cutting off any protest before it could begin.

Rowen scoffed, wiping his brow with the back of his glove. "We just left the castle a couple of hours ago, and we're already stopping?"

Darius shot him a look. "You and I both used our incantations more than once, Ingrid's been swinging that axe like a siege weapon, and Lyra is one spell away from empty. We can't afford to push forward into the Whispering Woods if we're already running on fumes."

Rowen sighed, stretching out his arms. "Fair point. Still feels weird, though. Like we're quitting early."

"We're not quitting. We're regrouping," Ingrid corrected, rolling her sore shoulder before hefting her axe over one arm. "And unless you've got magic potions stuffed in your pockets, we rest."

Rowen lifted his hands in surrender, but his usual grin was still present. "Fine, fine. If my favourite terrifying axe-woman says we rest, then we rest."

Ingrid rolled her eyes but didn't argue.

Lyra, who had been steadying her breath, smiled slightly at Darius in appreciation. "Thanks."

He nodded before turning back to the path ahead. "There."

Not too far away, a rock formation jutted out of the landscape—a small overhang, barely enough to be called a cave, but solid enough to provide cover. It was perfect.

"Let's move."

The group settled down in the shade of the rocks, the cool stone a welcome relief from the endless march forward.

Rowen flopped down dramatically, stretching his legs. "I hate to say it, but I think my legs are about to fall off."

"Good thing you weren't born a horse, then," Ingrid quipped, leaning back against the rock as she set her axe down beside her.

Rowen shot her a wounded look. "You wound me, Ingrid."

Lyra sat cross-legged nearby, already focusing on replenishing her mana. She took a slow breath, closing her eyes as she tried to centre herself, drawing energy back into her reserves.

Darius took a seat beside her, wiping his brow with the back of his hand. His whole body ached, more than he expected. Even though he had trained, fought, and survived worse, using incantations drained something deeper than simple stamina.

Sylara had been right. Incantations were powerful—but they demanded a lot in return.

"Alright," he said after a few minutes. "Let's talk about that fight."

Rowen groaned. "Gods, do we have to?"

"Yes," Ingrid answered instantly.

Darius smirked slightly. "We did well, but we could have done better. We need to go over what worked and what didn't before we end up in something worse than that."

Rowen exhaled dramatically but nodded. "Fine, fine. Let's hear it."

Darius leaned forward, resting his forearms on his knees. "Alright. We held our own better than we ever have before. We fought together. That was good."

Rowen nodded, rubbing his chin. "Yeah. I mean, I still move better than the rest of you, but I guess we were decent."

Ingrid nudged him hard with her foot, nearly knocking him over.

Lyra giggled, though she was still breathing evenly, focusing on her recovery.

"But there were mistakes," Darius continued. "Rowen, your Flicker Step is fast, but you lost balance twice. You were moving before your body caught up to you."

Rowen frowned but didn't argue. "Yeah. I noticed that too."

Ingrid crossed her arms. "And I still need to work on Titan's Grasp. I lost control the first time I used it."

"You adjusted well, though," Darius pointed out. "By the end, you had control over when to release it and when to hold back. That's the key to it."

Ingrid grunted but seemed satisfied.

Lyra finally opened her eyes, stretching her fingers before looking up at them. "And my magic... I wasn't careful with my charges. I shouldn't have used so much so fast."

Darius nodded. "It helped, though. Without Glacis Bastion, we would have been overwhelmed. But yeah, we have to make sure you don't burn through your magic too quickly before we even reach the next fight."

Lyra exhaled. "I'll work on better mana control."

There was a moment of quiet, each of them reflecting on their own mistakes.

Then Rowen smirked. "So, what I'm hearing is we're still pretty amazing."

Ingrid threw a small rock at his head.

He dodged at the last second, laughing.

Darius sighed but couldn't help the small grin forming on his lips. "Alright. We rest a little longer, then we move. We're not far from the Whispering Woods now."

Lyra nodded, her breathing steadier now, her magic slowly replenishing.

Ingrid adjusted her grip on her axe. Rowen leaned back, resting his arms behind his head.

They left the rock formation behind, stepping back into the corrupted land. The closer they drew to the Whispering Woods, the thicker the air seemed to become—like an unseen weight pressing against them.

They spoke less now, their senses alert.

The journey toward the Whispering Woods stretched long and

weary, the landscape shifting from barren ruins to creeping vines and coiled trees. The midday sun offered little comfort as they pressed on, and the closer they drew to the woods, the heavier the air became, thick with a presence none of them could shake.

Darius and Rowen led the way, their expressions grim. The last time they had entered these woods, they barely made it out alive.

And that same dread clawed at them now.

"I hate this place," Rowen muttered, gripping the hilt of his dagger, his usual humour absent. "Hated it the first time, hate it even more now."

Darius nodded, but he didn't respond. His mind was too focused, his gaze locked ahead on the creeping shadows between the ancient trees. The deeper they walked, the more the memories resurfaced—the contorted wolves, the unnatural silence, the thing that chased them before they ever knew what real nightmares looked like.

Now, the trees stood taller, their gnarled limbs curling toward them like skeletal fingers. The air was stagnant, suffocating, and that same unholy quiet had returned. No birds. No rustling of leaves. Just stillness.

It was exactly as they had left it.

Only worse.

The first sign of life came with a low, guttural snarl.

A beast—if it could even be called that anymore—crawled from the underbrush, its body a grotesque fusion of bone and rotting flesh, its eye sockets empty yet somehow watching them. More followed, slithering through the undergrowth, their spines protruding at odd angles, jaws slack with blackened drool dripping onto the ground, sizzling where it landed.

Darius' grip tightened on his sword. "Ready?"

Rowen cracked his neck. "Born ready."

Ingrid hefted her axe and lyra channelled her magic.

The battle began.

Darius moved first, stepping into the Phantom Edge incantation—his blade leaving behind a ghostly afterimage that struck twice. The first cut sheared clean through bone, but the second—the delayed strike—finished the job, severing the beast's head from its rotting shoulders.

Rowen flickered, his body momentarily disappearing and reappearing behind another creature, Flicker Step activating instinctively. He slashed its Achilles tendons before flipping over its hunched back, landing gracefully beside Darius. "nailed it!"

Ingrid had no interest in subtlety. She roared Titan's Grasp, her axe swelling in size as she brought it down with enough force to splinter the ground beneath them. The impact tore through multiple enemies, leaving behind only shattered bone and severed limbs.

Lyra stayed at the rear, conjuring Astra Bolts for precise shots, but when a creature lunged toward her, she spun her staff, muttering, "Frostlance!" A spear of glacial ice erupted forward, impaling the attacker before she followed up with a blast of Stormcaller, the lightning bolt searing its corpse into cinders.

They were winning.

Unlike last time, unlike when Darius and Rowen barely survived this place, they were pushing forward, carving a path through the horrors.

But it wasn't without its mistakes.

Darius miscalculated a strike, swinging his Crescent Fang too soon. The energy wave dispersed mid-air, missing its target. A creature took advantage, lunging for his throat.

Rowen had to yank him aside, nearly losing his own footing in the process. "Whoa, watch it! Guess that fancy arc slash still needs work!"

Nearby, Ingrid's Titan's Grasp slowed her movements after multiple heavy swings. One beast nearly caught her from behind, but Lyra—her instincts sharper than before—summoned Ignis Surge, sending a wave of fire in an arc that scorched the incoming enemy before it could land a fatal bite.

The battle ended with heavy breathing and sore limbs, but the difference was clear.

They didn't have to run this time or rest up too soon.

Rowen grinned, stretching out his arms. "Well, that was actually fun." Darius exhaled, watching the corpses dissolve into a black substance. "It won't be the last." They had only just entered the Whispering Woods.

And they all felt it.

The further in they went, the worse it would get. The forest pulsed around them, the same unnatural whispers drifting through the twisting trees.

"Who am I…?" "Where am I going…?" "Why…?"

Darius shuddered.

This was exactly how it felt before.

Only worse.

With weapons readied, they moved deeper into the Whispering Woods, their steps slow, cautious.

The deeper they went, the more unnatural the creatures became.

The Whispering Woods closed in around them, the air thick with something unnatural. Darius' grip tightened on his sword as the sound of snapping twigs and low growls echoed through the trees.

Then, they saw them.

A wolf, only it was no mere beast. It lurched forward, its three snarling heads snapping in different directions, their jaws lined with serrated fangs. Its fur was matted and writhing, as if something underneath it was constantly moving. Each head had milky white eyes, blind yet somehow fixated on them.

Beside it stood something that might have once been a deer, but its twisted, elongated arms dragged along the ground like grotesque tendrils. Its ribs jutted out, pulsing like they were breathing. Its head twitched erratically, its jaw opening far too wide as it let out a sound that was half a screech, half a gurgle.

For a brief moment, no one moved.

Then, the three-headed wolf lunged.

Darius dodged left, barely avoiding a lunging snap from the leftmost wolf head. He countered with a quick upward slash, but the middle head clamped onto his blade, holding it fast.

"Shit—!"

Rowen moved first. With a flicker, he vanished and reappeared behind the beast, slashing deep into its exposed spine. The wolf howled, all three heads snapping toward him at once.

It kicked out violently, its clawed feet barely missing Rowen's gut as he Flickered away again, landing back beside Ingrid.

The twisted deer moved next.

It lunged for Lyra, its elongated limbs whipping toward her like vines. She rolled to the side, raising her staff.

"Astra Bolt!" she shouted, firing a crackling blue sphere into its chest. The attack connected, but the creature absorbed it, its body rippling like liquid flesh.

Lyra's eyes widened. "It... it didn't work?"

"It adapted," Darius growled, finally wrenching his sword free from the wolf's jaws. "Aim for something vital!"

Ingrid let out a battle cry. "Titan's Grasp!"

Her axe expanded, doubling in size just as she swung down with monstrous force.

The wolf dodged, its unnatural speed making it look like it was shifting through reality itself. The ground shattered where Ingrid's strike landed, dirt and splinters flying into the air.

"Gods, I hate fast enemies!" she spat.

Rowen landed next to Darius, panting. "Alright, big guy, what's the plan?"

Darius exhaled sharply, analysing the creatures.

"The wolf is too fast to hit head-on," he said quickly. "We need to cut off its movement. Lyra—use the terrain against it!"

Lyra nodded, raising her staff. "Then let's see if this works!"

She flicked her wrist, casting Frostlance, sending a streak of ice along the forest floor. The ground froze instantly, creating a slick surface beneath the beast.

The three-headed wolf stepped forward—then slipped.

It was only for a second, but that was all Ingrid needed.

"Got you now!" she roared.

She activated Titan's Grasp again, her axe swelling three times its normal size as she brought it down with all her might.

CRACK!

The blow connected, this time landing on the wolf's middle head, splitting its skull open. Black ichor exploded outward, the wolf letting out an ear-piercing wail as it collapsed onto its knees.

But it wasn't dead.

It thrashed violently, its remaining two heads snapping wildly. Blood poured from its wound, but something else was forming—new, smaller heads trying to push through the gaping injury.

"It's regenerating!" Rowen yelled.

While they were focused on the wolf, the deer attacked.

It lunged for Ingrid, its unnatural arms stretching out and wrapping around her torso.

"Get off me!" she snarled, wrestling against the grotesque grip.

The thing tightened its hold, and for a second, it looked like it was going to crush her ribs.

But Rowen was faster.

He Flickered forward, reappearing at Ingrid's side. He slashed once, severing one of the creature's elongated arms.

The beast screeched, releasing Ingrid just as she activated Titan's Grasp a third time and swung upward, cleaving the remaining limb clean off.

"Thanks," she muttered.

Rowen grinned, his voice teasing despite his exhaustion. "Just returning the favour, big shot."

Darius saw his opening.

He gritted his teeth, feeling his energy draining, but he called upon Phantom Edge one final time.

His body blurred as he dashed forward, his sword striking through the wolf's chest.

Then, the afterimage followed.

The delayed strike tore through the wolf's last remaining heads, severing them in a clean, ghostly arc.

The beast collapsed, its form dissolving into black sludge that burned the frozen earth beneath it.

With the wolf dead, the deer staggered back, its movements becoming erratic.

Lyra saw her chance.

"One charge left…" she whispered.

She lifted her staff, summoning the power of Stormcaller.

"Now, disappear."

Lightning erupted from her other palm, crashing down upon the twisted deer in a massive, searing bolt.

The forest floor split apart, the creature letting out one last, horrific screech before it disintegrated in a burst of ash. The silence that followed was thick, almost suffocating. No cheers, no sighs of relief—just the ragged breathing of four warriors standing amidst the carnage.

Darius tightened his grip on his obsidian blade, feeling the weight of exhaustion settle deep in his bones. They had fought well, smarter even, but the further they pushed into these woods, the more unnatural the battles became.

The trees loomed taller here, their gnarled branches twisting into shapes that almost looked like reaching hands. The wind, which had been little more than a whisper before, now carried something else—low, murmuring voices that seemed to circle them, teasing the edges of their minds.

"Who am I?"

"Where am I going?"

Lyra shuddered. "The voices... they're getting louder."

Rowen wiped sweat from his brow, glancing around uneasily. "Yeah, well, so is something else," he muttered.

Darius turned to him, frowning. "What do you mean?"

Rowen crouched slightly, fingers brushing the dirt as he listened—really listened. A slow exhale left his lips as his gaze flicked to the dense foliage ahead. "Something's moving," he said. "But not like the other creatures we've fought. This is different."

Ingrid raised her axe, ready for another fight. "Could just be another beast waiting to be put down."

Rowen shook his head. "No... it's not coming toward us. It's circling us."

A cold prickle crawled up Darius' spine as he exchanged a glance with Lyra. The mage's hands hovered near her staff, her grip tight with tension but also trying to control her breathing to regain a magic charge or two.

Then, a sound—low, deep, and unsettling. Not quite a growl, not quite a whisper.

A rustling moved through the trees, just beyond their sight. It came from all around them.

Then it stopped.

Dead silence.

Not even the wind stirred.

The trees stood still now—but Darius could have sworn they had been closer just a moment ago.

The team stood frozen, waiting.

Then, with a sudden gust of frigid air, the voices in the wind rose into something more than whispers.

"You shouldn't be here."

A pulse of something unseen rippled through the forest, making Lyra flinch. Rowen clenched his jaw, one hand reaching for his second blade. Ingrid shifted her stance, steadying herself.

Darius' grip on his sword tightened.

"We keep moving," he said, his voice low but steady. "No stopping. No hesitation."

No one argued.

As they pressed deeper into the Whispering Woods, the darkness thickened around them. And though they did not turn to look, each of them felt the unmistakable sensation of unseen eyes watching them from the trees. Waiting.

CHAPTER 22

The Forest That Forgot Fear

The oppressive air of the Whispering Woods thickened around them, the unnatural silence broken only by the distant rustling of unseen things. The further they pressed in, the heavier the atmosphere became, as if the very forest itself sought to crush them under its weight.

Darius led the way, blade in hand, his fingers tightening around the hilt as his eyes scanned their surroundings. Every step forward felt more like an intrusion.

The memories of when he and Rowen first ventured here came back to him. How the air had felt wrong even back then. The way the trees had seemed to move when they weren't looking. The eldritch wolves that had given chase. And worse—the unseen entity that had hunted them, forcing them to flee.

Now, it felt like that presence had multiplied.

Rowen walked beside him, his usual smirk absent, replaced by an alert sharpness. His ears twitched at every sound. He hadn't said much since they'd crossed deeper into the woods. A part of him knew—they shouldn't be here.

Ingrid exhaled through her nose. "So, just to recap…we believe the Mawborn is the 'thing' you pair saw all that time ago, we was all also wiped out by it in black hallow."

Darius nodded. "That about sums it up."

Ingrid continued "do we actually have a plan?"

Rowen snorted. "We've got more tricks up our sleeves this time."

"Hope they're enough," Lyra muttered, gripping her staff tighter. "Because I don't like how this place feels. It's worse than black hallow."

She wasn't exaggerating. The trees stretched impossibly high now, their spiralled branches curling unnaturally like skeletal fingers reaching for them. The ground beneath their boots felt unstable, pulsing almost as if it were alive.

Then, the whispers began again.

At first, just murmurs carried on the wind. But soon, they grew louder—words spoken in a language none of them could understand, shifting and slithering in their ears.

"Who am I?"

"Where am I going?"

"Why am I here?"

Lyra flinched, shaking her head. "No. No, it's them again…"

Rowen's grip on his daggers tightened. "Guess that means we're getting close."

The ground trembled.

Darius raised a fist, signalling them to stop. His breath caught as he saw it.

Ahead, the trees gave way to a clearing, but not a natural one. The ground had been torn apart, uprooted violently as if something enormous had forced its way into the world.

And at the centre of that devastation, it stood.

It was an abomination beyond reason.

A writhing, shifting mass of mouths, interwoven in grotesque patterns, each gaping maw speaking in a different voice—some whispering, some wailing, some screaming with laughter that sent a cold shudder through their bones. Some of the mouths wept, thick tears of black ichor spilling onto the already cursed ground, evaporating into the air like a sickly mist.

The Mawborn did not walk. It pulsed, dragging itself forward in a way that defied nature, the ground beneath it warping and cracking with each unnatural movement.

Then its many eyes—because of course it had eyes, hidden between the ever-moving mouths—turned toward them.

And in an instant, the cacophony of voices became one.

A singular truth. A chorus of knowing.

"Who are you?"

Darius's breath caught in his throat.

The Mawborn was here. And it remembered them.

But the worst part wasn't the voices. It wasn't even the horror of its form.

It was the way that in its presence, their own names—who they were—felt like they were slipping away.

Rowen staggered first, his usual smirk gone, his hands clutching his head as though trying to keep his thoughts from unravelling. "No... No, I— I know who I am—" His voice wavered.

Ingrid gritted her teeth, her axe trembling in her grip. "Shut it out. Don't listen." But her own voice sounded distant, as if she were speaking through thick fog.

Lyra gasped, falling to her knees as if something had reached into her mind and started pulling. "I can't—I don't—why—" Her staff wobbled in her grip, her usually sharp eyes wide with terror.

Darius could feel it, too. His vision swam. His own name felt unfamiliar on his tongue, like an echo of something long forgotten.

This was how it won.

Not with claws or teeth—but by making them forget they existed.

He reached for his sword but froze. His body refused to move. His thoughts blurred, slipping like sand through his fingers.

Is this it?

Is this how we lose?

The voices grew louder.

"Who are you?"

"Who are you?"

"Who are you?"

Lyra screamed, gripping her head. The pressure was unbearable. Suffocating.

I need to make it stop—

She threw out her hands in sheer desperation—not with a plan, not with strategy—just sheer panic.

A wall of ice erupted between them and the Mawborn, shimmering and reflective.

And then—everything stopped.

The whispers cut off instantly.

The Mawborn froze.

Its many mouths twitched, curling inward as if recoiling from the sight before it.

Its own reflection.

For the first time, the creature hesitated.

Darius gasped, air rushing back into his lungs as the oppressive weight lifted. His mind cleared just enough to piece it together.

"The reflection." His voice was raw. He turned to Lyra, gripping her shoulder. "That's the answer. That's what Alara meant."

Lyra blinked fast, her chest rising and falling rapidly. "It's—" She swallowed, watching as the Mawborn twitched and recoiled at its own mirrored image. "It doesn't understand itself…"

Her gaze dropped to her hands, her breath hitching. Then, as the realization struck, her eyes widened.

"This is it!" she exclaimed. "This is what happened in Black Hallow!"

Darius, still rubbing his temples as his mind adjusted, looked at her sharply.

Lyra pressed forward, voice filled with sudden urgency. "I cast this back then! That's why it ran away! That's why we survived!"

Rowen staggered back to his feet, panting. "Okay—what the hell just happened?"

Darius tightened his grip on his sword, eyes locked onto the writhing mass before them. "We just found its weakness."

For the first time since the fight began—since Black Hallow—they had a chance.

Darius raised his sword. "NOW!"

The team charged.

Rowen flickered first, his body vanishing in three rapid bursts, appearing above the Mawborn as he brought both daggers down on one of the weeping mouths. The creature screeched, recoiling violently.

Ingrid's axe glowed, swelling to three times its size as she let out a roar and brought it crashing down. The impact sent shockwaves through the ground, splitting flesh and bone-like matter apart.

Lyra raised her staff. "Stormcaller!"

Lightning crashed down, striking the Mawborn's mass, sending its tendrils spasming and writhing.

Darius sprinted forward, greatsword raised. He could feel his incantations burning in his veins, but he had one shot.

"Crescent Fang!"

The energy arc ripped forward, cleaving through one of the larger, grotesque heads that had been whispering the loudest.

The Mawborn howled.

It was injured—but it wasn't dead.

And worse—it was angry.

The voices screeched, overlapping in a horrible cacophony. The ground beneath them split as dark tendrils shot forth, one nearly impaling Darius before he rolled aside.

A second mouth formed, stretching open with jagged rows of teeth—

And bit down on Rowen.

"ROWEN!"

His scream was muffled as he struggled, caught between the gnashing teeth.

Lyra's eyes burned. She didn't hesitate.

"GLACIS BASTION!"

The ice wall erupted, spikes blasting outward—the frozen shards speared into the Mawborn's flesh, forcing it to release Rowen in a howl of agony.

He collapsed to the ground, coughing blood.

Darius didn't hesitate. He moved before thinking, before anything else could happen.

He ran toward the creature—toward its core—and swung his sword with everything he had.

"PHANTOM EDGE!"

The afterimage of his strike lingered in the air for a second longer—then both slashes connected at once.

The Mawborn shrieked, its voices overlapping in a mind-shattering cacophony. Its entire form rippled, mouths distorting and twisting in unnatural directions, some stretching impossibly wide as if to consume the very air around them. The moment Darius's Phantom Edge landed, black ichor splattered across the ground, sizzling like acid as it ate through the corrupted earth.

But it didn't fall.

If anything, the Mawborn seemed to be adapting.

Tendrils shot forth again, faster, more precise. One lashed across Darius's chest, sending him skidding back with a grunt. Another wrapped around Lyra's ankle, dragging her toward an open, slobbering maw.

Rowen, still gasping from his near-death moments ago, flickered—but it was slower, sloppy. His body reappeared mid-dash, and he stumbled.

"NO!" Ingrid roared, moving before she even thought.

The Mawborn lunged.

Rowen wasn't fast enough.

The massive, gnashing mouth closed around him.

The air went still.

Darius felt his stomach drop as blood splattered onto the ground. Too much blood.

Lyra screamed, her magic surging wildly, uncontrolled. Ingrid froze.

No—no, this wasn't— Rowen. Rowen. Rowen.

The Mawborn reeled back, its mouths convulsing—then spat Rowen out like discarded meat.

He hit the ground in a crumpled heap, unmoving.

"Rowen—" Darius moved first, but Ingrid was faster.

She didn't check if he was breathing. Didn't hesitate.

Because something inside her had already snapped.

Her grip on her axe tightened until her knuckles went white. Her breath came out in short, ragged bursts— shallow, animalistic.

And then she screamed.

Titan's Grasp ignited.

But this time—it was more. Bigger. Heavier. The axe grew, and grew, and kept growing, towering in her hands, the weight should have crushed her arms—but she didn't falter.

She swung.

The first impact sent a shockwave through the battlefield.

The second shattered a dozen of the Mawborn's writhing limbs.

The third forced the monstrosity back for the first time.

Darius had never seen Ingrid this way. This furious. This powerful.

And she wasn't stopping.

Another swing—the axe nearly double its usual size, crushing into the Mawborn's core, forcing it back as its voices began to distort into panicked shrieks.

It was losing ground.

"Ingrid—" Lyra gasped, watching in awe.

"DO IT!" Ingrid bellowed, voice raw, her muscles straining to hold her axe up for another final strike.

Darius didn't need to be told twice.

He charged forward, his sword glowing with unnatural energy. This time—it wasn't hesitation. It wasn't fear.

It was certainty.

"CRESCENT FANG!"

The energy arc ripped through the Mawborn's centre—its true core—splitting through layers of twisting, gaping mouths.

For the first time—the creature screamed in true agony.

The voices shattered.

The tendrils collapsed.

And then—the Mawborn stopped.

A final, guttural wail rang through the Whispering Woods— And then its body collapsed inward, shrinking, imploding into itself—the mouths closing one by one, before finally...

Nothing remained.

Silence.

For a moment, no one moved.

No one spoke.

Then—a groan.

"...Okay, that sucked."

Everyone's heads snapped toward the source.

Rowen.

Still on the ground, covered in way too much blood, grinning weakly as he looked up at them.

Lyra choked on a laugh, relief crashing over her like a wave.

Ingrid?

She punched him in the arm. Hard.

"OW! Gods, Ingrid, I literally almost died—"

"Next time," she growled, glaring at him, "stay out of its mouth."

Darius let out a breath, his shoulders sagging.

They had won.

The Mawborn was dead.

But as he looked around at his battered, bleeding friends—he knew.

This war?

This was only the beginning, but for now The forest felt different.

No whispers.

No shifting shadows.

No unseen creatures lurking between the trees, waiting for them to falter.

For the first time since stepping into the Whispering Woods, the oppressive weight in the air lifted. It was subtle at first—just a change in the wind, the way the leaves rustled naturally instead of ominously. Then, as the minutes passed, golden shafts of sunlight broke through the thick canopy above, spilling warmth onto the damp earth.

The woods were… alive again.

The realization settled over them slowly, each of them standing there, taking in the unfamiliar calm. It was over. The Mawborn was gone.

Lyra exhaled first, a slow, disbelieving breath as she hugged her staff close.

Darius finally lowered his sword, staring at the now-empty space where the Mawborn had been. His heartbeat was still pounding from the battle, but something else took over now—relief. The quiet, bitter kind.

They had won.

And they were still standing.

Darius was the first to suggest it—setting up a campsite despite it being far from nightfall.

No one argued.

Their bodies ached, bruises and cuts covering every inch of them, exhaustion settling into their bones like iron chains. They had no energy left to push forward—no reason to.

The battle was won.

For the first time in weeks, they had earned a moment to breathe.

Rowen, pale but still smirking, sank against a tree, cradling his ribs. "So, I'm just gonna say it—we should kill terrifying, reality-breaking eldritch horrors more often. Because this? This sun? These birds? This is nice."

Ingrid sat beside him, arms crossed, her expression unreadable. She hadn't looked at him since the battle ended.

"Yeah," she muttered, "real nice."

Her voice was thick with something—relief? Frustration? Maybe both.

Rowen noticed.

For once, he didn't joke.

He shifted slightly, glancing up at her through the mess of his bloodied hair. "You're still pissed at me, aren't you?"

Her jaw tightened, but she didn't deny it.

Rowen sighed, running a shaky hand through his hair. "Look, I really thought that was it. For a second, I—" He hesitated, voice quieter now. "I wasn't scared of dying. I was just... pissed that you would be upset."

Ingrid's gaze snapped to him.

Rowen chuckled nervously, shifting his weight. "I mean—I didn't want Lyra and Darius upset either, obviously. But you—you'd be the most dramatic about it. Probably punch my corpse or something."

He expected her to roll her eyes, scoff, something sarcastic.

Instead—

She hugged him.

Not in anger. Not out of pity.

Just pure, raw relief.

Rowen froze, eyes wide. His arms hovered awkwardly, unsure if he was allowed to hug back.

Darius and Lyra, a few feet away, both caught the moment—but neither said a word.

Darius just smirked, turning his attention to the fire they had started building. Lyra, her exhaustion evident, just rested her head against her staff with a knowing smile.

Rowen finally exhaled, his shoulders relaxing as he leaned into the hug slightly. "So, does this mean you'll be nicer to me now?"

Ingrid pulled back just enough to glare at him. "No."

Then she shoved him back against the tree—gently this time.

Rowen didn't get much of a break after that.

Once Ingrid composed herself, she immediately took charge of treating his injuries—which, unsurprisingly, meant pain.

She wasn't gentle.

Rowen winced as she pressed a cloth against his busted ribs, rubbing in some bitter-smelling ointment. "You know, you're allowed to be delicate, Ingrid. Just a thought."

She ignored him. "Hold still."

"I am still—OW! Gods, Ingrid—are you trying to fix me or kill me?!"

"Both," she muttered.

Rowen groaned, resting his head back. "This is punishment, isn't it? Because I almost died."

"No," Ingrid said evenly. "It's because you do keep almost dying." Rowen grinned despite the pain. "Aww, you do care." Ingrid scowled. "Shut up and let me fix you before I change my mind." Rowen relented, letting her work. He could feel her hands shaking slightly, but he didn't comment on it. If she needed to pretend she wasn't worried—he'd let her. And maybe, just maybe—he'd stop pretending too.

Morning came slowly, the golden rays of the sun filtering through the dense leaves of the Whispering Woods, now devoid of its haunting presence. It wasn't the usual warmth that woke them, nor the gentle chirping of birds that had miraculously returned to the forest.

It was the sound of metal boots clanking against the dirt.

Darius stirred first, his instincts kicking in as his hand immediately reached for his sword. Rowen let out a groggy, "Gods, please tell me we're not fighting already."

Ingrid was already on her feet, her hand gripping her axe, eyes narrowed toward the direction of the approaching soldiers.

Within moments, a group of armoured knights stepped into view, their tabards bearing the insignia of the kingdom.

The lead knight, a gruff-looking man with a thick scar running down his cheek, raised a hand for his men to halt. He gave the group a once-over, clearly not expecting them to be alive.

"Darius," the knight addressed, his tone stiff, but there was a flicker of relief in his gaze. "The king sent us to search for you and your party after the land seemed to return to normal yesterday." His expression darkened. "We did not know whether we'd be finding bodies or survivors."

Rowen, still half-asleep, smirked as he stretched. "Well, bad news for the undertaker—we're all still breathing. Even the doomed hero over here."

Darius rolled his eyes. "Good morning to you too, Rowen."

"Best morning I've had in a long time," Rowen shot back, grinning. "Mainly because I'm still having mornings."

The knight exhaled, his stiff demeanour softening slightly at their banter. "His Majesty wishes to see you all at the castle. You have done the kingdom a great service. We are to escort you back safely, where you may continue to rest and recover."

Darius nodded, sheathing his sword. "Then let's not keep him waiting."

The group moved slowly, exhaustion still lingering in their muscles. The knights had brought wagons, likely expecting to carry the bodies of fallen heroes rather than the living, breathing, victorious warriors before them.

Ingrid crossed her arms, nodding toward Rowen. "You're riding in the wagon. No arguments." Rowen opened his mouth—whether to object or make a smart remark, no one knew—before Ingrid narrowed her eyes. He huffed dramatically. "Fine. But only because I like the view from up here." He lounged back on the cart, clearly enjoying being catered to, while Ingrid rode beside him, keeping an eye on his injuries. Darius, Lyra, and the remaining knights walked alongside the wagon, the journey back feeling lighter than any before.

The capital was still a few hours away, giving them time to simply be. Lyra glanced at the soldiers, then at the others. "So… when we get back, does that mean another feast?"

Rowen, from the wagon, shot her a lazy grin. "Damn right it does. And I, for one, plan to be waited on like the hero I am."

"You mean like the injured idiot you are," Ingrid corrected.

Rowen waved a hand. "Details."

Darius smirked, shaking his head. The weight of the prophecy, of their journey—it was still there. But for now, for this moment, they were simply friends sharing a victory.

The kingdom was safe. For now but as the castle towers came into view on the horizon, they knew—their journey was far from over.

CHAPTER 23

The Price of Peace

It had been ten days since they returned from the Whispering Woods, victorious but battered. Life in the capital had moved on, but Darius and his team had been anything but idle.

Ingrid had spent every single day visiting Rowen at Marisol's infirmary, her presence a constant even as she pretended it was just out of duty rather than concern. But when Rowen was finally well enough to stand, Ingrid dragged him to the training grounds, forcing him into daily sparring sessions. Her only reasoning? "That situation never happens again."

Rowen, still sore, still grumbling, had little choice in the matter. But even he knew she was right. He played along, grinning through bruises, but with each swing, each dodge, each gritted-teeth moment of determination—he got better. Stronger.

Lyra had buried herself in the library, training her mind instead of her body. The arcane texts of the royal archives had become her world, page after page filled with ancient knowledge. She still trained with her magic, of course, but Alara was absent—vanished from the castle after only two days of their return.

Darius, meanwhile, had spent his rest days differently. He had been seen more and more with Seraphina, their bond growing closer—so much so that King Aldric had started noticing.

And now, on the tenth day, As Darius and Seraphina rounded a corner toward the throne room, their conversation died at the sight ahead.

A familiar figure, Alara, strode through the halls—her otherworldly presence unmistakable. But this time, she wasn't alone.

Beside her walked a man Darius had never seen before.

He was tall, lean, and moved with a casual arrogance, hands resting lazily at his sides. His dark crimson vest stood out against the muted tones of the castle, and the wicked metal whip coiled at his belt gleamed in the torchlight.

Even from a distance, Darius could see the smirk tugging at his lips, the cocky confidence of a man who knew exactly what he was doing at all times.

"Who's that?" Darius muttered under his breath. Seraphina's brow furrowed. "I don't know." They both watched as Alara and the stranger disappeared beyond the throne room doors. The King's chambers. Darius and Seraphina exchanged a glance. Whatever was happening—whatever Alara had been doing these past days—it was about to change everything.

Darius and Seraphina lingered for a moment outside the throne room doors, exchanging a glance.

"What do you think that was about?" Seraphina asked, crossing her arms.

Darius exhaled. "I don't know. But Alara disappearing for days, then suddenly showing up with him…" He gestured toward the door where the mysterious rogue had vanished. "It's not a coincidence."

Seraphina hummed in agreement, then tilted her head toward the hallway. "Come on. Let's go find the others. If something big is happening, we should all be there."

They found Rowen and Ingrid exactly where Darius expected—at the training grounds.

Rowen was on his back in the dirt, grinning despite the fresh welt across his arm. Ingrid stood over him, axe balanced over one shoulder, hands on her hips, smirking.

"You getting slower, Rowen?" Ingrid teased.

Rowen groaned, wiping sweat from his forehead. "Slower? Me? I let you hit me. You've been so tense lately, figured I'd throw you a confidence boost."

Ingrid snorted, offering him a hand. "That so?"

"Absolutely." Rowen took her hand and let her pull him up before turning to Darius and Seraphina, flashing them a grin. "Ah, the lovebirds join us! Had enough moonlit strolls yet?"

Darius gave him a dry look, but Seraphina, to his surprise, only smirked. "Not yet."

Rowen coughed. "Oh."

Ingrid snickered, clapping him on the back as he tried to recover.

Lyra joined them moments later, arms wrapped around an armful of books, her robe covered in ink smudges. "Oh, good. You're all here. I found something interesting—" She paused, eyes narrowing at Rowen, who was clearly about to make a comment. "Don't."

Rowen grinned but held up his hands. "I was just going to say, you look like you had a thrilling morning in the library."

Lyra rolled her eyes. "More thrilling than whatever excuse you have for lying in the dirt, I'm sure."

"Listen, sometimes training means getting hit," Rowen said, dusting himself off. "I let Ingrid have her moment—"

"She made you have it," Lyra corrected. Rowen huffed. "Details."

Seraphina, watching all of this with a soft smile, leaned closer to Darius. "They really do feel like a family," she murmured.

Darius nodded, feeling an unfamiliar warmth in his chest. "Yeah. They do."

The moment was cut short by the arrival of a knight in polished armour, his heavy boots clanking against the stone as he approached.

"Ah, here we go," Rowen sighed dramatically. "Your Royal Highness, you're being summoned again, aren't you?" He glanced at Seraphina with a grin. "I swear, Ingrid's drinking buddy—er, I mean, your father—has got to let you breathe at some point."

Seraphina was already stepping forward when the knight cleared his throat. "Actually," he said, "I'm here for Darius and his party. You are all summoned to the throne room—immediately." The joking atmosphere snapped into seriousness.

Darius stiffened. "All of us?"

The knight nodded. "By order of the king."

The five exchanged glances.

"Welp," Rowen sighed, rolling his shoulders. "Guess we're getting promoted. Or executed."

"Rowen," Ingrid deadpanned.

"Just saying."

Darius exhaled. "Let's go."

As they followed the knight toward the throne room, the weight of the summons settled over them. Something was coming.

The grand doors of the throne room swung open, the heavy wood groaning as Darius and his party stepped inside. The air was thick with importance, an unspoken weight pressing down on them as their boots echoed against the polished marble floor.

At the far end of the chamber, King Aldric sat upon his ornate throne, his golden crown catching the flickering torchlight. He was not alone.

To his right, a handful of advisors, whispering amongst themselves. To his left, a knight clad in golden armour, standing stoic and unmoving, like a sentinel carved from steel.

And just off to the side—Alara.

But it wasn't her that caught Darius's attention.

It was the stranger beside her.

The man stood with an air of effortless confidence, arms crossed, his posture relaxed despite standing in the presence of the king. He wore a long, dark leather coat, its hem frayed at the edges, with a red sash tied loosely around his waist. Beneath the coat, a black fitted tunic hugged his lean but athletic frame, and his boots were worn and scuffed, the kind made for traveling—or running.

His hair was dark chestnut brown, slightly wavy, falling in loose strands over his forehead. A thin scar ran just below his right eye, a subtle imperfection on an otherwise sharp, fox-like face. His most striking feature, however, were his eyes—a piercing golden-amber, bright and watchful, like those of a predator that thrived in the dark.

For a brief moment, those amber eyes locked onto Darius—and in them, there was something electric. Almost excited.

Darius brushed it off.

As they approached the throne, the group dropped to one knee out of respect, their heads bowed.

Seraphina moved past them, stepping up the three small steps that led to the throne's platform, standing beside her father.

When she spoke, her voice was clear and authoritative, yet with a quiet warmth.

"My king," she addressed him formally now, "the heroes of the prophecy have arrived, as you requested."

The tension in the room thickened.

King Aldric studied them silently, his keen eyes sweeping over each of them. Then, he finally spoke.

"Rise."

As they stood, all eyes were now on them, And Darius could feel it.

King Aldric leaned forward in his throne, the flickering torches casting sharp shadows over his face. His gaze was steady as it swept over the four warriors before him.

"First," he began, his voice firm yet warm, "allow me to extend my gratitude—and my apologies. It has been ten days since your victory over the Mawborn, and though I should have spoken to you sooner, I have been consumed with matters of great urgency."

He paused, glancing between them. "But know this—the land breathes easier because of you. The corruption is fading, the people can rebuild, and, for the first time in far too long... we are safe."

A palpable sense of relief filled the air.

Rowen crossed his arms, a smirk tugging at his lips. "Not bad for a bunch of dead men walking, huh?"

Ingrid exhaled, shaking her head. "Feels... weird, doesn't it? No immediate threat looming over us."

Lyra glanced at Darius, smiling softly. "We actually did it."

Darius, however, didn't share in their relief—not fully. His fingers twitched at his side, his mind already running ahead. The Mawborn was gone. But it was only the first.

And the prophecy still loomed over him.

King Aldric's next words were proof enough of that.

"You have passed the first test of your prophecy, Darius," he continued. "The first of the demons has fallen. But we cannot pretend we were without doubt." His voice grew heavier. "There were those who feared... that you would never make it this far. That your destined failure would come sooner rather than later."

Darius stiffened, jaw clenching.

Rowen's smirk vanished. "Well. That's one way to kill the mood."

The king exhaled, his expression unreadable. "None of us know when your failure will come. But you have delayed it, and for that, we are in your debt."

Darius said nothing.

Then, King Aldric gestured toward the stranger, the one who had been standing beside Alara.

"You are not the only ones fighting against the darkness," the king stated. "This is Kastor. He hails from across the Azure Sea, from the distant land of Drakmyr."

Darius barely heard the name before his thoughts clicked together.

Alara's words. Her warning. Her cryptic words hinted at travelling to Sylara's land.

His gut sank.

They weren't done here.

Kastor stepped forward, his golden-amber eyes glinting like a flame catching the wind. He grinned lazily, as if the whole situation amused him. "Kastor Vale," he introduced himself with an easy nod.

Darius narrowed his eyes.

"Drakmyr is not like our kingdom," Aldric explained. "It is a vast land made up of several regions, each ruled differently. Sylara belongs to the region of Eryndell. Kastor hails from Dhalmora."

"Different lands, different rulers," Kastor added, his voice edged with dry amusement. "Not the 'one king, one throne' type of deal you've got going here."

Aldric ignored the comment. "Word of your success against the Mawborn travelled quickly. And with it came the news that Drakmyr, too, is in danger. Another demon lurks there—one that must be slain, just as the Mawborn was."

The king's eyes hardened.

"Darius," he said gravely. "In three days' time, you will sail to Drakmyr to answer that call. And..." the king looked towards his daughter "you shall go in my stead to fulfil my duties in Drakmyr also."

The room stilled.

Seraphina, who had remained silent, nodded immediately. "I am ready your majesty."

Aldric sighed, already anticipating her words. "I expected as much. You will accompany Darius to Drakmyr, but you will not be traveling together." He gestured to a figure clad in golden armour.

"This is Sir Alden Greaves. He will accompany you my dear to Eryndell, where you will meet my dear old friend King Theron Valcarys."

Darius barely had time to absorb that before Kastor interrupted with a casual smirk.

"And as for you lot," he said, pointing at Darius and his group, "you'll be coming with me to Dhalmora to meet King Marek Solvann."

A weighted silence followed.

Rowen let out a low whistle. "Okay. So. Just to recap... we're hopping on a boat, crossing the sea, and fighting another demon?"

"That about sums it up," Kastor said.

Lyra frowned, gripping her staff. "We just finished barely surviving the last one, and now we have to leave the continent entirely?"

Darius exhaled slowly.

He should have seen this coming.

Seraphina, however, was unshaken.

"I have known for some time that we might have to take this fight beyond our own borders," she admitted. "Sylara's arrival only confirmed it."

Aldric leaned back in his throne. "You have three days to prepare. There will be a feast tonight to celebrate the battle won against the Mawborn. Rest. Enjoy your victory while you can."

The weight of the king's words hung heavy as the four heroes were dismissed.

As they step towards the massive doors, the realization sank in.

"We're really leaving," Ingrid muttered.

Rowen let out a dramatic sigh. "Guess that means we've got three days to learn how to not get seasick."

Lyra blinked. "Wait—you get seasick?"

Rowen scowled. "I don't know, Lyra! I've never been on a damn boat before!"

As the grand doors of the throne room shut behind them, the tension that had weighed on their shoulders finally began to lift—if only slightly. The hallway stretched ahead, sunbeams filtering through the grand windows, casting warm patches of light along the stone floor.

Rowen was the first to break the silence, exhaling dramatically as he stretched his arms behind his head. "So, we're basically world-famous now. We kill one demon, and suddenly we're international heroes." He smirked. "Think that means we'll get free drinks in Drakmyr?"

"I think that means we'll be walking into more danger than we can even imagine," Lyra muttered, adjusting her staff on her back.

"I like my version better," Rowen said with a shrug.

Ingrid snorted. "Yeah? Let's see if you still like it when we're up to our necks in whatever eldritch horrors this land has lurking about."

Lyra hummed in thought. "Drakmyr... I wonder if their magic is different. I've never studied foreign sorcery before. There could be entire schools of magic I don't even know about."

Rowen threw an arm around her shoulders, grinning. "Oh no, Lyra's excited. That means we're definitely gonna be up against something terrifying."

She groaned, shoving him off. "You act like I go looking for trouble."

"You do," Darius, Ingrid, and Rowen said in unison.

Lyra huffed, but there was a hint of amusement in her expression. "Well, I wouldn't have to if you three weren't constantly diving headfirst into it."

As the conversation carried on, the group walked through the castle halls, the air around them lighter despite the storm on the horizon. But as they neared the staircase leading toward their chambers, Darius slowed his steps, letting the others pass him.

His thoughts were still turning.

Leaving. Drakmyr. Another war. Another demon.

He had fought for this land, suffered for it, nearly died for it—was still meant to die for it. And now, he was being asked to fight for another. He wasn't angry, not really. But the weight of it settled heavily in his chest.

He didn't notice Seraphina had fallen behind with him until she nudged his arm lightly.

"You're thinking too much," she said softly.

He glanced at her, exhaling. "I just thought I'd be fighting to save my home. Not... crossing the sea to fight someone else's war."

Seraphina studied him, then tilted her head slightly. "Isn't that what heroes do?"

He scoffed a quiet laugh. "I wouldn't know."

Her expression softened. "You'll do the right thing. You always do."

She didn't linger for an answer, didn't push the conversation further. Instead, she stepped ahead, joining the others as they disappeared around the next corridor.

Darius stayed where he was, just for a moment longer. He turned his gaze toward a nearby window, overlooking the capital.

The land was healing. The air was clearer. The people were rebuilding.

He had helped make that happen, and now, he had to leave it behind.

A deep exhale left him as he ran a hand through his hair.

Three days.

That was all the time he had left before they departed.

Locking that thought away for now, Darius straightened his shoulders and followed after his friends. The feast awaited them.

CHAPTER 24

The Night We Were Whole

The grand hall was alive with laughter, the clinking of goblets, and the scent of roasted meats and spiced wines. Lavish tapestries of past victories adorned the walls, flickering in the candlelight, while long banquet tables overflowed with food. It was a sight of abundance—a stark contrast to the bleak, harrowing journey that had led them here.

Darius and his party stepped into the hall together, their eyes widening slightly at the sheer spread before them. Plates of golden-brown Hearthland Hunter's Pie, thick-crusted and steaming, sat beside platters of Stormbrewer's Stew, its rich, fragrant aroma curling through the air. Roasted boar glistened under a honey-mead glaze, skewered alongside fire-charred vegetables, their edges blackened just enough to add that perfect crispness.

Rowen whistled. "Now this is how you celebrate victory."

They moved toward their seats, and the moment Rowen sat down, he wasted no time grabbing a flagon of mead. "To surviving a literal eldritch nightmare," he declared, raising it high.

"To still having all our memories," Lyra added, lifting her goblet of honeyed wine.

"To the next one we're gonna kill," Ingrid said, already pulling a plate of skewers toward her.

Darius smirked. "To not dying yet."

A round of laughter rippled through the group, and they clinked their drinks together before diving into the feast.

It wasn't long before the table descended into its usual mix of banter and friendly arguments.

Rowen, ever the menace, leaned over and dramatically inhaled the scent of Ingrid's plate. His nose instantly crinkled in disgust. "Oh no. No, no, no. You did not get those things again."

Ingrid, grinning wickedly, popped another Frostbitten Brinefruit into her mouth and chewed with satisfaction. "You're still weak, Rowen."

Rowen turned to Darius and Lyra in exaggerated betrayal. "She's eating them again." Darius shook his head. "I don't know how she does it."

"I bet she doesn't even like them," Rowen accused. "She just eats them for the drama."

"Oh, I love them," Ingrid said, popping another into her mouth with a smug expression.

Across the table, Lyra was less focused on the horrors of Ingrid's food choices and more on the pastries stacked before her. Spiced apple tarts, honey-drizzled cream puffs, soft cinnamon cakes— it was a dream.

Unfortunately, it was a dream interrupted.

A knight, polished armour gleaming in the candlelight, leaned over slightly and offered a charming smile. "A lady as beautiful as yourself deserves the finest dessert in the kingdom."

Lyra, mid-bite of a flaky golden tart, froze.

Darius, watching from across the table, bit down on his own grin. Rowen, on the other hand, nearly howled with laughter. Lyra slowly, carefully, placed her pastry back onto her plate, her face on fire. "Uh…"

The knight continued, clearly enjoying her flustered expression. "Would you allow me to bring you another, my lady?"

Rowen leaned in, elbowing her lightly. "Yeah, Lyra. Let the man bring you another."

Lyra kicked him under the table.

The king himself was present at the feast, seated at the head of the hall, surrounded by his most trusted knights and advisors. He had remained composed for most of the evening, exchanging words of wisdom with high-ranking officials.

Until—

"Wait. You're eating them?" Rowen's voice cut across the table.

Everyone turned their heads.

King Aldric, ruler of the land, sat calmly at the far end of the table… *eating a Frostbitten Brinefruit.*

Rowen looked shaken.

Darius actually stared.

Even Lyra, who was still recovering from her unwanted flirting, paused.

Only Ingrid grinned. She leaned back in her chair, victorious.

"Finally. A man of culture."

The king took another bite, unbothered. "They're an acquired taste."

Rowen buried his face in his hands. "I can't believe the king likes them."

One of the nearby knights visibly grimaced. "Your Majesty, that's… highly unorthodox."

Aldric smirked, taking a sip of his wine. "So is drinking with my daughter's companions and heroes. And yet, here we are."

Across the table, Seraphina's gaze flickered to Darius. He had been quiet, enjoying the feast but never letting his guard fully down.

With a small smile, she cut a piece of the spiced berry cake in front of her and slid it onto his plate. "Here."

Darius looked up, confused. "What?"

"You don't eat sweets," she said, raising an eyebrow. "But I *know* you'll like this one."

Darius huffed. "I don't do sweets."

Seraphina simply held his gaze.

Darius stared at the cake. Then, reluctantly, he picked up his fork.

One bite.

Seraphina smirked. "Well?"

He *hated* that she was right. "…It's fine."

She chuckled, taking a bite of her own. "Of course it is."

Darius shook his head, but his lips twitched up despite himself.

As the feast carried on, the warmth of celebration filled the air. Laughter mixed with music as a few knights challenged Ingrid to a drinking contest—one they quickly regretted. Rowen engaged in animated conversation with two kitchen staff, trying to bribe them for extra stew "for research purposes."

Darius exhaled, watching his friends enjoy themselves.

But amid the lively atmosphere, his gaze drifted to the corner of the hall where Kastor sat alone.

The man was leaning back in his chair, enjoying his meal with a detached ease that stood in contrast to the revelry around him. His sharp eyes occasionally flicked across the room, studying the people, analysing them the same way Darius might assess an opponent on the battlefield.

Darius debated for a moment before making his way over.

Kastor noticed him approach but didn't move—just smirked slightly and tapped a gloved finger against the rim of his goblet. "Didn't think the great Hero of Prophecy would bother with the likes of me."

Darius pulled out a chair and sat across from him. "Figured we should talk, considering I'm supposed to be following you across the sea in a few days."

Kastor's lips curled up at the corner, but there was something unreadable in his expression. "Smart."

A brief silence settled between them. Darius wasn't sure why, but something about Kastor put him on edge. Not in the way an enemy did—more like a gambler at a card table whose game he couldn't quite figure out.

"You haven't said much about your homeland," Darius finally said, keeping his tone neutral.

Kastor exhaled through his nose, swirling the drink in his goblet. "What is there to say? Drakmyr is… unlike your land. It's vast, harsh, divided among regions that rarely agree on anything. But it is my home." His voice softened slightly, almost with affection. "And I'd rather not see it turn into something unrecognizable."

Darius frowned. "Because of the demon?"

Kastor's fingers tightened on the stem of his goblet for just a fraction of a second before he let out a quiet chuckle. "That's the word for it, yeah."

Darius noted the evasion. He's hiding something.

"And yet," Kastor continued, "I've never seen it. Not fully. Only what it leaves behind." He took a sip of his drink before looking at Darius, the flickering candlelight casting shadows across his face. "I've heard the whispers, though. Some say it speaks to them. Promising things. It's got its claws in the minds of men long before they even see it."

Darius's stomach twisted slightly at that. The Mawborn spoke too. It stole memory. What if this thing does something worse?

He didn't realize his fists had clenched until he forced them to relax.

Kastor studied him, as if taking measure. "Makes you wonder, doesn't it? If you can win."

Darius narrowed his eyes. "I didn't come this far to fail."

Kastor smiled—not mocking, but not entirely kind either. "Good. Let's hope you're right."

While Darius had been speaking with Kastor, Seraphina sat beside her father, the king, watching the feast with quiet amusement.

Until he spoke.

"You've been spending a great deal of time with the hero."

Seraphina glanced at him from the corner of her eye, taking a measured sip of her wine. "You say that as though it's unexpected."

Aldric studied her for a long moment before shaking his head. "A princess should marry a noble. A prince. Someone of equal standing. That has always been the way of things."

Seraphina's grip on her goblet tightened slightly, but she said nothing.

"And yet," the king continued, softer now, "we both know that Darius is not just anyone."

She sighed, placing her drink down. "You wouldn't stop me. Even if I chose him."

The king let out a deep exhale, rubbing his temple. "No. Because the Hero of Prophecy isn't bound by our rules. But you, Seraphina…" His voice lowered. "You know what his fate is. You know what the prophecy says. You know how this story ends."

Something inside her coiled.

Of course she knew.

Darius was destined to die.

A doomed hero, a cycle bound to break him. To love him was to love a future ghost.

But even knowing that… she couldn't stop herself.

The king watched her for a moment longer before shaking his head. "Steady your heart, my daughter," he murmured. "Or it will break."

Seraphina stood. "Excuse me."

She made her way across the hall, catching Darius just as he finished speaking with Kastor.

"Mind if I steal him away?" she asked lightly.

Kastor gave her an amused look before lazily lifting his goblet in mock surrender. "He's all yours."

Seraphina led Darius to the far end of the hall, where the warmth of the feast felt distant.

Darius glanced at her, taking in her expression. "You alright?"

She hesitated. Then, "You're leaving soon."

Darius exhaled. "I know."

She crossed her arms. "I knew this would happen. I knew you wouldn't stay here forever, but…" She looked away for a moment. "I thought I had more time."

His chest tightened.

Seraphina shook her head, stepping closer. "I… I don't know how to do this."

Darius raised an eyebrow. "Do what?"

She huffed a quiet laugh, looking almost embarrassed. "Admit things."

Darius hesitated before speaking. "Then don't."

She looked at him, confused.

He offered her a small, almost helpless smile. "Just… show me."

There was a pause.

And then she stepped forward.

The space between them vanished as Seraphina cupped his face in her hands, fingers threading into his hair, and kissed him.

Then, his hands found her waist, pulling her closer, returning the kiss with everything he had.

There was no prophecy in that moment. No fate. No death hanging over his head.

Just her. Just now.

When they pulled apart, she rested her forehead against his, eyes half-lidded, voice barely above a whisper.

"Come with me."

Darius nodded, his voice caught somewhere between breath and heartbeat. "Anywhere."

She took his hand—fingers lacing with his—and gently led him from the edge of the hall. The warmth and chaos of the feast faded behind them, replaced by quiet corridors and the soft glow of lanterns. Neither spoke, but something passed between them in every glance, every step. A shared understanding. A choice.

When they reached his chamber door, she paused, turning to look at him. Her expression wasn't uncertain—it was full of intent, of trust, and something deeper than longing.

He opened the door, and she followed him in without hesitation.

Inside, the world narrowed to the gentle hush of closing doors and the flickering of a fire in the hearth. Darius set his sword aside for the first time in days. Seraphina's fingers brushed his cheek, trailing to his chest as she stepped into his arms again.

There was no rush, no urgency. Only the quiet unravelling of walls built too high, too long. They moved together in soft touches and whispered laughter. She pulled him down beside her, and he went willingly—his fate forgotten for just one night.

They didn't speak of tomorrow.

Tonight was theirs.

And as the fire crackled gently, the shadows danced along the stone walls, bearing witness to something rare and real.

Love, blooming in the eye of the storm.

As the evening wore on, the revelry in the hall slowly began to wind down.

Kastor was the first to leave, slipping away from his corner with a nod only the king seemed to notice. Aldric raised his goblet in quiet acknowledgment, their silent exchange unnoticed by the rest of the hall.

Soon after, the king stood, his advisors rising with him. He placed a hand briefly on Seraphina's now-empty chair, then turned to his remaining guests with a warm, satisfied expression.

"My friends," he said, "let the night be remembered."

With that, he and his royal guard departed, their golden armour glinting faintly in the firelight as they disappeared into the castle's deeper halls.

Eventually, only a few remained.

Rowen was still at the table, halfway through another helping of roasted venison, looking like he might just attempt to devour the entire table if left unchecked.

Ingrid rolled her eyes and stood, then promptly yanked him up by the back of his tunic. "Alright, menace. You've eaten enough to feed a small kingdom."

"But the honey-roasted potatoes—" he started, reaching for one more bite.

She groaned and dragged him away, his protesting words muffled by a mouthful of half-chewed stew. "You're going to explode in your sleep."

Their laughter faded with their footsteps, echoing gently through the high-arched halls.

And then, quiet.

The feast hall stood still, lit by the last of the candlelight and the glowing embers in the hearths. Empty platters and goblets reflected the golden hues, remnants of a celebration hard-won. Trays of half-eaten desserts remained abandoned, untouched but not forgotten.

It was a room that had known countless royal banquets—but tonight had been different.

Tonight, it had held heroes.

The echo of laughter lingered like a memory. The fire crackled softly, as if content. Outside, the moon hung full and calm over the capital, bathing the land in its silvery glow.

And within the castle walls, for the first time in what felt like an age…

There was peace.

Hard-earned, but real.

And for tonight—that was enough.

CHAPTER 25

When Strangers Start to Laugh

The road stretched long beneath the hooves of their horses, winding through rolling green hills and dense woodland, the scent of pine and fresh earth filling the air. The last few days had seen their homeland return to its natural beauty—wild and untamed yet no longer corrupted by the eldritch horrors that had plagued it.

Birdsong filled the morning air, a stark contrast to the oppressive silence that once clung to these lands. The rivers ran clear, and though the occasional wolf or wandering boar still lurked in the underbrush, there was no sense of unnatural malice anymore.

The world felt... right again.

Darius rode at the front, his greatsword strapped securely to his back, eyes scanning the path ahead. Behind him, Rowen and Ingrid rode side by side, the rogue in his usual relaxed posture, occasionally leaning back in the saddle as if he might fall asleep mid-ride. Lyra was just behind them, adjusting her hood to shield herself from the afternoon sun as she hummed a quiet tune to herself.

And trailing slightly behind, separate from the group, was Kastor.

It had been 2 days since their departure from the capital, yet despite sharing the road, Kastor had remained a shadow—always there, but never quite part of them.

Rowen, naturally, had something to say about it.

"You know, for someone who's supposed to be guiding us across the sea, the new guy's about as lively as a corpse," he muttered, just low enough for Darius and Ingrid to hear.

Darius exhaled through his nose. "Some people might had said the same thing about me not long ago though."

Rowen smirked. "Yeah, but at least you didn't have his creepy stare, or I never would've let you talk to me let alone befriending you."

Ingrid huffed a quiet laugh. "He's got a point."

Darius shook his head, but he couldn't deny that there was something about Kastor that unsettled him. Maybe it was the way he always seemed to be watching—calculating. Or maybe it was the fact that he hadn't shared much about his homeland's troubles.

If they were traveling halfway across the world to fight another demon, Darius wanted to know what they were walking into.

Noticing his glance, Kastor met Darius' eyes with a knowing smirk but said nothing.

Darius looked away.

Instead, he focused on the conversation that had been flowing between the others.

"Those last Three days in the castle just flew by," Ingrid remarked, rolling her shoulders. "Really going to miss the time off if I'm honest."

Rowen stretched lazily. "Time off? you were busy playing soldier in the barracks every day."

"Training," Ingrid corrected. "Unlike you, I actually take survival seriously." Rowen feigned offense. "I'll have you know I was very busy being a nuisance to the palace staff."

"Shock," Lyra deadpanned.

Rowen grinned. "Though, to be fair, I also spent a lot of time keeping Ingrid from drinking the royal cellars dry."

Ingrid scoffed. "That was one night."

"Two nights."

"Three," Lyra corrected.

"Traitors," Ingrid muttered, though there was no real bite to her voice.

Lyra, meanwhile, adjusted her grip on the reins. "I mostly spent my time in the library. Alara was… gone most of the time, but the few days she was there, she gave me some more insight into spell craft I can now manage 6 charges." She claimed proudly, "And I talked with the princess a lot."

Darius blinked. "Seraphina?"

Lyra nodded. "She's easy to talk to. We actually have a lot in common." A small smile tugged at her lips. "It was nice."

Rowen leaned toward her with a smug grin. "Oh, but Darius also spent plenty of time with the princess."

Darius sighed. "Do you ever shut up?"

"Never," Rowen said proudly. "But seriously, if I had a gold coin for every time I saw you sneaking around the castle gardens, I'd be a rich man."

Darius ignored him, though the slight upward twitch of Seraphina's lips from memory didn't go unnoticed.

The journey continued in relative ease, the group losing themselves in conversation and the rhythm of travel.

Until Rowen stiffened.

His head snapped toward the treeline, body tensed. "Hold up."

Darius immediately reined in his horse, the others following suit. "What is it?"

Rowen's eyes narrowed. "You hear that?"

A moment of silence stretched between them. Then—

A scream.

"Help! Please!"

A woman's voice, panicked, desperate.

Rowen didn't wait. He spurred his horse forward, and the others followed.

Within minutes, they found the source.

A cart had been overturned on the side of the road. A man and a woman—merchants by the looks of their clothing—were backed against the remains of their goods, a small horde of goblins circling them like scavengers.

And towering over them all, club in hand, was a troll.

"Well," Ingrid muttered, cracking her knuckles. "That's new."

"Goblins this far from the ruins?" Lyra asked.

"Not just goblins," Ingrid said grimly. "That's a mountain troll. They don't belong anywhere near here."

Darius cursed under his breath. "The castle guards did warn that not all beasts returned to their natural hunting grounds after the Mawborn's fall."

"Guess that means we're still cleaning up the mess," Rowen said.

The troll let out a guttural roar, raising its club.

Darius didn't hesitate. "Move in!"

The four heroes sprang from their saddles, their horses instinctively veering away as they charged into battle.

Leading the charge, Darius' sword flashing as he cut through the first goblin in his path. Rowen flickered, weaving between enemies, daggers flashing. Ingrid's axe came down in a brutal arc, splitting another goblin clean in two.

Lyra raised her staff, gathering power. "Stormcaller!"

A bolt of lightning streaked down, striking the troll's shoulder. It roared in anger but did not fall.

The goblins scattered, shrieking.

The troll turned to Ingrid, swinging its massive club.

She rolled aside just in time.

"Alright, ugly," she snarled. "Let's see what you've got."

Darius moved in, his blade flashing.

Rowen followed, striking at the beast's exposed flank.

The fight was fierce, the troll proving more resilient than expected. But the team had fought worse.

And then—it fell.

The team exhaled, stepping back, catching their breath.

But they had made a mistake.

One goblin had survived.

A single, cunning creature.

It leapt from the shadows, dagger raised—

Heading straight for the merchant woman.

And then, in a blur of movement—

CRACK.

A metal chain whip shot forward, snapping around the goblin's throat.

A violent yank.

The goblin's body hit the ground with a dull thud—its head landing elsewhere.

The team turned.

Kastor stood there, his whip still extended, the metal links gleaming in the sunlight.

For the first time, he didn't look detached.

He looked like a predator.

Darius stared.

Kastor smirked. "What? Thought I was just going to watch?"

Rowen wasted no time. As soon as the dust settled and the merchants finished gathering themselves, he practically bounded up to Kastor, eyes gleaming with excitement.

"That—" Rowen pointed at Kastor's chain whip, "—was the coolest thing I've seen in a long time. How the hell do you even learn to fight like that?"

Kastor barely spared him a glance as he coiled his whip back around his belt. "You practice."

Rowen wasn't deterred. He spread his arms, pacing beside him as the others gathered around. "I mean, yeah, obviously, but—damn. That thing moves like a snake. You had that goblin wrapped up and headless before I could even blink."

Kastor shrugged. "That was the point."

Before Rowen could push further, Ingrid approached, brushing dirt from her armour after having lifted the merchant's cart back onto its wheels. She gave Kastor an approving nod. "Quick reflexes. That save was clean."

"Yeah, yeah," Rowen waved a dismissive hand. "I could've done the same if I wasn't slightly distracted by—"

"By what?" Ingrid arched a brow.

Rowen grinned. "By you, obviously."

Ingrid rolled her eyes. "That's the excuse you're running with?"

"Are you saying I wasn't distracted by your radiant presence?"

Rowen said, his smirk widening.

Ingrid scoffed. "No, I'm saying you were too busy flipping around like an idiot instead of finishing the fight."

Before they could launch into a full-blown argument, Darius stepped in. He walked straight to Kastor, expression even, and extended a hand.

"That was a hell of a save," he said. "Could've ended differently without your quick thinking."

Kastor hesitated. His amber eyes flicked down to Darius's outstretched hand, then back up to his face. There was something unreadable in his expression, but after a brief pause, he clasped Darius's hand firmly.

"You're welcome," he said simply.

It was short, but it was something.

Rowen clapped his hands together. "Alright, great! We're all friends now— "wait." His head snapped around, eyes scanning the area. "Where the hell are the horses?"

The group turned, only now realizing that in the chaos of the battle, their steeds had bolted.

"...Shit," Ingrid muttered.

"Yeah, that's one way to put it," Lyra sighed, brushing stray hair from her face.

The merchants, overhearing, turned back to them. The woman, still dusting herself off, gave them an apologetic smile. "We're heading to Rivenwall, if that's where you're bound. It's only a couple of hours up the road."

The man gestured to the now-fixed cart. "You're welcome to hop in. Only downside is… well, you'll be sitting with all the herbs and spices."

Rowen's nose wrinkled. "So we smell like Ingrid's mead breath for the rest of the trip? Hard pass."

Ingrid smirked. "You say that like I won't make you walk instead."

Rowen's eyes flicked between her and the cart. "…I'm sure it's not that bad."

After a quick debate, the decision was unanimous: riding in the cart beat walking. One by one, they climbed in, settling among sacks of dried spices and crates of aromatic herbs.

As the cart trundled along the dirt road, the tension from the battle faded, replaced by the easy rhythm of travel. The warm breeze carried the scent of salt from the Azure Sea, and as they neared the coast, the faint sound of waves crashing against the shore reached their ears.

The first to break the silence—unsurprisingly—was Rowen.

"Alright," he said, leaning back against a crate, arms folded behind his head. "We've got time to kill. Might as well make it interesting. Ingrid, you must have some drinking stories from the past three days. Something ridiculous, surely."

Ingrid scoffed. "What makes you think I'd share any of those with you?"

"Because I know for a fact you spent at least one night drinking with the barracks lads," Rowen grinned. "One of them definitely had to get carried out, and I need to know who."

Ingrid considered, then smirked. "Three, actually."

Rowen whistled. "Damn. You are an inspiration to drunks everywhere." Lyra shook her head, smiling as she picked through a pouch of dried fruits the merchants had offered. "All these herbs and spices remind me of the smell in Alara's chambers."

Darius glanced at her. "Learn anything useful while you were with her?"

Lyra nodded. "She… taught me a lot. Not just about magic, but about refinement. Magic isn't just about what I learn—it's about what I make it into."

"Ah," Rowen said. "So, you're going to start shooting lightning out of your eyes?"

Lyra sighed. "No, Rowen. I'm not going to start shooting lightning out of my eyes."

She leaned back slightly, watching the rolling fields pass by, then turned to Darius. "So… when exactly did Seraphina set sail? She left the capital a day before us, right?"

Darius nodded, resting an arm over his knee. "She took the royal ship with her guards. They should've landed in the northern region of Drakmyr by now."

"Ah," Rowen chimed in, trying to sound clever. "Erendo… Erraldy… Er—"

"Eryndell," Kastor corrected smoothly from his corner.

Rowen snorted, turning his head back to Darius. "Huh. You seem to know an awful lot about her travel plans."

Darius didn't react. He just exhaled through his nose, eyes on the horizon.

Rowen grinned at the silence, nudging Ingrid. "See? He knows. He probably counted the sails as they disappeared over the horizon."

Darius gave him a look. "Would you like to walk the rest of the way?"

Rowen held up his hands in mock surrender. "I'm just saying—we get the back of a cart, bouncing around like sacks of potatoes, and she gets the royal ship?" He sighed dramatically. "Heroes of prophecy, and we're still traveling like commoners."

Darius shrugged. "This is more my style anyway."

Rowen scoffed. "Well, yeah. You like suffering."

Ingrid smirked. "He does have a point."

Lyra chuckled softly but didn't press the topic further.

The cart jostled along the dirt road, wooden wheels creaking in rhythm with the sway of packed crates and dangling sacks of herbs. The salty tang of the Azure Sea grew stronger with every turn, carried inland by the soft coastal breeze that tousled their hair and fluttered the canvas tarp overhead.

From the back of the cart, the world unfolded in slow, beautiful motion. To the left, golden fields stretched out toward the horizon, dotted with wildflowers and swaying grain, already rippling like waves in the breeze. Farmers could be seen tending to their work—some waving as the cart passed, others guiding oxen or gathering baskets of fresh vegetables into carts of their own.

To the right, the landscape dipped into marshy wetlands where herons strutted through shallow water and frogs chirped lazily in the reeds. Further out, they could see flashes of silver in the water—shoals of fish darting beneath the surface of narrow streams that cut through the terrain like shimmering veins.

And beyond it all, like a jewel set against the edge of the world, was the sea. The Azure Sea, vast and glistening under the afternoon sun, stretched out with its brilliant blue and whitecaps, the water sparkling with every gust of wind. Fishing boats bobbed in the distance, their sails like tiny triangles against the vastness of sky and sea.

Further along the road ahead, the silhouette of Rivenwall came into view—a humble cluster of buildings nestled along the rocky coast, their rooftops a patchwork of worn red tile and pale thatch. Seagulls cried overhead, circling the harbour like lazy guardians, while the faint clatter of ship rigging and the distant bark of dockhands rolled up on the wind.

The conversation continued, the group falling into a comfortable rhythm. Even Kastor, who had remained largely silent, was drawn in.

At first, his responses were short.

"Where exactly are you from? Is was Dhal-" Lyra asked at one point.

"Valkhast," Kastor interrupted.

Ingrid tilted her head. "I thought you was from Dhalmora?"

"Originally Valkhast, the eastern region. But I live in Dhalmora now—south coast."

"Oh...." Lyra waited for anymore information in which there was none. Not much to go on at all.

But over time, his answers grew longer.

"So what's Dhalmora like??" Rowen asked.

Kastor opening up slightly. "The streets are crowded, but the markets are good for business."

"Business?"

Kastor smirked slightly. "Acquiring things." Darius raised a brow. "You mean stealing things." Kastor merely shrugged. Rowen whistled. "Well, you'll fit right in with us."

The final breakthrough came when Rowen, as he often did, took it too far.

"Alright, alright," Rowen said, sitting up, "important question: Ingrid—would you rather fight a hundred goblin-sized trolls, or one troll-sized goblin?"

Ingrid didn't even hesitate. "The big one."

"Wrong," Rowen said, shaking his head. "Smaller ones. Easier to kick."

"Rowen," Lyra groaned.

"You can't just kick your way through a fight," Ingrid muttered.

"Of course I can," Rowen declared. "I kick my problems to the curb all the time."

"Shall I do that to my problem? That's you, you are the problem," Ingrid said dryly.

Rowen grinned. "I'd argue you're mine"

Ingrid grabbed him by the collar.

"Rowen—"

And then, unbelievably—

Kastor laughed.

It was short. Rough. But *real*.

The group went quiet for a moment. Then Rowen, ever the opportunist, turned to him with wide eyes.

"Was that—did you *just laugh*?"

Kastor rubbed his temple. "I regret it already."

But the damage was done.

And for the first time, the stranger among them didn't seem so much like a stranger anymore.

CHAPTER 26

Beneath the Flesh-Tide

The scent of salt and fish thickened in the air as the cart rumbled over the crest of a low hill, revealing the sprawling fishing village of Rivenwall below. Nestled between the gentle cliffs and the glittering blue stretch of the Azure Sea, the village buzzed with life. Wooden docks reached like fingers into the surf, crowded with vessels of all sizes—sleek ships with tall masts and battered old fishing boats alike.

Rows of drying nets hung between poles, swaying in the sea breeze. Fishermen hauled crates of glistening silver-scaled fish onto shore, their voices calling out in practiced rhythm. Children ran barefoot through the streets, chasing gulls and playing with sticks, laughter mingling with the cries of seabirds overhead. Salt-worn houses of pale stone and driftwood lined the edges of the main street, smoke curling lazily from their chimneys.

Darius brought the group to a stop just outside the village gate, where a lean man with a weathered face and a thick beard awaited them. He wore a cloak made of seal-hide and a wide grin of recognition.

"You must be the heroes," he said, extending a hand. "I'm Eldric, village leader and master of the docks. Welcome to Rivenwall."

Darius shook his hand firmly. "Good to meet you. Thank you for the welcome."

"You've done more than you know," Eldric said, nodding to the others. "Whatever they say up in the capital, we know it was your lot that saved this land. The skies are blue again, the sea's calm, and no more creatures crawling out of the forest. Rivenwall owes you."

Rowen beamed. "A toast would suffice."

Eldric laughed. "You'll have your fill aboard, I promise." He gestured behind him. "Your ship's ready and waiting, crew eager to set sail. We'll be reaching Dhalmora by dawn if we leave soon."

The group followed Eldric through the heart of Rivenwall, marvelling at the colourful market stalls and the sounds of village life. People paused to wave or offer baskets of goods, and Lyra looked like she could melt at the sight of a display of fresh honey cakes.

The dock itself was busy but orderly. The ship waiting for them was a sleek, double-masted beauty, its sails furled, hull clean and polished. Painted on its side in curling script was its name: The Silverwake.

As they reached the bottom of the gangplank, Eldric turned to them once more. "Safe travels to all of you. If anyone can fight back what's coming… it's you." His eyes settled briefly on Kastor, uncertain, but said nothing.

They boarded. Rowen was first to claim the deck dramatically. "I call captain!"

"No, you don't," Ingrid said flatly, marching past him.

"Too late. I already called it."

"You're not steering anything," Lyra sighed.

"Let the man dream," Darius added with a smirk.

The crew gave polite nods as the heroes explored the vessel. Darius exchanged a few words with the first mate, while Lyra leaned on the rail, taking in the horizon. Ingrid ran a finger across the blade of her axe, inspecting it. Rowen was already pretending to bark orders. Kastor, as always, lingered at the edge of it all, arms crossed, eyes scanning the sea.

As the ship pushed off from Rivenwall, the last light of the sun gleamed across the water. The sea was calm, painted in oranges and blues, stretching endlessly ahead.

Later, after settling in and watching the coastline shrink behind them, the five gathered together on the deck, the wind tugging gently at their cloaks and hair.

Kastor remained quiet for a while until Lyra nudged him gently. "You doing alright?"

He nodded slowly. "Just thinking."

Rowen plopped beside him, stretching. "Dangerous habit, that."

Kastor gave a sharp exhale through his nose. Almost a laugh.

After a pause, he spoke, quieter than before. "The nightmares started a little over a month ago. Small things, at first. Whispered rumours, strange shapes in the fog. Then... people changed. Started going mad. Like they weren't themselves anymore. Dhalmora's on the edge."

Rowen frowned. "That's... the same time everything started going sideways back in Elaria."

Kastor nodded. "It escalated fast. We thought it was just one incident. Then two. Then… entire towns losing contact. No monsters in the streets. Just silence. Like something had erased them. I heard the hero of prophecy had risen up in Elaria and fought back the beast plaguing them."

The group quieted.

"That's why you came," Darius said.

Kastor's eyes found the horizon. "I don't know if I came for answers… or to escape."

Ingrid placed a hand on his shoulder. "Doesn't matter now. You're with us."

Kastor looked at her hand. Then at the others. "You make it look easy. This… trust."

Lyra smiled. "It wasn't. But it's worth it."

Rowen leaned back, arms behind his head. "Welcome to the party, Kas."

"Kastor."

"Kas. We'll workshop it."

Kastor shook his head but said nothing. His expression eased.

They watched the sea for a long while, the stars beginning to peek through the sky as the sun disappeared.

In the distance, the silhouette of Rivenwall vanished beneath the horizon. A gentle wind carried the scent of the sea, and the only sound was the ship cutting through the waves.

Below deck, the clatter of plates and faint music signalled that dinner was being prepared.

"Shall we?" Darius said, motioning toward the stairs.

One by one, the party descended, their laughter and footsteps echoing into the night. Laughter echoed beneath the ship's deck.

Kastor, for once, wasn't on the fringe of the room. He sat at the table with the others, picking over a plate of salted fish and bread. Rowen was mid-rant about how "heroing should come with a pension," making exaggerated hand gestures that risked spilling Lyra's cup of honeyed wine. Ingrid smacked his hand away with a grin. Lyra rolled her eyes but laughed all the same.

"You lot eat like you've never seen a kitchen," Kastor muttered dryly, stabbing a chunk of potato with his fork.

"Not all of us had noble meals and gold-plated spoons growing up," Rowen quipped. "Some of us had to wrestle bread from boars."

"I highly doubt that's a real thing," Lyra said.

Rowen opened his mouth—likely to explain how it absolutely was a real thing—but Kastor cut in.

"If it *was*, the boar deserved to eat."

Everyone blinked.

Then Rowen laughed. "Well look at you! The shadow breathes!"

Kastor offered a faint smirk and shook his head. "You people are exhausting."

But the warmth remained in his eyes, and for the first time, it felt like he belonged at the table.

Darius sat back in his chair, quietly observing. This, right here—this was why they fought. The little moments. The connections. The light in the dark.

And then the laughter died.

It began with a dull *thud*—a sickening crunch from somewhere above. The ship groaned.

Silence swept the room. Muffled shouts echoed from the deck. Boots pounded wood. Then more yelling. Frantic. Panicked.

Darius was already on his feet. "Topside. Now."

They burst onto the deck, the night air slapping their faces. The sky had clouded over. Moonlight was smothered. The sea no longer sparkled—it churned, roiled, like something alive. But not from wind or storm. From something else entirely.

"What the hell is happening?" Ingrid shouted, eyes scanning the horizon.

Then a scream.

One of the sailors leapt at another, fists slamming into the man's face. Again. Again. Blood sprayed across the deck. The crew scrambled, trying to pull them apart.

Lyra gasped. "He's… he's not right—look at his eyes!"

The attacker's pupils had vanished—just white. Frothing at the mouth, he let out an inhuman howl as he tore at the other man's throat with his teeth.

Kastor's whip lashed forward—metal links wrapping around the attacker's neck and dragging him off his victim. The body hit the ground hard. Rowen was already there, planting a solid kick to the madman's head and knocking him unconscious.

"What was that?" Rowen panted. "That wasn't normal. That was not goblin-weird."

Kastor's face was stone. "That's exactly what I saw back in Dhalmora."

The words hung in the air.

Darius turned slowly, eyes scanning the blackened waves beyond the railing. The ocean seemed to… ripple.

Something moved beneath it. A massive bulge of water pulsed, then sank. No form. No face. Just… pressure.

Lyra clutched her staff tighter. "Do you hear that?"

They all fell quiet.

Faintly—almost beneath hearing—came a whisper.

"Come closer…"

"…life eternal…"

"…power beyond flesh…"

Darius's grip tightened on his greatsword. "The second demon."

"The Flesh-Tide," Kastor whispered. "It's here."

Another groan from the ship as something unseen bumped against its underside.

The deck tilted.

A wave crashed across the stern, sweeping crates and one screaming sailor into the dark.

"Hold on!" Ingrid bellowed, grabbing a rope just as another wave smashed into the side of the ship. Planks cracked. The mast swayed.

The crew scrambled to secure the sails, barking commands—but the water was no longer water. It moved with intent. Tendrils of black froth snaked up the hull like fingers.

"What do we do?!" Lyra shouted over the chaos, struggling to keep her footing.

"There's no fighting this!" Rowen yelled, eyes wild.

"We need to run," Kastor snapped, pointing out toward the horizon. "There! A whirlpool—cut past it!"

"Are you insane?!" the captain barked, hands on the wheel.

Kastor's whip cracked, latching onto the railing beside the captain. "Either that or drown. Your choice."

Darius met Kastor's eyes, weighing everything in that instant. Then he turned to the captain. "Do it."

The captain swore but obeyed, jerking the wheel.

The ship careened, catching the edge of the swirling maelstrom. Water sprayed, wind howled, and for one moment it felt like the entire vessel would be pulled under.

But Kastor was now helping the captain steer, guiding them along the current's edge with precision honed by desperation and experience. The ship bucked—screamed—

—and then shot out the other side, flung forward by the whirlpool's force.

Everything fell silent.

No whispers. No crashing waves. Just the lapping of real ocean.

The crew collapsed. The heroes stood, breathing hard, soaked to the bone.

Whatever it was—they'd escaped it.

For now.

The sea was still.

Not calm—*still*.

A vast, unnatural silence stretched across the black waters. The waves had stopped crashing. The wind, gone. The sails hung limp. The stars above, once glittering in the velvet sky, now felt distant… cold… like they were watching and waiting.

Kastor stood at the helm, jaw clenched, eyes locked on the horizon. He didn't speak. None of them did.

Darius stepped forward, his boots clicking softly on the wet deck. The air was thick—heavier than it should have been. Every breath felt like it had to be pulled in, like the ocean was pressing against his lungs.

Lyra gripped the railing near the stern, her eyes darting across the endless sea. "It's like it's… watching us."

Ingrid had her axe unslung, resting across her lap as she sat near the mast. Her eyes were sharp, her muscles tense, ready for a fight. But even she didn't speak.

Rowen shifted uncomfortably beside her. "Anyone else feel like we're in a really slow, really wet coffin right now?"

Nobody laughed.

And then, it began.

A low rumble—distant at first, like a storm grumbling over the edge of the world.

But it grew.

The water rippled beneath them, subtle but deliberate. Like something breathing just under the surface. Something *enormous*.

Another groan sounded from the depths behind them—long, drawn out, like a wail from a throat that had forgotten how to scream.

Kastor's grip tightened on the wheel. "It's angry."

The rumble turned into a vibration that seemed to rattle the very bones of the ship. Nails creaked in their sockets. Planks shuddered beneath boots. The masts trembled as if straining to hold steady against something that was never meant to exist.

The air shifted.

Cold, then colder. A chill that had nothing to do with the sea breeze.

Lyra took a shaky step back from the railing. "I don't think we escaped."

"No," Darius said, his voice low, steady—but hollow. "We just survived."

Behind them, in the direction they had come, the sea rippled again.

And then—

A *sound*.

Not a roar. Not a howl.

Something deeper. *Older*. A seismic groan that split the night and ran like a shockwave across the ocean. It wasn't just heard—it was *felt*. In the chest. In the bones. A primal, reality-breaking wail that made the stars flicker and the sea *tremble*.

Rowen stumbled back, hand bracing the railing. "That's not a sea. That's a thing." No one responded.

The crew stood frozen, pale-faced and wide-eyed, staring into the dark, into the black horizon where the sound had come from.

Nothing moved. No waves. No wind.

Just the quiet hum of *something* terrible—furious that its prey had slipped away.

A silence so loud it swallowed the world.

And then— Nothing.

Not a word. Not a sound. Not a breath.

Only the unshakable truth that whatever was beneath those waters was not finished with them.

And they were *still at sea*.

CHAPTER 27

A City Hung in Shadow

Dawn came slow. The first traces of light stretched weakly across the horizon, casting a dull glow over the battered ship as it drifted forward. The wood groaned with each shift of the waves, the hull scarred and splintered from the unseen horrors of the night before. The sails, though still intact, hung heavy from the mast, damp from sea spray and whatever unnatural presence had reached out for them in the abyss.

The scent of salt and damp wood lingered thick in the air, mixing with the faintest traces of something else—something foul that clung to their clothes and skin. A reminder of what had brushed against their reality.

The crew stirred sluggishly, their movements slow and deliberate, as if afraid that any sudden noise might stir the presence they had so narrowly escaped. Even the most hardened sailors bore dark circles beneath their eyes, exhaustion weighing down on them.

None of them had slept.

The heroes had stayed together on deck for the rest of the night, unable to bring themselves to rest after the nightmare they had endured. The ocean had remained eerily still, the absence of wind unnatural, as if the world itself had held its breath. But nothing more had come.

No further horrors. No more voices.

Just the unbearable silence stretching across the endless expanse of sea.

It was Rowen who finally broke the hush, rubbing his arms as he exhaled. "Still not sure if last night was real or if I've finally lost my mind."

Ingrid scoffed, voice hoarse from exhaustion. "If that's the case, we all went mad together."

Lyra sat cross-legged on the deck, chin resting in her palm. "Which... honestly, wouldn't surprise me at this point."

Darius stood near the bow, gripping the railing as he stared ahead, expression unreadable. His mind replayed the low, guttural tremor that had rattled through the ocean in their wake, the sound of something furious that they had escaped.

They had won this round. But only barely.

Then, just when it seemed like the world would remain suspended in that unnatural stillness forever—

A voice rang out.

"Land ahead!"

A surge of energy jolted through the ship. The heroes snapped their heads up, the exhausted crew rushing to the bow to confirm the call.

And then they saw it.

A jagged coastline stretched across the horizon, shrouded in mist where the waves lapped against the rocky shore. But beyond that—

Towering spires and sprawling structures carved into the cliffs themselves.

"Welcome," Kastor said, his voice steady despite his exhaustion. He stepped up beside Darius, arms crossed as he gazed at the approaching city. "Welcome to Drakmyr."

A few moments of silence stretched between them as the ship continued its slow approach, the mist beginning to clear as the city of Dhalmora revealed itself in full.

The sight before them was unlike anything the heroes had ever seen.

The city loomed high, built into the very cliffs that overlooked the sea, its labyrinthine streets winding up and down sheer rock faces, bridges and staircases weaving between towering structures of stone and metal. Unlike the warm and humble capital of Elaria, which had been a blend of medieval castles and village charm, Dhalmora was vast, imposing, and alien in its grandeur.

Massive archways and colossal statues of warriors overlooked the harbour, their expressions carved in eternal vigilance. The lower district—closer to the sea—was filled with an intricate network of docks, markets, and shipyards, the scent of freshly caught fish and burning coal mixing in the air.

Further up, dwellings and establishments clung to the cliffs, some built into the rock itself, their glowing windows forming patterns against the grey stone like fireflies in a cavern. Bridges of metal and rope stretched precariously across vast gaps, connecting the separate sections of the city like veins of a living organism.

Dhalmora was not just a city.

Ingrid let out a low whistle. "By the gods…"

Rowen, for once, was speechless, his wide eyes taking in every impossible detail.

Lyra gripped her staff, her awe tainted by something else. "It feels... different here. Like the air is heavier."

Kastor's gaze remained fixed on the city. "That's because it is."

Darius exhaled as he gripped the ship's railing, his knuckles white. He had thought himself prepared.

He wasn't.

They had set sail knowing they were heading toward danger, but seeing this massive, unknowable city before them made it real in a way that even the horrors at sea had not.

This was not Elaria.

This was a new world entirely.

And something was waiting for them here.

The closer the ship drew to shore, the more details of Dhalmora came into view—details that only deepened the stark contrast between this place and Elaria.

The harbour was alive with movement, bustling with workers hauling crates of exotic fish, barrels of dark ale, and sacks of unknown spices that scented the salty air. Unlike the simple wooden docks of home, Dhalmora's harbour sprawled outward in layers, built with dark stone, reinforced steel, and intricate carvings of warriors and beasts locked in eternal battle. Jagged cliffs loomed overhead, casting long shadows over the lower district, where open markets buzzed with merchants yelling in sharp, foreign tongues.

The ships themselves were different—sleek, dark-hulled vessels with massive sails, some trimmed in black and gold, bearing crests unfamiliar to the heroes. The people manning them were just as varied, a mix of rough-looking sailors, robed scholars, and warriors draped in furs and armour. Unlike Elaria's warm and welcoming crowds, Dhalmora's denizens moved with purpose and caution, their eyes sharp, their hands always close to their belts where blades and pouches rested.

The city stretched upward—a true marvel of engineering and architecture. Homes and buildings clung to the cliffsides, forming layers upon layers of civilization. Bridges of stone and iron connected the various levels, some so high that they vanished into the morning mist. Massive staircases wound up toward the heart of the city, while deeper within the cliffs, carved openings led to unseen corridors, entire sections of Dhalmora hidden within the mountain itself.

At its heart, far above, the fortress of King Marek loomed—a structure that defied logic. Built upside down, it hung from the cliffs, its spires and towers extending downward toward the lower city. From below, it resembled an inverted castle, as if the very land had tried to swallow it and failed. The dark stone gleamed faintly in the morning light, runes etched into its surface, flickering with hints of blue and gold.

It was overwhelming. It was breathtaking.

It was another world entirely.

The ship slowed as it neared the docks, the rhythmic creaking of wood and splash of waves the only sounds for a moment.

The captain, the grizzled man who had spent decades on the sea, let out a long exhale, his grip still firm on the wheel. "I won't lie," he muttered, rubbing a hand over his face. "Didn't think we'd see daylight again after last night." He turned to Kastor. "If not for you and your lot, we'd have all gone mad. The ship wouldn't have lasted much longer. So... thank you."

Kastor gave him a simple nod, acknowledging the words without basking in them.

The captain turned his attention to the rest of the party. "We'll stay docked for repairs, then head back to Elaria. But you lot—" he let out a short chuckle. "Looks like your journey is just beginning. I don't envy you."

Darius stepped forward. "Thank you for getting us here."

The captain waved him off. "Thank me by staying alive, eh?"

With that, the crew got to work, lowering the gangplank as Darius, Rowen, Ingrid and Lyra stepped off onto foreign soil for the first time.

The moment their boots hit the stone, everything felt different.

The air was denser, colder, carrying scents of brine, iron, and unfamiliar spices. Voices spoke in sharp dialects, the accent of Dhalmora rougher, more guttural than the flowing speech of Elaria. The people moved differently, some giving the newcomers side-eyes, others outright ignoring them as they continued their work.

Rowen took in the massive ships, the fishmongers gutting strange, multi-eyed sea creatures, the sharp-dressed merchants selling daggers alongside bread. "I'm starting to get the feeling we ain't in Elaria anymore."

Before Darius could reply, Rowen accidentally bumped into a dock worker.

The man—a burly, scarred seaman with a thick beard—stumbled back, his crate toppling to the ground, sending salted fish scattering across the stone. His expression distorted into rage.

"You blind, foreign bastard?"

Rowen blinked. "Oh, I—"

The man shoved him.

Darius moved before Rowen could escalate it further, stepping between them. "He didn't mean anything by it."

The seaman wasn't interested in apologies. He turned his head, shouting to his crewmates. "Oi! Looks like we've got some soft-skinned tourists!"

Several rough-looking men from nearby ships took notice, some standing from their posts.

Rowen raised his hands. "Alright, alright, no need to turn this into a—"

Another hand clamped down.

Not Darius this time.

Kastor stepped in, his grip firm as he stared the seaman down. His voice was low and commanding.

"Walk away."

Something in his tone—cold, unshaken by threat—gave the seaman pause. His crew looked between Kastor and the others, assessing.

Then, with a grunt, the man stepped back. "Fine. Just keep your little friend here outta my way."

As the workers moved on, Kastor let go of Rowen, giving him a sharp look.

"You need to learn how to move here," he said. "Keep your head down. Let me handle things."

Rowen scoffed. "Yeah? And what if I don't want to let you handle things?"

"You'll be dead before you step foot beyond the harbour," Kastor replied.

There was no arrogance in his tone. Just fact.

For once, Rowen didn't have a comeback.

As the group began walking further into the docks, Lyra fell behind slightly, distracted by the sights. That was when a pair of men—dressed in finer yet rugged clothes, the kind worn by those used to both wealth and violence—stepped into her path.

One of them, a dark-haired man with a silver tooth and a confident smirk, grinned at her.

"Well, well. Haven't seen a pretty thing like you before," he said smoothly. "You new to the city? Let us show you around."

Lyra's shoulders stiffened. "No, thank you."

The second man, taller and leaner, smirked. "Oh, come now. No need to be shy. Dhalmora can be dangerous for someone so… delicate."

Before she could answer, a shadow loomed.

Ingrid.

The moment the two men saw the broad-shouldered warrior with an axe bigger than their heads, their grins faltered.

One of them raised his hands, stepping back. "Just being friendly."

"Good," Ingrid said. "Then you won't mind leaving."

The men quickly dispersed.

Lyra exhaled, glancing at Ingrid. "Thanks."

Ingrid shrugged. "You'd do the same for me."

"Would I?"

Ingrid smirked. "No. But it's the thought that counts."

With their first encounters behind them, the group pressed forward into the city, Kastor now taking the lead.

The streets wound through the carved rock, twisting through tunnels and emerging into sprawling markets and elevated plazas.

To their right, a massive open-top arena stood—a colosseum of dark stone, its entrance carved with murals of warriors in battle.

Ingrid's eyes lingered on it. "What's that?"

Kastor followed her gaze. "The Arena of Dhalmora."

Rowen raised a brow. "Why does this place need a gladiator pit?"

Kastor's reply was simple, cold. "For amusement."

They moved on.

With each step, the streets became narrower, richer, more imposing. The people wore darker robes, gilded armour, fine silks woven with unfamiliar sigils.

Then, as they turned a final corner—

The Fortress.

Hanging upside down from the cliffs above, the castle stretched downward, a massive monument defying gravity. It was carved with runes, windows glowing faintly, balconies and bridges reaching into the open air.

Kastor stopped before it.

"This is it," he said.

"King Marek is waiting."

The towering fortress doors groaned as they swung open, revealing the vast interior of the upside-down castle. Darius and his party stepped inside, their boots echoing against the polished stone floor. The chamber they entered was unlike anything they had seen before, stretching upward—or perhaps downward—toward an arched ceiling adorned with jagged obsidian formations and luminous blue crystals.

Massive iron chandeliers hung from the vaulted ceiling, their flames flickering with an eerie, unnatural light. Strange sigils and arcane glyphs lined the stonework, etched into the very foundation of the walls, glowing faintly with an eldritch shimmer. Stained glass windows—far grander and more elaborate than those in Elaria's castle—depicted ancient battles, heroes locked in combat with monstrous entities beyond comprehension.

The air carried a scent of aged parchment, burning embers, and something distinctly metallic. A sense of power pulsed through the very walls, like a heart beating beneath layers of stone. The fortress felt alive in a way that was both magnificent and unsettling.

Rowen let out a low whistle, tilting his head as he studied the dark banners that lined the vast corridor. "Okay. I'll admit it. This is impressive."

Ingrid folded her arms, her gaze sweeping over the architecture. "It's... different from home."

"That's an understatement," Lyra murmured, her eyes trailing up the walls. "There's magic infused into the very structure of this place. You can feel it."

Kastor walked ahead, leading the way with practiced ease. "This is the Heart of Dhalmora," he said. "The fortress of King Marek. It is built within the cliffs themselves, a foundation of both stone and sorcery."

Darius studied the immense tapestries hanging from the pillars. Each depicted a different scene—one showed a battle against a monstrous sea of writhing flesh, disturbingly reminiscent of what they had faced in the ocean. Another depicted a group of warriors standing against a rising black tide.

Rowen nudged Ingrid, nodding toward a section of the wall where a great mural had been carved into the stone, depicting what looked like a grand arena. "See? Even their castle worships fighting," he muttered with a smirk.

Kastor overheard and responded without breaking stride. "The arena is sacred here. Strength is the foundation of our people. Victory earns respect. Only the strongest rule."

Ingrid smirked. "Sounds like my kind of place."

Darius raised an eyebrow. "And the people who lose?"

Kastor didn't answer right away. Then, without turning to face them, he simply said, "They are forgotten."

A tense silence fell over them. Lyra exchanged a glance with Darius but chose not to press further.

They continued through the massive corridor, the light shifting as they neared another grand set of doors at the far end. Towering iron gates embedded with silver inlay stood before them, flanked by two armoured figures—royal sentinels clad in dark, polished plate, their visors covering their faces entirely.

One of the sentinels stepped forward, his voice deep and commanding. "Kastor Vale. You return." His visor turned toward Darius and his companions. "And these are the ones?"

Kastor nodded. "The hero of prophecy and his allies."

The sentinel seemed to regard them for a long moment before giving a slow nod. "His Majesty is expecting you."

With that, the massive doors creaked open, revealing the grand hall beyond.

A throne room unlike any other, and at its centre, seated upon a throne of obsidian and carved bone, was King Marek of Dhalmora.

CHAPTER 28

The Kingdom Below

The throne room of Dhalmora was nothing like the grand halls of Elaria's castle. It lacked the warmth, the gilded tapestries, the sense of home that had lingered in the air despite its towering architecture. Here, the atmosphere was heavy, unforgiving, and void of comfort. The walls were charred black stone, twisted pillars stretching high into the cavernous ceiling like jagged ribs of a fallen beast. Torches flickered with pale blue flame, casting eerie shadows along the cold, polished floors.

And at the heart of it all sat King Marek.

His throne was a grotesque fusion of obsidian and bone, carved from the remains of fallen enemies, traitors, and beasts slain in the arena. Jagged vertebrae lined the armrests, while the high back of the chair was crowned with what could only be a dragon's skull. The eerie contrast between refined craftsmanship and brutal savagery made one thing clear—this was not a ruler who led through diplomacy, but through fear.

The King himself was imposing, a towering man draped in dark furs and reinforced steel, his armour bearing deep battle scars. His face, weathered and lined from countless wars, was half-covered in old burn scars, giving the illusion that part of him had melted away. His piercing amber eyes glowed beneath heavy brows, studying the newcomers as if they were prey.

The doors boomed shut behind the group, and the silence that followed was deafening.

Then—King Marek spoke.

"Well, well, well... look what the ocean dragged in." His voice was low and smooth, almost amused, but laced with something inherently wrong. It was the kind of voice that feigned kindness, that made you second-guess your instincts—because the way he spoke, he made it sound like it was *your* fault if you didn't accept his generosity.

He leaned forward, resting his forearm lazily over the skull-armrest of his throne. "So, you're the Hero of Prophecy, huh? The golden boy. The one who's supposed to slay the monsters and save us all." His lips pulled into something that might've been a grin, but it was too sharp, too calculated to be genuine.

Darius remained stone-faced, his jaw locked tight.

Marek's eyes flicked over him, then to the rest of the party, dragging his gaze over each of them as if measuring their worth. "I gotta say, I expected something... more." His fingers tapped rhythmically against the throne. "I mean, I hear this grand prophecy, I hear stories of this destined warrior, and then what do I get? A ragtag band of kids who stumbled off a boat lookin' like they crawled out of a crypt."

Rowen, standing just behind Darius, snorted. "Well, technically, we—"

Marek raised a single gloved hand, cutting him off without so much as a glance. "Nah. See, here's the thing—I don't much care for interruptions." His voice never lost its dangerous smoothness, but the weight behind the words made it clear.

Rowen, for once, actually shut up.

The King smirked, satisfied. "Now, look. I like to think I'm a fair man. A reasonable man. And I want to help you. Truly, I do." He gestured with both hands, as if offering them a gift. "You show up here, heroes on a noble quest, fighting against the great horrors of the world, and naturally, I should just bend the knee and roll out the damn red carpet, right?"

His voice dripped with condescension, and the sarcasm was thick enough to choke on.

"But see, here's the problem—" He pushed himself up from his throne, stepping forward, his heavy boots echoing in the silence. "I don't do blind faith. And I don't hand out favours like some soft hearted fool."

Darius held his ground as the King loomed closer.

Marek tilted his head slightly, like a wolf toying with its prey. "So, I'll make this simple for you. If you wanna play hero in my kingdom, you're gonna have to prove you're worth a damn." He leaned in just enough to let the smell of blood and steel fill the space between them.

"You see, Dhalmora ain't like your pretty little kingdom. We don't sit around waiting for heroes to save us. We fight, we survive, and we do whatever it takes to win." He took a step back, eyes gleaming. "So if you're really this great hero, if you think you can help my people, then you're gonna start by handling a little… problem."

Darius narrowed his eyes. "What problem?"

Marek grinned. "Oh, nothing too crazy. Just a little infestation down in the lower city."

Kastor's entire body tensed, his jaw tightening at the mention of the lower city.

Marek sighed dramatically, throwing his hands up as if inconvenienced. "See, the thing is, my soldiers? They don't come back from there. Something down there is eating them alive." His gaze sharpened. "And I don't send more men when there is a *hero* present."

Silence.

Then, finally, he clapped his hands together, the sudden sound making the tension crackle like static in the air.

"So! Go down there, clean up my streets, and come back in one piece. You do that, and maybe—maybe—I'll actually take this whole 'prophecy' business seriously."

He stepped back onto the throne's dais, lounging into his seat like he already knew they'd fail.

"So. What do you say, Hero? You wanna impress me?"

The room was dead quiet.

Then Darius exhaled slowly. He hated this man already.

And Marek knew it.

Darius was already turning toward the massive doors, eager to put as much distance between himself and King Marek as possible, when the king's voice cut through the tense air once more.

"Oh, and Kastor," Marek's tone was laced with a smug authority, as if he'd been waiting to savour this moment.

Kastor stopped mid-step but didn't turn around.

"You'll be going with them."

The words were casual, almost offhanded, but the weight behind them was suffocating.

Darius, Rowen, Ingrid, and Lyra all exchanged brief glances before looking toward Kastor, who remained rigid, his back still to the king.

"Keep an eye on our guests," Marek continued. "Make sure they don't get into too much trouble down there." He chuckled, leaning lazily onto the armrest of his bone-carved throne. "And while you're at it, I want you to think long and hard about something, Kastor."

Kastor turned slightly, his face carefully neutral, but his eyes flicker with something unspoken.

Marek's grin widened. "No matter how this little hero's errand turns out, you will return to my side. As my second-in-command."

A long pause.

It was a command, not a suggestion.

Darius's brows furrowed as he studied Kastor's reaction. His expression was unreadable, but his posture was too still.

Finally, Kastor inclined his head ever so slightly, not quite a nod, not quite refusal.

Marek smirked. "That's my boy."

With nothing more to say, Kastor turned sharply on his heel and strode toward the others, shoulders tense but face unreadable.

Darius didn't press him. Not here.

The doors groaned open, and the group stepped out of the throne room, leaving Marek's laughter echoing behind them.

The corridor leading away from the throne room was colder than before, the weight of what had just transpired settling in like an ache in their bones. They walked in silence until Kastor took an abrupt turn, leading them through a different passageway.

They emerged onto a high stone balcony, overlooking the sprawling city of Dhalmora beneath them.

It was a breathtaking, if intimidating, sight. Tiers of stone bridges, multi-levelled walkways, and massive stone dwellings carved into the mountainside stretched far into the distance. In the farthest reaches of the city, partially obscured by rising mist, lay the Lower City—a dark and tangled labyrinth of crumbling structures, flickering lanterns, and an eerie, pulsing glow that seemed to throb like a wound in the heart of the kingdom.

They could see tiny figures moving below, citizens of Dhalmora going about their daily routines. Some bustled through markets, exchanging goods and coin, while others moved with purpose—soldiers, thieves, travellers. Yet as they moved closer to the lower city something felt... off.

Lyra hugged her arms as she stared down at the Lower City. "The magic here feels wrong," she muttered, barely above a whisper.

Rowen, standing at the edge of the balcony, rested his arms on the blackened stone railing, eyeing the landscape with an amused tilt of his head. "So, let me get this straight—we save Elaria from a giant abomination, sail across the sea, almost die in an eldritch nightmare, and now, surprise, surprise, the new king wants us to prove ourselves." He let out a low whistle. "This whole 'hero' thing is really starting to feel like a scam."

Ingrid cracked her knuckles. "I don't mind. It's been days since I've had a real fight." Her tone was eager, but there was an edge to it, a barely contained frustration that hadn't had an outlet since they arrived.

Rowen snorted. "Of course, you don't."

Darius, who had been silent, finally exhaled, rubbing the back of his neck. "This isn't just about proving ourselves. Marek wants us in the Lower City for a reason." His gaze shifted to Kastor. "And I think you know why."

Kastor stood near the edge, hands resting on his belt, his expression shadowed as he looked down at the distant Lower City. "You haven't seen what this place does to people," he said at last.

His voice was quiet. But the way he said it stilled the air around them.

Rowen blinked, his usual smirk faltering for the first time. "Well. That's not ominous at all."

Kastor didn't smile.

The group lapsed into silence, gazing down at the darkened underbelly of the city. The wind was cold, carrying the faint scent of the salt air from the sea below, mixed with the faintest trace of rot.

Whatever was waiting for them in the Lower City, it wasn't going to be a simple test.

Kastor turned away from the view of the sprawling kingdom below, his usual indifference cracking just slightly. He exhaled through his nose, arms crossing over his chest. "The Lower City was the first to fall when the attacks began," he started, his voice low, measured. "The streets turned into battlegrounds overnight. People—families—were forced to flee upward. Those who didn't…"

His words trailed off, but his meaning hung heavy in the air.

Lyra frowned, stepping closer. "Didn't… what?"

Kastor's jaw tightened. "Some say the ones who were left behind weren't just killed." His eyes flickered downward toward the Lower City, his gaze haunted. "They say they became something else."

A cold silence settled between them.

Darius shifted uncomfortably. He'd seen enough in Elaria to know that rumours like that weren't always just rumours.

"So, let me get this straight," Rowen finally spoke, his usual light-heartedness sounding forced for once. "We're walking into a place filled with what? Monsters that used to be people?"

"No one knows for sure." Kastor shook his head. "But the Lower City's been a no-man's land ever since."

Ingrid folded her arms. "And the king just sends people down there?"

Kastor sighed, rubbing his face briefly before muttering, "The king isn't the same as he was."

That caught their attention.

Darius narrowed his eyes. "What do you mean?"

Kastor hesitated, eyes looking to fortress behind them. "When I first came to Dhalmora years ago, Marek was different. He reminded me more of Aldric. He cared for the people. He led the armies himself. He fought on the front lines." He let out a bitter chuckle, shaking his head. "Now? He barely looks at them. Barely speaks to me unless it's an order. He used to be my commander. Now I can't even tell if he sees me as a soldier or a pawn."

Darius studied him for a long moment. "Do you think it's stress? With the land falling apart?"

"Maybe." Kastor's eyes flickered, unreadable. "Or maybe something changed."

The words sent a strange chill through Darius.

He hadn't liked Marek from the start, but this? This was something else.

Then, as if to shift the subject before they lingered too long, he asked, "Marek called you his second-in-command. What did he mean by that?"

Kastor's expression didn't change. "Exactly what it sounds like. I'm the head of his army. The closest thing he has to a second-in-command."

Rowen let out a low whistle. "Hells, Kastor, I knew you had that broody 'mysterious badass' thing going on, but that? That's some serious power."

Kastor scoffed. "Not that it means much lately. I barely know what he's thinking anymore."

Darius frowned. "And now he's sending you with us?"

"That's what I don't understand." Kastor exhaled sharply. "I was sent across the sea to see if you were real. If the 'Hero of Prophecy' was anything more than a myth. And now, after seeing it with my own eyes, after watching you slay a demon, instead of bringing you to the battlefield, he's throwing you into the Lower City."

"And throwing you in with us," Lyra pointed out.

A brief pause.

Rowen rubbed his chin. "Well, I for one do think it's obvious."

Kastor arched a brow. "Do you?"

Rowen nodded sagely. "He wants us all dead."

Ingrid smacked him upside the head.

Rowen yelped. "What?! It's a valid theory!"

Ingrid rolled her eyes. "He's testing us."

"Testing me," Kastor corrected. "And you."

Darius exhaled, running a hand through his hair. "Whatever the reason, we don't have a choice. We take it one step at a time."

"Easy for you to say," Rowen muttered. "You're destined for this."

Darius shot him a flat look. "If I was destined for this, I'd have a lot more answers."

Rowen smirked. "No argument there."

The group lingered on the balcony a little longer, a moment of quiet before the descent into the unknown. The wind carried the scent of salt and something else—something wrong—from the depths below.

Kastor's gaze flickered to Darius. "You still trust this prophecy?"

Darius wasn't sure how to answer.

Instead, he glanced at his friends. Rowen, who never took things seriously but had never failed him in battle. Ingrid, who would walk through hell if it meant breaking through a wall in front of her. Lyra, who carried more power than she realized.

He looked at Kastor last. The one who had spent his entire life in a world already breaking apart.

"…I trust them," Darius said at last.

Kastor studied him for a long moment. Then, with the faintest smirk, he nodded.

"Then let's get this over with."

And with that, they turned toward the winding stone steps that led down—down into the depths of the Lower City.

The stone steps spiralled downward, each one feeling like a step into another world.

Gone was the grandeur of the upper city, the gleaming spires and bustling markets. The deeper they went, the more the light faded, swallowed by a heavy, unnatural gloom.

And then they reached it.

The Lower City.

A labyrinth of broken streets stretched before them, winding alleys choked with debris. The buildings loomed too close, their warped structures leaning over the narrow paths like they had melted in place. Some had collapsed entirely, leaving skeletal remains of stone and wood. Others stood whole but wrong, their windows and doors warped into unsettling angles, as if they were watching.

The streets were empty. Not abandoned—empty.

No stray cats picking through rubble. No rats skittering through the alleys. No voices.

Nothing.

Rowen exhaled sharply. "I don't like this."

"You don't like a lot of things," Ingrid muttered, adjusting her grip on her axe.

"This is different."

Darius scanned the streets. He knew silence. He'd spent his fair share of nights in desolate villages, ruins where nothing but ghosts remained. But this?

This felt waiting.

Lyra gripped her staff, her fingers trembling slightly. "The magic here… it feels wrong."

Kastor, who had been silent since they stepped off the last stair, finally spoke. "It is." His voice was low, cautious. "Nothing here is what it seems. Stay sharp."

As they ventured deeper, the air grew thick, like walking through something unseen but alive.

And then, the whispers began.

Soft at first.

A faint murmur on the edge of their hearing. Distant voices, just beyond recognition.

"Who are you?"

Rowen stiffened. "Did you hear that?"

"Why are you here?"

Lyra shivered. "I—I don't think we should listen."

"What are you?"

Darius clenched his jaw, forcing himself to focus. "Ignore it. Keep moving."

The voices slithered around them, crawling into their ears, their skulls.

"You left us."

"You watched us die."

Rowen winced, shaking his head as if to clear it. "Nope. Nope. I am officially done with creepy voice magic."

Then, something moved in the shadows.

Darius froze. His grip tightened on his sword.

They weren't alone.

At first, they thought it was just the dark, shapes shifting in their minds. But then—

A figure lurched from the alley ahead.

Misshapen. Wrong.

Its limbs were too long, its skin stretched and cracked, its mouth a jagged mess of teeth—too many teeth.

And then another emerged. And another.

Figures that had once been human.

Now corrupted into something unrecognizable.

Rowen let out a low curse. "I don't suppose there's a chance they just want to say hello?"

The creatures stared at them, twitching in unnatural movements.

And then—they rushed forward.

CHAPTER 29

The Betrayer's Crown

The creatures charged, their malformed bodies lurching unnaturally, bones shifting under thin, pallid skin. Their eyes—if they could still be called that—were milky, hollow voids that locked onto their prey with terrifying intent.

Darius struck first, his greatsword carving through one's shoulder. It barely reacted. A wet, sucking noise filled the air as the torn flesh stretched and reformed, sinew pulling itself back together.

"We have a problem," Darius muttered.

Rowen ducked under a grotesquely elongated arm, using Flicker Step to dart behind the creature and stab upward. His daggers slid into something that should have been vital—but instead of dropping, the thing twisted its head at an unnatural angle and grinned.

"That's unsettling," Rowen breathed before kicking off its chest and flipping away.

Ingrid barrelled through two at once, her axe cleaving one in half—only for its torso to drag itself forward, clawing at her boot.

"This is new," she grunted, stomping down and crushing the thing's warped skull.

A whisper slithered through the air—

"Help me..."

The team froze.

That voice—

Darius whipped around, eyes wide. He knew that voice.

It was Rowen's.

And then—

"Darius?"

This time, it was Seraphina's voice.

Lyra gasped as something lunged at her, hands gnarled into claw-like appendages.

"Lyra!" Darius roared, lunging forward.

Rowen was faster, Flicker Stepping in and slamming both daggers into its chest, forcing it back.

Kastor's chain whip cracked through the air, the metal coiling around its neck before he gave a vicious yank—the sound of vertebrae snapping filled the air. "Your mind will hear voices of loved ones, don't listen!"

Ingrid stood firm, keeping the rest at bay as she swung her axe in wide arcs, severing limbs and sending creatures reeling.

Lyra panted, clutching her staff. "They're not just beasts..." she whispered.

Darius's grip on his sword tightened.

"They were people," Kastor muttered. "People consumed by the Flesh-Tide."

A silence hung in the air.

Then, in the distance—

A low, wet groan echoed from beyond the streets.

The team turned.

Ahead of them, the ruined cityscape ended abruptly—

A pit.

Massive. Cavernous.

And at its edge, the walls moved.

Darius' stomach turned as he realized—they weren't walls.

Bodies. Fused together.

Dhalmoran soldiers, their faces tortuous in silent agony, mouths moving soundlessly as if still trying to scream.

Lyra gasped, stepping forward. "This…" She raised a hand, magic swirling in her palm as she reached out, trying to feel whatever force had done this—

And something fought back.

Her breath hitched as a force like cold hands wrapped around her mind, pulling, dragging—

She ripped away, stumbling back into Rowen, who caught her.

Then the pit rumbled.

Something crawled from the abyss.

A horrid shape, larger than a warhorse, patchwork flesh and bone fused into something inhuman.

It had once been a man.

And a rat.

A colossal amalgamation, its hunched frame covered in bloated, discoloured flesh, patches of matted fur still clinging to its grotesque form. Its arms—one grotesquely human, the other an elongated, skeletal limb with razor claws—dragged along the ground, gouging deep furrows into the stone.

Its face… or what remained of it… had one human eye, barely recognizable, staring from a twisted, gaping maw filled with jagged, uneven teeth. A second mouth had split open across its throat, gnashing and writhing as though it were trying to speak—but only in horrible, choked gurgles.

Kastor went rigid.

"…No."

Darius glanced at him, his grip tightening. "You know him?"

Kastor's jaw clenched.

"…Vikrom."

Darius stilled. "who?"

Kastor gave a slow, hollow nod. "I knew him as Vikrom he was the second in command before me."

The creature twitched, its grotesque rat-like snout sniffing the air—before it roared, a deafening sound that sent dust raining down from the cavern walls.

"Yeah," Rowen muttered, rolling his shoulders. "That's enough of that. Who's up first?"

Vikrom lunged, and the battle exploded into chaos.

Darius met the charge first, his Phantom Edge carving through Vikrom's bloated arm—but the beast barely reacted, twisting mid-lunge and slamming him with a sickening backhand that sent him skidding across the stone.

Rowen flashed in, his daggers dancing, but Vikrom's long, rat-like claws slashed wildly, nearly catching him as he flickered away at the last moment.

Ingrid came in hard, her Titan's Grasp expanding her axe as she brought it down in a crushing arc—

The blow landed, sending a sickening crunch through the cavern.

But Vikrom shrieked, his body convulsing—and then something ripped from his back.

New limbs.

Spined, skeletal appendages burst from his body, flailing wildly.

Rowen cursed. "That's—unfair."

Lyra raised her staff. "Stormcaller!"

Lightning slammed into Vikrom, forcing him to seize and convulse, but his misshapen mouth opened wide—

And he spat a vile black ichor, directly at Lyra.

She barely raised her *Glacis Bastion* in time—the ice wall shuddered under the impact, sizzling as the substance ate through it.

"Yeah, no thanks," she muttered.

Then—

A new voice joined the battle.

"Crimson Snare."

Kastor's chain whip ignited, but not with normal fire.

The metal links burned a deep, eerie red—like liquid blood. Each movement left behind a trail of razor-sharp energy, as if the whip itself had grown teeth.

With a single snap, the weapon coiled around Vikrom's arm, the bloody flames sinking into its flesh like it was ripping it apart from the inside.

Vikrom screeched in agony, its movements erratic as the crimson energy cut and gnawed at it with each passing second.

Kastor yanked hard, spinning Vikrom off balance—

And Darius saw his opening.

He surged forward, greatsword raised, magic burning through his veins—

And brought it down with everything he had activating a Crescent Fang at the moment of impact.

A final, brutal strike.

The blade cleaved through flesh, bone, and rot—

Vikrom screamed—

And then fell silent.

The monster that had once been a man collapsed, its grotesque form shuddering once—

And then it was still.

The silence after the battle was deafening.

The grotesque form of Vikrom lay motionless at their feet, its twisted body still steaming from Kastor's incantation. The stench of burning flesh filled the cavern, and for a long moment, none of them spoke.

Then Rowen exhaled. "Well… that was disgusting."

Ingrid rolled her shoulder with a grunt. "I don't like this," she muttered, nudging Vikrom's corpse with her boot. "What was the point of this?"

Darius was thinking the same thing. He wiped his blade clean on a tattered piece of Vikrom's former cloak and turned to Kastor. "Your king sent us down here. For what? Just to kill a few creatures? Or was there something else?"

Kastor frowned, gaze sweeping over the cavernous pit, the bodies fused into the walls, and the twisting, unnatural growths that clung to the architecture.

Lyra stepped forward, her brows knit in deep thought. "It doesn't make sense. We weren't given an objective beyond 'prove ourselves,' but to whom? And why? Was this just to see if we could survive?"

Rowen scoffed. "Great. Love that for us."

Kastor was silent for a moment longer, then muttered, "Maybe it wasn't just a test." Darius turned to him. "What do you mean?"

Kastor walked toward Vikrom's remains, standing over what was left of the man who had once commanded the Dhalmoran army. His expression darkened.

"They still retain something," he murmured.

Rowen raised a brow. "Something like what? Awful personality? A love for eating rats?"

Kastor shot him a look. "Memory. Instinct." He crouched next to the corpse, eyes scanning the ground. "Even when completely transformed... Vikrom still chose to remain here."

Lyra's eyes widened. "You think he was guarding something?"

Kastor nodded once.

A tense hush fell over the group.

Darius exchanged glances with Ingrid before stepping forward. "Then we search."

The cavern was filled with debris, ruined structures, and the remnants of a world long abandoned. The group spread out, shifting through old weapons, shattered stone, and things too malformed to recognize.

Rowen kicked over a half-rotted chest and sighed. "I swear, if this is just a sick joke from Marek, I'm throwing Kastor into the pit."

Kastor ignored him.

Darius moved along the cavern wall, eyes narrowing at something gleaming beneath a pile of broken masonry. With effort, he heaved aside a fallen beam and found—

A small, ornate box.

It was carved from blackwood, with golden filigree tracing delicate, unfamiliar patterns along its sides. It was too pristine, untouched by the rot and decay surrounding it.

Darius lifted it, frowning.

Ingrid peered over his shoulder. "That doesn't belong down here."

Lyra nodded. "It looks… expensive."

Darius opened it—only to find something unexpected inside.

A painting.

Small, delicate, and well-preserved, as if it had been placed there intentionally. The image was of a woman, beautifully painted, wearing richly adorned robes. Her eyes were sharp, piercing, but filled with sorrow.

Rowen, looking over his shoulder, blinked. "Who's she?"

Kastor stiffened.

Darius caught the subtle shift in his expression. His jaw tightened, and his hand moved swiftly, plucking something else from the debris before anyone else could see it.

A scroll.

Without hesitation, Kastor slipped it into his coat, out of sight.

Darius narrowed his eyes.

"What was that?"

Kastor didn't answer immediately, only adjusting his coat as if nothing had happened. "Nothing important."

Darius stepped forward, his voice sharp. "You're not keeping things from us, Kastor."

Kastor met his gaze, unwavering. "If it's important, you'll know when the time is right."

Ingrid crossed her arms. "You seriously pulling that 'mysterious rogue' routine?"

Rowen leaned against a broken column. "You do realize we literally just risked our lives here, right?"

"That scroll, it was the real target right?" Darius added.

Kastor's gaze darkened. "you're here to slay a demon, I'm here for other reasons."

Tension crackled in the air.

Darius clenched his fists. He didn't trust this. He didn't trust Kastor. But now wasn't the time to push.

Instead, he exhaled through his nose. "Fine. But if I find out you're keeping something dangerous from us…"

Kastor smirked slightly. "What? You'll kill me?"

Darius didn't blink. "Depends on what you're hiding."

A beat of silence.

Then, Rowen clapped his hands together. "Alright, love the tension, but maybe let's go somewhere that isn't filled with corpses, yeah?"

Lyra, still unsettled, nodded. "We should head back."

Kastor turned toward the pit one last time before muttering, "Yeah. Let's get out of here."

The Walk Back—And More Questions Than Answers

The journey back to the upper city felt longer, heavier.

The group moved with less excitement, the thrill of adventure having given way to unease.

Rowen ran a hand through his hair. "Alright, so what the hell is going on with this city?"

Ingrid frowned. "It's worse than we thought. If Vikrom ended up like that, how many more are there?"

Lyra hugged her arms. "Too many. And we still don't know how or why it started."

Kastor, walking ahead, was silent.

Darius watched him carefully. He knew Kastor was holding something back.

And that meant Marek was, too.

"Let's see what the king has to say," Darius muttered.

Rowen groaned. "Great. Can't wait for another cryptic speech."

The group climbed the winding streets, the towering upside-down fortress looming ahead.

Darius wasn't sure what awaited them inside.

But he was sure of one thing—

Something wasn't right.

The moment they reached the stone stairway leading back to the upper city, the sound of metal boots striking the ground surrounded them.

Dark Knights.

Dozens of them.

Darius instinctively reached for his sword—but the air was already tense, the weight of something inevitable pressing down on them. The knights were clad in jagged black armour, their helmets obscuring their faces, their weapons already drawn.

Kastor took a slow breath.

One of the knights, their leader perhaps, stepped forward. He turned his helmeted head to Kastor and asked, "King Marek is eager to know if the scroll was retrieved."

Kastor didn't even hesitate. "Yes."

It was one word. One word that changed everything.

Before anyone could react—before even a second had passed— the knights moved as one.

Weapons were yanked from scabbards, daggers pulled from belts, Ingrid's axe was wrenched from her grip so violently that it made a sharp clatter against the stone floor.

Darius' teeth clenched as he shoved forward, trying to break free—only to be grabbed by two knights, their grip unyielding.

"Let. Us. Go," Ingrid growled, struggling against the knights holding her.

Rowen twisted violently in the grip of his captor, his sharp movements more animal than man. "Oh, you bastards are gonna wish you'd—"

A sickening *crack* split the air.

Rowen stopped talking.

Lyra, who had barely begun to turn, was struck across the face. The force of the hit sent her crumpling limp to the ground.

Darius' eyes went wide. "Lyra!"

One of the knights hoisted her up effortlessly, slinging her over his shoulder as if she were nothing but dead weight.

Darius felt something in him snap.

He lunged, pulling all his strength into his arm to drive his fist straight into the face of the nearest knight—

SNAP

A *lash* of metal wrapped around his wrist mid-swing, stopping him cold.

Kastor's whip.

The chain burned against his skin, keeping his arm frozen in place.

Kastor stood there, his expression unreadable, but his words carried weight.

"I'm sorry."

Darius' stomach turned cold.

"You son of a—" Rowen started, but before he could get another word out, Ingrid broke free.

And punched Kastor square in the face.

Blood splattered from his nose, his head jerking sideways with the impact. The force of the hit sent him stumbling back, his hand snapping up instinctively.

It should have felt good. But the moment was cut short.

Because another knight immediately retaliated.

A fist, hard and unforgiving, slammed into Ingrid's skull.

She didn't even get the chance to curse before her knees buckled, and she collapsed face-first onto the stone.

Rowen's entire body tensed. The room spun around him. The fury in his chest erupted like wildfire.

"You *piece of*—"

He jerked, fast as lightning, twisting his boot just enough to grab the hidden dagger strapped to his ankle.

And in one smooth, lethal motion, he drove it straight into the neck of the knight who had struck Ingrid.

A gurgled cry escaped from the knight's lips, blood bubbling from the wound. The other knights barely had time to react before Rowen twisted the blade deeper, yanking it free and letting the knight drop lifelessly at his feet.

That was as far as he got.

A gauntleted fist slammed into the back of his head.

Rowen hit the ground, unmoving.

Darius' eyes burned, his mind raging, twisting, screaming, but the whip around his arm tightened further.

"You've served your purpose," Kastor said, voice low, conflicted, but still resolute. "The hero and his friends retrieved an item thought lost."

The knights stepped closer. Darius' vision blurred with fury.

Kastor exhaled, staring at Darius with something almost like regret.

"Now… you'll be cast out. Left to fend for yourselves. To kill the demon, as you intended."

And then—

A final blow to the head.

Darkness took him.

CHAPTER 30

After the Debt Is Paid

The first thing Darius felt was cold metal biting into his wrists. The second was a throbbing ache behind his eyes, a dull reminder of the blow that had taken him down. When his vision focused, he saw stone. Damp, cracked, and filthy with grime. He was chained to the wall, arms raised slightly above his head, iron shackles locked tightly around his wrists.

A faint drip, drip, drip echoed from somewhere in the cell, the only sound beyond the slow, steady breathing of others.

His friends.

Rowen was the first he saw, slumped against his own section of the wall, his arms spread wide by his chains. He looked exhausted, but his eyes were bright with fury.

Next was Ingrid. She sat rigid, her face bruised but fierce, the dried blood at her temple only making her look more defiant.

Lyra was beside her, pale, her dark hair matted, and her lip split. She was shaking slightly—not from fear, but from whatever magic had been drained from her when she was struck down.

Darius forced himself to breathe. "You're all awake?" His voice came out rough, but steady.

Rowen snorted, shifting against his bonds. "Aye, awake, aware, and currently festering in a king's personal piss pot. You took your sweet time."

Darius ignored the jab. "Are you alright?"

"Define 'alright,'" Ingrid muttered, rolling her shoulders against the stone. "I've had worse."

Lyra winced as she shifted. "I'm fine," she said, though she didn't sound it.

Darius exhaled, looking to Rowen for an answer.

The rogue's expression darkened, but he shrugged. "Nothing that won't heal." His voice was tight, jaw clenched.

Darius didn't have to guess why.

"... Kastor."

Rowen snarled at the name. "Oh yeah, let's talk about him. The rat bastard sold us out. You saw it. I saw it. Ingrid sure as hell felt it."

He turned his head to Ingrid, his usual smirk absent. "That whole punch Kastor in the face thing? Might have been the best thing I've seen all year."

Ingrid's lips quirked slightly, something almost like amusement in her eyes. "Glad I could entertain you, Rowen."

Rowen huffed, then scowled again. "But seriously—what the hell was that? He strung us along, let us think we were allies, then handed us over like we were nothing."

Darius looked at each of them before he spoke. "Before I went under, Kastor said something."

That got their attention.

"He told me we'd served our purpose. That we got the scroll, and that was all Marek wanted. Now, we're being kicked out."

Ingrid scoffed. "Well, he sure has a way of escorting guests out, doesn't he?"

Rowen glared. "I knew he was off the moment I met him. I should have gone with my gut."

"Maybe there's more to this, You also thought Darius was 'off' when you met him," Lyra pointed out.

Rowen shrugged. "Yeah, but at least he wasn't creepy."

There was a moment of silence, then Ingrid smirked.

"You stabbed a man in the neck for me, I hear" she said, voice mocking, yet oddly touched.

Rowen's eyes narrowed. "...Don't make it weird."

"Oh, it's already weird."

The group laughed, despite the setting. It was tense, nervous, but it was something.

Then—

Clank.

The sound of keys turning in a heavy lock echoed through the cell.

The laughter died instantly.

A group of dark-armoured knights entered, weapons at the ready.

One of them gestured forward. "On your feet."

They were yanked up by their chains, hands still bound, forced to march single file. The air was thick with the smell of old stone and rusted iron.

The halls were eerily silent, but as they walked—something changed.

A sound.

A distant roar.

Then another.

Louder.

Cheers.

Shouting.

Rowen's brows furrowed. "Tell me that's not what I think it is."

They rounded a final bend, the knights guiding them through a massive iron gate.

Then—

Blinding light.

The sound exploded around them, shaking the very ground beneath their feet.

Thousands.

The roar of a crowd, standing high above them.

They were in an arena.

The coliseum.

The same one they had seen when they arrived in the city.

Darius' gut turned cold as he lifted his head—

And saw him.

King Marek.

Watching from his balcony above, perched like a predator surveying his kill.

And beside him—

Kastor.

His face was unreadable. Unmoved.

Darius' fingers curled into fists as their bindings were locked down, chains hooked into the stone floor, keeping them in place.

And the crowd chanted.

Roaring for blood.

Marek stepped forward, arms wide, smiling like a king addressing his beloved people.

And he spoke.

"Welcome, heroes."

Marek's voice rolled over the arena like distant thunder. Measured. Cold. Performed.

"Really. I mean it," he continued, stepping forward on the balcony, hands outstretched as if inviting applause. "You came into my city, strutted about with your shiny prophecy and your smug little faces, helped me accomplish something in my lower district, spilled a little blood—" he laughed lightly, as if it were all a joke, "—and then you were expected to just walk out."

His eyes flicked down to the chained figures below.

"You were going to leave me," he said, his voice taking on a mockingly wounded tone. "Take what you wanted, get what you needed, kill your little demon, and then leave never to return across that pretty sea like good little heroes. Like I was some checkpoint on your quest log."

Darius's fists clenched in the chains.

Marek sighed. "But... you had to make something of it. You couldn't just do what I asked and left my fair city could you."

He stepped back—then, without hesitation, leapt from the balcony.

The crowd gasped as he landed in a smooth crouch, the black cloak rippling behind him. He rose slowly, face to face with them now. The King of Dhalmora. The monster in royal skin.

He moved between them like a snake, hands behind his back, eyes calculating.

"You know," Marek said conversationally, "I didn't start here. No, no... I was born in the dirt. Grew up scrapping in alleyways, eating rats and stealing from stall vendors. No crown. No legacy. Just fists and grit."

He stopped in front of Darius.

"But now?" A sick smile crept across his face. "Now I sit on a throne made of bone and shadow. Now I *command respect*. And what I've learned, dear prophecy boy, is that respect—" he leaned close "—has to be taken."

Darius snarled, "You call this respect? Chaining us? Threatening us?"

Marek stood straight again. "I call it balance."

He turned, addressing the crowd again. "But hey... maybe I'm too harsh. Maybe I overreacted."

He strolled to Rowen and crouched.

"Who hit Kastor?" he asked plainly.

No one answered.

Marek stood, pacing in front of them now. "No one? Really? Just a misunderstanding, huh?"

He looked up to Kastor, standing silently near the throne platform.

"Well then, Kastor," Marek called, "who was it? Who struck you?"

Kastor met his gaze. "I didn't see."

Silence.

Marek's jaw twitched. "Didn't see."

He let out a breath. Smiled again. "How convenient."

Darius frowned, confused. Why... why didn't Kastor tell him?

Was it guilt?

Or something else?

"Fine. Maybe you all had a bad day," Marek said, shrugging. "Maybe it's my fault for not laying out the rules properly."

He threw his arms open again. "Maybe I should just let you go."

A beat.

No one moved.

Even the crowd quieted.

"Yeah," Marek said, nodding to himself. "Yeah, maybe we'll call it even. Water under the bridge. My men... your little incident... Let's just chalk it up to tension."

A breath of relief passed through the heroes. Even chained, something in them softened.

Rowen dared a whisper. "...Is this actually happening?"

Ingrid didn't answer, but her shoulders loosened. Lyra dared to lift her head.

Marek turned to walk away.

He made it halfway back to the stairs leading to his balcony—

Then stopped.

His voice dropped, dark and venomous.

"Oh. Right."

He slowly looked over his shoulder.

"Who killed my man?"

The tension returned like a thunderclap.

No one spoke.

He turned fully, stepping forward again.

"I'm a fair king," he said. "But fair means debts are paid. And one of you—" he pointed now, sweeping his finger across them— "*murdered* one of my knights."

He walked closer again, slower this time.

"You see," he said, circling them, "people think when you wear a crown, you've got all the power in the world. But that's not true. Power is respect. And when someone *takes* from you, when someone kills your men—your *loyal* men—then people start to wonder if you're worth obeying."

He paused behind Rowen.

"Now, I don't care who did it. Maybe it was you, maybe it wasn't." He looked between Ingrid and Rowen, narrowing his eyes. It was just a moment but Marek spotted the look of lovers between these two.

A shudder ran down Ingrid's spine.

He didn't say anything more.

Just... *noticed.*

Then he smiled again.

"Well." Marek clapped his hands. "No use dwelling on it. Maybe it was all a misunderstanding. Well, It's been a pleasure, but...."

He stepped backward.

Back to the stairs.

The crowd watched, breathless.

Marek climbed slowly, regally.

He stood atop the balcony again, arms behind his back, looking down at them with a kindly expression.

"you're all free to go." he said.

Everyone held their breath.

And then—

CRACK.

A *wet*, *thunderous* snap echoed through the arena.

The sound of *something heavy* and *wrong*.

Ingrid gasped—then fell.

Her body slumped forward—but only the top half.

The crowd screamed.

Blood sprayed across the stone floor.

The other half of her slid to the side.

Darius screamed.

Lyra screamed.

Rowen roared.

Chained. Helpless. Screaming.

In the shadows beneath the balcony, directly under Marek, stood the thing that had done it— An eldritch creature, hunched and vile, held by four dark knights on chains. Its limbs were stretched and grotesque, its eyes bulbous and too many. Long, jagged claws shimmered with fresh blood.

Marek didn't even flinch.

He looked down at them all—

Smiling.

"After the debt is paid," he said softly.

And the world shattered.

Hello again hero, remember me?

ABOUT THE AUTHOR

Johnathon Axel Carr is a fantasy author, artist, and storyteller from Pembrokeshire, Wales. with a background in art, graphic design, and social media, he brings a strong visual flair and cinematic energy to his storytelling. he lives in Wales with his wife and children.
A lifelong lover of all things fantasy—dragons, swords, ancient ruins, and myth, The Cursed Prophecy is his debut novel: a dark, emotional epic where classic fantasy collides with eldritch horror—perfect for fans of Game of Thrones, Elden Ring, and anyone who believes a cursed sword should always be part of the plot.

DARIUS' JOURNEY WILL CONTINUE IN....

ECHOES OF THE FALLEN:
BOOK TWO OF THE CURSED PROPHECY SERIES

Printed in Dunstable, United Kingdom